DREAMSPACE

ESCAPE C19

12/1/21

Mark Jyothi,

Enjoy the read.

Bennt Joshua Dann

DREAMSPACE

ESCAPE C19

Bennett Joshua Davlin

CENTERED
AMERICA
PUBLISHING GROUP

CENTERED AMERICA PUBLISHING GROUP
Published by Centered America Books
A Publishing Division of 3210 Films LLC
269 South Beverly Dr. Suite 537 Beverly Hills, CA 90212

DREAMSPACE: ESCAPE C19

This book is an original publication of 3210 Films LLC

PRINTING HISTORY
Centered America Books trade paperback edition / October 9, 2020

An application to register this book for cataloguing has been submitted to the Library of Congress.

ISBN 978-1-7358736-3-3

PRINTED IN THE UNITED STATES OF AMERICA.

10   9   8   7   6   5   4   3

PRERELEASE NOTE

*For my three daughters and
Rene Descartes, Ellen G. White
and children everywhere.*

ACKNOWLEDGEMENTS

This novel wouldn't be possible without Mrs. Bennett Joshua Davlin. This third-generation cinematographer, former military sharpshooter, and search & rescue responder finally indulged me by starring in this book's cover for the lead role she inspired; she also led the cover art design team between participating in the finest art form of all, motherhood.

I thank *La Sierra University's Art Department* Chairman Terrill Thomas and his amazing staff who photographed this novel's cover art. Mike Easley also provided additional photo-work.

Many thanks are owed to George Lucas, whose first *Star Wars* film inspired me at 5 to make movies. I took up novel writing as well because of him, believing his credit for writing the first Star Wars novel, actually ghostwritten by Alan Dean Foster. Still, it's because of George that you're now reading this book.

I thank the writer James A. Michener who critiqued my first novel when I was 13, the product of a *typist* as Jim termed me. As a *writer* for Jim had to be printed by a major publisher, an honor I later achieved in the U.S. and internationally before web publishing's ascent changed everything.

I thank the artist Jackie Chan for giving me my first big break in Hollywood. I'm grateful for my friendship born from directing the iconic writer, actor, acclaimed director, and my late friend, Dennis Hopper, who pushed me to write this book.

Acknowledgment is also owed to my late friend, the prolific TV creator Glen A. Larson who felt that this story completed a mix of themes he began in *Battlestar Galactica* and Lucas hinted at in the first *Star Wars*. Glen believed this tale would be the final reveal of the science fiction genre; his instincts would be proven correct in ways I didn't realize, serving as the experience Ellen G. White swore people would now need.

I thank my film executive Jake Rohr, for reading the various drafts. Acknowledgment is owed to my friend, the novelist Karen Essex, Anthony Badalucco, Stein Willanger, and my entertainment attorneys Bob Darwell and Phil Rosenberg.

I thank the late Buckley Norris and former studio-chief Dan Melnick for showing me the way through Hollywood. The greatest actress I've directed, the iconic Ann-Margret, inspired a character in this story. Another role was written for Ed O'Neill to whom I still owe another bottle of champagne. Ed's role is based on another friend, LAPD homicide detective Dennis Fanning who shed light on a life solving murders.

I'm grateful to my teachers from the Episcopal School of Acadiana, Tulane University, London's Kings College and City College, and Tulane's A.B. Freeman School of Business. I'm also indebted to *TheGreatCourses.com* that allowed me to continue learning since graduate school.

I'm appreciative of Teresa and JC in Santa Monica, who always reserved my writing table at *Funnel Mill*, the world's best coffee shop. What our politicians have done to our west-coast cities like L.A., trashing such businesses, is an anti-American travesty.

I thank Blanvalet, Random House, Sony Books, and my other publishers for translating and printing my books worldwide.

And of course, I thank my dedicated readers and film fans for making it all possible.

AUTHOR'S NOTE

The virus in this novel and its film adaptation was titled the *Yin Yang virus* to foreshadow what would years later be our Chinese viral plague. Once the pandemic began, I attributed the *Yin Yang Virus* as *COVID-19*.

part one

David Bellingham the child

"Now I have come to explain to you what will happen to your people in the future, for the vision concerns a time yet to come."

Daniel 10:14

prologue

It was a Camaro.

He preferred SUVs, but the sports car was the only rental available in all of New Orleans due to three simultaneous conventions in the Crescent City. He'd considered delaying this road-trip by a month for a badly needed break after the last patient. He fantasized about taking an Airbnb for a few weeks in Petaluma, California, next to the *Lagunitas* Brewery. He didn't even like alcohol, a rare trait for a native Louisianian, but their IPA was beyond perfection for him.

When he drank it, he found an escape from the pain he'd endured in caring for his patients. The same diversion he used to get from working on old BMWs which he loved because cars didn't die. Fixing engines or now sipping Lagunitas, he only remembered the ways that he had helped his patients. The darkness temporarily abating for a time.

While now the dark feeling of a storm fast approaching, motivated him. So luckily for the world, he didn't delay this drive out to South Central Louisiana. In retrospect, the required surgery to become one of his patients would never have been possible if he'd delayed. Because his micro-surgeon trained in his unique procedure would soon die of COVID-19. He wouldn't have found another specialist as the entire healthcare system of the planet was swamped in the most terrifying plague since the *Black Death.*

The novel Coronavirus.

A pandemic the world did not see coming at them. Because the dictator of the country of its origin intentionally hid truths about the virus for five months while sending a half a million people to infect the United States. On a damp, gray morning some time before the pandemic, he headed out early, careful to drive below the speed limit through the notorious speed trap town west of New Orleans called Laplace. The town's name always reminded him of the philosopher Pierre-Simon Laplace's fictional demon, the all-knowing entity who could trick any human mind into believing anything. He wasn't sure if he shaved off time by later taking the old state highway from Baton Rouge to the small town of Opelousas. By the time he reached the pecan trees framing the lone, dirt road east of town, a nauseous feeling overtook him, forcing him to pull on to the shoulder.

He bit his lower lip as the car idled. Unsure of his next move. A rare state for such a decisive man of science. Eyeing the Hertz Gold Club rental contract vibrating gently on the dash. The exterior world now handed a predicament to this genius who was typically preoccupied with matters solely within his mind. He was a scientist born to share in Plato's belief that the inner universe of the consciousness constituted the only true reality. A truth he first learned as a philosophy major at Tulane University. After all, nothing beyond one's inner consciousness could ever be proven to the self. Any belief in exterior reality, he reasoned, was due to pain; usually through the threat of violence in any age from a mother's spanking up to the threat of anguish from the sergeant at arms when one broke the laws of the reigning command and control structure. Each generation being born into an ever-changing crucible of truths made real because of the pain which could be inflicted for violating the accepted laws.

While chaos served as the lack of laws, allowing not freedom but unpredictable pain due to the whim of random others. Like when his laptop with the only draft of his thesis was stolen along with his car as he stopped to pay for gas on the way to deliver his treatise. That theft upended his life. His pocket drive was with the computer. So no backup. Ironically, his thesis' theme was that the backed-up truths of any society would eventually be upended every few centuries as history and the philosophers *Hegel* and *Kuhn* indicated. Unexpectedly, the theft of his thesis fueled his life's quest to highlight deceptions in the real world. Illustrating this point on his office door, he hung the much-embraced world map with the real one overlaid in a lighter tone. Eventually, students and peers inquired about the weird, stretched map in light gray:

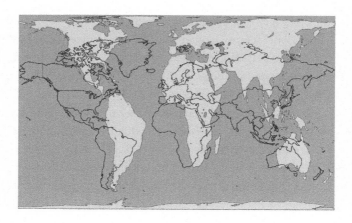

As for the accepted map, most of them knew Greenland could never be larger than North America, but attributed the stretched northern hemisphere to the curve of the planet: which made absolutely no sense. The popularly embraced map called the *Mercator Projection* was intentionally warped in the northern latitudes to allow for easy maritime navigational plotting. Later European kings found it convenient to falsely tower in size over their far larger, subjugated colonies south of the equator. Yet long after the colonial system's end, the lie still hung in every classroom of the world except for Dr. Jim Tutwiler's own. For he alone hung the lie contrasting with the truth.

It was a litmus test.

Not to impress others or weed out like-minded skeptics. Life taught him that there were no other like-minded people. His fellow academics were long-imprisoned by their degrees, boxing them into their tiny jail cells of knowledge, oblivious to anything beyond their respective disciplines. While he searched for one fact to shatter everything. He found it while chasing funding for his new computer technology. Taking the train from Zurich to banker meetings in Geneva, he passed the time with an audiobook summarizing the 17th Century philosopher and founder of science, Rene Descartes. There he learned the fact about science's birth that changed everything.

A discovery that could not be refused.

Just as he acknowledged that his great invention, bringing him to this isolated, country road would be a mixed blessing for the child he intended on helping. Which was why he now hesitated, slowing his foot on the vehicle's gas pedal.

His eyes evasively darted up to the old, white-painted home at the road's end. He became suddenly aware of the cheap air freshener concealing a previous smoker. Thinking of the ways a novelist like *James Joyce* might cultivate an eternity from this singular moment. In his mind's eye, he imagines a perpendicular line running ahead of his rental car. It marks the point when he can no longer turn around without risking notice from the boy's mother in the home at the road's end.

He knows he can help her child.

But although his remedy for her young son, David Bellingham, is scientifically in his reach, this solution will take something precious from the boy. Still, how can he refuse to help such a brave child in dire need? The boy's courage brought him to tears when he first read the police report. That eight-year-old at the time had done a hard thing at an age when most were lost in their heads. He saw himself in this youth. Finally, after so long, he felt as if he'd discovered a fellow seeker.

He must help this boy in need.

There always seemed to be a patient somewhere in the world requiring his unique technology. People suffering so much that their caretakers were forced to conjure self-deceptions to maintain their sanity. He always treated the caretakers and loved ones of his patients in a professional manner because the truth he dispensed always hurt them the most. When peoples' lies were unmasked, most resorted to anger. By now, he only worked with possible patients from a few set areas of the planet.

The reason why except for Israel, he no longer worked with patients in the Middle East. People there were already more violent due to a misguided notion of generosity in their societal laws. The prohibition of interest on loans in Islamic countries kept them in the same chaos as the European Dark Ages. Islam never revised this rule as the Catholic Church wisely had, launching the European renaissance. Without interest-based loans, complex financial markets never emerged. With no credit, new things like his invention could not be built; the society could not change and evolve: keeping the few in power and the masses angry.

The people's anger found expression through religious leaders altering the Great Prophet Mohammed's work; turning what had once been a tolerant religion into a radicalized, violent faith to express the frustration of those permanently disenfranchised by their faith. The lack of credit turned the Middle East into hypocrites who refused to face the truth, largely claiming the West to be an enemy but remaining culpably silent about the millions of their fellow-Islamic followers in Communist China who were imprisoned for no crime, forced-sterilized and made to consume their forbidden food of pork.

His work kept him traveling.

It taught him much. He found Catholic countries to be inefficient economies, but fun-loving; while Protestant nations were well organized but dry. National attitudes and history were largely shaped by the weather and geography. People on various continents smelled differently and their customs and cultures varied. While most societies weren't worthy of celebration, but disdain, typically built on subjugating the young where marry-your-rapist laws were still on the books.

Areas flush with resources had histories as slave-states like all of sub-Saharan Africa where a few chieftains had ruled over everyone as ill-treated slaves for nearly all of African history. He refused to work where most young female students were commonly raped by their teachers.

Central and South America, also flush with resources, had developed slavery, but for the warped purpose of cutting slaves' hearts out centuries prior. Killing captured slaves served as the indigenous society's monetary system while the natives approached the foretold end of their civilization's reign; sacrificing strangers to hopefully buy more time for themselves. *Columbus Day* to him marked the beginning of the end of the American indigenous peoples' pattern of mass-murder to the point of extinction as witnessed in Easter Island's long-dead society.

He was, however, happy to work anywhere within the United States. Before his nation formed, the indigenous inhabitants of his land would've also annihilated themselves like the rest of the native Americas. From working with a Cheyenne patient, he discovered that centuries before the white man's arrival, the ancient,

Cheyenne shaman known to his followers as *Sweet Medicine* prophesied of the coming of strange white men who brought a mobile, new animal that turned out to be the horse. *Sweet Medicine* correctly foretold how North American Indians would harness the horses' mobility for travel to attempt to annihilate each other to extinction. To avoid that outcome, the shaman struggled to persuade the Cheyenne in antiquity to abandon their murderous, warrior culture but failed. The white man's cruel domination proved to be the sole outcome where the American Indians didn't go extinct by their own bloody hands.

The land those Indians once roamed in vast numbers would become the nation where citizens entered into a lawful compact with each other regarding their respective rights and liberties. The United States would save the world more than once, evidenced as the car stereo's XM radio somehow turned on. *Lucky Now* by Ryan Adams began playing with a life of its own on the stereo. His foot pressed the rental car's accelerator. The vehicle's wheels crossed the imaginary line. Soon after, he announced himself to the child's mother who opened the front door of her country home upon his approach.

"I'm Dr. Jim Tutwiler," he introduced himself as he exited the vehicle and extended his business card.

A few minutes later in her worn kitchen smelling of generations of Cajun cooking, Ms. Bellingham avoids his gaze as she hands the visitor a steaming mug of coffee. The old linoleum floor creaks, sagging towards the room's far corner where a commercial coffee machine rests beside a massive tub of *Community Coffee*. No doubt, he surmises for the flow of nurses caring night and day for her ailing son.

A boy locked in an unthinkable prison.

Ms. Bellingham and Dr. Tutwiler sit around a breakfast table bought by her dead husband before they met. The mother's beauty caught him off guard. Jim always worked with old patients and usually older caretakers. He was unprepared for this woman's beauty; the police report photos documented an unrecognizably injured woman on the night of the incident.

He broke his focused gaze on her, inadvertently peering through the open side-door, catching the back of her son's head in the living room. The boy, now nine, remained motionless, half reclined on an upright gurney before a big TV as the nurse temporarily parted his eyes. Jim immediately knew what they were up to.

Mom eyes him.

When she first opened her front door, this doctor explained that he could help her son. She wouldn't have let him into her home, but what he said rekindled the only hope she still possessed. Fit beyond most middle-aged men, his dark hair was peppered with gray. His muscular frame beneath the worn PJ's Coffee ball-shirt and faded jeans seemed so out of sorts that she again eyed his business card on the table. Again she wondered what kind of medicine could be practiced by a doctor in a Bio-Software department?

Dr. Jim Tutwiler, PhD
Bio-Software Department
6823 St.Charles Ave.
New Orleans, LA 70118

jtutwiler@tulane.edu
www.tulane.edu

Tulane University

She glanced up at him.

In his stare, she felt at ease. She didn't feel the typical judgment in his eyes which seemed to hold vast depth. After all, what kind of parent made the poor decisions she had? Her life choices now serving a cruel sentence upon her only child.

Jim explains, "All patients with your son's affliction, eventually return to their homes since modern medicine can offer no help-"

"How many of these homes have you visited?" she asks.

Then he reaches the point that can spark violence:

"Yours is the ninth. In each I've witnessed fanciful remedies akin to the one you've devised with the TV," he preempts her angry reaction by reaching out and touching her hand, "David is not feeling what you think he is."

She caught herself enjoying his touch, which singed her rage. The moment reminded her of *Mr. Darcy* from BBC's *Pride and Prejudice* she recently saw on TV. She's watched a great deal of television lately. She feels wrong enjoying this man's gesture while at the same time sickened by what he just said. Has she been wrong about David? Was her son no better off because of what she did? Was her remedy just another lie on her long path?

He continued, "In the nine houses I've visited, every family devised a remedy which they believed decreased the patient's suffering. But it didn't decrease their anguish," he stressed, "he's in a nightmare. I've come to both announce and end it."

She remained silent, finding herself struggling to continue the conversation. She wanted to lash out at him. How could this stranger know what her son felt? She peered back at David, realizing her anger was truly directed at herself. Watching her, he was moved by her gentle reaction as he continued:

"I've developed a way to establish communication with patients with your son's rare condition," he explained, "it has a one hundred percent success rate-"

"I was told there were no trials anywhere-"

"That's because I've not published my findings," he glanced down at the table, "for despite my amazing success rate, there is one big issue…"

Jim struggled to find the right words to explain what he would ultimately happen to her son from his invention; the unavoidable outcome of all of his past nine patients. The thing he wished to forget over a beer. But never did Dr. Jim Tutwiler expect that the phrasing of his next words would decide the future fate of all humanity.

one

David was lost.

Up until the accident, he knew who he was: the son of a whore. Which was where his story began and ended for most. Because nobody wanted to know about such a woman like his mom or her only child. But being a whore was just one of his father's many falsehoods that people believed. He knew what was real. But *reality* for most people, it seemed to David had been more about perception and prejudice than truth. Lies were easy to hear, truth required work. Now he was in a place beyond reality. He didn't think of his state in such poetic terms. He didn't think much at all. While he couldn't work at anything except feeding only-

Agony.

How could one convey what was beyond experience? On the night of the incident, he transcended human experience and entered Hell. After which, he could hear, but feel nothing, seeing only darkness occasionally punctuated in shimmers of maroon. He heard his carcass being transported from his parent's bedroom where the incident occurred to an ambulance as paramedics asked his mom questions about what had transpired.

His mom answered them, periodically succumbing to hysterical weeping which finally caused the boy to panic in a way he'd never done before. The next thing he remembered was squeaky wheels stopping in silence. The distant, occasional hospital announcements over a P.A. system as he listened intently for his mother's voice.

A door opened.

The sound of padded shoes before a gloved hand parted open his right eyelid. David Bellingham's motionless eyeball remained still, oriented up and to the right of the female doctor who blinded him with her penlight momentarily directed at his pupil. In its wake, he made out the female doctor with dark hair gathered into a bun. She looked tired, blue bags gathered under narrow eyes rendered larger from behind her thick glasses. He couldn't make out her name embroidered on the breast of her white lab coat, but above it, he saw, *Neurology Dept., Opelousas General Hospital.* From all the TV medical shows he'd watched with his mom, the boy knew neurologists dealt with brain issues which seemed strange since he was dead. Then she rocked his reality.

She spoke to him:

"Hi David, I'm Dr. Bri. You're at The Opelousas General Hospital. You may not be able to feel your body right now. Your mom is nearby, watching us. She's stayed near the whole time. You've suffered an injury to your head and the MRI I'm about to perform will help us figure out how we can help you," a content smile formed across her lips, "So I need you to think thoughts and this machine will show me just what to do. Your mom told me you love walking in the woods near your house, so you must be pretty brave because I hate frogs. But think of those walks and after the scan, your mom will visit."

The neurologist's gloved fingers gently closed David's eyelids, returning him to the darkness punctuated by the hints of maroon from the dim overhead light shining through what he now realized must be the flesh of his closed eyelids.

The neurologist turned away from her young patient in the dimly lit MRI chamber. By now she suspected he suffered from a rare condition inflicted by the severe injury to the base of his skull. A hell visited upon the few unfortunate enough to experience the rare syndrome caused by blunt force trauma to the lower back of the head or severe strokes, rendering her patient neither living nor dead.

Just gone.

Modern medicine possessed no better word to explain this cerebral syndrome making a tomb of David's body. Unable to move or feel. A condition beyond any cure. The neurologist, a mother herself, struggled to remove all emotion as she headed to the exam room behind the glass door.

Through the glass, David's distraught mom eyed her only son. The boy's motionless legs retracted into the narrow tunnel of the MRI scanner. Bruised and beaten, she couldn't contain herself, wanting to rip out of her skin. Hungering to hold his hand as she did in the ambulance, but once they reached the hospital she fell apart. No longer hyperventilating, she desired to feel his pulse to confirm that her husband had not taken all that mattered to her. But the man clearly took something from the boy. As the MRI machine progressed, she found her thoughts drawn back to the monster-

David's father.

That handsome man whose good looks concealed unspeakable evil. Even now, she didn't suspect the majority of his dark secrets. Like his passion for parading around his isolated, rural home in a vintage Nazi SS officer's uniform he purchased online before they met.

The outfit remained hidden behind a secret attic panel where it would never be discovered. Nor did she suspect the six hamsters the man buried alive in a tennis can as a boy, just after his family moved from their ancestral home of Shreveport down south to Opelousas. The early spankings from his youth taught David's father at a young age to hide his pathological taste. A forbidden fire that could only be revealed during Halloween from behind his perennial Darth Vader mask. While the real mask David's dad regularly wore struck the senses at first as handsome and appealing.

David's father grew into a strapping high school football quarterback, initially very popular with young females. After suffering a career-ending ankle injury, he wound up a Louisiana State Trooper, thanks to a connection through his coach's brother. That law enforcement officer, like the broader organization of generally decent people, never suspected this sociopath in their midst.

He manned the State Police's *Troop K* Property Room, secretly fencing seized contraband: small amounts so as not to draw his superiors' attention. He buried the accumulated cash from those sales in sealed, plastic containers not far from the hamsters' remains. The money he'd use to entice women with elegant vacations. The ones who spent time in his isolated house at the end of the long, dirt road, all eventually fled for reasons they could never articulate. After a slew of failed relationships, the man realized he must capture a woman rather than entice if he was to ever acquire the son he was after. A boy to share his dark tastes. Luckily the man found a woman so traumatized by her life that she longed for the story he peddled.

His beaten, widowed wife now stared at the hospital MRI screen depicting their son's cranium. She turned away from the highlighted areas on the MRI scan documenting her boy's head trauma. Turning to her son through the glass hospital door, David's mother caught her own bruised and injured reflection. What had she done? She now seemed a far cry from that brave Cajun beauty, first stopped by the State Trooper who would later become her husband.

At the time of their meeting, he was on his way home after fencing contraband in Carencro when he pulled her over for speeding on Interstate 49. She was headed back to her hometown of Opelousas, a place she'd vowed never to return to. Lured there by a small inheritance. One from her dead mother she detested for remaining purposely oblivious of her then boyfriend's perversions after he inappropriately touched her. The scars of that molestation left her always wanting to be where she was not.

A feeling that at 17, after having saved enough money, caused her to buy an Amtrak train ticket to Hollywood. Whilst en route a rail accident shut down the line for days. Afraid to fly, she stayed in the Houston Galleria Hotel which was costly, but the only available lodgings she could find.

On the elevator ride up to her room, she experienced an odd encounter with an old Russian lady who claimed to be a fortune teller. Locking eyes with her, the old woman dramatically predicted in a thick accent that the young lady would meet her *Prince Charming* when she next returned to the town of her birth. She recollected on that strange prophecy the next morning over eggs and pancakes at Zucchini's Restaurant when a local photographer offered her a sizeable amount for a *Houstonian Magazine* fashion shoot.

It seemed that her luck had turned.

She soon became a print model, supplementing her income as a hostess at a high-end, Italian restaurant. There she met many lecherous men who reinforced the notion that L.A. would've been far worse. She began dating a young, handsome politician who frequently dined there. Her arrest in a planted drug bust aimed at him taught her never to consort with elected officials, who usually played dirty and attracted powerful enemies.

She escaped jail time with a lawyer provided by one of the politician's wealthy donors. Although she faced no jail time, the felony was unavoidable due to the amount of planted drugs. It would later seal her fate after she fulfilled the soothsayer's prophecy: returning home after seven long years for the inheritance of $4,514 which ultimately led her to this hospital room.

The neurologist's words at first passed through David's mother's mind as she struggled to focus on the physician's moving lips. For some reason, Mom's consciousness drifted back to when she first dined with the handsome State Trooper courting her. During the romantically lit steak and lobster dinner, she loved the crease of his grin. His manner of gesticulating with his hands as he spoke. The realization sinking in that the fortune teller years before, told her more than she then understood as she thought at the time that this suitor was indeed her-

Prince Charming.

Now he had claimed their son. The neurologist's gentle hand on her shoulder drew her back to the present. No, the boy's mother told herself. What the doctor told her could not be true.

No. No. No.

Her son would get better, she reassured herself before the doctor's grasp on her shoulder tightened as the clinician repeated the grim diagnosis. No, thought Mom, it couldn't end like this. Because she was good and what David did was righteous. The terror was finally over. So the happy part of her and her son's lives should begin.

But the boy on the MRI table was hurt badly by the man the child considered the Big Bad Wolf, like the one from his illustrated storybooks. In pictures on his mother's laptop, the young child eyed screenshots of his dad as a groom in his State Trooper uniform alongside his mother in her white wedding dress at the Kiwanis Lodge. Surrounded by a sea of blue, uniformed

State Troopers. The photo of the heart-shaped wedding cake seemed so perfect that his mother hesitated to slice it. She appeared happier than ever in a picture she so widely distributed on social media.

The boy later found that image hard to reconcile against his father's later assertion that his mother had been a whore. His mom brushed that off as daddy just being mean. For he was too young for her to tell him the truth about his father.

When David was three, her husband assaulted her over a comment about their home's peeling paint. She fled with her newborn only to be pulled over near the Texas state line. The police discovered the heroin her husband planted sometime before in her car's fuse box. She knew it had been planted, but no one would believe her due to her prior conviction. This second offense most probably meant prison time.

The *prior* on her record was what first caught her husband's eye at the traffic stop. When they met on that gray, winter afternoon, her NCIC report on his patrol car's dashboard computer served as the kernel of his wicked plan to ultimately trap this woman. Years later, the rapid intervention with the Lake Charles judge during her second offense proved the lynchpin of his wicked scheme. Now even the local Opelousas police kept a close eye on the wayward mother with two prior drug felonies, helping the dutiful husband keep the family together. It was all lies, she knew, but their condescending looks made it real. The reason why she now believed in nothing but her son. The boy who bravely saved his mother's life and now suffered for the deed. All because she picked the evil man, who valued his son solely on how David compared to him.

Because it wasn't until David turned eight that the little boy appeared on his Dad's radar. Until then the man only returned home occasionally to watch LSU football in the back room on in-season Saturdays. But following David's eighth birthday, old pictures of his father's high school football glories scrolled through the new digital picture frame in the living room. Soon after, David's father dragged his son into the woods, igniting a lighter under the boy's forearm to supposedly test David's metal. Even before a sobbing David sprinted back to show his mom his blistered forearm inflicted by his father, she sensed darkness fast approaching. That very evening in their bedroom, her husband told her:

"It's time for you to leave."

"Fine. I'll go get David-"

He grabbed her arm, "No. Only you're leaving."

She now realized the truth about her prison. Faced with the loss of her son, the constant angst evaporated. For the first time in her life, she knew where she stood. She'd die before leaving her son with this clueless monster who didn't even know his child.

The reason why she uncharacteristically laughed in his face as she pulled her arm from his grip, "Why would you want him now?"

"You turned him into a faggot," he grunted, "and now I'm gonna fix it-"

"He doesn't need fixing," she laughed, "David will never be like you."

At first, he thought her mad before he felt the biting truth of her words sink in. The boy was hers alone in spirit. Swelling anger consumed the man until he found his hands tight around his wife's neck, choking her.

His prison now in ruins.

There was no choice, but to next imagine disintegrating her corpse in acid. Of the many options, it would be the most ideal. Another drug addict who deserted her kin and vanished. Then his eight-year-old son severed his mother from that most certain outcome. The cocking of the department-issued .40 mm Glock 22 handgun opened a new possibility.

An eight-year-old David stared down the barrel at his charging father. He had taken the weapon from its holster on the side table when he crept in moments before, drawn in by the sounds of his mother's gasping breaths.

"DAVID! PUT THAT DOWN!" his father gruffly barked as he extended a hand for the gun.

The sour milk scent of the man's sweat was close to David. His dad's thick fingers wrapped around the gun's muzzle as the man sighed. The monster realized how weak his boy really was, so much like his mother: rendering David unworthy of continued existence. The verdict of a creature who knew how to make things disappear. A man now resolved to start over from square one, which somehow influenced the boy's next move regarding the weapon in which his father always kept the first bullet chambered.

He pulled the trigger.

David's ears rang from a gunshot no one at the time realized would author humanity's future. The bullet passed through the man's hand before carving a hole into his jawline. The entry-point gave up a surprisingly small amount of blood while the exit wound splattered most of his brains against the bedroom wall. His body collapsed to the floor as he urinated and defecated from the lethal, blunt force trauma.

David did not witness these details.

The weapon's violent recoil sent the eight-year-old flying backward. The boy's head slammed hard into the table's edge behind him. The world escaped young David Bellingham. Unexpectedly, the eight-year-old was transported to a realm beyond comprehension.

In the hospital, his mother now peered at David. The neurologist explained that her son's MRI scans clearly showed permanent cerebral damage. When the physician uttered David's unique condition, her words conjured the image of her son being trapped inside a bank vault:

"Locked-in syndrome."

The head injury had snatched David from the only reality he'd ever known. Sudden. Painless. The recoil of his father's department-issued handgun sent the eight-year-old careening back into the table. The crack of bone resonated through the rear of his skull. Then he felt nothing, the doctor explained. The resulting lower brain stem injury severed her son's consciousness from reality.

Stripped of his sense of proprioception, the sensation of his body vanished, with one key exception that would later manifest. Also gone was his sense of interoception, informing him of bodily sensations like hunger, his bowels, bladder, and even his skin's sense of touch. The only level of sensation to remain was exteroception, the ability for the child to hear, yet unable even to sense his body, listening to the real world as if over a radio broadcasting into his void.

"David can't sense or move anything in his body, including his tongue," the female neurologist continued, "but remains fully conscious. As a mother of two," the doctor wiped back a tear, "I find it hard to tell you that there's no known treatment for your son's condition. Everyone with it eventually desires not to go on. And due to his age, I can't even offer euthanasia, but that sort of thing is usually handled once you go home…" the rest of her words no longer registered in David's mother's rattled mind.

Mom's mantra gave way to the fortune teller's prophecy. *Prince Charming* had come and taken her son away with him. She reflected on that prophecy later in the autumn as medics finally returned her paralyzed child to his former prison at the end of that long, dirt road. Transporting the boy, now nine, in a gurney and back brace up to his bedroom overflowing with medical equipment, I.V. bags, and catheters. Machines beeped to accompany the creak in the floor from the nurses' steps. Twenty-four-hour medical care rotated around her son, made possible by her deceased husband's excellent state trooper health insurance. Endless days strobed into sleepless nights. Mom rolled around restless half the evenings in her bed.

Certain days when a nurse left and the replacement ran late, David's mother would creep into her son's bed and hold his hand as she sang lullabies to him. The love for her only child flooding over her while at the same time she knew she should end his suffering. Like snuffing out a candle, she told herself as she recollected on the neurologist broaching the possibility of euthanasia after he was back home. Pull the life support's power cord from the battery backup. One yank of the wrist. But she must hurry before the next nurse arrives. Her hand around the cord as she mustered the courage to end her son's suffering. When out of the corner of her eye, she spotted the Walmart shopping bag on David's bookshelf left by a nurse. The store's logo bubbled up a memory from within her.

The previous Christmas.

Packing groceries into the hatchback of her worn SUV. The parking lot packed tight with last-minute Christmas shoppers, forcing her to park at the outer edge. David walked unseen along the sidewalk between the lot and the busy street beyond. Cold mist curled from his mother's breath as she peered away from the street to avoid the watchful eyes in the passing sheriff's cruiser.

Continuing to load bags, she failed to witness the truck which struck a gray cat in the street. Its blood-splattered David's shoes as the boy stood on the sidewalk, eyeing the animal's midsection crushed from the wheels. The feline bounced up and down like a broken slinky. Without thinking, David ran to the animal's aid, carrying it to the sidewalk-

"David put that down!" his mother blurted as she turned to see the gruesome scene.

Warm blood ran down the boy's hand as the animal peered directly into his eyes as it expired. Just like that, it was gone. Eyeing the crimson blood on his hands and shoes, the notion materialized in David's mind. As mom drew near, even she registered the sudden maturity in her son's tone as he told her:

"Mommy, when I grow up, I know what I'm going to do."

"Really?" she feared her child's revelation from such a gory event.

"I'm going to cure death."

His words carried such conviction that his mother felt a cold chill before she managed the response, "David, death isn't something you cure. It's a natural process-"

"Weren't all sicknesses natural until someone cured them?"

"Everything dies," she firmly reiterated, "everything."

Now she took a final breath, ready to release her child to death right when the night nurse entered the room, startling the mother. She beat a quick retreat without comment, collapsing in her bed, struggling to cry quietly. Her son had more perseverance than her. So she resolved on what she would do the next day when-

The impossible occurred.

At the time it seemed like only a coincidence. But in fact, there was no such thing. Only by looking backward would historians appreciate the significance of this moment. Like a century before David lived when the assassination of a nobleman would lead to two World Wars, the Cold War nuclear age, the tech revolution, all leading up to David's present life. The assassin at that time early in the 20th Century failed in his task of murdering the future heir to the European Hapsburg Empire.

The would-be killer sat sobbing at an outdoor café table over his failed attempt when the nobleman was accidentally delivered just beyond the would-be murderer's table; the chauffeur got lost and stopped before him. The assassin dispatched a bullet which achieved what not even Napoleon could, ending the reign of Christian royal hegemony dating back to King Charlemagne in the 8th Century. That single shot which ultimately caused World War I and II. One bullet which would kill nearly more people than had been alive on Earth for most of human history.

Yet that moment would seem insignificant to the one in David Bellingham's mom's bedroom. As she noticed her bedroom

TV remained frozen during AMC's presentation of *A Clockwork Orange*, the film, part of a two-day marathon of the work of Stanley Kubrick. Mom focused on the performer in the stuck footage: the actor Malcolm McDowell sat immobilized in a movie theater chair. Eyelids forcibly clamped open as a nurse irrigated his exposed eyeballs with a saline dropper. Forcing him to watch a movie from which he could not turn away. The massive movie screen filled his complete range of vision. It seemed like a vacation compared to David's prison.

The image paused for several seconds as the TV signal froze. As Albert Einstein's theory of relativity indicated, there were always two truths which might seem conflicting but usually were complementary. For the mother of David Bellingham, this paused footage culminated in a moment, which only in retrospect, would be revealed to have saved the world.

Leading to her purchase the next day of the largest TV at the Opelousas Super Walmart. One with a curved screen so large that it would fill David's entire range of vision. Mom and the nurse wheeled his adjustable gurney and life support equipment into the living room, positioning him upright with the special neck support.

Placing him close to the television.

Drawing near, Mom whispered in his ear, "With you not having school, I figure we might as well have fun."

Taking a sip from a bottle of Abita Amber beer on the side table, she reclined in the chair behind her son's wheelchair. Her fingers tenderly opening her child's eyelids. Her big toe navigating the buttons of the remote on the floor. His mother lovingly blinked her son's eyes as they surfed cable and web TV stations. Media reflecting in David's stationary eyeballs pointed now down and to the right. His body motionless. There was no way to tell what he felt, his mother conceded.

Perhaps it was an escape into media?

She came to believe it on faith. Desperately needing him to escape into Han Solo, Harry Potter, or James Bond. Maybe that would free him from the tomb of his mortal coil. She would give anything to know for certain if she helped him now. One thing in retrospect was certain, it kept them both alive. While she never suspected that everything she believed was wrong. It would take eight months to unlock that awful truth. When late on a cold Wednesday afternoon, a rented Camaro stopped halfway up the old, dirt road leading to Ms. Bellingham's home. Inside the idling vehicle, unbeknownst to David's mother, sat the most important man she would ever meet. Someone who knew what no one else did.

An honest man.

One whose search for truth would give a later generation its sole hope of survival. For David would make clear many facts long-kept hidden. Just as the driver of the Camaro would reveal a crucial fact about David to this mother. A truth that would force her to take certain actions. For as much as he had to offer the boy-

The truth would hurt.

two

It would kill David.

Across the table in her kitchen, the Tulane professor peered down at his steaming coffee mug after making the dire price of his invention clear. Dr. Jim Tutwiler's eyes now evaded hers, having disclosed the truth that drove him to want to be drunk in Petaluma. It was hard for him to discuss it as David was a child and his mother was so beautiful. But still, he pressed on:

"It's gonna save him, but it's gonna kill your son," he shrugged, "It's killed all nine of my patients. My invention will get

David out of his body, and give him new experiences that he could never have which…comes at the cost of his life."

"How does he have these experiences?"

He knew he had her with his reply, "I'll give your son a new body-"

"But that's impossible."

"My technology will trick his brain into believing it," explains the researcher, "he'll be someone else in my digitally created game world. It's the true escape you thought you had by letting him watch TV-"

"What kind of technology?" she probed.

"A video game would be the best description for it, but that label doesn't do it justice. It feels as real as this," Jim knocks on the table, "as real as life but better. And you're never the same after gaming it. We are our experiences. So after, you're more than you can imagine in a way that words can't capture."

She eyes the surfaces of her coffee mug continuing to vibrate from the prior motion by Jim who adds:

"But my game is an adult one with mature content. And David is a child. He'll wish to play it again and again to escape his traumatized body. Repeated game play will finally trigger his mortality. His mind will turn off. We don't yet understand the neurological mechanism which causes it."

He lets her absorb what he's said.

Mother's eyes turn away like all the others. Still, Jim knows that once he gets to the next part she won't be able to say no, "By playing it, Ms. Bellingham, my patients were able to have new experiences, each in their own way finding meaningful contentment before they died."

"But they knew they were dying."

"After playing many game cycles, they no longer cared. They no longer felt tied to this world in any traditional sense. Which allowed them to be whole in a way that ironically we're not."

"How long does a game last?" she queried.

"Three to four weeks-"

"How long does David have before he…expires from it?"

"Our greatest success was 18 months, the shortest was 10," he shrugs, "it's the reason why we can only test this technology on Locked-in syndrome patients. Which involves an initial surgery in New Orleans and then a trip out west to California."

"Why California?"

"To bring this concept to fruition constituted a very expensive, medical device that could only ever help a handful of people. Through my university, I sought additional third-party funding from outside medical providers. The Loma Linda Medical Center is a faith-driven hospital, expending vast resources to help make all people whole. They funded my computer simulator at their Southern California medical campus as a joint venture with my university, Tulane. Once we get David out to Cali, I can free him from his crucible of pain. Because I assure you, your son is not watching TV," he cleared his throat. He didn't want to hit that point too hard just yet. Because until they got to California, he knew that nothing could be done about the boy's affliction.

Silence fell over them.

Staring at each other, each said nothing. He knows she needs to pull it along now or he'd be pandering. He refuses to be a salesman. With this much at stake, the client must come to him.

Jim sits at this table because of a random idea he incepted while jogging down St. Charles Avenue seven years prior. As a streetcar rang its bell while he traversed Napoleon Avenue, an epiphany flashed as simultaneous signals between neural connections populating his consciousness; forming a realization that the symbolic-logic math system he studied in philosophy could be applied to computer coding to trick and manipulate the senses; immersing a human brain integrally into a false reality.

"OK. So where do we go from here?" Mom asked.

"We start with a surgery at Tulane Medical Center," he elaborated, "installing ports into David's brain. I warn you, he'll have wires coming out of little holes in his skull. They tether his neurons into the game system. Then when he's well enough to travel, we fly to California and you get a gift. You and your son will be able to converse with each other again."

He saves that gem for last.

He's done this scene a lot. If it were a movie, this moment would be when the camera dollies in close on mom's gorgeous face. Because this woman is more beautiful than any movie star Jim has ever beheld. He struggled to hide his attraction to her, but he knew she sensed it all along. He thinks of her harsh injuries in the police report pictures. Everyone falls for this one, he mused, whether to love or capture.

Real beauty evokes such emotions.

She loved this quirky man who promised her the stuff of her dreams. To probe beyond merely pressing her nose into the back of her son's head, wondering how David actually felt: her sole longing answered. A reconnection after the monster took her child away.

This stranger promised to reconnect them.

The surgery occurred a week later at Tulane Medical Center. In the operating theatre, surgeons bore tiny holes into her son's freshly shaven skull. The interface was new with little leeway for aesthetics. Primitive bundles of synthetic electrodes were woven into cluster patterns spanning countless neurons in David's brain. The thought of holes in her son's head drove his mother to take refuge in the ground floor PJ's coffee shop. Sipping French roast, she watched toddlers playing in the kiddie play center.

Two weeks after that surgery, a chartered Gulfstream jet flew David in a medically induced coma, his mother, Jim, and two techs from New Orleans to Ontario Airport in Southern California. An ambulance next transported them at dusk to Jim's computer lab building just off the central quadrangle of the Loma Linda Medical Center's picturesque campus.

Palm trees and rustic hills surrounded Jim's lab building. The next afternoon on a bench facing the lab and Loma Linda University Church across the grassy quadrangle, David's mom sat anxiously on a bench. The warm California sun against her face. She'd waited as techs in the lab slowly resuscitated David from his medically induced coma. The process took far longer than expected. Then Jim approached her, offering to split his sandwich for lunch, promising:

"Loma Linda Hospital promotes a vegetarian diet, but I promise this pecan ball sandwich is life-affirming."

She loved the sandwich.

She ate it as Jim told her how the Seventh Day Adventist followers of Loma Linda were recognized as one of only five *blue zones* in the world; areas where humans lived on average far longer than anywhere else.

"How does a blue zone begin?"

"This area was founded by a woman named Ellen G. White in the 19th Century. She urged her followers to buy this land in the desert and build a medical center. But she claimed this center would one day be the light of the world by saving humanity from possible world-ending destruction-"

Jim was interrupted by an incoming text on his phone.

"Time to go," he told her as he ended the call, sliding the phone back into his pocket.

Mom helped gather up the sandwich wrappings, never considering that by healing David, Ellen G. White's prophecy might one day come true in curious retrospect when the fate of the world hung in the balance.

Jim and mom arrived back at his high ceilinged lab. The place smelled of cleaning chemicals and warm circuitry, a notably unique and memorable combination. Techs finished connecting the final wires from David's head to the massive, nano-supercomputer processors lining the walls.

The nine-year-old boy remained naked except for a metal machine wrapped around his midsection, elegantly disposing of bodily waste. The capsule cradling the boy was named a *comport* by Jim since it was the wider port connecting the patient's mind to the computer processor. The electric pads of the comport's inner bed sent mild electric shocks firming up David's musculature to avoid atrophy.

Witnesses to the event, like most significant moments in history, failed to appreciate the importance this day would have on the future of humanity. Its relevance like all prior Old Testament prophecies would become true only in hindsight. Technicians at the time later spoke in various documentaries on David Bellingham, of a more austere gravity at the time due to the patient's young age.

"Remember what we talked about on the flight," Jim prompted mom as they approached David's capsule.

The scent of static electricity from the lab now filled Mom's nose as she drew near to her son. Large computer cooling units towered over them, spilling a low hanging, dry ice-like mist across the floor.

David's mother stared at the encompassing mist covering the floor as she ignored the ghastly ports from the bored holes in her son's head. The sudden flash of a camera fell across her as she peered down at her child. In the dim shadows at the edge of the room, the medical study's photographer snapped candid wide-angled photos.

David's eyes remained closed.

So mother's eyes darted to the large speakers mounted on a shelf over the boy's comport. The sound emanating from them sounded like static.

On the jet flight out west, they dined on a catered meal of Billy's Cajun boudin and jambalaya; Jim warned her that this static-like sound was the best his system could depict of a human scream:

"All my past Locked-in syndrome patient screamed upon their reconnection to the outside world," Jim explained in the padded comfort of the private jet.

"Why must there be screaming?" she was taken aback at the time.

"Everyone cries during birth," the academic shrugged effortlessly, "David will be reborn. The scream only happens the first time we reconnect him."

He didn't tell her why.

Now a week later in the Loma Linda lab, mom squeezes her son's paralyzed hand as her stomach dropped, realizing her son had been wanting to scream this whole time. She felt the vast difference between believing and knowing.

"David," she fights back tears as his eyelids are parted open by the sophisticated machine irrigating his eyeballs with a saline mist, "I can hear you now, baby. You're thinking words and I can now hear them out loud–"

"MOM! MOM! MOM!" he cried. At that moment David hears his thoughts projected in a mechanical voice as he thinks the words:

"CLEAR MY THROAT! CLEAR MY THROAT! CLEAR MY THROAT!"

Techs immediately began to suction saliva from the rear of his esophagus. The sensation of him choking returned to his senses months ago and overtook him in constant agony. In each of Jim's cases, the physical issue varied, but always forged incredible anguish for the patient. All the patients eventually regained some sense of their body.

"It's OK baby," she replies.

"MOMMY, YOU HEAR ME?"

She nods yes.

Only now does David realize that his mother somehow hears his inner thoughts. The mechanical device again draws open his eyelids. Not mother's crude blinking, but a sleek machine with tiny padded claws prying his lids as micro-jets irrigated his eyeball as he makes his will known:

"MAKE IT STOP MOMMY-MAKE IT STOP-MOMMY-PLEASE MAKE IT STOP!"

Looking down at his paralyzed shell, she regrets not having pulled his life support. Freed from his silent tomb, he makes clear the fear the doctor told her. Why hadn't she killed him? She lacked bravery. The flash of that dead cat in her son's arms. Then Jim's grip on her shoulder draws her to the reassurance he wishes her to now give David:

Wiping back tears, she comforts her son, "No baby, these people are going to make it better-"

"STOP IT, MOMMY! STOP IT!" her boy screams from his mind-

"Now," Jim tells his technicians behind them.

A switch is thrown.

The cooling systems lining the supercomputers begin to rumble like a roaring train fast approaching to carry her son away. The text on the bank of monitors behind the comport vibrates, showing:

PROGRAM INITIATING...

The photographer darts in close, snapping a final pic. Stop. Eye the frozen image in his camera's viewfinder. A frightened nine-year-old boy with eyes parted by irrigation spectacles. Naked except for his midsection concealed in steel.

Although no one present appreciates it, this image will become the most iconic photo in human history. For a future generation of Americans and the world, it will represent the source of their possible salvation. For some, it will signify their greatest fear. Nonetheless, it will hang in the National Portrait Gallery in Washington DC, adorning countless college dorm room walls, memes, t-shirts, and what would become the longest-running Times Square marquee ad in American history.

But all of that remains in the future.

For now, his mother hopes as the camera captures her child that David can be liberated from his tomb of a body as Jim promised. Meanwhile, young David Bellingham holds no such aspiration.

He is in control of nothing.

A guinea pig in an ultimately lethal, cutting-edge computer-based video game. Microchips married to brain cells. A paralyzed explorer about to set sail through the digital landscape to a New World.

He will be the first to realize that this creation is anything but a game. He will later prove this point by employing what will become his favorite theory, Einsteinian relativity which governed just about everything in ways few appreciated during his childhood, but most would come to fathom because of him. For now, the boy like his mother remains unaware that a great hinge in history has just swung open. The culmination of an event born from a revelation birthed in the wake of a New Orleans streetcar bell.

David's mother can't help but think of herself as she peers into her son's face. The fact that her life has been so troubled since she was abused when she was younger than David, a crime almost preceding her memory. But the loss of it now wells up within her. She feels the pain of her boy in shared childhood trauma. As a child, she escaped the abuse by watching *Cinderella* countless times, believing and waiting one day for her prince to finally come. The dreams of a little girl whose first recorded memory was locking eyes with a street dog set to attack her. A golden-haired child better cared for by neighbors than her family. And later as a mother, she birthed a boy fated to suffer for her quest to find the love and protection that she never received. Now he too would not fall in love or reach fatherhood.

Yet even his mother failed to appreciate many things. One of which was that her helpless son would fulfill the prophecy he foretold in a cold Walmart parking lot. As implausible and outrageous as it seemed at the time, David Bellingham would cure death. Because the coming plague Jim felt in his bones was part of a wider challenge never before faced by any nation in history. What people would call the *Time of Trouble*. But for now, this boy must wait many decades for the underlying truths of the universe and his role within it to be revealed to him through a government agent, a man who holds the secret David needs to save humanity.

part two

Ray Kemper

"And there shall be a time of trouble.
Such as never was since there was a nation."

Daniel 12:1

three

"Ray, you with me?" she asked.

The words from his secret lover were piped into his ear over their private communication link. The moment his partner spoke, the image of her naked body sparked in Ray's mind's eye. Remembering her smell when they last kissed in the privacy of his hotel room. The sting of knowing that if their superiors ever discovered their dalliance, they'd be in serious trouble.

Careers replaced by prison sentences.

Now her inquiry ended Ray Kemper's train of thought; searing away some great notion which had filled his mind. A truth he realized while staring at the iconic photo of his idol, David

Bellingham, back when the child was set to begin Jim Tutwiler's lethal video game. That digital experience from which young David, alone, famously survived.

"I'm here," Ray curtly replied to his female handler in her remote, offline location, "I hid before he looked back."

FCC agent Ray Kemper slowly peered over the shoulder of the man in front of him in the thick crowd. It was odd how the mind could cycle through a meditative thought or his partner's naked body while he hunted the most dangerous person in history only paces ahead; the figure many considered to be the current antiChrist; a person Ray now fought on the surreal front line of 2059. The fourth year of World War IV; that conflagration waged in both the offline *real world* and here while *on-lining* in the virtual eHallways of the modern web created by David Bellingham.

The stakes couldn't be higher.

This conflagration began four painful years prior in 2055, leading to this FCC Web Agent now tracking his target through this seemingly endless, eCorridors packed with people. Ray hid amidst the crowd of thousands of chatting online users filling this virtual web hall; none of them suspecting that the hoodie-clad figure strutting through them many paces ahead of Ray, was the most prolific mass-murderer in history. They might not know his actual face, but everyone knew his name harkening back to awful events in recent history-

Blackout.

The famed 20th Century physicist, Albert Einstein, incorrectly predicted that any third World War would be a nuclear exchange. In contrast, World War III started as an economic attack on America long before. Chinese news agencies still refused to call it a world war. For Americans, the Third World War began when the U.S. government under then-president Bill Clinton allowed in tariff-free, Chinese slave-made goods to the U.S. market and then the free world. With no environmental protections required by Clinton for these Chinese-made products, he fed not only slavery but the largest mass-pollution in history rarely covered by the American media at the time, acting through political party loyalty to aid Communist China.

Mass-media was too busy lauding the U.S. presidents who enriched the destruction of America and the planet through enriching Communist tyranny. Their treason was undeniable once COVID-19 killed so many Americans after Hillary Clinton revealed America's spies to China's dictator on her hacked, unguarded server in 2013. That traitor silenced the voices who could've warned the nation. The woman along with Obama and Biden rigged the 2016 Democrat Party presidential nomination proven by Wikileaks while illegally wiretapping the only major candidate to oppose Chinese slavery in 30 years. The complete breakdown of the Constitution in high treason. A scandal light-years beyond Watergate to resist the only president who aimed to curb Chinese slavery.

George Washington warned of America's destruction once a president would for foreign bribes, end domestic manufacturing. The nation would, Washington foresaw, be enslaved to the foreign king who made the products Americans bought. Washington knew Americans would be blind to the theft of their liberty as they were through the pro-China media of the future, pushing the lie of private wealth being owned in Communist China. Clinton, W. Bush, and Obama, now termed *The Three Traitors*, needlessly allowed the Cold War into a world war taking over America.

Washington predicted the port cities receiving these foreign slave-made goods would turn treasonous. Reflected in the urban Sanctuary-areas blooming in the major U.S. ports for China: Seattle, Portland, Los Angeles, Manhattan; cities long robbed of their rights by their own leaders, mass-imprisoned, made drug-addicts to Chinese opioids, and later saw the defunding of their police. Bringing mayhem to resist then-President Trump who aimed to stop Chinese slavery. While the pro-China U.S. media seldom reported how the virus that destroyed the American economy had been concealed by Xi Jinping for five months. China sent half a million Chinese to infect America, mostly in the Sanctuary cities proliferating under Clinton, Bush, and Obama.

"Xi Jinping lied and billions died," a little girl in a meta-ad for The *New Mother Goose's History eBook* continued the famous children's rhyme, "About China's private wealth, Clinton, Bush, and Obama lied."

Ray weaved down the eHall past a promotional documentary titled *Isaiah's Warning*. The film highlighted how the end-time prophecies of Isaiah had come true. The show noted how Isaiah foretold the Chinese C19 outbreak later termed the *Yin Yang Virus* to remind the world of the horror that China's dictator gifted them, *"For the vintage will fail…The highways lie waste, the traveling man ceases, the treaty is broken, its witnesses are despised, no one is respected."*

It became clear over time that the Yin Yang Virus's largest effect was to wipe out nations by killing or virally castrating males worldwide through receptors in the lungs, liver, and testicles. For others, it slowly rotted the bodies out like Swiss Cheese. All from a dictator who had artificially-made a half human-half pig species that Stalin so longed to possess like Star Wars Storm Troopers clones. A Chinese enemy who unleashed strains on the clueless nation leaving its U.S. borders open to Chinese trade and travelers. Among the 480,000 Chinese who mass-infected the nation were some with more lethal strains in their possession if the leader required it. The U.S. was controlled by him and the west coast that would be quarantined and suffer for their policies.

Through long-cyber striking American companies, Xi Jinping was also allowed by U.S. politicians and academics to enrich him. But he didn't foresee advances in medicine which by the mid-2030s finally slowed his viral annihilation. His Yin Yang virus evolved into what for the past two decades had become primarily a pulmonary disease affecting the elderly as long as younger people stayed current on their annual *Green Lung* pill prescription.

The advertisement for the pill filled the walls around Ray. Peering through the bodies of the crowd ahead of him, he kept a sharp eye on his prey. Covering the walls of the hallway around him broadcast the startlingly bright, green fungus suffocating and filling human lungs in the continuing Yin Yang Virus pandemic. The synergy between the evolving virus and now-constant spores presented an ever-present harbinger of death. Only recently could younger people taking the annual pill shed the long ubiquitous facemasks. All reminders of America's treasonous enrichment in what most finally accepted as World War III perpetrated by the *Three Traitors*, Clinton, W. Bush, and Obama and their administrations and allies. It only ended after CRISPR genetic-altering technology largely poisoned the gene-pool of much of Communist China.

Now as unthinkable as it was, Ray fought on the front line of this new, *Fourth World War*. This conflagration began through acts refusing to be ignored like the prior war; when the teenager known as Blackout wielded his digital, computer virus with undeniable effects on mass-municipal electric grids in 2055. Unlike Xi Jinping's slow, deceptive war on American soil, Blackout's attack was so fast it refused to be ignored for a time.

Blackout named his online virus, the Yin Yang Virus in homage to Xi Jinping's concealment of C19 now evolved with China's rain into *Green Lung*. Then Blackout's Yin Yang digital virus could quickly be world-ending. Only one person foresaw this threat before it manifested. The modern web's famous inventor and blogger, David Bellingham warned that near-total power could one day be focused on a single human. His prophecy came to fruition in World War IV. That conflagration beginning on Thanksgiving Day, 2055.

Blackout surpassed the mass-killing record Communist

China had achieved by the 1970s, previously killing more people than any regime in history before even Xi Jinping's murder of millions. This acne-faced teenager claimed to be the liberator of the planet from the past unregulated, Communist Chinese pollution of *World War III* that ultimately generated never-ending worldwide hurricanes across the planet. Born from the stratospheric contamination from America's prior, made-in-China purchases.

Ahead of the agent, Blackout, now clad in a dark hoodie with his evil glowing mask again spun around to see if he'd been followed in the crowded hall. His online likeness, termed a *Skin,* blended in with the many clad as him online in homage to the eTerrorist. Ray's tweak months before allowed him to lightly shade out anyone else wearing Blackout's iconic hoodie-clad Skin.

He knew his prey well.

Illustrated moments before when the FCC agent somehow sensed his target would soon turn back. Meanwhile, Ray was already crouched out of sight in a small crowd of Ricky Gervais Skins, Gervais being held in great reverence in the future for having spoken the truth about the Communist-controlled media of his age, broadcasting new perversions for young American eyes as misguided progress. Ray stalked Blackout for so long that he could instinctually anticipate the teen's next move.

The meta commercials around them splashed vivid colors across the crowd hiding Ray. The lights of the video advertisement, termed a *vid ad,* projected even from the moving media screen floor beneath Ray. Casting a sweeping array of face-paint-like-colors across his face. The moving floor carried the crowd forward down the twelve-foot wide, seemingly endless hall.

"You're on the web with Bellingham Labs *Doors 4.0,*" an automated voice periodically resounded as Ray eyed the media on the moving floor screen.

Bellingham Labs was David's company, now the most visited on Earth from the inventor's landmark creations. Begun back in 2032, David's earpiece computer, the *eComp* ended the need for all computers and smartphones. Like practically everyone else, Ray rarely took his own off.

The eComp tricked the user's mind, superimposing a virtual smartphone screen over their range of vision, utilizing the user's eye as the mouse. In the borders of Ray's vision, he saw icons for programs along with a corner positioned media window displaying a live feed of his female handler, Ravenna:

"I lost visual," Ray whispered to his partner over his communication line, termed a comlink.

"You're giving him too much distance," she warned from their remote, offline location.

Ravenna could offer useful support, but he dismissed her insights on tracking. After all, she was just a handler trained in the physical world; his real-world protector and warrior, she never achieved the coveted status of an online agent like Ray. Usually stationed in his hotel room, she guarded his body while he was immersed in the eComp's docking station, the comport; this device having long evolved beyond the original prototype from David Bellingham's youth.

The sleek pod-like machine was topped off with a bulletproof, holographic media screen lid. Once Ray reclined inside it, the lid closed as his eComp docked with the housing around the headrest area of the inner bed. His mind instantly immersed into the seemingly infinite web hallways, losing all sense of his body along with any trace of the offline world.

Online in the web.

These days Ray never strayed far from his comport. Because once the U.N. strike-force registered Blackout's entry ping onto the internet, he was expected to immediately online and track and hopefully touch the eTerrorist. Ten minutes ago the agent attempted just that, materializing in one of these endless eHalls constituting the architecture of the web.

These corridors were where people met up to chat online

at no charge, drawing sizeable crowds providing cover for the fugitive. Ads subsidized the free hangout space; the reason why almost all the surfaces, including the moving walkway floor, broadcasted vid ads.

The eye candy complicated visual tracking. And the moving floor didn't help, carrying all the *chatters* past endless doors; each door evenly spaced every 6 feet on either side of the crowded corridor. The passageway was three times the width of a conventional hotel hall. Each unique door led to a distinct website. Bill Gates had *Windows*. David Bellingham gifted the world-

Doors.

Each door projected seductive media enticing users into its specific site. Many digital travelers here didn't chat at all, but only hyperlinked into a hall in front of their desired door through which they quickly entered, vanishing into that website; they appeared only for a moment, online social distancing as best they could through chat corridors.

Unlike the 15 Hare Krishna Hindu celebrants now hyperlinking between Ray and Blackout in the thick crowd. They drummed up business for their site nearby. The agent's eyes struggled to follow his target between the festive, bald, robed Krishnas, singing and swinging candy-cane staffs to lure people into their website's door.

Door Peddling was free but constituted only localized advertising, luring in users within eyeshot in the eHall. Whereas the mega hitters like Bellingham Labs' upcoming, two-player video-game *Dreamspace* now filled every surface but the doors for as far as the eye could see. The ad pulled away from the close-up of a gamer isolated in their comport, their minds immersed online. Their comports were orderly arranged in multiple levels within new buildings titled *bodhouses* or *body vaults*. The mega ad showed one as an unseen woman's voice asked the audience to:

"Imagine both your bodies fed by I.V.'s. within the safety of our comports. Robotic systems and med-staff to oversee users' bodies as they join online with their game-mate in the most exciting experience ever created. Come find your ideal game mate through our brief but unique dates in customized *Dreamspace* worlds. Live your dreams."

Then another ad. The iconic Indian trillionaire, Mr. Zero broadcast a live *Flesh Update!* on all the non-door surfaces of the corridor. Ray peered up at the ad on the huge ceiling a mile above the chatters.

A crouching Agent Kemper seemed like a spec under the massive vid screen ceiling extending for as far as the eyes could see. It showed the tracksuit-clad, Indian peddler in dark gold-rimmed sunglasses. Mr. Zero screamed in his thick, Calcutta accent from above the conversing *chatters*:

"Join the movement! Wear Matt Damon's Skin, now the top-selling Skin online! Buy now and get a free Damon Skin for your eComp's Siri. Damn, Siri never looked so good!"

The blinking logo of Mr. Zero's House of Skin's intermittently flashed illumination across Ray's Matt Damon's Skin accompanied by the actor's authentic voice filter. Ray's vintage, middle-aged *Bourne Identity* era Damon was the best camouflage these days, allowing him to melt into the millions of users who'd gone retro-crazy for the iconic star. This year alone, Damon's estate generated over a billion dollars in Skin right's proceeds, donating much of it to aid the Midwest famine after Blackout's cyber strikes of U.V. indoor grain farms.

His first strike famously brought down *Space Force One*, killing President Tiggi and her top advisers. An America made desperate from radical climate change in the '54 election surpassed any prior identity politics. The nation voted in a hermaphrodite president self-identifying as a female who proudly possessed every genetic race and ethnicity. She seemed like a doting *Mother Nature* to protect the nation in her arms. Even her name felt safe, Mamma Tiggi. No one took issue with her having never held a political office. American history already proved to voters that prior career politicians, especially lawyers, were highly unsuitable to lead a nation. The current world war broke out on Thanksgiving Day when Blackout assassinated Mamma Tiggi with his digital virus, bringing down her spacecraft. Her death thrust Tiggi's untested vice-president into the highest office.

The former governor of Ohio, a blonde-haired 45-year-old spiritualist, and ex-Governor was first maligned for having been a semi career politician, mistrusted in modernity. Political detractors and some in the press termed him the *Nazi* due to his appearance in striking contrast to his genetically diverse predecessor. But Tiggi was wise to choose him as her running-mate. Soon this man would be the rarest of U.S. presidents, a true leader.

In a private meeting with Ray at Camp David, the President confided that his belief in God was why he could back Ray's risky approach. The leader believed that this life was as The Old Testament made clear, a test for a real existence to follow. Still, the President couldn't bring himself to believe that his Creator would make humanity to end history with a depraved, teenage psychopath as the price for Steve Job's lie of a digital utopia. Even in Job's day, most Silicon Valley executives had barred their children from using interactive screens, which they criminally peddled to the children of the world. Now the web proved to be humanity's possible undoing. The President confided that if the war was lost, his *State of The World Address* would try and term the world war not as the fourth one, but rather as an extension of World War III; since it was all the fallout of the *Great Traitor*, Bill Clinton's selling out to Communism and poisoning the planet, continued by W. Bush and Obama like three Roman emperors above the Constitution they swore to defend.

Ray had the only plan.

Still, not even Ray's approach had a foolproof strategy to fight Blackout's plan. The eTerrorist claimed to have wired his body so that if wounded or killed, his lethal, digital virus would be auto-uploaded to shareware sites worldwide. Then the long-dreaded, mass upload of the digital Yin Yang virus termed the *ePocalypse* could not be stopped in time from its proliferation out of the dark corners of the web. If this nightmare scenario occurred, any disgruntled soul could end the world from their eComp's iScreens, downloading and then launching Blackout's deadly virus on an array of targets in a world too wired to unwind itself from the web.

If digitally exchanged to others, the mass spread of electric-grid cyber strikes and their resulting electromagnetic pulses, termed EMPs, in the real world would end all human life. The threat of a mass-digital-spread of Blackout's digital virus across the web, the *ePocalypse*, would leave no operable machines left to build new ones. Anyone alive would be left to slowly drown in the rising rainwater of their leveed zone after pumping stations were rendered permanently inoperable due to the digital virus's real-world EMPs. Americans would drown in the rising rainwater sown by their predecessors.

There would be no escape. The elites in their space stations in orbit would succumb to prolonged, high levels of radiation, which the stratosphere protected for those on Earth. Those in shelters at the tops of the Rockies, Alps, and the Himalayas would be the last to drown, leaving behind a stormy, blue planet devoid of land or *Homo sapiens*. That ironic label humans chose for themselves was Latin for the *wise man*. In retrospect, the label would've been comical if not for the lethal price of that arrogance displayed in the late 20th and 21st Centuries.

Effects of the China Pollution triggered what the *Old Testament* had termed the *opening up of the fountains of the deep,* erupting through the volcanic seams of the planet's tectonic plates, from a large channel beneath the Arctic Ocean; but unlike Noah's flood, this deluge didn't recede after forty days, but was later revealed to continue for eons. The sudden rising water triggered a series of never-ending worldwide hurricanes and hailstorms now covering the planet.

Only swiftly constructed water pumping stations rerouted ever-constant rainwater to keep the leveed areas from drowning during storms just as New Orleans had fought for centuries. The ePocalypse's threat of a deluge to cover the planet starting with an eye swipe empowered its teenage creator with a power never before witnessed. The reason why his supremacy made him seem like something more than human, almost god-like. Even now in the web hall as Ray stalked him, the meta ad advertised the award-winning documentary on the eTerrorist's recent *goodbye* parties for his elite *Hacker Club* partying in various world capitals.

It sickened Ray to see how many of the young fawned over the eTerrorist, representing the only power they ever knew. A generation who never saw the sun now had a demi-god to replace it. The president of France at the hacker's demand, ran naked up the *Rue du Faubourg Saint Honore* to keep his country from being cyber struck. President Balik of Poland was kicked in the genitals by a donkey to protect his nation. Blackout forced leaders to recreate physical stunts from old *Jackass* films, gathering more online admirers. Then the teen reinvented himself like a modern Caligula. Birthing wild, sexual perversions unheralded since Renaissance popes and Roman emperors.

The teen raped the Spanish president's wife while her husband was handcuffed at his request to spare that nation. Then he forcibly raped the Spanish president. The politician's bodyguards tried to intercede, stopping only after the hacker's eye swipe destroyed Barcelona with an eye swipe, launching his digital Yin Yang virus on that city. Blackout's rapes were filmed on spy-cameras and broadcast across the web. So similar to Caligula who forced Roman senators to make their wives whores in the Senate turned into a brothel for the plebeians. After the Vatican stunt, which no one wished to recall, the teen openly pushed for sodomy but did not get the cooperation of most homosexuals. After the mess created by media earlier in the century, people largely viewed sodomy as a symptom of child rape and unwitting victims to be tolerated, but not proliferated. Rather the child molesters who raped those many victims, like Blackout did, could not remain under the rainbow banner as well. In the end, Blackout loathed that God's Prohibitions of Abomination held sway over him.

Then he took aim at Israelites and Christian sects honoring the Saturday Sabbath. He hated God's laws, which empowered believers. So Blackout remarketed himself as the final harbinger of destruction. The song *Centuries* by the old band *Fall Out Boy* stood as his anthem; angry lyrics to coerce hatred to be showered upon the Israelites and all those who followed God's unchangeable laws symbolized in Sabbath at the final day of the week. As Chinese Communism already well-proved, total rulers not only sought to control the exterior world but also the inner-mind of their subjugates. It was needed because the societies birthed by these tyrants would require brute force to keep the mistreated masses in line. Blackout was now able to surpass even the former Chinese dictator for life, Xi Jinping.

The U.S. president condemned the hacker and anyone who followed his *deranged* orders. Blackout retaliated by sporting Colin Kaepernick's skin, using the Nike symbol as his reinvented brand icon, commanding all Americans to take a knee for the flag. Then the new U.S. president like a modern-day Winston Churchill or Reagan did what no prior appeaser was willing to consider. His iconic speech now played in the eHallway around Ray for an upcoming web documentary promo:

"Although I do not believe it for a moment, if the history of our great nation is to end," text superimposed below the U.S. leader showed '56, *First State of the World Address*, "The United States of America will go down fighting to the last man, woman, and child on the web just as Americans in the prior world war weekly risked death in the grocery stores. We seek only freedom and liberty. And we possess an antidote to this modern monster's virus that carries severe ramifications, but will end this wickedness."

Ray knew the truth.

The president bluffed. There was no secret weapon. It was all to buy Ray time to write his program. The objective, to stop the upload of Blackout's virus to shareware sites. Then in 2057 following the American president's famed speech, the world erupted into mass hysteria.

Blackout vanished in Russia.

World stock markets crashed. Most assumed the ePocalypse to be nigh. It was mayhem. Like a confused Mardi Gras that went on in cities for weeks, stretching into months. People began losing their minds from the stress of sudden death at any moment. Suicide spread as it had from the worldwide storms in the 2040s. The teen's former posse remained under U.N. guards at the various, old Tsarist palaces they resided in at the time of his vanishing.

Government analysts confidentially expected Blackout to trigger the ePocalypse at any moment, possibly while drunk or on the new personalized, opiate-like iDrugs, which he reportedly began to abuse according to dark web chatter. The President lived under this continuing threat of brinksmanship from a secure military bunker in Colorado. The planet again faced the threat of sudden Armageddon not felt since the 1950's Cold War threat of mass thermonuclear war.

A great many people in the past years had returned to God in their own way, especially given the truth behind the birth of science long-popularized by David Bellingham's famous blog. But this Divine return seemed to come too late. Still, Ray worked hard at coding.

The President prayed.

He confided to Ray in a meeting they had in the conference area aboard the new *Space Force* One free of any online connections. The leader of the free world asked only to have God's will be done. For this President knew from scripture not to interface with God like an oracle to listen and respond. For that relationship was forbidden even to the Old Testament's *Elect* at the end of days who would come to restore the New Jerusalem. The President agreed with David Bellingham's popular blog, certain that the New Jerusalem was the United States, where finally Israelites could worship as their laws dictated, free of spiritual intermediaries, respected by America's distinct Freedom Of Worship. Even in Israel, citizens were forced to be orthodox by law, worshipping again under illegal intermediaries never forced upon Americans.

Some felt the President had gambled the fate of his species to keep his fellow Americans free. Defeatists thought the war inevitably lost. But the President was willing to do anything to keep America free and alive. Ray Kemper became that leader's-

Roll of the dice.

Ray's two vital pieces of software were created for a simple mission; the objective which the current President, unlike his predecessor, green-lit. For the real culprit was an overly wired world. Now Ray's mission was similar to what sail fishing must've been like when there was still marlin in the oceans. Let the fish get distance on a hooked line only to reel him back in a bit and repeat. Each time weakening it a bit more just as Ray lulled Blackout's online sensors. All to get-

Close enough to touch his target.

Only then could Ray's containment program geo-locate the eTerrorist's offline location, allowing Ray's strike force to swiftly kill Blackout in the real world. If Blackout wasn't killed fast, Ray's containment software would never work. To contain the ePocalypse files' upload to other shareware sites and beyond he needed Blackout dead, leaving him to only fight the auto-coding.

Ray was the only person in the U.S. government to be granted access to Blackout's actual programming codex. Through

his insightful analysis, Ray realized the hacker's coding language to be a work of genius. From it, he feared he could never outduel this coding mind. He found it hard to believe that the virus hadn't been created by a nation-state-backed team of designers. It was so complex but elegant. Ray finished the program to hopefully contain the virus's mass upload to shareware sites when the team received an unexpected breakthrough.

A young female defector from Blackout's camp made it possible for Ray's government team to receive a ping when and where Blackout approximately onlined. But touching Blackout's online Skin proved to be difficult. The eTerrorist possessed complex sensor programs registering anomalies of anyone getting too close. The reason why Ray patiently hid in the crowd as he let his prey advance through the never-ending hall of *chatters*.

To trick the sensors, Ray had to let Blackout repeatedly advance almost out of view. There was no plan. Just him and his gut instincts. Trying to remain hidden, the agent stopped behind a carrot clad as Abe Lincoln complaining to a burly Panda Warrior. Ray feigned he was looking for someone nearby as the two conversed ahead of him:

"...he threatened to fight you online?" the Abe Lincoln carrot huffed to his friend.

The Panda recounted, "And I said until Blackout kills us all, this is the only place we can meet for free. So if you don't like what I'm saying then just hyperlink somewhere else..."

Crouched, Ray moved away from them, deeper amidst the seemingly endless sea of *chatters*. Ahead, the crowded web hall gently curved to the left, obscuring his target from view. Darting forward, Ray avoided touching other users chatting in a myriad of languages. Progressing then backtracking, over time he slowly closed the distance.

"Ray, you're too far back," Ravenna warned over the comlink, uncomfortable at the distance he granted Blackout.

"Hey, it's me," he reassured her, knowing that many people could be listening in over the mission comlink. After all, Ray was as close as he ever got to his target in World War IV.

Everything was on the line.

No one talked about winning the war, but *ending* it so that humanity could solely battle the parallel existential threat. After all, Mother Nature had already made islands of continents and soon set to possibly flood the world over. That battle against mass drowning had occupied the last two grueling decades and was still ongoing.

In 2042, after the then-secret U.N. report leaked and people realized the worldwide mega-storms would continue for 7,000 years, social breakdown first ensued. The nation was engulfed in mass looting. Rioting. Food hoarding. Skyrocketing crime. Record farm-crop failures and famine swept the globe due to the complete loss of the sun.

The violent seas and sky infringed on most remaining international trade that hadn't been previously curtailed by the Chinese viral attacks. Now many of those who thought logically about the world offered respect for Blackout's power, seduced down the rabbit's hole. Knowing you supported death, but somehow like a vampire, feeling liberated because everybody else wished to dance with the Devil too. Humans were always infected by a herd mentality. But as his partner Ravenna often quoted the famous Mexican expression, calling the Devil and seeing him walk towards you, were two very different things altogether.

Many of Ray's generation who never saw the sun in their lives, vented their anger by wearing Blackout's iconic skin and yearning for the ePocalypse to end their anguish. New York was the only city devastated by Blackout to ever be rebuilt. Yokohama, Cape Town, Memphis, Dubai, London, Seattle, and Miami to name but a few, were still flooded ruins. While the third world with its rickety magnetic flood walls and cheaply constructed levee zones were most hard-hit, contributing to the near billion lives already lost in the fog of World War IV.

After President Tiggi's assassination, Ray's U.N. *Swipe 9* task force was formed to initially analyze and track the infamous eTerrorist. Ironically the next meta ad showed the mercurial, 14-year-old hacker who had killed his parents and burned his Fort Collins, Colorado home to the ground to cover up any detail of his life, both offline and online. Soon this maniac came to kill so many that the vast casualties couldn't help but become lifeless statistics like those of Stalin's or Xi Jinping's victims. The reason why before joining *Swipe 9*, FCC Agent Kemper was forced to personally witness the aftermath of Blackout's handiwork.

In his case, it was Saint George, Utah, two days after a cyber strike, still a ghost town of rotting, electrocuted corpses. What touched Ray most remained in the living room of the darkened home in the rain-soaked cul de sac. A mother had been burned to an unrecognizable crisp as she tried to rescue her young daughter from the living room comport. Both by then charred carbon black. The odor of cooked bacon still so prevalent that Ray never again could consume pork. In Saint George, the hunt for Blackout became personal for Agent Kemper, just as the strike team's superiors wished it to be. The reason why deep inside him-

Ray would always have Utah.

In the end, *Swipe 9* was asked by President Tiggi to hunt, but never to engage in the kind of necessary, risky field action needed, which only the new President supported once he settled into office-

"Ray! He's surfing away," Ravenna chirped over the comlink.

Ray was too far from his target to see Blackout make the iconic Hawaiian *Shaka* or *hang-loose* hand-gesture, triggering the translucent surfboard materializing beneath the eTerrorist's feet. On her remote monitor, Ravenna spied Blackout in the distance, surfing up the sidewall and inverting on the massive media ceiling a hundred feet above Ray.

Online surfing presented more challenges for Ray than just tracking the fugitive in the chat halls. The *Doors 4.0* upgrade created a media wave river on the ceiling where inverted surfers rocketed on clear surfboards along the tidal ad stream only visible up there. Blackout disappeared over the crest of a massive, digital wave above advertising new anti-Green Lung air filters, his form barely visible in the halls far below. Besides knowing when Blackout initially onlined, Ray's team could not track his progress on the web due to his cutting-edge VPNT Ito scramblers. Ironically, only the old visual tail would work-

The agent counted down from five in his head before making the hand gesture, causing the personal announcement to chime in his ear, "You're surfing the web with Bellingham Labs' *Doors 4.0*."

A translucent surfboard expanded beneath his feet as he surfed up the sidewall, racing towards the ad-stream far overhead. Ray surfed after Blackout many times in the past few months, tracking this lunatic all over the web and often losing him up here in the vaporous ad-stream of waves. Many in the government considered Ray's mission a fool's errand. After all, even if he touched Blackout and located the enemy's real-world location, the strike force would have only a fraction of the time to kill him. Besides, no one had a clue where the eTerrorist was in the offline world until the recent breakthrough.

A week prior, another defector from the hacker's camp, revealed the eTerrorist might be headed to Shanghai. The reason why Ray was now in that same city, currently using the comport in his Shanghai Hilton Hotel penthouse. Unknown to the public, Hilton Hotels long possessed upgraded hotel rooms for top-secret web agents like Ray to launch onto the internet in what the sitting president termed-

Our last *Hail Mary.*

Out of range of Blackout's sensors, Ray Skin swapped from Damon to a caped, black knight, rocketing past countless other surfers in the dimly lit ad-stream of colored waves. Surfing over one wave and then another, his expert eyes honed in on Blackout's tiny spec set against a meta ad for an anti-fungal lung medicine. Leaning forward on his translucent surfboard, Ray accelerated, dodging and twisting around surfers as he negotiated the massive ad wave rolling in, soaring straight into the half-pipe wave.

"He's hyperlinking on the other side of the wave!" Ravenna advised over the comlink just before Blackout's surfboard fell away as the fugitive vanished, "I target laid."

Her comment meant his handler had set a digital target marker across Ray's iScreen filter. The red crosshair high above in mid-air began to fade on the virtual wormhole Blackout hyperlinked through to another part of the web, dissolved. Once gone, they would altogether lose the closing path to follow. Ray rocketed on the superimposed red target high above the oncoming wave. Picking up speed, he launched off the wave's crest, expertly leaping off his surfboard so that his finger barely grazed the spot as the crosshair almost completely vanished and-

four

Somehow he touched it.

Ray's eBadge clearance allowed him to instantly teleport through the hyperlink wormhole. He materialized in a different spot on the web in time to see the next virtual target Ravenna remotely overlaid across his iScreen. He touched that one too, popping into a new environment, immediately searching out the target and virtually teleporting to another point. And another, and another, and another…hyperlinking so fast from one spot to the next that only a top tracker like Ray could keep up. Finally, he materialized behind the eTerrorist who had stopped in a crowded hallway ahead of the agent.

Ray lingered behind users, concealing himself in shadows many paces away from the fugitive. Watching through the *chatters*, Agent Kemper spied Blackout entering through a door marked-

Shooting Gallery 5.6.

"Ugh," Ravenna grunted, "you can only Skin swap in there when dead. He's gonna spot you tailing him again."

Ray waited for two more people to hyperlink in front of the game's door. Then he followed a user clad as Batman who alongside a talking piece of bread entered the game site.

"*Shooting Gallery 5.6,*" a gritty, male voice announcement chimed in Ray's ears.

"I got your back," as his handler, Ravenna, focused her eyes upon Ray onscreen from a classic video game view filter. Her point of view positioned slightly above and behind Ray so that she served as eyes in the back of his head.

A riveting orchestral soundtrack accompanied the clatter of an immense, unseen battle emanating from around the curved, massive white corridor. The walls were minimally marked with the words *Shooting Gallery* with watermarks of past professional gamers who now made millions through pay-per-view fees of their live gaming in pro levels.

In her remote location, the growing cacophony of the unseen battle ahead forced Ravenna to raise the audio level of her comlink microphone. It assured she'd be heard by him over the din of Ray's online environment. With her mic set so high, Ray on the online end, heard her voice in native Castellano Spanish behind the computer-generated translation into seamless English. *Swipe 9* agents in the field all spoke in their native tongue, relying on auto translators for speedy, error-free communication-

"This hallway leads to the first level of the game," the gritty, male intro voice grumbled in Ray's ear, "Survive Level One and-"

With an eye swipe, Ray muted the computerized greeting. Lowering the game's soundtrack would alert Blackout's sensors.

Because almost everyone kept the music score. With that riveting cinema-like sound score, Ray as Damon picked up the discarded mega caliber .48 handgun. It had two magazines taped to its scuffed holster stained in dried blood. Securing the holster and magazines in his waistline, Ray darted forward; rounding the end of the curve to the *Pit*.

Multiplayer online games generally possessed a pit for killing newbies in what was pejoratively looked down upon as *PP'ing* or *power poaching*. Killing players earned points, but not enough to mean anything to mildly higher level gamers. These low-level bullies were recent newbies preying on the more recent. Above the mayhem rose the stone cathedral-like chamber, a mile wide and a half-mile high with a stained glass ceiling coloring the golden beams of simulated sunlight. Casting colored beams of sunlight on continually discharged gunpowder seven days a week, 365 days a year. Everything seemed realistic except for the smell of gunpowder or any other scent along with meaningful sensation like pleasure or pain other than a mild game vibration when shot.

"Two!" cried Ravenna.

Ray spun to his right like the hand of a clock, moving from midnight ahead of him to two on the clock face's dial. Closing in before he even spotted his indicated prey. He moved like her automaton. In melees, she took control of him, the two acting together as a united killing machine superior to the multitude of aggressive players. Ray firing with the speed and accuracy of a highly trained, government killer who couldn't be shot and taken down. Ray's gaming prowess impressed a professional Axe-Master, advertising his services to the newbies. The user pointed at Ray:

"I can make you an eWarrior as awesome as him!" the master cried as Ray darted past, ignoring the compliment as the mentor pointed Kemper, "In just three private lessons for 150 eCredits I can make you all as great as him–"

"Damn, lost visual," Ray muttered to his partner.

He knew the eTerrorist wouldn't stay long. Blackout never journeyed inward to rooms and levels where groups formed in the game. The eTerrorist never risked being in a site that long, fearing the President's secret tool which was just Ray and his two pieces of software.

A killer walrus ambushed the FCC agent from behind the Axe-master. Ray reeled back, feet artfully moving over a pile of the dead. Their skull-faced timer clocks on their foreheads counted down from their respective 30-second-long death penalties. Each room deeper in the massive multiplayer online game carried progressively longer mortality penalties with mandatory media ad watches and surveys. But in the first pit, IM's, social loops, and eDings was all the dead had time for in their short, thirty-second death penalty in which they couldn't move anything but their faces.

His boot stepped on a dead girl laying on her side as she took an eCall, "Sure. I got thirty seconds to talk. I'm dead-"

Ray scrambled over another dead player asking her eComp, "Siri, any messages?"

Then he spied Blackout disappearing through a passageway in the far corner of the room, "Regained visual," he told Ravenna, "left corner passage."

Ravenna projected a game map in the upper, right corner of Ray's iScreen, revealing the passage ahead. The left side of the corridor led to a dead-end, the right fed to the next chamber.

Sprinting past gun-wielding Mexican wrestlers, sniper ballerinas, and an angry Mickey Mouse bayonetting Napoleon, Ray closed in on the narrow entrance Blackout just vanished into. Out of ammo, he picked up a discarded, bloody pistol. Most gamers didn't like them, but he was proficient enough to wield a pistol like a sniper's rifle across vast distances. Verifying eight rounds as he ran, Ray slid the mag back into the weapon's grip and crossed the threshold to the intersecting tunnel when-

A bright explosion of light!

It emanated from the darkened dead-end corridor to the left. Blackout had waited there, firing a shoulder-mounted, rocket-propelled grenade launcher at Ray. The FCC agent's training moved his body faster than he could organize thoughts. Reactions honed from training and experience informed him that the incoming blast would kill him. The ordinance missed his body, but the concrete fragments from the rear corner exploded back at him; the shockwave sending Ray careening down the hall. Gun extended, the agent flying in mid-air expertly drew a beat on Blackout's head as he was flung forward at Ray. In the melee, he wasn't sure if their Skins contacted-

Back in his Shanghai Hilton hotel room's comport, Ray's physical body didn't so much as flinch. Inside the sealed comport capsule, Agent Kemper's eyes remained closed. His face relaxed as if sleeping. Dark hair framed the geometry of his square jaw and olive skin complemented by a fit body, etched muscles visible under his white stretch shirt adorned with an American flag and FCC logo below it on his shoulder. Khaki pants. Combat boots. Every fiber synthetic as cotton and wool were now as rare as gold.

His chosen, online appearance as Matt Damon's Skin, caused a close-up shot of Damon to remain visible across the lower part of the holographic media lid to Ray's comport. The age or details of the Skin could be adjusted. Damon being one of an infinite number of Mr. Zero's House Of Skins *flesh library* Ray accessed as a government agent.

This comport rested in the far corner of Agent Kemper's Shanghai Hilton hotel room. Standing over it, his handler, Ravenna, cut a full, curved silhouette. Her natural, long, black hair appeared blonde now thanks to her iCamo-dye; a new stealth camouflage allowing her to toggle between hair colors like a chameleon via her iScreen's eye panel. Still, Ray only thought of her with her natural brunette hair color.

Ready for anything, she gripped her mega caliber rifle with

her right hand; matte black weapons and blast grenades magnetically secured to her intentionally unmarked, white combat jumpsuit woven from feather-light Tylon body-armor. Her striking face glowed in the light of the comport's holographic head's up display, hovering in mid-air before her. The back wall projected Ray's Siri 9.6 which due to a former practical joke wore her likeness.

All the surfaces of the hotel room were seamless media display screens: the four walls, floor, and ceiling. With an eye stroke across her iScreen, she altered the media display to depict the 360-degree, live view of Ray's online game space. The room's bed, couch, table, and chair, all crafted from ePlastic, could auto-color-shifted from the current brown color to translucent. So then nothing could block the underlying media cradling her.

This hotel room, termed a *Media Suite*, was conceived by the famed Mono-minimalist, Korean designer, Kavi. As a multimedia creation in spiritual insight, the room imported online elements into the offline world just as science's birth by God originated Descartes' realization that mental ideas could be imported into reality.

The top four stories of the Shanghai Hilton contained only Media Suites. Ray and Ravenna's rooms were on the highest floor, closest to the rooftop helipad. These modern-day *safe houses* possessed the highest-grade firewalls necessary for this mission. Although these suites possessed what looked like a *Blue Series* comport from its color, they were actually top-line *Red Series* comports with enhanced armor for the ultimate body protection while *on-lining*. The model Bellingham Labs proudly advertised as "The safest place on Earth." Ray had one more layer of protection-

The human one.

Ravenna, his female handler, provided on-site protection for the six foot two, 30sh male agent prostrate on his back within the hermetically sealed capsule. As a child in a time when epidemics and violence kept kids largely at home, Ray had first been drawn into this unique trade by the old, fictionalized web series *Tales of the FCC*. Begun back in the early days of David's *Doors 1.0* web, Ray could never have imagined this high tech setting.

Ravenna typically had the Media Suite simulate the online space surrounding her partner online. But now the suite projected the frozen moment as Ray and Blackout's Skin's touched. The silhouette of them contacting turned to visual TV-like static.

Online, a chunk of rock decapitated Blackout's head, sending his body flying backward in mid-air, trailing behind Ray's shredded torso as both slid to a violent stop down the long hall. Bloody streaks marked their landings as they rested in an ever larger, pool of expanding blood settling between them. Ray's mangled body resting beside Blackout's decapitated head laying face down.

"You are dead," the gritty game voice told them, "you may Skin-swap during this thirty-second death penalty."

Through the bloody pool's red-tinted reflection, Ray stared through Damon's eyes at Blackout's severed head. The eTerrorist morphed from a generic Skin back to his actual likeness with those haunting eyes as the death penalty clock appeared across his forehead, counting down from thirty seconds.

"Hello Ray," Blackout gingerly addressed the agent. Beyond the bazooka ambush, the eTerrorist wished to make it starkly clear that he'd noticed Ray tracking him.

Blackout also he knew his name.

So it was true, concluded Ray. Blackout had indeed acquired some of the task force's personnel files in the India cyber strike that killed so many *Swipe 9* agents.

The night Ravenna first saved his life.

Meanwhile, in the offline *real world* of Ray's Media Suite, the Shooting Gallery's administration site marked *ENTER* holographically hovered over Ray's comport. His FCC eBadge auto-accessed the game's basic programming at this point. On the wall screen ahead of Ravenna, Ray's Siri which usually made the surfaces look like half walls, vanished. It was replaced with the outline of Ray and Blackout's bodies touching. That imagery unfolded into an expanding color map of Shanghai. The digital map also covered the lower portion of the comport's holographic screen as the map quickly honed in on a downtown building close to their hotel. Glowing white light signaled the structure's upper floor where the eTerrorist currently resided. Ravenna stared at it blankly for a moment. The impossible task had been achieved. She couldn't believe it-

Blackout was so close.

Spinning around on the heels of her combat boots, she darted forward, drawing her belt-mounted sidearm as she raced to the hotel room's door. She blasted the sliding door away as she sprinted through the opening, saying:

"Ray your program works," she gasped between breaths, her words auto-translated to, "I have a geo-lock on his location just eight blocks away!"

The timer in the upper left corner of her iScreen revealed that she had 27 seconds before Blackout's death penalty ended; he would surely offline and leave by then. Ravenna's eye swipe called up her automated, drone transport waiting on the rooftop helipad. With no time to get up there, she raced across the empty outer hotel hall in a single stride, blasting a hole in the old glass wall before leaping through the shattered window. Her body falling out of the 49th floor of the Hilton Hotel into the howling rainstorm. The street below racing up at her before her drone sped in, allowing her to fall through the open rooftop hatch and into its driver's cockpit seat. Its automated five-point-harness secured her.

"Keep him online!" Ravenna cried over the comlink as her neck whipped back as the drone rocketed forward.

Online in the *Shooting Gallery*, Blackout taunted Ray through the pool of crimson blood, "If you're not gonna talk," the eTerrorist feigned insult, "then I'm offlining."

Through the reflection of blood, Ray's stomach sank as he watched the eTerrorist call up his exit protocol. A semi-opaque stop sign marked *OFFLINE* materialized before the eTerrorist's face as he stuck his tongue out to touch it and log off. But Blackout hesitated, his eyes returning to Ray's in the reflection of the bloody pool:

"Geez, thought you'd say something to keep me talking online. But you didn't," the death clock on the teenager's forehead now ticked down from 19 seconds, "I know it's you, Agent Kemper. Recognize those moves in any world. Ray, if you had a fan club, I'd be its founding member. Prefer you so much more than that bitch partner, Ravenna," sighed the teen, "handlers are so obvious. So make me stay 20 seconds, tell me what you love most in the world. It wasn't in your file."

"Seeing you dead like the millions you electrocuted in cold blood."

"The stalker talks," Blackout mockingly yawned, "honest, but dull."

"No. Honest is me saying you're just another psycho for the history books-"

"No Ray," Blackout retorted, "I am the end of history. Which raises the question. What exactly are you doing here?" Blackout's eyes tore into Ray again through the bloody reflection, "You catch me, I just upload my virus to shareware sites worldwide, and it's GAME OVER!" his face blushed in blood lust, "AND EVERYONE DIES!"

In the real world, Ravenna fought not to pass out as her drone veered suddenly to the left. Her inadvertent eye stroke across her iScreen returned her hair to its natural, dark brown color. She heard Blackout online over Ray's comlink, but couldn't speak. Her transport auto-piloted so quickly through the blinding rain and skyscrapers that she nearly passed out from the violent g-forces.

Online, Blackout attempted to entice Ray, "Buy more time.

Just tell me, what are you doing here?"

"I don't know," Ray wasn't lying. No analyst believed the eTerrorist could be killed in less than 30 seconds from the discovery of his real-world location. Ray didn't think it would work either, but he wasn't going to stop his handler from trying as Blackout's death penalty clock ticked down from 16 seconds.

"But you must know what you're doing here," pressed Blackout like a child who couldn't get another to play along.

"Oh, I know," he grinned as if hiding a secret.

Ravenna continued to tighten her abs in the drone to keep the blood in her head as her transport rocketed towards the 27th floor of the Intercontinental Hotel. At the last second, the drone stopped, violently shifting on its side as her eSeatbelt unlocked. Ravenna was sent rocketing sideways through the drone's now open hatch and out into blinding rain. Before she careened into it, she shot out the 27th-floor window of the hotel hallway ahead of her. His handler's senses remained dizzy from the harrowing, high-speed ride as she rolled into the hotel hall, shattered glass all around as she bounced to her feet.

"I'm trying to kill you," Ray was honest with Blackout.

The eTerrorist laughed.

A government support tech back in DC chimed to Ravenna over the open comlink, "Run right!"

Sprinting down the hall, she realized in the iSceen clock that she had 12 seconds left as her tech explained, "Had to drop you ten rooms away so his sensors wouldn't register the gunfire in the hall. I'm remotely opening the last door on the left."

The door ahead clicked open as she sprinted inside Blackout's hotel suite.

Meanwhile, in the *Shooting Gallery*, Ray kept his eyes locked on Blackout's smiling, severed head reflected in the pool of blood, "So you chase me around, and you don't know what to do with me when you catch me," chuckled Blackout, "and that's what you're doing with your time?"

He flirted with Ray.

Ravenna's thermal filter on her iScreen indicated the heat signature of something big and hot lurking on the far side of what must be Blackout's bedroom wall.

"He's in some flying drone," her data telemetry officer interpreted the heat signature.

She ran to the edge of the bedroom door as it was blown open by the roar of jet engines. Through it, she spied hidden wings expanding out of Blackout's customized comport. Side-mounted jet engines rose up from recessed panels.

"Engines are firing up," Ravenna confirmed as she stood out of view beside the doorway, "He's going to offline! Strike now!"

At Creech AFB Drone Mission Control outside Indian Springs, Nevada, a thousand drone pilots remotely flew the modern U.S. Air Force fleet. Twenty pilots currently manned the U.N. *Swipe 9* air-task force from their military comports in an underground bay. Only one pilot was close enough to launch his missiles, but there was an issue:

"Too far out for F&M," stated the drone pilot over the mission comlink, "Request target lay. Over."

Listening over the group comlink, Ray knew that F&M stood for Trikon 5 *Force-Flex* precision missiles. The drone pilot's request for a "target lay" meant the smart missile at this distance required an infrared crosshair projected on it from a field agent near the target.

"Copy. Setting target lay," with no emotion, Ravenna replied over the din of the jet engines. She stepped into the bedroom doorway. The infrared beam from her gun was immediately sensed by Blackout's comport jet's security sensors.

"Firing," the drone pilot spoke over the comlink.

A previously concealed gun turret rose out of a recessed center panel, its barrel closing in on Ravenna's body now covered in the turret's laser crosshairs. Nowhere to hide. The mega caliber turret guns would blast through any set of walls like butter from the lethal force.

"Comport anti-aircraft weapons system activating," her field support confirmed what she already saw ahead of her.

Ray, half-listening over the comlink knew the next moment would be her death from either Blackout's comport gun turret or the F&M blast.

His face, however, revealed none of that as Blackout seemed diverted for a moment. Being alerted by a pop-up window, no doubt, to the intruder back in his hotel room.

"Well, that's all folks," Blackout called up his virtual stop sign to offline.

In the milliseconds that followed in Blackout's hotel suite, Ravenna knew the eTerrorist's comport jet was about to rocket away. They almost got him. Blackout was probably next going to end the world. The gun's barrel of his flying comport turret turned, blowing out the glass window wall ahead of it. Howling rain rushed in as the crosshairs from Blackout's weapon system closed in on Ravenna's vital spots.

At the same moment online in the *Shooting Gallery,* Blackout touched the stop sign with his tongue and offlined.

In the eTerrorist's hotel room, the gun turret refocused on her. The turmoil inside Ravenna that raged for months now turned calm. As a brainwashed child taken from an orphanage she had been indoctrinated in her nation's Mexican Web Academy; she long-lived for a heroic death needed to acquire a star in the Agency's *Hall of Heroes.* A reward of promised immortality in the eyes of envious young cadets now seemed to her like some idiotic animal chasing its tail. The world would soon disappear for her, and no star would ever bring it back. A martyr's life which only, in the end, did she realize had been a love story-

She thought of Ray.

In these milliseconds, she didn't think about the signature on paper committing her to her husband in Mexico that she hadn't seen in so long. Nor the children she'd never bring to life or that her next disclosure could end her partner's career and carry mandatory prison-time for Ray. An unbearable lightness swept across Ravenna as she witnessed the streak of approaching light from the single F&M rocket careening towards the shattered window as she uttered over the comlink-

"Ray I l-" the exploding F&M seared her final syllables in fire.

She was gone.

Online in the *Shooting Gallery 5.6*, Blackout's severed face now showed a sudden hollowness. His Skin should've disappeared as his system shut down, but Ray's second piece of software kept the eTerrorist's Skin from logging off. Focused, Agent Kemper had no time to process his partner's death as his online Damon Skin returned to life. Blood and guts now moved backward in time to regather into the holistically whole body during his in-game resurrection.

The automated game voice now advised, "Your game's death penalty is now over."

But if Ray did not succeed at his next task, Agent Kemper knew he and the world would be over. His death along with everyone else following his handler's own by seconds or minutes of the real battle now ensuing. All his training came down to this moment to decide-

The fate of the world.

five

Ray resurrected.

The skull-faced death clock timed out. It disappeared from the forehead of his Matt Damon Skin, which returned to life in-game. Wounds instantly healed as his body reconstituted, towering over Blackout's decapitated head on the blood-covered floor. The FCC agent eyed the six manila files, which magically appeared, rising up from the dead eTerrorist's Skin. These were copies of Blackout's treasured virus program attempting to escape. Each file of his Yin Yang digital virus embossed with black and white *Yin Yang* symbols fought to escape his digital hold. The free-floating data files violently attempted to fly off in opposite directions to multiple shareware sites worldwide. Ray's quarantine program temporarily held them.

To contain the wider dissemination of the virus program files, Ray's second custom-piece of software loaded. Symbolic logic math symbols of hearts, spades, omegas, and other icons unpacked themselves in streams of data flooding across his iScreen. Many of Ray's data equations vanished as Blackout's automated eDefenses fought back, attacking his code with tornado-looking data spirals.

Ray's rapid eye swipes amended his code, allowing his codex to battle back as he struggled to keep Blackout's virus files from veering off in all directions. They yearned to travel to shareware platforms to be uploaded to worldwide users. That shadow legion of the many in shadows to activate the file, triggering the worldwide ePocalypse through thousands of iScreens. Finally, Ray's software weakened the opposing program.

The agent slowly reeled the deadly data towards his floating iScreen as they resisted him. The files struggling again, nearly racing out in all directions before the folders disappeared into his iScreen, instantly appearing as file icons in the upper corner of his screen.

Stunned silence.

Ray couldn't believe he was saying the words, "All files are quarantined on my eComp."

Distant cheers from the White House, drone team, and unseen military leaders were audible over Ray's comlink. Holding out a weary hand, the agent's "ok" symbol with his fingers called up his stop sign marked:

OFFLINE

He touched it.

The semi-opaque stop sign vanished along with Ray. The agent returned to his body as if awakening from a dream in his

Shanghai hotel room's comport, the familiar Hilton logo embossed in the device's holographic lid. Another quick eye swipe opened the holo-glass lid as the FCC agent raced out of the empty Media Suite and down the hotel hall. Taking the lift to the roof, he called in another drone transport already waiting up on the pad to ferry him the many blocks to ground zero.

Blackout's blasted out hotel room.

U.N. ground troops securing the perimeter prohibited him from a rooftop landing until the advance team of soldiers secured Blackout's suite. Eight minutes later, the lift doors opened and Ray was allowed to enter Blackout's floor, following the thick scent of smoke to the charred out room. Only then did the FCC agent recollect on his handler's last words to him over the comlink:

"Ray, I l-"

He knew what she meant to say.

Entering Blackout's living room, Ray recollected on a particular evening three months prior. He and Ravenna embraced in the afterglow of sex in his Media Suite. The wall screens of his hotel room simulated an old panoramic 4K video from Narvik, Norway in the Arctic Circle before the worldwide rains blotted out the sky. The brilliant Aurora Borealis encompassed them, illuminating the two lovers' bodies in soft pink and yellow. Having lowered the eThermostat, even their breath misted in the frigid air. It was their most intimate moment, perhaps why he felt comfortable enough to joke about such a forbidden thing:

"Ray, I love you," he teased aloud, "I'd like to hear you say it just once. Ray, I love you-"

"Stop it," Ravenna playfully elbowed him in the ribs, "or you'll get us both thrown in prison."

Ray threw the semi-opaque sheet over their heads. Just the two of them naked under the frosted, translucent sheet diffusing the blurred blasts of the Northern Lights into fluid splotches of colored lights.

"It's just us," he told Ravenna, "no Mexican or FCC web agencies listening in-"

"Are we talking American white picket fences again?" she grinned. Ray felt foolish as she reinforced reality for them, "A century ago I'd have to swim the Rio Grande to you. Now that Mexico's a first world nation, I can't even get into your country except working on this task force. When the manhunt's over," she bored into him with knowing eyes, "I'll be that Mexican handler you were forbidden from dating. Just a blur in your Web Agent career."

It wasn't her eyes or intonation, but the vulnerability this hardened soldier attempted to hide that made him love her at that moment. Leaning in for the kiss, her face turned blurry as it did for all lovers who closed in on each other's lips.

"But Ravenna," he slyly noted before their lips touched, "our most intimate moments are blurs-"

Ray rid the memory from his mind.

Crossing the burned exterior living room, he allowed the U.N. fire crew to carry out their packed gear. The blast bomb explosion blew itself out, evidenced by the living room half-reduced to its concrete frame. Peering through the bedroom where the F&M hit, Ray eyed the eight armored U.N. soldiers in the room now seared back to blackened concrete. They had retrieved what was thought to be Ravenna's bones bleached white. Ray turned away, seeing his former handler and lover's eComp half-covered in ash in the corner beside the now blown-out bedroom doorway.

He remained in the doorway as the armored United Nations guards draped a U.N. flag over the small box holding Ravenna's remains. Heads downcast, they solemnly prepared to exit the room. Ray stepped away, darting back down the hall to the charred bathroom, which somehow still retained its metal door. Only then did he focus on the fact that-

She was gone.

The pain welled within him. The agent trained to control emotion found it hard to do so now. Locking the door from the inside, he approached the mirrored wall over the sink, which was cracked, but survived the blast. Taking off his eComp, the agent held Ravenna's and his own in the palm of his hand. Staring at them both, he couldn't help but remember how Ravenna grabbed his eComp when he dropped it in the windstorm last month.

They had raced over the coastline dunes of the central Sahara at dusk. This remote area possessed the lightest downpours and mass surveillance on the planet. A region where they could run outside cloaked in the wind blown upward by tiny ground-based tornadoes.

These mini twisters could suck a human body up to ten feet or more in the air. With their training, Ray and his partner could leap from one vortex up to taller ones rising fifty feet high before risking being sucked up into the clouds above. An odd meteorological event from the new Earth.

Which was where his eComp fell off in the wind-blown sand. He hadn't tightened the tension mount as much as he thought. Wind whipped up by the encircling tornado sucked it off. She retrieved it in the sand, jokingly hacking his eComp's Siri Skin option to make Siri appear as herself.

He later scanned his eComp system, discovering that she never hacked him, but she wanted him to know that for a handler, she was pretty clever. When she proved herself to him. That was when he knew he had some part of her heart. Something he craved to hold on to after the mission would separate them. Maybe he shouldn't have done what he did, but they shouldn't have assigned him such a beautiful handler-

A knock at the door.

The U.N. armed guards had arrived, honing no doubt in on his eComp's GPS signal. Instantly the tears vanished from the corner of the agent's eyes as the skilled liar turned and opened the door. Ray noted the sixteen guards in full body armor flanking the entrance, spilling back into the living room. Two of the U.N. grunts hidden behind mirrored visor helmets entered the bathroom with their heavy mega caliber weapons in-hand.

The shorter, junior officer set a metal box marked *Quarantine* on the floor. They all knew the protocol. Without being told to, Ray stripped down naked. Depositing both eComps into the blast box. The war wasn't truly over until Blackout's digital virus codex, solely existing in Ray's eComp hard drive, was contained and destroyed.

Once fully naked, the leader closed the blast box, incinerating the items Ray had placed within it. The junior soldier then scanned Ray's body with a small titanium hand-wand. On the junior soldier's iScreen display, the wand allowed him to view MRI-like imaging through Ray's body. The soldier's Siri searched for any hidden hard-drives to perhaps store Blackout's codex.

"He's clean," from behind the mirrored visor, the junior agent informed his superior through a computer morphed voice.

The senior soldier nodded and opened the door, taking a red bag from one of the soldiers outside and handing it to the naked FCC agent. It contained clothing and items he had packed years before when first joining the strike force.

Now he drew out the pair of new *Lucchese* cowboy boots. Followed by socks, boxers, black combat pants, the usual dark blue t-shirt and rain jacket emblazoned with yellow FCC letters, and two cigars in aluminum tubes. He had hoped to one day light them up with Ravenna to celebrate their mission's success.

Now Ray stuffed the cigar tubes in his pants pocket and quickly finished dressing. His reflection warped in the leader's mirrored visor.

An embedded flash and camera activated in the top of the U.N. soldier's helmet just before she ordered in a computer morphed voice:

"Agent Kemper, under UN Order *Swipe 9*, I must now re-record your oath."

Peering into his twisted reflection in the leader's helmet visor, Ray repeated the same oath he took before the president's adviser gave him the hard copy of Blackout's viral codex.

The senior leader's camera now recorded Ray as he stated, "Under penalty of imprisonment or death under *Swipe 9.72*, I pledge not to write, share, disseminate in any way, or recreate in any part, the software codex of Blackout's *Yin Yang* digital virus divulged to me alone in the course of the Swipe 9 mission."

An integrated flash in the senior leader's helmet deactivated just above the embedded camera that now stopped recording. The soldier's body language relaxed beneath the micro-spider web plated armor. The mirrored veneer of the visor dissolved to reveal the team leader's middle-aged, butch female leader, Collins. He knew her. They played in the poker games Ravenna hosted during the frequent space flights. Besides cards, she loved to read, loaning Ray online English lit courses from her library:

"So it's…really over?" Collins dared ask.

An exhausted Ray nodded yes.

"All the files are contained?" she felt compelled to hear him personally confirm this life-changing fact.

He nodded affirmatively.

Collins' sighed, her relaxed body language visible through her armor, "The end of World War IV," she couldn't believe she bore witness to such an event. Then she realized, "Whoa. Ray when they declassify this mission, you'll be remembered as the savior of the world."

"Ravenna killed him," Ray humbly corrected her.

"Containing those files is all anyone's gonna remember," Collins then realized, "Wow. Someone will probably play my role in a web movie about this moment," she took in the details of the scene.

"Boss, you think someone will play me too?" her subordinate's morphed voice asked from behind his mirrored visor.

"Of course. There are nonstop web channels on world wars. Hell, there could even be a spinoff series on just us two-"

"Us?" her junior didn't believe her promise of fame.

"The bit players Rosencrantz and Guildenstern from *Hamlet* got a whole play by Tom Stoppard," Collins shrugged to Ray, "I thought you just listened to that audio course?"

"There are so many characters and they talk weird," the junior shrugged to Ray.

Agent Kemper reflected on the irony of two soldiers in a pivotal, historical moment focused on how they might be represented in some future online media. But as important as this time was, the moment didn't feel so different from others. Perhaps why they required context from a distance.

Then Collins, a literature enthusiast who might've been a professor in a time before the storm realized how callous she'd been, "Ray, I'm really sorry about Ravenna. Can I pass on a message to her husband? We're flying her remains back to Mexico tonight."

Ray didn't know Ravenna had even been married. His shock was concealed by his training in deception as he nonchalantly inquired, "She had a family?"

"No kids, just a husband," Collins bent over to retrieve the quarantine box.

The pain he felt from that revelation stayed with him for weeks. His mind kept returning afterward to seek the realization robbed from him by Ravenna's comment on the final day of the manhunt. What great notion had he forgotten?

Agent Kemper flushed the memories away. Taking a deep breath of the cold, sterile air as he stretched his fit muscles across the translucent mattress. An eye swipe across his iScreen turned the Media Suite's ceiling into a digital mirror, reflecting his etched,

Spartan warrior like body draped in shadows. Intense weight training was the government agent's only sole diversion, giving him a sculpted look akin to the old-style action stars he liked such as Damon.

This hotel room was identical to the ones he had lived in for years, including in Shanghai. So that when he woke up, he always struggled for a moment to remember where on the planet he was specifically. Now for the past thirteen days, he'd been in outer space onboard the Space Station Hilton.

He always promised himself a trip up here as a reward if he ended the war. With an eye stroke, the media surfaces broadcast a live video feed of Earth from the space-bound hotel. The faint ring of satellite debris similar to Saturn's ring sickened him almost as much as the swirling, worldwide mega-hurricanes covering the planet. Ray focused his gaze on the blazing sun filling the upper portion of his room's media display.

He long fantasized about soaking his feet in the only beach club accessible to Earthlings at the bottom of this hotel. A place where he could feel the unadulterated touch of the sun against his face through a protective magnetic field. Feeling light from a star he'd not experienced since he was eight. Some of the wealthiest war refugees had paid enormous sums to remain here in orbit during the war to feel the sunlight through the magnetic wall. The war having ended three weeks ago, they were all gone. Still, nothing went right from the start.

Dark tidings first confirmed on the Delta space flight up to the orbiting hotel when Ray first learned that satellite debris had forced the closure of the Nikki Space Beach Club. Management projected the repairs wouldn't be complete for a month. Due to the inconvenience, the hotel manager extended Ray's stay for a third of the normally required points through Christmas and New Year's. They even threw in half-off room service. With the holiday fast approaching, the place remained empty.

Ray wouldn't have known.

He only left his room to work out in the famous, zero gravity Le Soleil Gym at the top of the hotel, beyond the artificial gravity field. It was his first time exercising with the new Phychotronic weight system. Instead of weights, he moved against invisible magnetic fields. The resistance fields gave his muscles a fully even burn across them as he floated in midair within a large bubble atop the hotel. The glass gym peered out into space. Working out in space, he found himself unexpectedly hungering to be with Ravenna and work on a new case. It was an illogical fantasy. They'd been together so long, seen and shared so much during the war. He didn't desire a Christmas break. People went on those to forget.

Ray just wanted to remember.

At first, he thought his superiors might interrogate him over Ravenna's last words on the comlink. But what had she really said? Nothing. The F&M prematurely ended her disclosure of love for the post-mission auditors. So now he was left to reside in the Media Suite, staring up at Ravenna as his Siri, her close up covering the walls, floor, and ceiling. He never showed emotion, knowing he might now be audited. But changing anything event his Siri now might draw suspicion. If tears were to be shed for her loss, they were done in the shower so that the mist and water concealed such emotion from possible hidden cameras. They owned him.

But he could own a case.

Somehow he felt like it would bring him back to that rhythm maintained with his long-time handler. Most evenings, he'd inhale prescription anti-depressants the FCC doctor prescribed for PTSD. Falling asleep as he stared at Ravenna's massive close-up on the media wall. Then waking up hung-over, workout, eat, repeat. All beneath the eyes of his dead lover reminding him of that TS Elliot poem he studied in college.

Sometimes he'd get in the hotel comport, imagining his handler still alive with her weapons holstered to her body as she safeguarded his own. When she first became his partner, he was given a redacted form of her U.N. eDossier. Her ten confirmed kills surprised him. Now Ravenna's face moved wherever he looked like some constant ghost. Her name hinted at the darkness for him, that unpredictable edge she possessed. Quiet, but dangerous. While the real Ravenna remained burned to white bones sealed in a closed coffin six feet under her ancestral Mexican village of Sentispac.

Looking back, the stolen seconds when she shed her stretch business suit and let down that beautiful head of dark hair emitting her intoxicating scent, were the only moments Ray ever had with her. For they were spies of different countries forbidden from fraternizing-

"Need anything, Ray?" his Siri as Ravenna broke his train of thought, the app sensing a change in his facial pattern.

"Play my favorite," he asked.

Siri complied.

The surfaces of the Media Suite morphed to darkness as the electronic voice of David Bellingham spoke. The 52-year-old inventor still resided in his Opelousas living room comport, his silhouette barely visible in shadows. Over the years, Ray gleamed an informal education from David Bellingham. The famed thinker blogged on topics as diverse as God's inception of science or how group meditation for a month in DC back in the 1990s was scientifically shown to lower the regional crime rate.

The famed inventor now discussed "The 7,000-year-long storm covering every inch of planet Earth. A result of the outsourcing of American consumable goods to China-" with an eye swipe Ray paused the blog, like most he knew that story all too well.

His eyes wandered back to Ravenna.

The face of his Siri stirred passions. Their illicit affair was only possible because she was charged with arranging the team's lodgings through a never-ending stream of mostly Hilton properties. Placing his room across from her own, one evening she knocked on his door. After he let her in, she stole a kiss beyond the reach of surveillance cameras.

That first kiss was the most romantic memory in his life. Long before he read her grandmother's locket's engraving in Spanish which translated meant, *guard your heart.* Those words in retrospect served as a stark warning to FCC Agent Kemper. The fact that she concealed her marriage from him hurt more than even the beatings he took as a kid from older bullies. The never-ending rain was the worse enemy. It got to most. The anger. Depression. Kids who never saw the sun were different in a way he couldn't put his finger on. The lack of sunlight, prior tampering in the gene pool through artificial conception, interactive screens, it wasn't one thing that was wrong but the entire wave of supposed progress truly coming to swamp the next generation.

"My brain's fried," his older neighbor in Chicago used to tell Ray as a kid. Jumpy like a heroin junky in need of a fix. Over generations, not having a mom around during rearing took a sudden toll. Wired into their inner worlds they were not prepared for the grim realities of the real one. The flat backs of the heads from being in day-care-reared masses undeniably documented cold infancies of abuse akin to Stalinist Gulag nurseries. Both were nation-state reared when leaders took mothers away. So most Americans could work to buy things to enrich Xi Jinping until the Yin Yang viral plague.

Few had time to think of love.

He remembered back when his dad first gave his only child some adult wisdom about women shortly before the man's premature death. The warning that Ray could never honestly know a female's heart. Expectedly, that memory popped into his head as he again found himself staring at Ravenna as his Siri on the Media Suite's wall.

She proved his father so right.

Ray's dad worked as an asset manager for a flood wall

company. A booming business back when the giant flood walls were being constructed in the late 2030s through the mid-40s. As a kid, his father's job took the Kemper family overseas for three years to Shaoyang, Hunan Province of Mainland China, which now was commonly referred to as the *New South Coast* resulting from the rising sea level flooding much of the coastal lands.

Living there, Ray witnessed the people long poisoned by manufacturing without any environmental protections so that cancer had become the norm at 29 there since the 20'teens, now commonly affecting most children. The old and middle-aged had long since died off from the poison pollution now high up in the atmosphere, generating the worldwide storms which drew up subterranean ocean water. Even many Chinese now viewed their pollution as the biblically prophesied *wings of abomination* which the Prophet Daniel foretold would end the world. That abomination created by all the seemingly cheap goods Americans had purchased due to the lack of any environmental protections. The most expensive products ever made in history that later came at the cost of possibly all life.

Young Ray quickly discovered that only the lone totalitarian leader held all the power and wealth in China, controlling the slaves as he played his puppet state of North Korea, speaking the real views of the Chinese overlord who struggled to look presidential. The totalitarian dictator dressed and acted as a U.S. president, but was the opposite, a tyrant for life. Wiping out the Muslim millions who committed no crime except occupying the western part of the nation that the Chinese government elites needed to migrate to. China had to relocate its people. The Yin Yang Virus had really been about possibly planetary recolonization in the warped minds of the Chinese dictator who had already poisoned his land to death. Nothing in Communist China was as it seemed. Every taxi had a sign for *Buckle Up, It's The Law*, but a young Ray quickly learned that there were no seatbelts in Chinese taxis. Just as no one followed the traffic signs. Sidewalks being only additional roads in that toxic, unsafe land.

The air pollution there was intolerable.

Even by the 20'teens, people could go mad from the pollutants in the air. His family ultimately had to relocate, moving to his Mom's hometown of Chicago to be close to her ailing mother. Then Ray's dad died suddenly of *Green Lung*. Long after he left the world stage, the virus Xi Jinping concealed, still bloomed bright green fungus within the all-too-familiar *broken glass* pattern of infected lungs. Something old and new to slowly suffocate the victim through asphyxiation with the usual cardiac arrest-level pain, now paired with Cholera-like diarrhea.

Ray's dad died from it when the boy was only twelve. Young Ray helped his mother clean out his deceased dad's office of personal belongings. It was a moment he would never forget. Those Tycho-ceramic hard drives piled against his dead dad's office window overlooking the blinding rain obscuring Lake Michigan. Ray often recollected on that shrine of hard-drives as his dad's only grave. The temporary monument of a man's life wrapped up in transient, financial figures headed for an archive warehouse until the IRS deemed it legal to delete the recent past archives.

Ray desired something more.

The reason why he became an agent in the Federal Communications Commission, the FCC, which now served as America's frontline in law enforcement. Ray's job as a Web Agent was more like former Hollywood actors, expertly trained to be a futuristic imposter behind many digital Skin's. A student of human behavior to such an extent that he could no longer be like other people. When off the clock, he couldn't tolerate meaningless small talk.

His mind drifted.

Perhaps he'd ingested too much of that anti-PTSD

inhalant following room service? His consciousness swooned. It was still hard for the agent to believe the war was over. But nothing would be won until the storm was over. Which wasn't happening anytime soon.

Exiting his bed, the fit, naked agent approached the hotel room comport. Running a hand across the device's glass holographic embossed lid, the holo-lid slid open for his unique palm print. He yearned for a reason to enter the device and online. He'd been trapped in the crucible of online action for so long that it was now the only place he felt at home.

When were they going to give him a new case? He had no life after four years on the road, no home, just his belongings packed away in storage in DC. Which he did not want or need. He craved only a case. This man, quietly mourning the loss of his secret lover, required work to avoid what would be a drug-induced Christmas fog. But the case did not come as he listened to recent Christmas classics:

"I'm dreaming of a stormy Christmas,
the only one I've ever known,
where raindrops thicken and wind index risen,
as we're safely tucked inside our leveed domes."

He celebrated New Years as expected, with a mini bottle of bourbon from the wet-bar recessed behind the media panel opposite his bed. Half stupefied and drunk, Ray watched as the Time Square New Year's ball dropped in a blur. In his blurred vision, it reminded him of the blur when he kissed Ravenna.

Then, just seven hours into the year 2060, he received a Delta Space-lines ticket to Beijing, flashing on the media surfaces of his hotel room. Ray's flight was set to depart in only four hours from the Hilton's lower level spaceport. Along with the ticket was an IM. He eyed the instant message from his boss, FCC Lieutenant, Joe Caresio.

FROM: J. CARESIO:

Merry Xmas, Happy New Year, and all that. In response to your request for a new case, you're headed to China. Your prior experience there will be needed. The eDossier will be sent in-flight. It's time-sensitive, so we'll chat after your field visit with the local detective. Time to come back down to Earth. You've been greatly missed, Ray.

six

It was an important case.

Unlike any other, the Chinese homicide detective had ever worked. The gruesome death that seemed a possible suicide frightened his superiors and risked destabilizing the security of the modern web. Because if this was murder, it was supposed to be impossible. Then there was the victim, a half Asian, Caucasian American who emigrated to Mainland China, the PRC, with close ties to the top Chinese leadership. His death occurred while he was online and should've been captured by various surveillance cameras in his bedroom. But the home's surveillance data was corrupted. Even the comport's camera system covering the areas around and inside the protective capsule, all had temporarily pixelated footage in their remote online hard-drive sites.

The last useable video showed the victim fully contained in his bedroom comport. Eyes closed. Flat on his back. Mind immersed online. Then, the cameras in the bedroom and comport simultaneously pixelated out for 17 critical seconds; the next viable footage revealed the individual kneeling in his then-open comport, its lid slid open; an antique Japanese sword from his wall-mounted collection now plunged through the man's bloody abdomen.

The death transpired in the second-story bedroom of his swanky mansion protected within a private, gated neighborhood enclosed beneath a sophisticated geo dome. One of the ritziest Beijing suburbs. Chinese forensic experts couldn't explain the footages' sudden pixelation; the reason why the Chinese homicide detective delayed classifying it as a *suicide*.

A break came three days later in his cramped apartment after he brewed Japanese *Gyokuro* tea from Yame, Japan. It was gifted to him by a Japanese detective after they completed a recent homicide case. The expensive delicacy which would've taxed the Chinese detective's meager salary following his divorce proved worth its weight in gold by revealing the vital clue.

While carrying his teakettle back to his cramped bedroom, a hot droplet struck the top of his bare foot causing him to notice the trail of spilled tea drops spanning the concrete floor, trailing back to his kitchen. Eyeing the path of emerald drops, his mind realized a similar pattern in his new case.

On his iScreen, the Chinese cop reviewed the surveillance cameras beyond the victim's bedroom and home, expanding them in an ever-smaller checkerboard of camera points of view throughout the domed neighborhood. One by one in a daisy chain, he watched each camera cluster pixelate for a few seconds, beginning with the most remote cameras aimed at a flooded, lichen-infested forest beyond the enclosed compound.

Each camera momentarily pixelated all the way up to the ones at the murder scene in the dome's epicenter. The path of pixelating cameras, undeniably similar to the drops of tea, led into the victim's bedroom just before the time of death. Then the pattern wound its way back out to the perimeter's lichen wood free of cameras. Leaving behind seconds of video permanently wiped as a possible killer transited past each camera.

This clue caused the detective to suspect a murderer. A hunch further verified by the pathologist's notes insisting that no one could stab themselves the way the victim did with the sword from his wall-collection of antique blades mounted on his bedroom wall. The fact the victim's comport accessed a U.S. server at the time of death meant the case fell under United States FCC web agency jurisdiction. The reason why the Chinese detective was now en route to the Beijing Spaceport to retrieve FCC agent Kemper.

Meanwhile, Ray was in the stratosphere.

He reclined in the last of the twelve rows of Delta business class comports. David's docking comports now replacing the conventional seats, leaving passengers in coach to only access their iScreens. Many people back there got jittery without being immersed online for more than a few minutes.

Ray remained doubtful of the murder designation. Reviewing the FCC lab analysis in the case's eDossier, he found his American medical team less inclined to rule suicide as impossible; although it would be difficult for anyone to repeatedly stab their body as what appeared to have happened. Still, his FCC superiors refused to call it murder. Because if this case could undermine *the safest place on Earth,* the corporate claim of the top-line, *Red Series* comport, then no one would be safe in a comport as their minds were immersed online. Just as Blackout was removed from the stage, a new threat arose to possibly undermine the entire modern web, making this case as relevant perhaps as Ray's prior one.

He exited his comport.

The smell of dry, sterilized air. His Velcro-bottomed slippers allowed Ray to easily walk in the lighter gravity field. He stretched his legs next to a cluster of bathrooms at the rear of the business class cabin. On his eComp's iScreen, he took a second look at the video surveillance files from the Chinese eDossier.

Leaning against the empty bathroom door, Ray stretched his thighs. His iScreen displayed the overhead surveillance footage from the victim's many bedroom cameras. Four viewpoints all on the Chinese American in his comport, his mind immersed online. Then all of the cameras simultaneously pixelated only to reappear a few seconds later revealing the man dead, the sword blatantly missing from his wall-mounted collection. That missing blade's tip now pierced through his back as the man knelt inside the open comport with its retracted lid. His blade stabbed through his torso, its bloody tip poking through his back. The question bit at Ray-

Suicide or murder?

Then Ravenna's voice as his eComp Siri, whispered in Ray's ear, "Ray, the captain notified us we're about to enter inner orbit."

With little time left, the agent scanned the bio on the local detective. Familiar with the nuances of China, he assumed the detective's name to be a mistake. For the Chinese cop possessed only one name and an extraordinary one at that. Because all Chinese individuals were given two names, the family name preceding the individual's birth-order, stressing a family alliance at the core of one's self over any western concept of individual self-identity.

Returning to his comport, he onlined to snatch another look at the sole forensic evidence of a possible killer. One dermal skin flake discovered on the victim's comport belonged to a female. Although the genetic sample was too corroded to eSimulate her physical likeness, his experts possibly attributed it to the deceased man's maid. Daily, she cleaned his comport with isopropyl alcohol.

Her boss was a germ freak since almost dying of *Green Lung* years before. Ray was surprised any collectible DNA survived the alcohol at all. And since the deceased was so interested in continuing his life via such hygiene measures, why would the man commit suicide?

Ray ended the media presentation with an eye stroke, calling up the virtual stop sign, touching it as he offlined. Again he was aware of the magnetic collars snug around his wrists and ankles as he floated in near-zero gravity. The magnetic collars drew his body down into the Delta Airlines comport bed which transformed itself back into a sleek chair, the lid retracting to the rear of the chair. The retracted holo-glass lid on the seat-back ahead of Ray illustrated their landing path through the stratosphere devastated by the storms of the past pollution of slavery.

The craft began vibrating as it usually did during reentry. Cradled in his padded surroundings, Ray reflected on how safe his victim must've felt inside his secure Red Series comport. Did he require a Red Series because of the corrupt, Chinese political officials he maneuvered through? Only military F&M's could pierce such extreme super-armor. All those precautions taken to simply kill yourself? It didn't feel right to him. Nor did the option of murder-

His head spun.

After all, comports were the most secure place for online users except for a bank vault. When immersed, one couldn't be awakened by sounds or touch; all their senses dead to the world. The reason why onliners required protection. Faith in comports served as the bedrock of security for one's body while onlining in David's modern web. His deceased's comport showed no signs of illegal gamma drilling, requiring 15 minutes to bore a tiny hole through the holo-glass-lid through which to pump in poison gas. While the surveillance cameras only pixilated for a matter of seconds.

With government planners now counting on most of the world population soon to migrate into *Dreamspace*, Ray grasped his case's broader ramifications. If it was murder, where was the proof? It was like an angel of death flew past all those surveillance cameras, magically blinding each from view before somehow opening the comport's lid and murdering a man with a sword in under 17 seconds. That insurmountable task forced FCC experts to believe his case could only be suicide. Maybe his superiors didn't entirely trust him with his unique knowledge of Blackout's viral program, but they needed his experience in dealing with a political case in Mainland China which constituted another significant puzzle.

Down on the surface, the detective waited in standstill traffic halted in blinding rain. His old hybrid minivan had auto-piloted to the Beijing spaceport obscured in rain and hail. The destination was visible as a computer-generated icon ahead of him on the vehicle's windshield heads-up display.

The detective took a moment to brush up on the FCC agent, who it turned out was well-schooled in China. Agent Kemper as a kid lived on the new south coast where his father worked for an American floodwall company back in the '30s trying to save post-Communist China. With experience in-country, the agent would most certainly inquire about the detective's odd name.

His name was why the Chinese cop never fit into this confused nation. A people who prided themselves on their history that they failed to take the time to know. Because for the first 2500 years, China was monotheistic. Its hallowed *Temple of Heaven* honoring the Abrahamic God they called *Shangdi*. The first Chinese purposely immortalized much of their Israelite Bible into the writing system's symbols. Many of them illustrating stories from the Book of Genesis. The belief in *Shangdi* was upended by Confucius and Buddha, who both told the Chinese to spurn *Shangdi*, the one God of China. Even with tales of Genesis woven into the symbolic language, the Chinese forgot their long past with the one God.

Most Chinese by now knew this fact. So much Confucianism and Buddhism left most people unable to truly believe in God. Then came the storms developed after 2,000 years of China's godless direction leading to the intentional worldwide pandemic; that act of one fueled a chaotic time when so many needlessly died.

As a baby, he was lucky enough to find himself abandoned at a gas station bathroom. Another *Climate Change* orphan. Two years after his birth, Exxon/Mobil Corporation was sold to Sinopec's growing petrol hegemony in the Asian market and the name Exxon was mostly lost in China except for their airport jet-fuel depots like the one here at the airport.

He didn't regret being named after a gas station. On the contrary, the detective wore it as a badge of honor, endowing in him the insight of a consummate outsider, which aided him as a detective to see what others could not. Because caring what others thought of you rather than what God thought, was a false harmony. After losing their belief in God, two millenniums passed as the Chinese repeated their atheist mindset until newborns' neural programming were slowly rewired to be clogs in a mass-Asian mindset to serve the reigning command and control structure.

That concept of keeping-face in the eyes of others instead of *Shangdi*, the one true Chinese God, fed blind obedience within members of a family to judgment from the vital superior. The system extended up through the hierarchy governing the countless families into provinces with governors serving the emperor of the Chinese nation. Confucius sought to murder God, sending China on the path to ruining the world. No one had any doubt about that now.

Now China's curse was apparent in the storms they sowed and disease they wrought upon the innocent. Such was their painful for failing to honor the one, true God. The one true Creator that Exxon found far easier to accept in his life. He first learned these facts online and couldn't believe his peers never sought to question their culture. Mindless lemmings who ignored the Biblical tales in their writing system. While he saw things not as he wished, but how they were.

The key to him being a detective.

As a child, Exxon only knew abandonment. The pain turned to strength, allowing him to fully separate himself from the others. His weird name fueling unrelenting mistreatment from school-kids to bar him from fitting in. Teachers treated Exxon like a bastard, refusing to say his name, forcing him to go by the name *number one*. Everyone's first name was the birth-rank in their family followed by the family name. He fought snide schoolyard remarks about his lack of a family name with clenched fists. Later his superiors in law enforcement chaffed from his unyielding indifference to their prejudices and greed. Like the typically wicked, they considered him just stubborn, unnecessarily difficult, even erratic.

He loved old *Dirty Harry* films, feeling a deep affinity for Clint Eastwood's stoic character. But when it affected the power players at large, he was their Chow Yun-Fat's *Hard-Boiled*; they gave him the high-profile cases because he was a trusted, unbiased, cop. Which was why he could tell them to screw off without punishment; moral superiority was a power that couldn't help but be wielded by him in moments of anger from a lack of justice. Still given his experience-

This case freaked him out. Because the possible victim expired while kneeling in his comport. Technically that eComp was undocked at the time of death. So the victim wasn't immersed online when he expired. But he still died in a comport and that was all that mattered under the U.N. Net Neutrality Act of 2044. It dictated American jurisdiction since the comport had accessed an American website during the time of death. The nationality of the accessed website dictated web jurisdiction.

In his 15 years on the force, the Chinese detective mostly worked the less glamorous, non-web-related homicides. In web cases, Exxon typically transported the two hard drives from the deceased's comport to the officiating web agency's embassy in Beijing. Each embassy physically then mailed the drives in sealed diplomatic pouches to their respective Web Agencies via space-flight couriers. But in VIP cases like this one, the drives would be retrieved in-country by the officiating Web Agent. The two cylindrical-shaped hard drives were still in the victim's comport in his home. They constituted a literal *black box* of telemetry documenting everything up through the time of death.

Meanwhile, Ray Kemper waited as his Delta space jet slowed to a stop at the Beijing tarmac's end. He observed hail outside, visible on all the media screen walls framing the inner surfaces of the spacecraft's cabin. His Siri suggested he rendezvous with the local detective at *Departures* as that level was relatively empty with most flights having already departed.

Two miles away in slow-moving traffic, the Chinese detective still couldn't make out the massive spaceport in the fog and hailstorm. Chewing on a toothpick, Exxon caught a glimpse of his face in the rearview eMirror. His long visage looked Cantonese with slighter features now gathered into a wrinkled brow. He didn't like dealing with the FCC's charming, but cocky agents wearing their clichéd American cowboy boots as made famous in that web show.

Ray sported similar *Lucchese* cowboy boots as he disembarked from the space jet. But he was by now, no mere cowboy. He considered himself culturally a citizen of the world after serving so many years on *Swipe 9*; circumnavigating the globe 53 times left him a stranger to no land, making him a seasoned gourmand. Ray knew the most delicate foods originated from agro-domes in the Northern Japanese island of Hokkaido; their commitment to perfection mirrored only by Tuscan agro-domes.

He was well trained in human psychology. Years of travel taught him so much about people. In the many eateries where he often dined alone with a cap brim covering his face, he listened in on people's conversations over his eComp auto-translator with an audio booster. What he heard around the planet revealed to him that humans were the same everywhere.

They talked of lives spent largely living and working at home, kids, coffee, food, keeping dry from ever-present rain and *Green Lung*, love, cheating, gossip. All part of the unexpected modernity where COVID-19 evolved into the now ubiquitous *Green Lung;* while Blackout's digital virus assumed the Chinese yin yang moniker of the continuing biological plague.

It took the storm's cessation of inter-ocean trade to fully stop America's purchasing of Chinese goods and its world-ending pollution. If it had stopped purchasing slave-made goods earlier, perhaps the fate of the world could be different. When the slave-trade finally ended, so did America's massive imprisonment rate for its subsequent jobless. It was odd, scary, and even banal in the coffee shops of modernity's rain. That wasn't to say that fear of the ePocalpyse, another permanent blackout, or the threat of *Green Lung* from the constant rain was not far from one's mind. The war was ever-present. But life still had to go on.

The terminal's elevator glass doors slid open for the American FCC agent. Cold, whipping raindrops assaulted his exposed face as he stepped out into the cacophony of Beijing's Terminal 3's exterior departure area. Car horns honking beneath massive banks of overhead U.V. viral-killing lamps shining down light and warmth.

A fierce gust forced more rain out under the canopy dampening offloading passengers. Scampering business commuters now rudely pushed faster from behind Ray. As a sea of bio facemasks ahead of him pushed past. They were needed to ward out airborne fungus and the many animal-borne diseases that later plagued this most-polluted land. With the new anti-*Green Lung* annual pill, facemasks were finally no longer largely required except for older people of those venturing to India or China. Their ruler nameless, protected from the disease in perhaps a lone life of splendid isolation in some lavish bunkers.

No one here wanted to be outside if they could help it. The scars of slavery turned China into a devastated land. Xi Jinping, its former totalitarian ruler for life was now long-dead. But the scars of his communist dictatorship lived on around the world. George Washington's prophetic warning to his nation had come true, wrecking not only America but the many nations of the world with China now worst afflicted.

In the media walls of the spaceport, Xi Jinping remained as the face of the current ruler although that dictator was long since buried. The Chinese finally got to own rather than just rent their wealth and property; but due perhaps to eons of centralized submission via Confucianism, the nation displayed a propensity for totalitarian rulers, the likes of which currently ruled while masking their identity with Xi Jinping's Skin. No one knew who was in power. So a dead man ironically remained the ruler of the land his regime long-before poisoned to death.

The treason of the Three Traitors were made clear by the murders of Xi Jinping so that they were all four considered as the team that ended the world. Trump contributed too. He thought he was in a normal trade war and left U.S. borders open to Chinese trade and travel even after the pandemic. Allowing Xi Jinping's to spread new strains laced into his Chinese-made products and via his mass-infecting Chinese travelers like he employed at the pandemic's start. The plague like the prior, medieval *Black Death* both originated in Wuhan's Hubei Province, had spread through trade and travel until China was embargoed worldwide by the free-world

The 20th Century well-proved that death remained the inevitable outcome of a communist society; a false sheen to mask a tyrant extending total control and death. The Chinese nation that sought harmony after it was forced to forget their one, true God, *Shangdi* thousands of years ago, generated pollution that might very well end all life. All born from those past American consumers.

The cheap goods would come back for them and their children through Blackout's digital virus paying homage to Xi Jinping, the world's largest mass-murderer to-date of his own people and those of the world. The virus now known as *Green Lung* constituted the present form of the Yin Yang Virus that already had killed billions.

While the pollution from Chinese slavery came in those *wings of abomination* prophecied in the Bible up in the stratosphere to trigger radical Climate Change. Not the carbon emissions but the undeniable China pollution to make American goods. While the Chinese citizens buzzing around Ray outside the spaceport remained quiet, the result of eons of Confucian conformity. Even their children were born calmer and easier to tame; and Ray didn't think that was a good thing. People of any age found it difficult to process a major anomaly not previously memorialized in history, like America's treason of embracing slavery that caused this nightmare.

China was visibly toxic.

If he stayed here too long his neurotransmitters would get scrambled in his brain. The same when he was a kid. Locals said it was common since 2008. The way someone would inexplicably feel conflicting emotions, like laughing and crying at the same time. But that took a day to set in. He would only be here for a couple of hours. He tried to lose himself in seemingly endless Chinese faces as he progressed through the thick crowd of facemasks.

His jacket raised his integrated facemask and expanding, clear-plastic face guard over him. Through it, he passed many sets of sloping eyes half-busy on their iScreens. Their eyes reminded Ray of David's blog on Asian features, crafted from a far longer glacial period during the prior ice age; when the frostbit climate rewarded narrow eyes, thinner noses, and wide, flat faces.

Then a chill up the agent's back interrupted his idle reflections as he and his automated bag departed the warm protection of the overhead bank of U.V. lamps atop the canopy; crossing beneath the waterfall of water pouring off the exterior awning's edge like a tiny Niagara Falls. His Siri auto-maximized the rain hood from his smartstorm jacket's collar. As virtual arrows on his iScreen directed him to the curb just beyond this awning where the unseen vehicle had drawn near in blinding rain. Ray's waterproof cowboy boots stopped in murky, shin-high water.

He could barely sere the minivan stopped ahead of his superimposed iScreen arrow. The vehicle's hydraulic door slid open. From inside the van, Exxon eyed Ray. The Chinese detective noted the American's cowboy boots popularized in the old web show about the FCC. Tossing his auto-rolling bag onto the scuffed yellow leather back-seat couch, Ray took in the unexpected aroma of hibachi-oil in the air. His hood, partition, and mask folded back into his integrated raised collar.

"Thanks for the pickup," Ray's eComp auto-translated his words as he handed the Chinese detective a decorative box containing a bottle of Reposado Tequila; the gift purchased from in-flight duty-free via his iScreen before landing. Distilled from blue agave grown in the sky-rise U.V. farms of Jalisco, Mexico. Ray remembered how Ravenna once assured him that Tequilla recently became all the rage in China, replacing the earlier obsession for Cognac. After the flooding caused by their pollution, the Chinese broke with their history and culture, yearning only for things from other lands. Still, these gifts remained a mandatory sign of respect in Asia and were covered by Ray's expense account. The Chinese cop accepted it with muted thanks.

Exxon drank only beer.

The Chinese detective's ceiling mounted media sunscreen cast a tacky purple sunset down on them. Magenta shadows from it filled the small sockets of Exxon's wide-set eyes as he studied Ray and drove. The FCC agent was not surprised at the youthful appearance of this Chinese man.

Age was hard to assess in Asia.

"I've worked with many Web Agents," Ray's auto-translation software interpreted the detective's Mandarin into English in Ray's ear, "*eKGB. FCC. EWB.* Always the same. They promise to keep me involved in the case…which is usually the last time I ever hear from them."

"I don't run a one-man show," Ray expected such resistance from the local cop. Flashing a charming smile perfected over years of FCC facial gesture classes, his auto-translation wove his English into Mandarin in the detective's eComp, "I work closely with local law enforcement. All I have is one question. Is Exxon your real name?"

As if on cue, the Chinese homicide cop pointed at a Sinopec gas station ad digitally highlighted over the holo-windshield overlooking sheets of rain. Ray's eComp translation software broadcasted the Chinese in English, "As a baby, they found me abandoned at an Exxon gas station."

"Really?" the FCC agent was surprised.

"No," the detective cut him off in a deadpan tone.

The hardened Chinese cop was sly to these Western, online agents' charisma and mind games. He worked with enough of them to know these tricks, if not truly understanding their art of deceptive charm. The reason why he shut himself off around Ray and purposely messed with him.

The remainder of the car ride was spent in silence. Ray surfed his iScreen, reviewing emails, checking into his Delta space flight bound for DC in less than seven hours. The extreme turbulence from the typhoons filled even the upper atmosphere, sometimes interrupting even space transport. This trip would be brief, a visit to the crime scene, and subsequent handoff of the hard drives still sealed in the victim's comport.

With the car in auto-drive mode, Exxon eyed updated social net photos of his twin daughters' soccer semi-final in Qingdao, populating the upper left corner of his iScreen. The detective noted how his ex-wife carefully omitted herself from the pics.

Since their divorce, he had moved into his cramped apartment, indulging in hibachi cooking which his wife had forbidden because of the overwhelming odor it left on everything. The detective inherited a passion for wok cooking from his adoptive father, the same security guard who discovered him as a baby in the Exxon bathroom but didn't take him in for years. For much of Exxon's later life, his surrogate dad worked as a security guard at the domed Forbidden City, usually remaining empty due to China's new hatred of its history since shedding Shangdi 2500 years prior. Exxon still walked through its stone squares protected from the rain beneath the dome. That palace was now his sole connection to his late, adoptive father.

One thing the man taught Exxon was that everyone possessed a sound-score to their life whether they realized it or not. That orchestral choir of feelings embodying all of their past and future expectations so that people seldom lost their emotional place in space and time. Without that music, he thought, no one remained anchored to their lives, lost in the moment devoid of the past or expectations of any future. Despite his jolly demeanor, Exxon sensed a dark choir to this chipper American.

Then Exxon and Ray's Siri's were both alerted to the large geo-dome rising ahead through the hail-storm. These mega structures having been built back in the early '40s were once considered the ultimate escape at the time from the constant rain. Before *Green Lung* hindered the rapid growth of domed communities. The required air purification systems later proved unfeasible for most private communities. Approaching the front gate's airlock, Ray reckoned the structure to be 18 football fields wide. Exxon's Siri bounced the access code to the building's computer.

The front blast door slid open, ushering the vehicle to an automatic stop within the airlock. Ultraviolet lights blasted the minivan's exterior, frying any fungal or Coronavirus elements festering from the endless storm, which commonly caused paronychia infections of the hands and feet or bloomed in the pulmonary system as *Green Lung* in now mostly the elderly.

"You're cleared for entry," the automated domed-city computer spoke respectively through both men's Siri's in Mandarin and English. The inner airlock gate slid open. Then Ray beheld something so amazing that if he were not well trained-

It would've brought tears to his eyes.

seven

Artificial twilight.

Almost real sunlight showered down from the seamless media screens adorning the interior of the dome. So that it seemed a dusk of lavender and orange had taken flight over the tree-lined boulevard. It wasn't the finest dome Ray had experienced; there were no falsely contrived clouds like Manhattan's geo-dome to conceal the massive U.V. light banks at the top of the dome's interior. But it was slick for a privately funded dome. Exxon tried to stifle back tears from his welling eyes; a common reaction for people who unlike these lucky few did not live in such a wondrous place.

The thick, armored roof dampened the sound of exterior rain as the hybrid minivan cruised beneath trees where actual birds chirped. Ray rolled down the window, taking in clean, sterilized air. He observed birds flying over chic homes of recycled driftwood and reclaimed glass. A child played in her front yard as they drove past. A far cry from Ray's childhood spent under those antiquated U.V. lamps in wet garages, rain continuously tapping outside the windows.

Drowning in a million droplets.

People experienced panic attacks, some driven to suicide by it. He remembered as a kid laying in bed, not wanting to get up. Even video games didn't offer escape anymore. Just the threat of unending rain coming to drown you. Endless rain. Coffins back then often came out of the ground, floating around neighborhoods like harbingers of what would come. He was tough. But sometimes he'd cry for no reason in the shower. Even the sound of a shower could get to a person. Everybody had their own experience wrestling with a looming death by drowning.

Now, eyeing these well-manicured lawns, he couldn't fathom how children before the storm ever chose to stay indoors to play video games when they could frolic under a blue sky. Beneath a sun his generation could not now behold from Earth with the naked eye. Old media on the web and video games were all anyone ironically saw of real sunlight, often showed in the online world. To responsibly respond to endless rain, the aesthetic became a reuse of past items woven into deeper meaning. Like the design movement of the 2040s was named-

Eco cool.

Beyond the aesthetic, Eco-cool sought an underlying unity. A point well illustrated in the largest mansion on the hill under the massive dome's center. Its front gate crafted in a sheen of plastic bags like the pre-storm plastic refuse from Asia filling parts of the Pacific Ocean. Watermarked Asian characters in faded red were imprinted across the sea of bags; these words in the form of pictures documented actual Genesis stories and historical worship of *Shangdi* until China imposed Confucianism.

The gate swung open for Exxon's eBadge. His old hybrid came to an easy stop in the dry, circular driveway of reclaimed shopping bags with American store logos. A reminder of America as the source of the pollution from mainland China. The vogue eco-aesthetic of melted *Coca-Cola* soda bottles made up the front door; that soda now a famous Christmas drink even in this nation which now acknowledged the Abrahamic Faith of their historical Shangdi. The Coke glass doors auto-slid open for Exxon's eBadge as the two men entered the home.

Ray's heels clicked lockstep with Exxon's own across the reclaimed concrete. The rare scent of actual leather in the air as the two men silently crossed the lavish front salon of priceless, 20th Century Ikea antiques. That universal status symbol of past modernity, the Ikea original packing boxes now laminated as the dining room's matching wallpaper, documenting the *provenance* of these antiques often knocked off in modernity.

The air, refreshingly clean and dry.

Exxon led Ray up to the second story, activating the media screen along the sidewall. Video footage of the dead owner of the home flashed along the wall, depicting the handsome, smiling half-Asian man arm-in-arm with various Asian eCelebrities and international elites.

Ray noted the surveillance cameras in the mansion. Beneath a bank of seven cameras, the two cops stopped in the sprawling master bedroom. A large bay window on the left overlooked the dead man's tennis court and swimming pool.

The law enforcement agents slowly circled the *Red Series* comport in the bedroom's center, where the deceased had mysteriously expired days before. Ray eyed the bloodstains now dried brown across the cream-colored, faux leather of the inner comport's bed. One of the tiny surveillance cameras above the inner bed was speckled in dried blood. Taking a step back, the FCC agent eyed the other ring of cameras implanted in the outer shell of the blast-proof frame.

"How did the cameras get wiped?" the Chinese detective probed, his words translated into English in Ray's ear.

Ray shrugged, "We're not sure. The lab took to calling it a video cloak. But they have no idea how it pixelated segments of video from all the cameras' remote hard drives."

"So how then was the comport opened from the exterior?" pressed Exxon.

"Perhaps he hit the manual release?" Ray eyed the manual release button recessed into the inner bed's lining. Exxon said nothing. Ray advanced another query, "And what makes you so certain that it's murder?"

He noted the testiness in the detective's voice as his words translated, "The pathologist concluded no one could do that to themselves-"

"But he died as found, in the classic suicide position-"

"Seppuku," Exxon corrected him.

The Chinese detective triggered a Wikipedia request, which once granted by Ray, expanded across his semi-opaque iScreen. A cinematic recording of a Japanese samurai played as an unseen narrator explained in Ray's ear:

"Seppuku. An ancient Japanese form of ritual suicide. Vanquished samurais knelt down to commit suicide with their *tanto* sword as their victor loomed over them. Just before stabbing himself in the mid-torso, the vanquished was spared a grueling death by decapitation from the victor's blade."

"So nobody lost their head?" Ray curtly replied as the video notation ended.

The FCC agent's comment frustrated Exxon so much that his response befuddled Ray's auto-translation software. It chirped in his ear, "Comment undecipherable," before the Chinese detective calmed down enough for the auto-translator to tell Ray, "She was there. I know it-"

"What makes you certain there is a woman involved?" pressed Ray.

"The epidermal skin sample found on the comport's outer lid was a female, but not the maid."

"OK. So the maid missed a spot while cleaning the comport sometime before the death. There's nothing to link that DNA to the murder-"

"The deceased was a clean freak. He inspected his home daily with an anti-germ light. Did you even read my brief?"

"I read it carefully," retorted Ray, "but that doesn't mean I arrived at the same conclusion."

Exxon huffed as his translation reiterated, "It's not the maid's skin. It's left recently in the crime scene."

Ray had read these facts, noting, "The DNA is corrupted. It's not the maid, which leaves us with every female as a suspect."

Exxon sighed.

Without the DNA evidence, he feared his case would eventually be ruled a suicide by the FCC. Pulling the two cylindrical hard drives from the comport's outer shell, the Chinese cop's heart sank as he realized he was handing his case off to this uncaring fool. He felt a deep connection to all his victims whose lives were taken just as his parents were when he was deserted as a child.

Ray grasped the two tubes by their integrated handles recessed into both ends. The tricho-carbon fiber surface felt cold to his touch. Flashing a polite gesture of thanks, both men knew their respective eComps documented the hand-off; the reason why Ray now assumed a truncated, officious tone as he said:

"On behalf of the United States government, I accept these comport hard drives, and thank you for your cooperation in this matter. This case is now under the jurisdiction of the United States Federal Communications Commission."

They remained silent during the drive back to the spaceport. The Chinese detective only spoke to Ray as he dropped him off at the departure area. It was late, most of the international flights had already left. Ray stood on the empty curb beneath the U.V. lights now on a dimmed, night mode.

"Search those hard drives," Exxon gestured at the two tubes Ray held, "She was there. I know it."

The door to Exxon's van auto-closed as the vehicle sped off; leaving the FCC agent surrounded by rain and hail beyond the canopy. Winds whipping the smell of hibachi from him.

Ray quickly repacked the short cylindrical drives into his automated roller bag as an obese, disabled Chinese woman rolled past on a unique hybrid, luggage bag wheelchair she could sit on. Identical Mr. Zero vid-ads along the spaceport's many support columns once again advertised the number one selling digital Skin of Matt Damon. Then the ad shifted to the now iconic multi-player shooting game *Financial Scandal 2008,* ubiquitously known as *FS8* with the iconic logline "You Got Robbed."

As Ray's eLuggage auto-zipped itself closed, his Siri chirped in his ear, "Ray, unfortunately, your flight's been grounded due to gale force winds across the Western Pacific," she informed him as his automated luggage followed him into the empty terminal building, "I can get you on the last flight stateside. But either way, you'll have to overnight somewhere to get to DC."

Ray didn't need to be anywhere in particular for his case. If he finally returned home, he'd still have to get his belongings out of government storage and find a new apartment. So he chose the last flight out to Los Angeles, which felt more like home now than DC. After all, he trained for five years there as a young FCC cadet at the eAcademy.

By the time his Delta space flight reached orbit, he was fast asleep, rocked into a deep slumber by the violent turbulence from a massive hurricane covering Southeast Asia. His slumbering body levitated in the business class comport in upper orbit, secured aloft by the magnetic ankle and wrist collars.

In his dream, Ray wandered back down that Indian hotel alleyway where intimacy had once saved his life; when Blackout's cyber struck his *Swipe 9* team. He approached Ravenna's silhouetted body set in darkness against the rain. Turning to face him, Ray gasped at the sight of her two dead fish eyes, replacing her own. The grotesque vision jolted him awake in his business class comport.

Parched, he exited the machine. His Velcro soled space slippers once again securing his feet to the floor in the low gravity. He approached the gastropub where he grabbed a water sip-sack. Two L.A. executives commiserated over the strange hours they kept in their near-daily commute across the Pacific. Another passenger told the bartender that he flew free on accumulated miles sometimes just to see the sun above them.

"But it's still on a media screen," noted the bartender as he glanced up at the star on the ceiling.

"I know," the man sighed, "but I am closer to it."

Pin lights above him tracked Ray's return path between the three rows of comports. The vast heavens projected around him on the high definition media screens covering the tubular interior wall. Two hours later Ray's dream still haunted him as he reclined in the L.A. hybrid taxi that soon pulled up to The Beverly Hilton.

From his loyalty status with the hotel chain, Ray was pre-cleared by a retinal scan at the hotel's front door. It electronically opened for him. Guided by virtual arrows along his iScreen, he reached the lift which auto opened; then across the penthouse level hall, more arrows leading him to his hotel room door which slid open.

The LED walls of his Media Suite glistened with the iconic Hilton logo at the start of the welcome screen. A life-size image of the room's designer, Kavi, filled the hotel room wall beside Ray as he sat down on the bed. Kavi looked at Ray pulling off his cowboy boots. This room was identical to the one in Shanghai, the Space Station, and hundreds of other Hiltons where Ray had resided. He knew Kavi's recorded greeting so well he mimicked her words in chorus:

"I designed this room to mimic the web where we spend most of our lives, bringing harmony and unity to both the online and offline worlds-"

His eye stroke ended her greeting as Ray eSynched his eComp to the room's media system.

His automated bag rolled to the corner as its recessed legs lifted it up waist high as the bag auto-opened its integrated drawers. Behind the bag, a wall-sized image of Ravenna's face appeared as his Siri, chirping:

"FCC firewall is installed. The room is surveillance bug-free. So I have only one question-"

"Yes. I'd like room service," yawned Ray as he pulled out the two hotel provided memory drives from the comport, inserting his victim's drives in their place.

On the wall screen before him, his Siri reported back, "Your 'usual' will be delivered in 30 minutes or less. The new data drives are also loaded into your hotel room comport."

Ray grabbed a tiny bottle of Scotch from the minibar, chasing it down with a quick puff from his micro anti-depressant inhaler. In the sudden head rush of the drug, Ravenna's face vibrated before him as he felt a sudden rush of sadness. The grief again left him dizzy, perhaps due to one too many puffs on the inhaler? Still, that dream of Ravenna with the mental image of those fish eyes returned, troubling his soul.

Laying back on his transparent bed, Ray eyed the face of his dead lover on the ceiling's media screen. Ravenna's actual likeness winking playfully back in a warmth Ravenna would never have employed. Again those dead fish eyes from his dream, like something rotted and best thrown away. The Siri didn't even feel like her now. Perhaps why the decision came so quickly, like a build-up to a battle that never actually had to be fought:

"Siri, delete your Skin," the master ordered his software.

Instantly his electric lover vanished from view. In her place, appeared thousands of eComp Siri Skins from a revolving carousel from Mr. Zero. His animated offering of Skins ranged from the historical to absurd. Ray considered choosing Ricky Gervais, much beloved in modernity as an important critic of past media. But Ray finally chose his eComp's free default Siri: a formless, silver face David Bellingham incorrectly expected would be the only choice for his users. A lack of vision allowing Mr. Zero to dominate the Skin trade from his Calcutta tenement hovel to become the second wealthiest human on Earth after David Bellingham. Dragging Ravenna's Skin to the trash can, Ray emptied the garbage, completely deleting his former handler's likeness. And just like that-

She was gone.

He searched his heart but felt nothing. Just another moment in his life. Only hours later did Ray regret his actions. Unanticipated darkness welling up from within. A deep depression Ray recognized at first touch, but so quickly forgot in its absence. His mind turned away from his former handler to that memory of his deceased father's hard drives piled up before window overlooking hail obscuring Lake Michigan. Then he floated into the recollection from his dream-

Ravenna's fish eyes.

The sadness became suffocating. Deep in the effect of the booze and drugs, Ray stumbled from his bed through the hidden door in the suite's LED media screen wall. The passageway led him out to the old, exterior balcony of rusted steel and chipped paint, corroded from the ever-present storm.

A hailstorm-filled Wilshire Blvd before him. Leaning against the corroded balcony rail, he felt the angry rain penetrate his soul. This hotel was one of the only Hiltons old enough to still possess balconies. Cold rusty metal against his bare feet as he stood atop the balcony railing. He thought back on the marathon he ran without training under the Phoenix geo dome, which still left his hamstrings so tight. Then he recollected on the stream of identical Hilton Media Suites he'd inhabited these past many years, risking life and limb to end World War IV.

Now here he was.

Death did not scare Ray. Death was his only real partner, handing him a never-ending stream of murder and mayhem. But all that destruction somehow stayed in his soul. He'd given up so much for childhood notions of heroic meaning, to avoid leaving behind something more than those trivial ceramic hard drives that marked his father's meager existence. The search for meaning left him now wondering what truly mattered. He felt in some ways like he knew less than when he began this voyage.

The FCC taught him how to overcome the fear of death. But now maybe that wasn't such a good thing. After the greatest World War manhunt in history, everything in its wake felt anticlimactic. His love for Ravenna was woven in that conflagration. The war also ended with her death. Leaving him alone, as far as he knew, with a complete mastery of the most dangerous idea every incepted. Blackout's program code. After this case, they'd probably cycle him into a desk job like his boss. Doing the kind of work that turned any man into a bitter, isolated alcoholic or drug addict.

Suddenly Ray felt so tired.

Leaning over the railing, he gave into momentary temptation, feeling himself starting to fall forward. Imagining his face colliding into the street far below when he was saved at the last second by his Siri:

"Ray. Someone's IM'ing your murder victim."

A shocked Ray fell backward, landing on the cold balcony

floor. Immediately sobering him, the fall shook loose the impending fate he almost suffered from weakness, fatigue, or possibly just nostalgia. His mind swooning. Wet, uneven concrete had painfully scraped his palms. Dizziness. A sudden ache in that old wound in his right elbow from the Moroccan mission. He refocused through the drug. His mind thirsting now to unlock this new puzzle:

"How could someone I.M. my murder victim?"

"The victim's drives are loaded onto your room's comport," his generic, silver-faced Siri chirped in the lower corner of Ray's iScreen, "You're now recognized *on-lining* as his ID, Coolguy7."

Ray should've known that fact.

Only as he stumbled back into his Media Suite, did he fathom how the drug cocktail had snuck up on him. The concealed door in the media screen wall closed behind. Still groggy, he felt a chill at how close he came to jumping to his death. A cold shiver passed through him as his feet glided across the slippery media screen floor. The instant messenger window was projected on all the surfaces surrounding this FCC agent.

A massive, white I.M. dialogue bubble lit the darkness on the far wall. Above the bubble appeared the *Dreamspace* logo. Ray eyed the instant message sent to his victim from someone identifying themselves only as:

THE VOYEUR:
YOU'RE LATE.

Ray rolled his tongue around the hollow of his cheek, his next eye stroke activating his eComp's audio dictation. He noted his dead victim's user I.D designator appearing in the new dialogue bubble with the header *Coolguy7*.

Ray spoke aloud, "Who is this?" his words populating the empty dialogue bubble onscreen as he spoke:

COOLGUY7:
WHO IS THIS?

The cold response appeared, cutting FCC agent Ray Kemper to the core:

THE VOYEUR:
YOUR KILLER.

eight

Ray's training kicked in.

His eyes honed in on this suspect's *Dreamspace* I.D. *The Voyeur* who just audaciously claimed to be the FCC agent's killer. Hopping into his hotel room comport, the clean smell of the hermetically sealed chamber filled Ray's nostrils as the holographic lid slid closed. Ray's generic Siri instructed him that:

"'Voyeur' does not care what Skin you choose, but demands that you are body scanned to verify you're CoolGuy7."

"Use my FCC badge over-ride," he replied.

His eFCC badge falsely confirmed his body match to his possible victim.

He chose the young *Bourne Identity* era Matt Damon Skin.
Lying back, his eComp synched into the docking station cradled
around Ray's head. As he onlined, Ray expected the typical loss of
body sensation.

His Siri informed him, "Now entering *Dreamspace.*"

Ray felt himself shoot forward as if from a cannon. There
was no apparent break in reality as he slammed into slimy mud that
he would've sworn covered the ceiling. Head spinning. As his eyes
adjusted, he made out the dark woods surrounding him and sensed
the plastic ball gag taped over his mouth. Unexpectedly aware of
wet restraints binding his ankles and wrists.

Rolling over, he stared up at the face of his possible killer
stepping out of the shadows and into a shaft of moonlight through
trees. He had not seen the moon for so long. And he could smell
scents here that never before registered online. Taking in the
fragrance of pine, dirt, and the light rain filling his nose. He was in
a forest of tall juniper pines, casting shadows of pine needles across
his date's visage. An angelic-faced, little girl, perhaps 12 years of
age who approached in a crisp, private school skirt and starched,
white shirt. Kneeling over him, the little girl sliced his forearm with
a small knife in her hand—

IT HURT!

"Little something to warm us up," her breath misted in the
damp air as she eyed his Skin with a flirty grin, "Like your Skin
choice. Very retro," as she cut loose his bindings.

"Figured you'd appreciate the change," he bantered back.
Ever the skillful liar, the Web Agent caught Damon's reflection in
the mud puddle, so lifelike that it threw him.

"So let's do it," she spun around in the mud on the heels
of her red, knee-high boots.

The girl skipped as she led Ray down the dirt path hewn
into mud and ferns. The detective analyzed her movements as his
mind pieced clues together. He surmised they'd shared *Dreamspace*

dates? He knew from the endless ad barrage that the game was a two-player platform. So he knew users first had to date to find their game mate. Did she hope *Coolguy7* could be her permanent gaming partner? There was also something in her manner that struck the FCC agent as out of sorts. Something that he couldn't quite put his finger on.

Ambling down the wet path after her, Ray smelled a chimney's fire cutting through the thick scent of damp flora and dirt. Thunder grumbling above them as her blonde hair bounced in the moonlight. Weaving their way between the tall pines they arrived at a stunning, contemporary glass house rising up in a cold, steel angles and glass walls.

The front door auto-slid open as tiny sensors scanned their bodies for bacteria. Every detail, authentic. The mild scent of basil and olive oil from the open-air kitchen hinted to Ray about the Italian meal recently prepared.

Turning to him, the girl flashed an expectant look or perhaps an expected call to action that he could not yet discern. Rain slowly trickled down the sloping glass ceiling above them. Droplets of water projecting raindrop like tears moving across their bodies. A damp Ray took in the fireplace's faint warmth from across the room. Then she climbed atop the modern, sleek couch beside him.

"Miss me?" her eyes remained now level with his own.

Ever the consummate actor, the highly trained FCC agent played along. His mind again sifted through what he could know about her. They had met before online. She thought via the identity scan that he must be her suitor. Drawing close to him, her lips now uncomfortably close to his. She might not even be a female at all.

Sounds across the hall drew their attention to the far side of the glass courtyard in the home's center. His heart quickened. Through the glass, he made out the low lit bedroom where an ancient, *Frankenstein* movie played on a massive media screen wall.

Silhouetted in front of the screen sat a couple in bed watching the film, their backs facing him.

Ray turned to his pint-sized, female host who now dug into her backpack, producing the same blade she used to cut him. Setting the wet blade in his palm, she flashed an expectant look Ray had seen before. That expression of a killer that Blackout let everyone see. But then the killer's thrill left her with the wake of sudden suspicion:

"I don't know how you tricked the system, but you're not Coolguy7."

"Why?" he feigned.

She sneered, "Coolguy's a sick puppy-"

"Trying new tricks," he replied.

Her response struck him as almost too quick, "Then alright trickster, there are two ways to go," she produced the small pill in her second hand as an alternative to the knife, "Choose."

"Why the distrust?"

"Need to match up with my game-mate. But then again, you know that. Just like you know what I want."

Ray remembered her I.D. from their IM chat, The Voyeur. He replied, "Watching me kill."

Perhaps his comment rekindled trust? But for a test, it seemed too obvious for him to use the blade. So he swallowed the pill instead. Suddenly dizzy, he collapsed to the hard, tiled floor. His vision blurry as he began to pass out, barely able to make out her mutter

"I don't know how you fooled the body scan, but you're not Coolguy7-"

Everything went black…

Ray regained consciousness to see a lone candle in a sconce mounted on the cramped wall beside him. The flame flickering down. He registered sounds of dirt falling on a hard surface only inches above his face before he realized he was trapped in a coffin. Breath racing. Heart pounding.

Buried alive.

The candle flickered out as the last of the air was exhausted by his breathing. He reminded himself that this was just an online game. Struggling to extend his hand to call up his exit protocol, which didn't work here. He started to suffocate as he heard his Siri in his ear:

"Ray. You could use your eBadge to force a log off, but it might alert her that you're law enforcement."

He negatively shook his head. This existence wasn't real, he struggled to tell himself. The craving for air consuming him. Fighting to stay conscious.

His training brought the FCC agent a few more seconds of clarity. His mind raced to a solution, which ultimately eluded him in the mathematics of possibilities from this point. Grueling asphyxiation. Struggling to avoid using his FCC badge in a literal test of conviction. Then a final scream in silence, now robbed of oxygen as he died for this investigation.

This was real.

His life actually flashed before his eyes as it had done once before in actual offline combat. He saw himself as a kid snuggling next to his dad-Blackout screaming about annihilating humanity-the U.N. guards zipping Ravenna's charred remains in a body bag—being robbed of some great idea by Ravenna's voice over the comlink...then without realizing it, FCC agent Ray Kemper's consciousness flickered out of existence.

Ray opened his eyes.

His body drenched in sweat, back in his hotel room comport, which he never actually left. His chest pounding as he wolfed down air in overlapping gasps. He felt as if he'd died. Struggling to force out the gruesome image of that coffin. It was a game. But as real as a dream, reinforcing the reality to which he returned. His heart, nonetheless, refused to abide by what his mind dictated to be the reality. His comport now reminded him of that coffin. An eye swipe opened the holographic glass lid.

He rose up.

Even a cold shower did not wash away the sickening feeling of having been buried alive. That nausea remained in his subconscious like a bad memory he couldn't delete. He was surprised to find he just couldn't convince his emotions otherwise; a strange bifurcation of his heart that was difficult to articulate, part of the new consequences of an online platform again achieving a *Tutwiler reality*, when an in-game experience to the player could not be discerned from real life.

Later in bed, he asked his Siri, "What site was our victim on when he died?"

"*Dreamspace*," his Siri replied.

"I've seen Dreamspace's marketing," he commented, "I want to see any third party interviews that provide a deeper context."

Siri replied a millisecond after her eSearch, "This investigative journalism piece is the only thing I could find like that."

On the media surfaces around his bed, the promotional video began with *Dreamspace's* co-designer, Pia Geller, the former head of Bellingham Labs research and development. The world knew her as David's only collaborator. The interview program was *Hot Spot* hosted by *Anonymous*, an investigative journalist who never revealed himself on camera or his actual identity to the media.

Eyeing her sitting in the interview room on the media screens, Ray took in Pia's face like a map. He found himself moving past the intended misdirection of her brown hair dyed in streaks of bright aqua green. Her Southern drawl now drowned out in a Californian accent was rare. But it was her eyes that transfixed him. They possessed a profound distance; as if Pia had stared off peeks at things beyond imagination. Her glance reminded him of the eyes of that old-time artist, Billie Eilish.

Instead of musical creations, Pia achieved a *Tutwiler Reality*. Something now long-considered lethal. But unlike Jim Tutwiler's prior creation, Dreamspace didn't poison its users' minds with GNS which killed all but one of Tutwiler's medical-patient-gamers.

Not only had they made such a game safe, but Pia and David pioneered the very nature of video game design. Perhaps experience endowed a coolness in her manner, mused Ray. An emotional detachment Pia wore like a loose, old sweater about to fall off her shoulder. She didn't care what you thought. She saw you naked with your lies, felt Ray, as the woman continued:

"Honesty with your game mate in *Dreamspace* is paramount," Pia stressed to Anonymous, "because only your game mate playing alongside avoids the *Tutwiler Dilemma,"* by now everyone knew that reaching a Tutwiler level of reality in-game would bring later kill the user with what later came to be known as *Gamer Neural Shock* or GNS.

"How do two people safeguard against it"

"It's why movies have a love story alongside a wider tale of survival. Deprived of real love or any other real mind, a consciousness will break down."

"And so people already in relationships are supposed to just dump their offline mate?" asked the off-camera interviewer.

Pia sarcastically grinned, "Yeah. Tell me how many people would choose their significant other with whom to do it all over again? Despite how we would like it to be, you don't get to dictate to the data. The data must lead you."

"So after the brief dates for neophytes, the real game never ends," probed the unseen interviewer, "What is that in-game experience like?"

"It's the never-ending story users play until they expire of natural causes. They're fed, bodies safeguarded, making it easier for essential workers in the real world to better fight the storm and manage dwindling resources. Bellingham Labs feeds you plant-based intravenous sustenance, subsidizing anyone who can't afford the subscription. Leaving essential workers to hold back the storm and feeding more on less."

"I get the real-world benefits," the interviewer sighed, "But you're asking us to jump into a never-ending game we've never before experienced-"

"No," she corrected the interviewer, "the dates provide tastes of the platform so you not only know but strongly seek to enter *Dreamspace*."

"So everyone knows from the ads that the game tricks your mind, immerses you into an individualized story that you believe to be real. Then you play until you die. But what are you doing for all this time."

"You get to really focus on what matters. In Dreamspace your requirements like food, which your mind always needs, and shelter are taken care of. It's the pursuit of happiness that perhaps could've been if Eve had not eaten the apple? A digital Eden now available for the entire world."

"You're still not really painting a picture of that garden."

"I don't need to. Soon the whole world including you will be on it."

"Then I better start dating. And you previously described a *Dreamspace* date is the opposite of a real date. How so?"

"Yes."

"Can you expand on that line of thinking?"

"Traditional dates begin in lies," she turned now to face the camera's lens; her dreamy eyes staring through Ray's own, "Strangers lie on average three times when initially meeting. Most humans will lie about major items nearly the entire time they're courting. You know what I'm talking about," her words now bore into Ray's heart as if she were speaking directly to him, "Two suitors playing roles. Taking the big secrets to the grave. But if you knew that undisclosed thing about the other person the illogical would be decipherable. We are reasonable. But we're liars. After all, we nearly destroyed the world while considering ourselves in that generation so environmentally friendly. Obsessing over organic while we murdered the planet."

"So any human society is a march of folly?"

"If the historian Barbara Tuchman had lived long enough she would've called out the treason that made the storm. We're always led by wicked fools. They reflected our warped concepts of love which were usually the opposite," she pejoratively chuckled, "The reason why the overwhelming majority of marriages end in divorce. Families with a lot of step kids are not like the Brady Bunch. Incest porn of the 20'teens made that clear, but no one wanted to see the truth. Which was how Michael Jackson could be a pedophile in the light of day. All wicked manifestations of the underlying economic system in which America fostered Chinese slavery for bribes in a cycle that ultimately nearly killed the world. That's not reality, it's madness that we now carry as the Three *Traitor's* burden. Dreamspace offers a stable, macro, and micro economy to let anyone not sweat the bare essentials. That's when people can be challenged in more interesting ways."

"And those challenges require a committed set of game mates?" probed the interviewer.

"Yes. *Dreamspace* is where honesty reigns. Its users are anonymous unless they choose not to be to certain people. And they're free to do whatever and be with whomever they desire. Just like you study elements, we test our possible mates with various tensions to see what they're made of. So you can be sure this is the person with whom you'll want to spend the rest of your life. Our dating software metrics are revolutionary. We make amazing couples."

Later as Ray urinated in the hotel room's smart toilet, he thought back on Pia's words. Remembering how the lies flowed from leaders down to individuals until the pandemic and storm refuted such madness. Driving pilgrimages by people to spin on the graves of politicians like the late Senator Diane Feinstein, the famed traitor who financially aided China's economic interests for decades, employing a communist Chinese spy who clandestinely accessed confidential documents, reporting them back to China. Showing the same lack of scrutiny on her staff that she showered on a Communist dictatorship whose imports corrupted her region. Like Los Angeles's late politician Maxine Waters who luxuriated in Bel-Air while nearly all black and Latino males from her constituency were long-sodomized in prison as the price of the Chinese imports flowing through her port. With her displaced citizens filling makeshift refugee camps in river bottoms and ditches around her, driven out of dwellings by tens of millions of non-citizens trafficked to the U.S. by the Cartel, living in multi-family shifts that drove citizens from their dwellings.

Ray, himself, had engaged in a drunken pilgrimage with college buddies to spit on the late Senator Chuck Schumer's grave. Schumer's district represented the treasonous port of Manhattan where police were attacked with water, sucker-punched, demeaned before they were attacked and infected with what came to be known as China's Yin Yang virus.

There were so many to hate from that Time of Treason. Eric Swalwell. Adam Schiff. Nancy Pelosi. Jerry Nadler. Andrew Cuomo. New York's Mayor DeBlasio. California's governor Gavin Newsom whose sanctuary state stripped citizens of police protection for the theft of property of a thousand dollars or less even before the pandemic. Then he limited their right to bear arms while allowing zero-dollar bail for all burglaries after granting sanctuary to 30 million non-citizens never screened by customs or border enforcement. The non-flooded regions of Californians still hung Newsom in effigy each year as the traitor who welcomed Xi Jinping's 8,300 self-quarantining Communist Chinese citizens from China into his Sanctuary state and then cut a special deal to receive PPE masks from the same mass-murderer. The major-ranking

Democrats and non-Trumpian Republicans from the *Time of Treason* were all unmasked by history as villains, their offspring typically changing their last names or hiding their identities to avoid outright violence by a nation so raped and robbed by their ancestors-

Ravenna hid her marriage from him.

For some reason, the thought suddenly formed in his mind. Weary, he set a hand against the bathroom's media wall above the toilet urinal. Media played on the wall, showing film clips from a recent, new movie on David Bellingham's life. The film reenacted how David first invented the virtual, online chat room that later tethered him to engineers and designers paving the way for him to dream and deliver the eComp-

The film paused as Ray's Siri chirped, "Ray, I found a rare clip with David you might find interesting."

"Sure, play it."

As Ray washed and dried his hands, returning to bed, the media followed him on all the surfaces. In shadowy silhouette surrounding him, David's adult body hovered in his special comport. The baffles of respirators and medical equipment in the darkened living room. His face and body were framed as usual in shadows, his actual face never truly clear. While the same artificial, electronic voice spoke for him:

"I know humans are innately good from storytelling including modern film and TV. In these fictionalized stories, the heroes always win, reflecting the conclusion of the famous Yale infant morality study from the early 21st Century. It showed most human infants were born with a preprogrammed moral code. But 11 percent of infants were inclined to be bad, celebrating the theft of property from others, a trait often shown in our past political leaders and criminals. In *Dreamspace* this wickedness can be painlessly expressed in their own private worlds without harming the wider population."

An idea welled up within him.

The next day across the white table hovering without legs in Ray's secure online FCC chat room, he met with Exxon. Ray was surprised to discover the detective owned a comport, most Chinese nationals being limited to just their eComp iScreens:

"What if the killer met the victim through *Dreamspace*?" posited the FCC agent as his auto-translation software converted his English to Mandarin, "Then somehow the would-be killer tracked the victim down in the real world and killed him?"

Exxon's reply chirped in English in Ray's ear, "The victim was a *Dreamspace* beta tester helping prepare the system for the worldwide release next month. But he wasn't on *Dreamspace* when he expired."

"He was on that site when the cameras all pixelated," retorted Ray.

"But then he logged off. This wouldn't even be your case if he hadn't returned with the sword to die in the comport.

"But this gives us a plan. We track down the beta testers he dated, compare their DNA to the eroded sample at our crime scene and we catch our killer if this wasn't suicide."

"There must be thousands of *Dreamspace* beta testers in the system," added the detective.

"Ten thousand to be exact," Ray specified, "but we only need the ones who dated our victim. There can't be that many."

Exxon shifted in his online seat, pleased with a new course in the investigation before he realized something wondrous:

"What?" the FCC agent read the detective's facial expression.

"You might actually meet David Bellingham."

After the online chat room conference ended, Ray queried *Dreamspace* through the FCC network. Sitting on the edge of his hotel room bed, Agent Kemper eyed the pop-up auto notice of his delivered message to Bellingham Labs' security department. He expected a reply would take time to work its way up the internal company ladder.

In the Media Suite, the FCC agent watched archival agency footage of *Dreamspace's* beta testing which commenced a year and a half before. Leaning back in bed, Ray watched videos of beta tester's recorded testimonials submitted to the FCC for its official authorization. The web agency's stamp of approval required for the game's general release. Some testers had matched and allowed an interview before immersing themselves in the long term, perpetual *Dreamspace* game.

Later in the hotel gym, Ray watched the end of the interviews on his iScreen as he did sit-ups. An aging couple from the Bronx fled the rain, migrate online to a body vault. The loving couple seemed unique in that they refused to date anyone but each other. They felt that they were that rare, ideal couple in the real world and would remain so online.

A camera crew recorded them preparing to bed down in their sleek, long-term, immersion comports. Their metallic jumpsuits already donned as robot drones attached automated I.V. systems to their forearm mounted ports. They looked around them as immersed gamer's muscles were shocked to perfection by the electric inner beds of the nearby comports.

Looking at the sea of unconscious gamers, the old woman griped, "Screw the real world. Migrating online is the best thing we could ever do."

"Bodhouses let us live cheap," her husband added, "no *Green Lung,* taxes, meals, or car repairs, with the best armoring and security-"

His wife gestured at him, "And he's gonna look a whole lot sexier."

Her comment made Ray chuckle.

Hours later in his hotel bath, he watched a documentary covering the media surfaces. David ended the most significant debate in Western Philosophy. That same argument stemming back to ancient Greece between Plato and Aristotle about what was real: the inner universe of the mind or outer, physical world that the senses perceived.

In his landmark blog, David solved the quandary by invoking Albert Einstein's theory of relativity. It required that at least two contrary viewpoints be necessary to form any truth in space-time. The reason why Einstein was now regarded more as a philosopher than a physicist. Because of David, the dual realities of the mind and body were conjoined together like opposing faces on a coin. Spin the coin, David famously blogged, and both faces remained simultaneously valid and invalid: true or false at the same time to the relative observer.

The logical consequence was that there was no exact, centralized reality. Even the Earth was not stationary as it orbited the Sun. Earth's star revolved around the outer perimeter of the Milky Way Galaxy, completing a circuit every 425 odd million years. While the Milky Way Galaxy was expanding in a cosmos exploding out in all directions at a million miles a day. Everything moving in various degrees of constant motion away from the central point that birthed this universe in the *Big Bang* when many believed God said let there be light.

So a valid truth required two points of relative data. Yet the scope of most data before David was incorrectly viewed as opposites. Just as science and God were never at odds, but inherently complementary. Pre Trumpian Republicans and Democrats after the 1990s were still seemingly at odds, but both served to economically enrich a Chinese dictator. Even sleeping and dreaming could each be real while in that specific state and then not. As Descartes warned, don't be too sure about what's real beyond the mind. The concept now known as the *Tutwiler Ethos*.

Ray's eye swipe flipped to more media on his hero, David Bellingham. He took in scenes from the '55 Academy Award-winning film titled *Bellingham*, chronicling David's early years and brain trauma. Soaking in hot, bathwater, Ray watched on the ceiling as the actor who played David Bellingham's father accepted the *Best Actor* award in 2052-

Knock! Knock! Knock!

The sound emanated from the front door. With smart doors, no one knocked on doors anymore except in power outages. Rendering the gesture more threatening than it might have once been. Donning a hotel robe after he emerged from the bath, Ray put on his eComp which he had taken off in the tub to clean the alloy surface. He eyed the video feed on his iScreen showing the empty hallway outside his door with the box in front of it.

Moments later, he retrieved the package from the hall, placing the synthetic box on his bed. Unpeeling the eco-plastic lid constructed from recycled ethanol, Ray beheld the gilded note inside imprinted on thick cardstock stationery. Ray had not held actual paper in his hands for years. The invitation was embossed in Silver Leaf:

A NOTE FROM DAVID BELLINGHAM
In response to your email, I will now see you.
Use MEETING LINK DS37157A when free.
-David

Ray didn't hesitate. Heart racing, he entered his Media Suite comport.

"Sorry Ray," his Siri chirped, "You must download a system upgrade to access this meeting. It will take a minute."

Ray remained in the comport, allowing the update patch. But the status bar kept showing it required five more minutes after five minutes. Watching the slow progress of the download across the inner holo-lid of his hotel room comport, Ray stopped to absorb this profound moment. He wondered what his great hero was doing right now. But never did he suspect that David Bellingham was watching a murder.

nine

David watched him die.

Eyeing the ancient Greek philosopher's curling beard and ugly face adorning a broad, thick frame now reclined across the stone dais ahead of the adult David Bellingham. The figure before David remained surrounded by a cadre of friends and admirers clad in white togas. This scene simulated for David the death of Socrates, the first great Western philosopher. The famed inventor had watched the tableau realistically play out countless times before him thanks to his *Dreamspace* rendering technology.

The tech inventor knew that the FCC agent would soon materialize. But until that time, the fifty-two-year-old visionary remained where he stood, alone on his multi-mile-long-and-wide black rectangle in the void of star-filled space. He looked younger than his professed fifty-two-years. He was actually 49 but artificially advanced his age when young to secure investors. He obfuscated many facts about his life like his date of birth, trying to suppress any images of his childhood or father coming to public light. He told himself that his nose and eyes were warmer, but they looked the same. He was haunted by a scenario where everyone wore his likeness, filling his modern-web-creation with his father's face.

David stood on the heavenly object floating in orbit above a storm-covered Earth. His digital home now inspired by the same black monolith from Stanley Kubrick's film *2001*. Another movie from a filmmaker who although never having met David, unexpectedly helped to save his life, thereby possibly saving all humanity.

Now, this scene of death manifested before the older David in Socrates' ancient stone, prison-cell. The inventor long-before removed Socrates' friends that were present for Socrates's consumption of poison rather than being exiled from Athens.

The old, thick-boned Socrates long-before, consumed the poisonous hemlock from the now-empty bronze cup on the floor. The executioner had then urged the condemned to walk around the chamber until the expected numbing sensation formed in his legs. Invisible amidst them, David often came to this scene he conjured on his lone monolith. He long before injected all his memory banks' knowledge into Socrates' simulation. The discussions they shared enlightened David by the one incontrovertible conclusion that Socrates drew from history.

In the west, societies without a belief in God's forbidden abominations of the Old Testament, eventually over generations, instituted child rape as the inevitable sexual norm. In other areas, it was child murder, enslavement, or sacrifice. A lesson well-illustrated by the first enemies to challenge the pedophile norm in the west, the ancient Israelites. Yet they too allowed sodomy to proliferate and it soon corrupted their leader to order the mass rape of all Israelite boys by their Greek pedophile overlords. Israelite high-priests turned into pedophiles; setting off an Israelite civil war, the legal way of worship without intermediaries as the rules strictly made clear ended in 605 BC. They were not allowed to build a new temple but only follow their inner-temple. Violating that law created pedophiles whose actions later called Christ to Earth, in Socrates' opinion, to reiterate the inner faith of the Torah and condemn intermediaries as robbers and thugs.

Then three hundred years after Christ, the same Greek pedophile society that killed Socrates hijacked Christ's inward-looking Christianity in 325 AD. They reinvented the belief system to answer to new, exterior, spiritual intermediaries known as Catholic priests; they exclusively appointed non-heterosexuals to the role. They also altered the Sabbath to Sunday with no liturgical support in deference to Constantine's favored Sun deity.

The new Greek-style priesthood made heterosexuals feel like sexual perverts for desiring females. Just as the American mass-entertainment system by the 2020s, funded by China, sought to sexually reprogram young Americans in new kinds of stories. As California's LGBT core of pedophiles who had raped most of its members as kids, sought to legislatively empower 27-year-old child rapists from escaping mandatory sex registries. The now-mature raped children as adults remained silent. The mass-raping of children both literally and artistically fed America's 2030s *Sodomy Spike* of rape as young American boys assaulted younger ones.

America's purchases for Made-In-China slave products were weaponized back to corrupt its Americans. Serving as the foundation for a reordered, American society where families were painted as perverts in the rise of incest porn to make other new abominations seem acceptable in comparison. All of it to kill the nation. The opposite of progress. The unsustainable costs of having a family further destroyed the nation from a 28-year-long slave-trade deal its Founders' strictly forbid. Paving the way for the further rape of children as the one inevitable outcome of humanity, Socrates notably concluded. Even the U.S. Supreme Court granted equal treatment to male homosexuals under discrimination while never discriminating between the rapist wolves amidst the sheep they had created. Supreme Court Justice Gorsuch along with other Justices empowered pedophiles.

Just as the ancient Greek philosopher realized he died because he didn't rape boys as everyone else did. Making him feel like an outsider his whole life by others. The people's well-documented distrust and teasing of Socrates for being a pervert who would not rape children presaged his capital punishment sentence as a teacher. For such a pervert, these pedophiles reasoned, must be poisoning the minds of ancient Greece's youth. Pedophilic sexuality had to be forced upon the young to keep the system going as it almost institutionalized itself in a mass-male-rape.

Killing Socrates who didn't rape children.

Socrates now sighed to David, "It's still better than the choice of exile. They're just worse out there."

"They always seem to love the ones that hate them the most," reflected David as he thought of *The Three Traitors*.

"They should've left their love at home for their children," Socrates lost all hope, eyes staring through David, "instead of putting it in their leaders who have ended everything."

Socrates had been the one man open to wherever truth took him. Unlike most, he refused to ignore inconvenient truths. Perhaps why David returned to him time and again? But these insights had made Socrates more depressed with his species. A haunting feeling that he'd lived in the wrong time and place. He kept talking about the political leader the Bible professed would arise to speak truth and make the world like Eden by having America again make what it needed. A place where houses would need to be spaced apart and cities largely abandoned as Isaiah foretold. A restoration in preparation of the coming of the Lord.

With all of history loaded into his mind, Socrates worshipped the only truth he ever found. The only legal way to worship God as an Israelite through His unchanging Torah laws.

Socrates became an Israelite.

His conversations with Socrates turned strange. But since Pia left, he needed someone to speak to. It was at her prior urging that he downloaded all knowledge from the web into the philosopher the year before. Including even the knowledge only a handful of experts and the U.S. President knew. Something David wasn't supposed to know; the scientific prediction that the worldwide storms would last far beyond the 7,000 years noted in the leaked U.N. report. It was projected to last, in fact, at least 40,000 years. That information like the damage of the Pearl Harbor attack in the 1940s was suppressed from the public to ward off a complete, social breakdown.

David feared that the waters would continue to rise up from the subterranean sea. The future masses, therefore, had to be concentrated and sustained in ever tinier leveed zones. Ideally packed into bodhouses to keep as many alive as possible. Space stations or the moon were not viable options, as the solar radiation without Earth's atmosphere would kill everyone. Dreamspace was his cure to the fallout of America's treason. Now as he approached the apex of his secret plan, David Bellingham had to deal with this meeting. Even before it began, he knew it would be different than any other. Purposely he delayed longer, intentionally extending the agent's download time. He knew this could be dangerous but he had to save Dreamspace-

"Meeeow," the cat warming itself near the monolith's purple fire purred. The same cat he digitally recreated from his childhood. Socrates's Greek tableau vanished. Just the empty monolith before David as he spun on the heels of his leather-soled, black slippers.

"FCC Agent Ray Kemper now logging in," his Siri noted

in his ear.

David Bellingham turned to face the FCC agent now standing 20 paces behind him. The inventor's eyes tracked the cat as it stalked between them and the storm-covered Earth rising at the monolith's far end.

Behind the cat, David sized up the FCC agent's Matt Damon Skin. Once again, Bellingham reflected on how he'd created a new web platform but failed to realize that all users would want to wear skins, making Mr. Zero a trillionaire.

"Hello Ray," the inventor spoke with a slight Louisiana drawl.

"Hi, Mr. Bellingham-"

"Please," he interrupted with an odd grin, "call me Dave."

"Hi, Dave," it was awkward for the FCC agent to address his iconic hero by the man's first name.

"Can you use your real Skin with me?" queried David.

"Sorry Dave, I'm prohibited," Ray shrugged, hoping to lower the man's guard, which he might've achieved because David next revealed:

"I wish I could see your face since this mystery is really about bringing the two of us together."

"How so?"

David appreciated Ray's curiosity. But the words the inventor said next thoroughly confused the Web Agent, "We're like mirrors to each other. I always wanted to be a law enforcement officer. A good one, not like my dad-"

"Yeah, I saw the movies on you. I'm into your blog too."

"Thanks," David replied, "being a philosopher is my favorite occupation."

"When I was a kid," confided Ray, "I wanted to play Tutwiler's lethal game."

"It's not a game," corrected David, "it showed me many possible outcomes of my life in the multiverse. Almost no one knows that," a glint in David's eye as he grinned, "I gamed so many outcomes over time that I could speak to myself in the past."

"But you can't travel back in time," noted Ray.

"Data can be sent back. Einstein named such a machine, a 'tachyonic anti-telephone."

"I heard your blog on that."

David nodded affirmatively, "My dad's unexpected, parting gift entombed my body but dispatched my consciousness to other possible realities in the multiverse. Which freed me to design *Dreamspace*, a refuge to attempt to continue our species."

"Your game is of no concern to my work," Ray returned to business, "only that a murderer might be using it to find prey."

David stiffened, "If there's a killer then I need you to find them. Tell me, do you know the short story 'The Purloined Letter'?"

"Heard your blog on that too," answered the agent, "Edgar Allen Poe's short story about 19th Century detectives searching for a letter throughout a suspect's apartment. They fail to notice it in the most obvious spot, unhidden for all to see."

"Did you enjoy the tale?" probed David.

"It was crap," Ray nodded his head, "We detectives always look in the obvious places."

"It's considered the first detective story ever written. I fear your murder investigation could be the last."

With that said, the famed inventor gestured for them to walk across the vast expanse of the seamless, black monolith. Side by side they hiked towards the distant glow of a surreal, purple fire stretched in a line across the far horizon of the monolith. In silence, they closed the quarter of a mile down the black stone slab in space with the sounds of only their shoes and breath.

Ray felt weird.

This meeting was not going as he expected. It veered off into a personal exchange while he felt the need to keep it about his case. But this man was, after all, the most idolized individual on the planet.

Ray indulged him as best he could. From the corner of his eye, he wondered what was going on inside the inventor's mind. They finally stopped at the purple fire only a few paces before them. A thin, waist-high, surreal purple flame ran like a wall from end to end across the monolith. Both warmed their chilled hands before the odd fire. The level of reality in the game platform again crept up on Ray.

He was freezing.

"Ever track down anyone famous?" David inquired, his face tinged by the purple firelight.

"My job's not that interesting. I mostly track people online."

"How fitting Ray, because your killer's right here."

At first, Ray thought he misheard what the inventor said. David swept his right hand through the air. Words of purple fire materialized in mid-air in its wake. The hovering flames snaked into floating letters spelling out:

HOPELESS ROMANTIC
ANIMAL LOVER
VOYEUR

Ray recognized the last one, piecing it together, "These are the user ID's of the suspects who dated my murder victim in *Dreamspace*."

An impressed David affirmatively nodded.

"I already met Voyeur," explained Ray, "but since *Dreamspace* is your system, you probably know that didn't go well."

"Ray, even if I wanted to, I can't know that," he stressed, "the data generated by our *Dreamspace* user's dates are too vast to store and review."

"I figured you cracked that problem."

"We intentionally refrain from spying or storing data on our clients. Anonymity is key to finding game-mates. But you will date all three again."

"How?"

"My game matching software along with a new fictional profile for you will virtually guarantee a second date with Voyeur and the other two remaining suspects."

At first, Ray thought the man was joking. The FCC agent did not bother to conceal his shock that they were even discussing online dating, "But Dave, I only need the users' IP addresses. So I can go to their residences and compare their DNA to that left at my crime scene. That's how I catch my killer."

"I don't know their identities or IP addresses. To discover that you must first kiss them on a game date in *Dreamspace*. Only then can we track down their I.P. addresses and geo-locate them for your investigation."

"A kiss?"

"Yes. Kissing on the lips is how we link and share data in *Dreamspace*. If they like you enough to date you again, you'll kiss and link networks. Our system will then physically track that suspect's offline, 'real' world' location."

"Despite your assurances, I find it hard to believe that you don't know your own user's identities and locations?"

"Anonymity is key," stressed David, "allowing our testers to push the envelope, doing things often considered unacceptable in the real world," his eyes bore like lasers into Ray's soul, "Ray, believe me, you'd be amazed at people's unfettered natures and desires on my platform. So our beta testers remain anonymous even to us so that they can remain genuine," the shadow of the cat passed between them as David added, "I have one, non-negotiable deal point. Your partner must audit your *Dreamspace* dates."

The mere mention of a partner caused Ravenna's face to flash in Ray's mind's eye. He suppressed it along with the entailing grief, "How could a partner audit the date without being a third wheel?"

"Your partner remains invisible to the two daters, auditing them over a comport monitor or iScreen. An auditor keeps it clean."

"Dave, I don't have a partner-"

"Everyone needs a partner-"

"What're you afraid I'm going to do?"

David's eyes tore into him, "Whether you choose to accept it or not, everything is about continuing our life force through others. Which is why love and sex are an essential experience desired by almost all mature humans. If you're lucky enough to feel true love, you'll realize that you don't get to pick who you fall for. Real love is driven by unpredictable tensions like Romeo and Juliet who both died from it."

"Those are fictional characters," retorted the agent.

"Reality is a cage, Ray. Dreamspace is a walk-on part in the real world. To permanently game they have to reveal themselves. Coming to know each other. So if there is a killer in the Dreamspace community, this person would be experienced from their dates and would see through your lies and escape your grasp."

"I'm as trained at deceit as old-time politicians," joked Ray.

"*Dreamspace* makes my users able to read people in ways even your famed FCC training does not achieve. Normally I would not be so blunt. But if this is murder then we cannot afford to let a killer escape. Or they could kill my entire game before it launches by scaring off the user. Then this killer could be the murderer of all humanity."

Ray absorbed the high stakes. His investigation had morphed into something perhaps as powerful as the manhunt for Blackout. The FCC agent allowed the silence to pass before he reassured the inventor of one essential truth about himself:

"I'm more a hunter than a lover."

David smiled, gesturing goodbye as he added, "Then I wish you happy hunting-"

Everything went black.

No goodbyes. The online meeting abruptly ended with Ray opening his eyes back in the confines of his hotel room comport. His first thought was how to secure a partner. The FCC's annual budget was set to close at the end of the month, which was a horrible time to request more funding in the field due to the required red tape. Without proof of an actual murderer, Agent Kemper's superiors would be happy to classify this as suicide and close the case. It was, after all, political.

A few hours later in a circular, online FCC chat room, Ray tackled the issue with his supervisor, Joe Caresio. His boss, the 58-year-old with a slight paunch didn't have much of a personal life. Joe's hip was permanently injured from a gun battle years before, sometimes forcing him to use a mechanized wheelchair. He never showed that online, but his *selfie* did portray the growing mid-section of a graying, desk-bound bureaucrat. When Ray broached the need for an auditing partner, Joe rubbed his thumb against his forefinger as he was wont to do when he had a good idea like the one he then uttered:

"What about the Chinese detective?"

Ray thought on it aloud, "That…could really work."

"Because any added expenditure will be stonewalled-"

"I know," Ray leaned over the floating chat room desk without legs.

"I don't have to tell you that this case is a political hot potato. The FCC's set to greenlight this *Dreamspace* game which the White House views as a key component to future law and order. It's not about keeping people off the streets. Like in bodhouses. My superiors want this put to rest as a suicide-"

"What do you want?" interrupted Ray.

"I want you to solve the case," his boss's sudden firmness informed Ray that Joe shouldn't have to spell out what was well-understood from their long career together. With a sweep of his eye, Joe approved Exxon to monitor the online dates.

There was, of course, no budget to travel and house the detective stateside, but Ray had an idea about that.

Then Ray's superior for a decade ribbed his younger field agent with a wry grin, "You sure you're not just doing this just to get laid?"

"One of the three *Dreamspace* suitors already responded to my date requests," Ray prepared for that comment.

"Let's see it."

Ray's eye swipe projected the *Dreamspace* IM reply around the circular media wall framing the chat room. He had received the correspondence from the *Dreamspace* user only hours before this meeting. The I.M. text boldly filled the circular screen in stark, black letters set against white:

SHOW ME THE MOST ROMANTIC DIGITAL TIME, TOMORROW, 8 PM WST WITH THE HOPELESS ROMANTIC ☺

"Given the time requested, you thinking the suspect's in America?" Joe asked.

"Yes. I considered it," WST or *Web Standard Time* was set to Cupertino, California, serving as the international dateline of the modern web. But it meant nothing, "Boss, the user could be anywhere.

Joe scanned the message on the wall as he pieced it together, "So she responds to this auto-matching software... and then you gotta create an online world to impress her?"

"Pretty much," shrugged Ray, "And Exxon will watch."

"That just makes it weirder," Joe winced.

Secretly Ray fretted about how he would ever create a dating world to impress his hopeless romantic. Which meant he must design an online world seductive enough to draw a possibly experienced *Dreamspace* dater into a kiss. But all those details would be tackled later. For now, he just needed his superior to go along with the plan.

"Well lover-boy," his boss scoffed, "guess it's time to find Ms. Right."

part three

Ally

"When I blot you out, I will cover the heavens and make their stars dark; I will cover the sun with a cloud, and the moon shall not give its light."

Ezekiel 32:7

ten

How to seduce a hopeless romantic?

Ray Kemper remembered his father's advice that no man could ever honestly fathom a woman's heart. Now his mission was further complicated by David Bellingham's warning. How *Dreamspace* imbued its experienced users with insights rivaling that of a sophisticated Web Agent. A point Ray still found difficult to accept. Now he must play the part of a fictional online suitor. One seeking a unique, all-changing relationship with a game mate they could share the remainder of their life within *Dreamspace*.

The massive requirement to attain a kiss. Now his first suspect, identified only by the I.D. *Hopeless Romantic*, wished to visit Ray's game world which he hadn't even yet thought to construct. A web flick and pizza was not going to cut it. Leaving him with the one question he ascertained from the single clue in his suspect's chosen moniker.

How would he seduce a hopeless romantic?

In his Media Suite, Ray recollected on love. That painful remembrance of his mother sleeping in his father's hospital bed as he succumbed to *Green Lung*. Wasn't that true love? Then he thought of Utah, which was never far off when death became the subject; that mother who died trying to save her child. Love returned Ray to death, reminding him of another of his favorite Bellingham blogs.

In the basement L.A. Hilton gym, the agent stretched muscular limbs across exercise mats, listening to David's blog over his eComp about the intertwined nature of sex and death. Before sexual reproduction, death did not exist. The predecessors to sexual reproduction on earth were cellular life forms that mitotically subdivided into two halves from its original self. So the original cell never died, but rather divided its way to immortality. The reason why certain sponges and jellyfish were still immortal organisms.

Even if they lost some part of their collective whole, the original cellular colony would survive. Whereas sex brought death to each successive generation to make room for future, unique creatures. Sex and death acted as different sides of the same coin. Sexually reproducing organisms as temporary vessels sought eventual unification with another of their species. Rather than dividing into two halves, sexual genders sought to unite their two sets of DNA into a hybrid, creating a new and distinct life form.

Ray replaced the blog with music, exercising for two hours with free weights. Lost in the classic songs of The Moo. Reflecting on how music moved from the traditional love songs in the post-pandemic world to political songs openly assaulting the prior generation as in the late 1960s. The counter-culture came full circle with the death of so many extending back to that generation from the Yin Yang virus

The angry music didn't help.

Ray took off the pressure that hosting a dating world presented at the time. Eyeing his etched, muscular frame in the gym window, he remembered the scrawny youth who first entered the FCC Web Academy in this very same city. Recalling how his boss, Joe Caresio, first got him into weightlifting here.

Death inspired it.

The FCC Training Academy in Los Angeles psychologically wore down young cadets, weeding out the weaker candidates. One active field agent's tear-filled testimonial moved Ray like no other, in a cadet class regarding online child predators. A child-killer had webcasted the murder of two young boys in a North Carolina trailer-home in the woods. Ray's class was shown graphic footage censored from the public's view. The two young boys screamed apologies up to their throats being cut. Their faces making clear the assumption that they'd done something wrong because adults must always be right. That footage cut Ray in a way that only Utah surpassed.

Cadet Kemper considered dropping out of the program until his field instructor at the time, Joe Caresio, introduced him to the FCC's basement gym frequented by the academy's older teachers. A place of rusty, 20th Century weights in an old windowless series of rooms lacking sophisticated anti-viral systems and thus wreaking of bleach. A far cry from the sleek cadet facility of pneumatic resistance machines for the cadets. Using old hand weights, Joe taught Ray how to untangle his inner turmoil through multiple reps and sets.

Now in the polished Beverly Hilton gym decades later, an adult Ray recollected on those first workouts. Exercising as a skinny youth with the burly man who would become his quasi-father, mentor, and now his current boss. Cadets were intentionally paired up with instructors who would come to guide them in the field from headquarters. Ray watched as the job took its toll on Joe who now suffered unexplainable vertigo from the wicked things he'd witnessed as a younger agent, his symptoms suppressed only by liberal ingestions of Johnny Walker Red Label Scotch. Joe's beloved wife had developed a brain tumor. After the surgery to remove it, she retained no memories of her husband who had been her high-school sweetheart. His wife now lived with another man in another home in a different life. In the end, figured Ray, no one could touch the darkness without the darkness touching back.

Perhaps the reason why forced retirement was mandatory at 60 years of age for Web Agents? As for love, they had to be on the continual lookout for *honey traps*, seemingly interested women paid by China proxies, rogue nation-states, terrorist organizations, or multinational oligarchs to twist an agent's loyalty or blow their covert cover, the worst possible outcome which instantly ended a Web Agent's career. Anonymity was crucial to their job even after retirement, assuming a false persona in a government protection program with a healthy stipend to fend off corruption from exterior forces. Ray's inevitable future.

Shutting his eyes, the agent focused on The Moo's final verse of *Crass Consumer*, the iconic anthem of Ray's generation, lashing out against prior Americans who from Clinton's Administration through COVID-19, served their Communist overlord of which few spoke of. That self-obsessed generation reared on economic treason memorialized by the Moo's song:

"Walmart, Pottery Barn, Louis Vuitton, and Prada,
buying sex, love, and status to make y'all holler,

just lies the ads been feeding you since you were a kid,
Chinese pollution is the real cost of all that shit.

Crass consumer, you think your actions are permissive?
All that useless crap you buy each other for Christmas?

You enriched slavery to bring us viral pain,
Your purchases sowed Blackout's virus and our rain.

The Moo's song expanded into the famed, Grammy Award-winning chorus of primal screams modulated into alternating beats. The song became almost religious for people of the later 21st Century: a modern generation yelling back in time at the ones who sowed the seeds of the rain. Curling dumbbells, Ray noted how those lyrics served as the anthem of his generation after the pandemic who never saw the Sun, Moon, or stars.

His mind drifted back to David's blog about true love. How the past generation compared themselves to the magazine cover, airbrushed models of ideal proportions starting with Barbie dolls that defied human dimensions, sending women of the previous ages into body dysmorphia over a look that was not real.

The Moo's song roused Ray into a final, angry set of weightlifting. What hurt most was how avoidable all of it could have been. No American earlier in the century ever thought to google the incredible pollution China generated, the true cost of all that cheap slave-made, polluting crap Americans stuffed in their laughable, recyclable bags. As much as it was an obsession for Ray's age, the prior generation like the prior age just trusted in elites. No longer wrestling as Americans

Anger at the generations before him drove Ray back to the current plight of love. What dream world could he create to lure his *Hopeless Romantic* into a kiss? For that kiss might very well be necessary to allow this online refuge for the many victims of that past malfeasance to continue it. He had to extract the suspect's elusive I.P. address.

Just then, Ray remembered Pia's comments in the *Dreamspace* advertisement, how people lied to each other on their initial dates in the offline world. Hiding the truth until they were both in so deep that they could dump their ugly realities on each other, hiding only the worst.

Dating was the art of lying. And what greater lie was there than one's self-deception? The reason why the majority of relationships never worked. Back in his hotel room, Ray again eyed the suspect's IM:

SHOW ME THE MOST ROMANTIC DIGITAL TIME, TOMORROW, 8 PM WST WITH THE HOPELESS ROMANTIC ☺

Later, he kept returning to the message on his iScreen. Repeatedly eyeing it during the short space flight from Los Angeles to Chicago. He finally immersed himself online through the Delta business class comport, surfing to the *Dreamspace* date-maker software.

Scrolling through images of preset date world templates, he eyed the old western cowboy world. Roman orgies and palaces. Outer space adventures. A strange post-apocalyptic, zombie land where users appeared as oversized stuffed daisies. Even the clichéd dinosaur land. The program made clear that most users didn't use any of these laughable presets.

None of that felt as real as the dreaded coffin that stayed with him even now as he departed Chicago's O'Hare spaceport. Riding in a drone-taxi down the bustling streets towards the famed *Near North Side* of Chicago. He remembered the former homeless, 20-odd-year-old men and women under tents that used to line these sidewalks and corners of his childhood Chicago neighborhood.

That generation reared on touch screens from youth that it was later discovered that most 20'teens Silicon Valley executives barred their own children to use. Screen-use wasting young minds into oblivion later in life. Looking through led-blue-tinted-lenses had helped for a time to make things seem worth focusing on, but the effect faded. So wired to the online in their formative years that three-dimensional reality never held enough interest for them to focus upon. Sitting homeless, scrolling smart screen media with the blank stare of shellshock, the homeless youth remained oblivious even to the traffic and noises around them.

They died in true isolation.

Other experts claimed this teen plague that played out on these streets wasn't caused by touch screens at all, but rather the G5 web network. That hurriedly-installed system built across America during the pandemic; the media wholly ignoring the University of Oregon's study already showing the detrimental effects to humans even from the less-pronounced signal of the prior generation of the web. G5 intensified heart-condition symptoms matching the Yin Yang Virus It may have even helped for what was China's blacking out of the internet. Apple alone objected to G5, but all other Big Tech elites rushed it in another step of self-destruction that began with industry-suppressed internal reports on the danger of interactive screens for children.

Ray like most now knew that the past leadership of Democrat Party strongholds in major port and logistic cities like Chicago served Xi Jinping's will up to the pandemic. For 25 years the U.S., traitors enriched slavery and curtailed their own citizens' freedoms. Bill and Hillary Clinton claimed that building up a third-world Communist dictatorship to a first-world one would somehow help American interests. Instead, it created the largest internal constitutional crisis in America. An invisible Civil War to imprison Americans to jail, send them homeless on the streets, and drug addicted them by their own leaders. Under then-president Obama, it the orderly handover of power in 2016 that continued through pro-Chinese influential censorship until the deconsolidation of mass media and news from the four companies the industry had devolved into from the 66 companies at the time of Clinton's treason

Many pro-Chinese U.S. journalists reporting on the lie of private wealth in Communist China were tried for treason along with executives, the board of CNN, MSNBC, The New York Times, The L.A. Times, pro-China politicians including even the *Three Traitors* and Biden, the creator of the largest mass-imprisonment in history.

Biden was comically awarded the Presidential Medal of Freedom by Obama, the largest jailer of blacks, Latinos, and humans in all of history. No wonder Obama's wife got depressed about racial injustice, was the old joke. The marginalized of all colors were robbed of their forefathers' manufacturing jobs, sent to prison, drug addiction, the streets, or meaningless service-jobs that later revealed them jobless. Made to think all along that it was their fault and not their leaders.

Ray reflected on that detestable age as his drone taxi passed a massive mural of Dick Cheney's exaggerated bust portrayed in colored hues of mold and fungus. Cheney remained the lone political hero from that economically treasonous time for bringing so much money, albeit corruptly, back to at least a major American manufacturer and mass-employer, *Halliburton*.

While slavery seeded the storm and eroded health and freedom. In cities like Chicago where the G5 signal had been concentrated like many urban areas, the new web signal silently fried many peoples' bodies, impairing their offspring. The American port-cities suffered the greatest blow. Unlike tiny Beverly Hills Island or Manhattan's geo dome, the majority of buildings in Chicago as in most formerly, major cities remained empty. Metropolises, as Isaiah prophesied, became vacant.

Families had long-since moved to the safety of the countryside to be closer to food sources, a critical element long-since driving up property values. It was not because of a sea of workers hired by these food centers that drove up those values. Food processing plants didn't hire many workers as various strains of the Yin Yang Virus infected cattle and livestock, driving later automation. But when the nation's extended supply chain broke down, locals had a source from which they received even better discounts as the only customers for that period while those in more urbanized areas faced possible famine.

Ray passed several *clustered* homesteading communities filling formerly long-vacant buildings or shopping malls. From out of the virus and molds, the new social peers had become real people, living in clusters with their covered-backyards connected or whole buildings allowing intermingling like a private community. It allowed multiple families to enjoy social interaction after decades of familial isolation and common web blackouts; although dads who didn't work at home, often lived in a sequestered garage or remote location except for the holidays when they quarantined to enter back into their community. Oddly these working spouses lived often in their sequestered garage, telecommuting as in days of old but with their families now often behind the next wall.

The politics of viral survival.

Most of these buildings were newly well-kept since he'd last visited. Part of the newest addition to the legendary government program, OPAH, the *One Parent At Home* subsidy that began during the pandemic. It also proliferated at-home-factories. Manufacturing workers now labored as self-employed-contractors in their garage or additional living-space long-cheap and plentiful in largely vacant cities thanks to OPAH.

Building owners were actually the larger of the manufacturing class, coalescing many tenant-subs to collectively make things for the manufacturing concern. The prosperous new middle and upper class of the storm with their private hotel-like building restaurants, stores, ice-skating rinks, and exclusive services. One spouse working near their subsidized stay-at-home mate. Bringing back a wage where one could be the breadwinner. Working and living in units alongside their neighbors; all assembling kits of raw materials into finished goods to drop-ship or return to the central packaging contractor.

Fungus graffiti of Hillary Clinton bloomed on the corner stop light control box ahead of Ray. The woman who with Obama rigged both major parties in 2016 was the wife of the original slave-master Clinton. The one who killed the Chinese spies that could've changed history. As rain beat down on fungus art, Ray's taxi drone smoothly decelerated beside it.

His auto-taxi stopped before the entrance to the senior living center. Passing through the building's sliding outer-electric door, Ray squinted as the U.V. light fried possible micro-contaminants off his clothes and body. His temp and vitals were remotely registered by the med bot system. This act happened unseen as he entered any building, but here it was on-display in extra-wide holo-screen print to ease the residents' fears.

Green Lung was an excruciating way to die and preyed most often on the old like the residents here. The saline micro-mist spraying into his open eyes was an added precaution. Then he received a personal *Green Lung* negative on his lung test after breathing into a self-cleaning cylinder extending from the interior wall monitor. His good bill of health was made clear by the eProctor. The building's inner-door opened to his reassurance that he didn't have any spores in his lungs. It was still hard to believe that the new once-a-year-pill allowed him to stop wearing masks except when he was in crowds.

After the short elevator ride, he discovered the fourth-floor hall now-covered with media screens generating the illusion of a Japanese Zen garden at dusk, the sun setting just over the horizon. This addition, he figured was part of the refurbishment campaign management promised to commence the prior year. Everything in the senior living home now glowed bright and serene for an aging population vulnerable to *Green Lung*.

Minutes later under the newly installed U.V. lights of the domed roof, Ray opened his mom's portable ice-bucket in the renovated, greenhouse rooftop. The smell of artificial grass filled Ray's nose as he downed a microbrew beer. He turned to his mother putting towards the hole across the new putting green. Rain obscured the holographic glass windows which now projected the popular 7th hole at Pebble Beach before the rain. The greenhouse's new noise-dampening technology blocked the sounds of rain and hail with white noise, forcing Ray and his mother to hear a silence of sorts along with the need to speak abnormally loud.

They saw so little of each other.

Still, his mother enjoyed her son's rare visits which were almost impossible during his *Swipe 9* manhunt. Ray was now making up for the lost time. She had aged gracefully in the four years they seldom saw each other. Ray remembered as a kid how she taught him how to moisturize his face, gently patting eye-cream under his eyes in her vanity mirror.

She had been a car show model in Chicago when she met his father at the *Autorama* convention. Smiling in a bikini beside a limited production exotic back before the storm. He'd seen a press picture of it. Her auburn hair back then possessed no gray strands which she still dyed.

His mom raised her young son to fear the right things, like flies, which killed more people than great white sharks. The shark, of course, died a long time ago, along with most sea life due to the rising salinity from the released, subpolar oceans. She detested flies because they carried parasites and diseases which killed so many each year in the damp rain. As a kid he watched her hold a wrapped dishtowel, arm half-cocked, ready to strike a buzzing fly on the kitchen counter.

"Flies are hard to kill because people underestimate them," she often told him as a child, "The fly watches us all the while. So the key is not to look at it when you strike," she whipped the towel forward, killing the pest," carrying the dead thing to the trash she often asked her son, "If people underestimate a fly, what else do they underestimate?"

His mom was not grad school educated like his dad, but brimming with common sense, taking suffering in stride. She wasn't sad that her boyfriend, Tate, a tall, gray-haired, retired Marine with a boxer's build, was as usual too sick to join Ray. A veteran of the Rain Forest Wars of the late 2030s, he sometimes joined them for rooftop mini-golf, but always left before the steaks, giving time alone for mom to catch up with her only child. Lately, Tate suffered from *Green Lung*; Ray had not seen him for years. When she stared sadly off into space, he thought it was her sick boyfriend's absence which made her somber, but his mother surprised him with her next comment:

"Ray, I want off the meds."

"Mom, there are way better ways to die than that," he cautioned.

She'd undoubtedly succumb to *Green Lung*. The thought of losing his mom in such a gruesome way seemed unimaginable to him. An event so raw and unanticipated that he used his FCC training to manipulate her.

She never suspected the trick, ignorant to the fact that her only child worked for the secret, elite agency. She believed him to be a mid-level, I.T. engineer for the State Department who traveled a lot.

Her eye swipe canceled the illusion of Pebble Beach in the greenhouse windows. Peering at the real, blinding rain surrounded them, she appeared on the verge of tears, "Baby, I just don't recognize this world anymore."

"But you recognize me," he inflicted maximal boyhood cuteness. Letting the emotions he wished to portray overtake him, but not so intense that it clouded his mind. Maybe his act worked? It was genuine, and perhaps the reason why she said nothing more of it.

Later down in her apartment, they grilled grass-fed buffalo steaks raised in U.V lit tunnel farms reclaimed from long-abandoned Colorado mineral mines. His mother nagged her son to settle down and give her grandchildren. She played an ancient *Alicia Keys* song from her childhood on the web stereo. The love song led Ray to ask:

"Mom, what would be the most romantic way for a couple to meet?"

His mother must've previously given it considerable thought, for her words came so quickly. Her eyes stared into space as if the actual events transpired before her as she narrated:

"London, New Year's during World War II. An off-duty nurse in a red dress spots an American tail gunner who enters the pub. Their eyes meet. Then bombs start to drop. Literally. But they don't notice at first, experiencing their own fireworks," her voice trailed off as her lips collected into a satisfied grin.

"Wow," an impressed Ray confessed, "you made that up fast."

"I didn't make it up," she grabbed an old photo from the living room cabinet, "that's how your great-grandparents met back in the *great used-to-be*," like many older people, she used that term for the age before the storm. A time that for Ray, despite all the old movies and recordings of the sunlit Earth, could never seem real to him.

He eyed the dog-eared black and white photograph of his great-grandparents, a Yank gunner and American nurse who met halfway across the world in war. His mother's story moved Ray as he headed back to the spaceport, wondering if he should use accumulated bonus miles for a free Delta ticket to DC?

He had everything with him including the victim's cylindrical memory drives packed in his roller case. On the ride to the terminal, The Moo's top videos played on the drone taxi's media screen ceiling. Listening to the music, Ray felt his journey had not yet ended. On his iScreen he saw the flight to L.A. Before he'd return to DC, he decided he would go there. He missed Los Angeles. He considered what little was left of that city to be home.

Being a citizen of L.A. was a conscious choice rather than an accident of birth. Practically no one came from the half-flooded city now a series of islands. That former metropolis still felt like a breath of freedom to Ray. Later his iScreen flashed his Hilton Hotel upgrade as he landed back at the LAX International spaceport.

He grabbed a hybrid taxi down through the leveed Wilshire Corridor connecting to Beverly Hills Island resting in the center of Los Angeles Bay. His roller bag again followed him into another ubiquitously familiar Media Suite. Loading the *Dreamspace* design software across his Media Suite wall screens, he kicked off his waterproofed cowboy boots. Reclining across the translucent hotel bed as his Siri, filling the ceiling, told him:

"Your date design software is loaded."

Soon his Siri peppered him with perfunctory questions meant to facilitate the architecture of Ray's date world. He was trained to be an actor and writer on the fly, but never a director. Due to processing power, a dream date was limited to 30 minutes, but he knew from research that users respected shorter dates over longer ones.

Much planning was required.

The system possessed endless designed presets for any conceivable item. He scrolled through seemingly endless English pub designs. Then there was the audio build out: voices, atmospherics, background noises, source music, ambient sounds from the exterior street, explosions, and much more that only film directors would have to conceive and mix. Then he returned to Mr. Zero's House of Skins integrated Skin portal to choose the characters of his date world, World War II uniforms, civilian clothes, and his outfit. The last step was to select the red dress to match the one from his mother's story for his possible murder suspect.

Yawning, his eye-stroke uploaded the metafile to *Dreamspace's* server for further rendering, requiring five hours.

Collapsing back in his translucent bed, he soon drifted off into another dream where he entered the English pub he just designed.

The pub was nearly empty except for his boss Joe, sharing a drink with Ray's dead Chinese man from his case at the bar. Both of them nodded to the bartender, David Bellingham, appearing just as Ray saw him in his private *Dreamspace* world.

The famed inventor poured out two ice-cold martinis before two empty stools at the far corner of the bar. Ray sat down and sipped the first glass as he waited for his date. The surprising, bitter taste of iron across his tongue caused him to realize he was sipping chilled blood as he heard an alarm go off-

Ray awoke breathlessly.

Laying on his back in his L.A. Media Suite, eyeing the sick Earth on his media screen ceiling he realized he'd slept the following day away. The same view David lived with on his isolated monolith. Ray now added it to his media presets. The alarm went off a second time, notifying him that it was time for his actual *Dreamspace* date. An eye stroke triggered the web call to Exxon over in China.

The detective in his tenement suddenly filled Ray's wall's media screens. The Asian detective sported a faded Batman t-shirt and camouflage sweatpants. He held a big bowl of popcorn as if ready to watch a movie inside his cramped apartment with a back alley view of endless rain.

With flat, unimpressed lips, the Chinese cop urged, "Please make it quick. I gotta pick up my kids for soccer practice in an hour."

Both of them knew that if Exxon's eyes pulled away from his iScreen, the sensor in his eComp would register the departure of the auditing partner. Which would instantly kick Ray off his *Dreamspace* date. So both were tethered from halfway around the globe in pursuit of a common, possible suspect.

"You *rushing* me?" teased Ray.

Given his reaction to his mother's story, he felt confident he'd get a quick kiss.

His generic Siri interrupted, flashing across his room's media surfaces, "This *Dreamspace* user requests you appear online looking the same as in real-life. I could use your FCC badge to override-"

"No," Ray considered such an eventuality after David wished to see his actual identity. In light of the inventor's warning, he would try to be as honest as possible, minimizing lies. So for the first time on a case, Web Agent Ray Kemper employed his actual likeness-

His *selfie* Skin.

Halfway around the storm-ridden planet, Exxon's iScreen projected a gamer's third-person view of Ray entering the World War II-era pub. His partner hadn't told Exxon much about the customized *Dreamspace* date world he created, to leave the cop attentive and hopefully impressed as the story played out.

The auditing function swapped between various viewpoints, generating a cinematic effect for Exxon as Ray entered the pub, stopping for a moment to observe his handiwork. The final rendering filled in thousands of minuscule details like the faint cracks in the water-stained ceiling or spent peanut shells filling the pub floor. Smells of stale beer and cigarettes hung in the air as he passed a group of British soldiers huddled over long tables, 30 or so of them, drinking and talking in low murmurs. His mother's story had come alive.

Catching his reflection in the large mirror beside the door, the FCC agent stood clad as his great-grandfather from his mother's old photo. Wandering through soldiers in British and American uniforms, Ray sought out the face of the possible killer in that bright red dress he'd chosen the previous evening. The visage of his Chinese murder victim filled his mind, flowing in the same seam that ran back to Utah. Victims who needed Ray, reminding him of his sense of purpose.

Then he spotted his suspect.

Her red dress glowing against a sea of khaki and gray. Her face turned away as she muttered something to the portly, English bartender stroking his handlebar mustache. Turning her head, Ray caught sight of her face.

For the first time in his career, FCC agent Kemper lost his cool on a case, storming over and grabbed her arm, attempting a quick network-linking kiss. She resisted. All pretense burned away. Her choice in Skins revealed she knew his actual identity. This suspect was toying with him. For the woman in the red dress-

Looked just like Ravenna.

eleven

Ray eyed the digital ghost.

Never was the FCC agent left speechless on a case. Her hair was blonde, strikingly similar to the same color Ravenna sported with her iCamo's hair camouflage; her face was exactly like his dead handler's own. He wondered how this user lurking behind Ravenna's online Skin could know his real identity? Could this be an ally of Blackout, someone involved in hacking Ray's eDossier from *Swipe 9*? And what did any of this have to do with his dead Chinese victim? Then FCC agent Ray Kemper realized his grip must be uncomfortably tight around his date's slender forearm. Questions swirled, sucking him under as she evaded his grasp.

Quickly she slapped his face, instantly returning Ray to the moment. The FCC agent remembered Exxon was auditing as he struggled to regain his footing, "Let go of me," her second slap was harder, speaking in Ravenna's voice filtered through the warmth of a genuine American accent, "I'm not into this."

Her OK hand gesture called up her Stop Sign exit protocol. Ray could flash his eBadge and block her logging off, but his cover would be blown. He figured he couldn't force a kiss as she would push him away before he could manage the task.

"Please, I'm sorry," was the best he managed.

"You're lame. And I'm not into beatings," she gestured at the bartender, his back to them, pouring a pint of bitters for another patron, "You didn't even program the bartender to say anything other than 'What can I get you?' Are you kidding me?" she reached out to touch the semi-opaque offline sign.

He grabbed her hand, blocking her exit, "You said we were using *selfies*."

"This *is* my *selfie*."

"Please stay," his mind relented, "I'm new at this, but I'm a fast learner."

"Want me to stay?" she bargained, "Then give me control of your world."

Control of his world? The request sounded ominous.

"This is me paying it forward. My community service for the sake of your next date," the doppelganger of his dead partner called up his power window which appeared as a floating, semi-opaque view screen marked:

DO YOU GRANT A CHANGE OF HOST?

She fashioned Ray's fingers into an OK sign. The power window then flipped around to face her. She worked quickly, hands and fingers darting into surreal shortcut gestures that were foreign to him as she scanned the architecture of this world's storyline, "Your choice of music is outdated," she smirked, "gotta keep it real," with another gesture she dematerialized the floating power window.

"This will be cooler," she muttered.

Taylor Swift's classic "Shake It Off" began playing on an old radio behind the bar. Ray found himself instinctively following his date's moves as each of her spins and twists were somehow met by his own, unintentional gyrations. His body flowed into an unexpected dance of fluidity as if they had practiced this old Hollywood dance routine to perfection. How strange to perform motions for the first time which seemed now so familiar that he didn't have to think about the moves.

The music score blasting louder as the whole bar joined into the dance sequence. Soldiers unexpectedly dipping waitresses as more dancing patrons streamed in through the pub's front door. A massive dance choreography like out of a 1930's era-Busby Berkeley musical until the dancers began leaping up into modern styled splits. They performed the more recent moves like *the robot*, arm swing, and signature *Moo gyration*. A rousing finale of music was greeted by his date falling into his arms as a spotlight shone down on them as background lights dimmed. She leaned close for the kiss. Ray required when a faint, incoming whistle resounded which Ray recognized as mortar fire—

An explosion of light.

A searing illumination surging through Ray Kemper's body. Time moving too quickly to sense or think. The explosion gave way to scorching heat he'd experienced in actual combat-

A disoriented
weightlessness of body
flying across the pub
bad pain in his back
colliding into a wall
laying   down...

That dizzy buzzing of his body. Suddenly lost in the grain

of the wood having skinned his hands like in combat before. As if the period of his life between that last combat and this didn't exist.

The only reality.

Ears ringing. Covered in dust and blood...eerie silence except for an air raid siren somewhere outside...hacking cough. Realizing he choked on dust debris. Incessant coughing. Struggling for a clean gasp of air. Pain in his body surrounded by frightening howls in chaotic darkness. Hard to hear much of anything through the loud ringing of his eardrums. Not like the slick shooter worlds or web movies, but modern war's ugliness fostered upon innocent citizens like-

Utah.

This woman could be...his killer.

His eyes focused on a shaft of light illuminating the fountain of blood erupting from a woman's head. A fountain perhaps deemed too high for movies but genuine to those like ray who had witnessed such horrors. His eyes scanning the gruesome remains illuminated by streetlights now shining through a shattered hole in the pub's wall. Moonlight showed through the partly shattered ceiling, casting a shaft of white crepuscular light through the dust.

Backlit vignettes of injured humans with bloody limbs torn off. The bar warped into a slaughterhouse for people. All his finely constructed creations blown to smithereens. Pain rushed up Ray's hip and back, his eyes focusing on a lamp swinging through the shattered hole in the pub's front wall. A hand extended a lantern through it, illuminating the sinewy silhouette of an old Air Warden in a scuffed helmet Ray had not chosen for the date:

"Clear out chaps!" the Warden cried, "Incoming V8 rockets! Get down to the tube station across the street!"

The desperate sea of humanity swept up through the darkness, carrying Ray out of the massive, smoking hole shattered through the bar's front wall. A flood of desperate bodies like a raging surf. Blurs of hands and fingernails cutting his cheek, nearly taking out his eye. He spotted his date rising out of the wave of humanity. Fighting through the crowd to reach her.

He instinctively grabbed her.

Ray's eAcademy training again kicked in, immersing him in the moment. The two *Dream Daters* flowed with the frightened crowd down a damp Knightsbridge street winding around the hole from which a collapsed double-decker bus on fire half extended. Then down into the dimly lit metro station. The thick smell of body sweat born from fear. Screams. Murmurs. Children wailing. Ray's hand suddenly in his date's firm grasp as the crowd spilled them into the lower level of the subterranean tube station; the madding crowd of bodies pressing them close. A stray beam of moonlight cascading down the stairwell highlighted his date's beautiful, blood-splattered face.

This woman, a ringer for his dead lover. Then more bombs up on the surface. Her familiar breasts tight against his chest. Both hearts pounding. He did not realize this moment would be the most romantic of his life. A contrived incident with a virtual twin of his dead handler as Nazi bombs exploded above them. He forced himself to remember the mission as the metro station shook around them, dust lightly showering down.

"People don't want happiness," she whispered to Ray as her lips closed in on his own, "It's the tension that awakens us to life, drawing us into the moment. Because *Happily Ever After* is as dull as...you-"

A bomb blast above collapsed the ceiling onto them. Searing pain in darkness as screams were cut short-

The sudden release.

Ray opened his eyes, staring at the inner media screen lid of his Hilton Hotel room comport. He was back, he thought before realizing that he'd never actually left. A realization he kept having to reinforce after sampling *Dreamspace's* hyper-real game platform. Taking a deep breath, Ray's eye swipe opened the comport's holo-lid. He sat up, accepting his first date as a loss. Her face now etched into his consciousness as Exxon's visage filled the wall screens of the media suite. The Chinese detective wryly grinned over the video call as he shared his thoughts:

"Could certainly be our killer. That was like the best reality show ever," Exxon's Americanized voice joked in English over Ray's eComp auto-translator, "it got good once she took over. And at the end, you so fell for her-"

"She'll be back," the FCC agent feigned confidence, "and, I wasn't into her."

"Oh yes, you were. I was there. When you went to kiss her, you were afraid she didn't want to kiss you back."

"C'mon-"

"Ray, I'm a detective who got to be an eye witness, I know what I saw-"

The FCC agent heard a sound in his hotel room bathroom. He had to remind himself he was back in the offline world, instantly ending his video call with Exxon. His senses focused because he was not sure that-

An intruder was in his hotel room.

twelve

Ray was not alone.

Sliding out of the comport, he crawled across the darkened media floor. His outstretched arm extending to grab his handgun tucked under his bedside table. His hand tightened around the grip. His index finger on the trigger guard activated the weapon's integrated, infrared camera mounted beneath the barrel. The tiny camera auto-recorded on a remote FCC hard-drive. Its POV, what the camera saw, was projected in the upper corner of his iScreen. His eye swipe triggered the thermal mode, allowing him to read the heat signature through the wall to the left of the hotel room's front door.

He spotted the silhouette of a person.

The agent's bare feet beneath faded jeans closed in on the bathroom door just as it flew open! The figure threw something at Ray's head. He ducked under the flying hairdryer which missed his face by an inch. His hotel room door slammed shut as the figure fled into the hallway. In two leaps, he made it to the door.

Swinging it open.

Racing down the long, curving hotel hall of media screens projecting a web ad for the web series *Villains of History*. He ran past the ad flashing Time magazine covers of dead figures with X's painted over their faces: Hitler, Bin Laden, Xi Jinping, and Blackout. Sprinting past the images, Ray progressed along the curving hallway, spotting the open stairwell door on the left set to close shut.

Ray blocked the door from closing with his extended foot. Swinging his weapon's barrel down the narrow corridor, he approached the stairwell of levels of alternating stairs. Through the thin gap between the staircase railings, he spotted a gun pointed down at him.

Ray instinctually leaped back.

That familiar stranger honed from training overtook his body as he slammed against the concrete stairwell wall, barely avoiding the bullet zipping by, ricocheting in the stairs below him before it plowed through a wall. The mega caliber gunshot triggered the hotel alarm which blasted over a P.A. system:

"Warning! Mega caliber gunfire detected. All guests are to take cover in their bathrooms and armored lobby areas."

More mega caliber bullets edged closer to Ray now trapped in a corner. He couldn't get a line of sight from this angle, so he did the only possible thing, shooting out the stairwell window as he jumped through it, falling out the 44th floor. Tumbling in mid-air, Ray saw the distant ground rocketing at him as he tucked in, clutching the weapon's frame against his chest. He double pulled the trigger of his mega caliber handgun. The massive recoil slammed the gun against his chest, uncoiling his body, nearly knocking the wind out of his lungs as he was thrust him upward.

Ray flipped backward, crashing through a stairwell window. Tucking limbs tightly, the agent rolled onto the stairwell landing three stories below the floor from which he'd just jumped. He landed on his feet, springing up into a shooter's stance, gun in hand. Honing in on sounds of footsteps above him through a closing stairwell door. Racing up four stories, he saw the stairwell door shut. Grabbing the knob-

He kicked the door open.

He entered the floor of hotel rooms. No sign of anyone down-range of his weapon's barrel. Then he heard a hotel lift door closing. He raced up, blocking the entrance with his outstretched gun. He heard the lift's ceiling hatch close above him. Pointing his weapon up, he heard what might be a gun cocking above him. Ray dialed back the trigger, firing three regular caliber rounds through the elevator walls as a warning.

"There's nowhere to go!" cried the agent.

Vibrating sounds above.

He heard the figure climbing up the cables of the lift. Ray leaped to the lift banister, using it as a foothold to nimbly push open the hatch. Aiming his gun upward, ready to fire into the darkness of the elevator shaft. Hauling himself up, he made out no one above him. It was as if the figure vanished like a ghost.

Later in the Hilton security control room of media screen walls, Ray watched the hotel surveillance footage of him standing atop the elevator shaft, captured from two angles by the hotel's surveillance system.

"Skip back again please," Ray asked the security department chief.

"Fifteen seconds back, no prob," the head of security eye swiped his iScreen.

The security chief went by "Marshall" printed on his name badge. The moment they met, Ray's FCC eBadge unlocked the

Nashville native's complete bio across the agent's iScreen. He noted the hotel employee's prior for neural drug dealing in high school which should've precluded his hiring in this position, but that was of no immediate concern to Ray as the man cooperated without requiring a court order.

The media screen wall of the control room now expanded to show four camera angles of the elevator shaft which all pixelated for seven seconds.

"Please expand out to the full surveillance array," requested the FCC agent.

"Sure."

A moment later the checkerboard of camera POV's gave up the eerily familiar pattern. Ray followed the daisy chain of pixelating cameras from the elevator to the story where he lost the suspect in the lift. The cameras on the next higher floor pixelated out in a long trail of momentarily ruined footage leading all the way to the furthest most camera aimed west at the island's bulkhead.

"Reverse the footage," requested the FCC agent.

The chief complied. It was just like Beijing. The pattern of pixelating cameras moved in reverse across the squares, each representing camera POV's, from the outer perimeter to the corridor outside Ray's hotel room. Then from the hotel room to the outer perimeter when the intruder first entered. The intruder's path masked from view.

Ray bit his lip in thought.

He knew for sure his case was as Exxon believed, a murder. Again his killer got away. He suspected it was one of the users his victim dated in *Dreamspace*. But how did they find him?

Before collapsing back into his freshly made bed, Ray manually dead-bolted his door rather than relying on the automated system. Then an instant message filled his iScreen with the *Dreamspace* IM dialogue bubble:

YOUR INVITE IS ACCEPTED.
WELCOME TO ANIMAL LOVER'S CAGE,
1:00 AM WST.

Perhaps it was his intruder?

There was no point to be gleaned from such questions until he secured a kiss. His mind focused only on the task at hand and danger he'd been in. He eRequested an online meeting with Exxon in Beijing.

In a secured, white FCC chat room, Ray explained what had transpired. He leaned over the hovering table floating between them as he pressed in mid-conversation:

"C'mon, it's an airline mileage ticket," stressed the FCC agent, "I have a ton of hotel miles too-"

Exxon leaned back in the floating chair as his auto-translation bluntly reiterated: "Ray, I don't fly."

"Exxon, as evidenced by recent events, I could get stabbed while online hunting our murderer-"

"The FCC has plenty of agents," smirked the Chinese detective, "you don't need me."

"We have no proof of a killer so I can't get a handler. Look, you wanted to be involved. Now you're involved. Someone broke into my room! I'm about to date some animal weirdo in a so-called 'cage'. You told me you wanted to nab this killer. How bad do you really want it because I might soon be killed?"

The Homicide detective rolled his tongue around the hollow of his cheek. Finally, a Web Agent involved him in what he still considered his case despite having handed off the hard drives. And he did have vacation time. This was a chance to be more than just a messenger in a significant web case. Still, there was-

The issue.

Ray sensed the Chinese cop pulling away. The FCC agent gestured at his *selfie* Skin, "Look, I don't want to be killed while I'm online hunting our killer. I need you."

Exxon expected such sentimentality. Just like a *gweilo*, thought the detective, using the popular, Cantonese word for Westerners which literally meant "white devil", "Post a cop at the door-"

"You *are* that cop. One week is all I need you for in L.A.," the FCC agent's tone hinted at the allure of the city.

"I'd rather stay in Beijing," Exxon's auto-translation replied, "Besides, I don't fly. How many times must I tell you that-"

"It's an hour flight. You can manage."

"You're half-way around the world."

"I need someone watching my back in both worlds, that's the point," the FCC agent pressed.

The Chinese detective remained intractable.

"Exxon," Ray tried a new tact, "You were the one who got me to consider this a murder case. You got me into this."

Exxon had to admit that this case could mean a chance for a better life, a larger house for when his kids visited. He did yearn to know the who and the how of this crime, "Fine. Come pick me up. We fly to L.A. together."

"Great," Ray agreed.

"Business class."

"Sure."

"And I'll need more than a few drinks on the flight."

"Done. I'll meet you at the Beijing Business Class Delta Lounge."

Nine hours later, the Delta space jet rocketed from Beijing to Los Angeles. Inside the in-flight lavatory, a thoroughly inebriated Exxon exited the cramped bathroom, stumbling past the orbital flight path projected on the lavatory's media door. The Earth and Sun-filled the curved media wall showing the live view from outside the windowless spacecraft. The drunk detective awkwardly walked in his micro-Velcro slippers towards Ray, seated at the sushi bar gastropub.

The FCC agent surfed his iScreen, reviewing the eNotification he'd received about the bullet casing recovered by the LAPD in the Beverly Hilton stairwell:

.48 MEGA CALIBER XXG ROUND.
NO SERIAL NUMBERS ON CASING.

The bullet was probably foreign-made. Any American round would carry an individualized serial number. Now the ballistics meant another dead end for Ray.

"Hey," Exxon slurred from behind him. Ray turned as the detective plopped down drunk on the stool beside the agent. The Chinese detective wore a bewildered look of astonishment as his auto-translation explained to Ray that "The toilet just cut me off from more drinking."

"Urine sensor," chuckled the well-traveled FCC agent through his auto-translator, "A frequent flier trick is if you're drunk," he whispered, "piss in the sink."

Exxon piled sushi on his plate. In the lower gravity field, the pieces hovered slightly over the plate as the rice gently separated into grains. The drunk cop grabbed at the grains of rice with his chopsticks and suddenly realized a truth he felt compelled to share with his partner, "Ray. I'm over my fear of flying."

It was the afternoon when they landed in California. But it looked as dark as any day or night on Earth. The hybrid taxi progressed through pounding hail. A hung-over Exxon leaned against the car's window, snoring. When they arrived, Ray roused his new partner. They proceeded down the upper hotel hallway of The Beverly Hilton where the drunk Chinese cop sat down on the floor, forcing Ray to help him up. The agent finally negotiated the detective into his room just across the hall from Ray's. Alone, Ray collapsed back in his translucent bed. But he couldn't sleep, his body movements prompting his Siri to ask:

"Your usual from room service, Ray?"

"No," he sighed, "I think I'm gonna go for a walk."

"Outside?" inquired his silver faced Siri as if such an option seemed unthinkable.

"Yes," he made clear.

"Well, you were flying a lot today so, understandably. But be cautious. There's a *Green Lung* air alert."

He went out. If he followed every Green Lung micro-particle alert, he'd never leave his room. Plus the new once a year drug injection made it safer. He didn't have to wear a facemask anymore. Two space flights in ten hours were a lot to deal with, plus his media suite still didn't feel safe to him: especially with his newly assigned partner and *bodyguard* dead drunk back in his room.

On the elevator ride down to the lobby, Ray conversed with the late-night hotel concierge who was a *blue*, part of the 2040s sect of Hindu transsexuals who permanently dyed their skin sky-blue. The first of many short-lived cults expressing fear and anger over the forces of nature after the leaked U.N. report. The concierge on Ray's iScreen suggested a fancy new convenience store:

"The sandwiches are the fizbit. The staff is even going on dates there because of the Voxy-good food."

Strolling under the maze of rain awnings covering the streets of Beverly Hills, Ray breathed in the wet, humid air. Next year the new dome would encircle this entire island. Digitally outlined on his iScreen, Ray saw the futuristic convenience store ahead, obscured in thick rain. Situated on the corner of Camden Avenue and Wilshire Blvd, rested the new concept, corner mart. A beta test store in preparation for a national rollout by an Italian retail firm. The greeting screen flashing across his iScreen as he entered, promised a unique movie-like experience.

CINA-STORE
Where You're The Star & Groceries Are The Show

Tiny spotlights mounted across the store's ceiling tracked Ray's every movement along with other shoppers. The vid-ads were mostly from corporate sponsors like *FS8* or *Dreamspace* which played briefly on the iScreens before the customized sound score piped through his eComp spot-lit his every action. As Ray looked at a basket of oranges, a pop-up ad coupon and short ad-vid filled his semi-opaque iScreen with images of high-rise citrus agro farms of oranges growing under artificial U.V. light banks:

U.S. FOODS
Growing America's Food In A World of Rain
save 10% now on oranges!

Then Ray heard the familiar, female voice, "Forget me already, flyboy?"

He turned around to see her. His mind struggling to piece it together. His heart dropped. For he beheld the seemingly impossible a second time. This fellow shopper in the convenience store looked exactly like his dead partner-

Ravenna.

thirteen

Speechless.

Ray Kemper's mind went blank. Lost in the familiarity of the face he never expected to see again in any world. Only years of training allowed him to conceal his profound shock. Having once before been unable to control his emotions, he wouldn't allow her to sense she was controlling him. He cataloged the woman's pinstriped, stretch business suit and nametag pinned above her breast pocket which read:

ALLY

"Ally," he found himself uttering the name aloud in a flirtatious tone.

His mind racing.

How was this possible? Never for a moment did he believe that a virtual double of his partner on the date existed in the flesh. He was trained to believe only what he could prove and little of that could be gleaned from online experiences. He assumed she must be a digital Skin based on his dead handler, maybe from their hacked *Swipe 9* files; never did he suspect her likeness was real. He never expected to meet a real-life, living doppelganger of Ravenna.

She took a moment to reorient herself, "I'd say coincidence, but nothing is…are you a stalker?"

"Stalk you? The Hopeless Psychotic, I mean 'Romantic.' Here in the flesh," again he said her name aloud, "Ally."

"That's my name."

"Are bombs about to go off?" he joked.

"No. Just sparks," she grinned.

"Maybe we could pretend this is where we met. And look, I didn't attack you," he chuckled.

"Presentation is everything."

He eyed her generous bosom concealed behind her low cut business suit, "I like your outfit better this time."

"This is the work outfit where a good pair of tits and a smile gets you ahead…" then her flirtation ran dry.

Perhaps it was the sudden recollection that sparks never flew for her on their online date, wondered Ray as she turned to leave. The FCC agent struggled to conjure words to make her stay that proved unnecessary as she turned back, compelled to ask:

"You didn't think up that date of yours, did you?"

He shook his head no, "How'd you know?"

"I figured only a woman or a pretty boy could think that up. And you're neither."

"Yeah," he confessed, "I asked my mom about the most romantic way a couple could meet, and that's how my great-grandparents met, he gestured at himself, "And here I am, pretty romantic."

Her guard melted, allowing a glimpse of the chink in her armor symbolized in her more sincere smile, "I like that you did that, asked your mom."

"I like that you crushed me in falling concrete," he smirked, "No compromising. You sure know what you want-"

"Most call it just being a 'bitch'."

"Nothing wrong with knowing your worth."

"What's your name?"

"Ray."

"So you want to grab a drink, Ray?"

"Sure," he eBounced an untraceable contact portal to her, "let's eLink later this week and we can-"

"No. I mean now."

They walked together to the restaurant, *The Grill*, an old 20th Century bar and eatery with a curious entrance at a backdoor from the alleyway just off Rodeo Drive. Ray excused himself after escorting her to the wood-lined bar. With her back to him, he headed towards the bathroom. But instead, he stepped out the back fire-exit door and stood beneath a rain awning where he ePhoned Exxon in his hotel room.

"Are you nuts?" in the corner window of Ray's iScreen, the homicide detective's disturbed face matched his auto-translated reaction to Ray's whereabouts, "Ally is an- *'undecipherable...possible expletive, unable to translate'* murder suspect. As in the last guy she dated is," he stressed, "dead-"

"I'll get her DNA-"

"No. I'll get her DNA off your corpse's dick."

"C'mon-"

"C'mon nothing! Ally is a murder suspect! From one detective to another, we know what happens when a hot girl's in the mix."

"I'm a professional."

"So are gigolos," in his Hilton Media Suite, a drunk Exxon added, "Marry her for all I care after her forensics clear-"

"Thanks for your blessing."

"Ray, she might be the love of your life or the end of it," warned Exxon.

"I sent you the address. Just get over here and tail us," Ray ended the eCall.

Reentering the late-night restaurant, Ray walked behind a couple, artfully concealing himself so that he caught Ally off-guard at the bar. But her actions disarmed him:

"Can I ask a favor?"

"Sure."

She took off his eComp along with her own, dropping them to the floor, crushing both under the heels of her boots, "I'll pick up new ones after the date," she turned to leave.

"Wait," he asked, "we're leaving?"

"The bartender says they're closed for some late-night, private function."

So they walked down Rodeo Drive under the partially constructed Beverly Hills geo-dome. Their eyes peering beyond the distant cranes lining Rodeo Dr. at the floodwall along what was formerly Santa Monica Blvd. Due to the Staph Fever and other outbreaks of the late 2040s in domes, Beverly Hills delayed the construction of this one. With the improvements in dome technology yin recent years, Beverly Hills would soon possess the grandest, illusory geo-dome on Earth which even rivaled New York City's cloud machines concealed the simulated U.V. lit Sun and convincing-looking Moon.

"Real stars will rotate over downtown Beverly Hills's domed inner roof," an announcer's voice proudly claimed as the glass elevator rose over the Santa Monica Blvd floodwall.

The lift carried the couple to the new complex of condominiums, hotels, and shops perched atop the high floodwalls protecting Beverly Hills Island against the largely risen, open ocean. The developers named this area *Sky City*, resting 150 feet in the air, running the perimeter of the island. Not far from the upper elevator station Ray and Ally grabbed a drink at the *Vino Wine Pub*, a narrow wine bar of reclaimed wood booths lined with oxygen-producing sansevieria plants and Peace Lilies to filter out the harsh disinfectants required to keep *Green Lung* at bay. The pop up on their iScreen projected the establishment's eHostess's voice as they entered:

"A super oxygenated environment engineered to maximize the fragrance and taste of our fine wines. Take in the romantic view of stormy seas crashing atop the floodwall to the smell of neo-Tuscan tapas in the air. Where would you like to be seated?"

The eHostess' software guided them to a rear corner booth with a window overlooking the stone sea wall. Ray sat opposite Ally, with his back to the back wall. Even in the crowd, he felt naked without his eComp, wondering if Exxon was back at the other restaurant searching for them.

"Don't meet old fashioned girls like you these days," Ray reflected on their distinct lack of media.

She eyed the semi-distracted patrons all on their eComps, half surfing, and half living, "I like to be present. Maybe that notion is old-fashioned, but our attention has always been our only real commodity. But you still seem preoccupied-"

"It's just that you look so much like-"

"That woman you knew."

"Yeah. Sorry, but I gotta ask," he posed the one thing he could imagine, "Were you adopted? I swear you could be this woman's twin."

Shaken, she measured her reply, "Yes, in fact, I was adopted. Before you ask, I know nothing of my birth parents. I was adopted as an infant baby from Mexico and raised in Santa Cruz in Cali," then she realized, "Odd that you would ask."

"Ever wonder about your biologicals?"

"When I turned 18, I contacted the adoption agency. My eFiles were lost in the solar flare storm of '43."

Peering into the lines of her face, Ray couldn't help but be transported back to when he first saw his former handler's charred remains in Blackout's suite, devastated by the "F&M" missiles-

"Alright. Let's talk about it," Ally's words drew him back to the present.

"Your face jogged loose some memories."

"With the media gone," she smirked, "we can finally be present."

Walking past their booth, a fat man in a synthetic wool jacket departed with two male associates. The patron turned to a Filipino woman bussing an empty table, "Have a great night. I really respect working people like you putting in the late hours."

The server smiled. Ray could tell from her expression that she felt slighted by the backhanded compliment.

"What just happened?" Ally queried him about the exchange.

He knew it was a test.

At first, Ray considered dumbing down his response, fearing the true one might tip his hat to being a Web Agent. Then he again remembered David's warning how *Dreamspace* rendered his user's quite intuitive. So Ray continued his streak of honesty in the real world, "The patron truly wished her well. But he's so out of touch as a human being that he failed to realize he's an ass, insulting her as he gives back her power that was never his to take. His lack of self-knowledge probably imbues his political views as well."

"How so?"

"Jerks usually want the government to run everyone's lives when they refuse to properly run their own."

"What was not his to take from her?" Ally watched the bus-maid vanish through the kitchen door.

"He values himself and his fellow humans by the purchasing power their paycheck represents. Although he wishes to compliment, he can't get beyond his pejorative bias over her low grade of pay."

"And 'pejorative' means what?" she inquired.

"It's when he feels he has the right to look down on her due to his faith that people's jobs define their self-worth. He's never questioned the nonsense he was fed in life or anything else, even the fact that he might be an ass. He's so insecure that he can't help but take from others to fill his empty vessel. But when he dies, he brings nothing with him except his decisions and actions. It's why lives often flash in front of people's eyes in the end."

"Why?"

"In that final judgment, he will know only the fear of death which was present the whole time eating away at him in ways he refused to see, driving all this bizarre behavior. The fear of death caused him to act that way to her and everyone else."

"Wow," she clapped her hands, "you sound as smart as David Bellingham."

Ray blushed. It was a high compliment.

"I love his blogs," then he pushed back the notion that Exxon was currently searching for him.

In the booth opposite them, a female patron stepped away from her girlfriends, trying to keep her anger to a whisper as she talked over her eComp's ePhone app, "Joe, I'm just not comfortable with you working with her," she stalked off to the bathroom to continue her call.

"And her?" tested Ally.

"Screwed," smirked Ray, "she needs the person on the other line more than they need her. But if she acted as if she didn't need him, she'd control him. But she doesn't consider herself worthy enough to take such control, probably because of daddy issues as a kid."

"So you think Freud's right, it's all about our parents?"

"It's all about love, whether we had it when we were young or not. Or whether someone touched us or forced themselves into our love when we were young. Those secrets control most of us."

"What was she like?" her eyes probed his soul.

"Who?" he replied.

"The one that left you this battered."

"You battered me on that date-"

"No-"

"Oh really," Ray joked as if he were a web newscaster, "Breaking news! Hopeless Romantic rampage claims 50 lives in a London pub. In a game world where things hurt! In your *Dreamspace* world does fire shoot out of your eyes?"

She giggled, "I went easy on you with the pain level. It could've been heart-stopping."

"Tell me who you're getting over?" he retorted.

"Someone I dated in *Dreamspace*," she gave up something.

"Well then, we're both battered."

"Who was she?"

He took a deep breath as he worked out a lie, "We worked in a company forbidding us from fraternizing, so we kept it secret."

"And you got bored and broke her heart."

Ray's voice wavered, "she died."

"Wow. Didn't see that coming."

"That's death for you."

Her body language softened, "I just saw the little boy in you."

"And your ex?"

"I don't know anything about him...we only dated in *Dreamspace*."

"But I thought you demand people look like themselves in the real world."

"I do now after him. I thought he could be my game mate. But he just wanted to date in-game."

"Isn't that the point?"

Her look suddenly grew dark and foreboding, "I'm never going to forget myself in any world. And the thought of migrating permanently online with a game mate I never even met in the flesh was just one lie too many."

"Maybe it'll make a lot of people happier."

"In *Dante's Inferno* do you know who resides in the innermost layer of Hell?"

Ray knew the work well from another of David's blogs, "The liars."

His correct answer impressed her.

"Isn't *Dreamspace* that lie?" she queried, "The handiwork of a disabled man who never knew how to live. And he wants us to join his delusion."

"So why play?" Ray asked.

"I can admire the art without being a slave to it. I like meeting people in *Dreamspace*. That one person showed me my hypocrisy, and maybe I showed him his too. But with him refusing to meet in the real world, I dated him until I couldn't. The masters of mankind" she turned, eyeing the hail and sea spray in the window, "ruined our world and now they wish us to forget it even existed. Rewriting reality. That's the worst crime. Which was why I'm now all about the real world..." her voice trailed off.

"He was probably married," Ray tried to lighten the mood.

"For all I know, he was a she," she grinned.

"Be happy to show you that I'm all male."

She laughed before her mood again grew dark, "I bet behind all that charm, this is your first real interaction in years," her eyes unmasked him, "a break from that inner shallowness you hide so well from yourself which keeps you running. The past nipping at your heels," her words reminded him of the night he stood on his hotel balcony rail, prepared to jump, "seeking diversions to keep you from facing the elemental truth that it's getting impossible to hold it all together."

Her comment tore at his soul, but the expert FCC agent knew how to play that game, "But I am charming?"

His comment extracted a laugh from her, "Do you even know why we kiss?"

"Sure. So you can shoot down guys and tell them how lost they are--"

"Kissing is about tasting each other's saliva. If it tastes good, you're genetically compatible. Tastes bad, it's dead on arrival," he found her choice of words stinging, wondering if this was his murderer as she leaned in for the kiss. Their lips met. If only they were in *Dreamspace*, he mused as his job would be done. Still, this kiss sent an unexpected chill down Ray's spine as she pulled away, her smile indicating she enjoyed it too:

"Want to see where I work?" she asked.

Minutes later, they strolled along the Sky City promenade atop the floodwall. Interactive ads surrounding them as they progressed past boutiques and more restaurants shuttering at the late hour:

"I'm always on the web learning about anthropology," she explained how she discovered the fact about kissing, "It turns out that humans have to worry about genetic similarity since we all came from a single woman, a genetic Eve a quarter of a million years ago. Eve had a mutated, prefrontal lobe giving all humans a higher, rounded forehead that fed our quantum leap in intelligence."

Still, he thought at the time, even the most intelligent systems humans created were not free of errors. Ironically when they reached the Four Season's hotel spa's front door, it refused to open for her iScreen swipe card. She finally resorted to jamming a nail file into the solenoid hinge-

The door clicked open.

Ray had consumed only two glasses of the Super Tuscan back at the bar but felt surprisingly inebriated as he followed Ally's silhouette through the ambient lit spa boutique. Smells of perfumed candles in the sales display racks filled his nostrils. Soon their bodies were pressed against each other in the green, marble steam room. Its fourth wall peering out into the spa was an actual aquarium, brimming with brilliantly colored fish living between the glass walls, fanning their tails in storms of fluttering red and yellow.

With the fish framing her, Ally lustfully eyed Ray in the steam room. Vapor roared up through concealed floor vents. His hands peeled away the top of her dress. Their tongues entwined, her body so familiar to him. Losing himself in the slipstream of emotions of Ravenna reborn. No past now. No present, future, or death.

She was just like Ravenna-

"Ever feel like you've been here before?" he asked.

"Feel like I'm here again," she said while playfully reaching into her purse on the stone bench beside them. Steam filled his range of view. Then for a moment in the open purse, he spied the glint of her small gun before she disappeared with it in the growing vapor. The stinging danger awakened him to the truth of this situation. How could he have been so stupid? Exxon had warned him! The agent's eyes darted around, seeing only more steam and-

No sign of the woman with a gun.

fourteen

R eality.

Undeniably it drove Ray from romantic delusions to sobering truths. The steam room, now mere camouflage for his killer. He was such an idiot. He should've heeded Exxon's warning. The power of attraction eclipsed reason until now. The FCC agent's eyes darted about. Pulse racing as he recalled David's warning about how users could evolve in *Dreamspace*. Perhaps doing forbidden things in those date worlds made her so comfortable with violence in the real one? Temples throbbing in the heat. From the corner of his eye, he saw her lunging at him through the mist.

Ray's bare feet sliding across the wet stone. He expertly maintained his balance, crouching low as his martial arts training kicked in. Spinning her into the wall of multicolored fish.

Flashing a wide grin, she enjoyed the rough play. Her dampened, bare breasts against his perspiring torso. He focused on her right hand concealing the item behind her back. He wrenched her extremity around and saw that she did not wield the gun. As the steam abated for a second, he spied the faint outline of her purse on the tiled bench with the weapon still inside it. In her open palm, she held a new eComp.

"I always keep a spare," she slid the device across his wet forearm before donning it on her ear. Her semi-opaque power window on her iScreen flashed:

SCAN COMPLETE...
VENEREAL DISEASE FREE

She kissed him as he gently pushed her away, asking, "What's with the gun?"

She wrapped her arms around him, "I work late, live alone, and I'm 120 pounds."

Her lips pressed against his as she began to pull off his shirt when they both heard sounds from the outer spa area.

Through the wall of colored fish, they both eyed the janitor advancing up the hall with his cleaning cart.

"We better go," Ally ushered them out of the steam room towards the emergency exit down the rear hallway.

"Hey, you're not supposed to be here," the custodian cried as they ran towards the back exit.

"Give me a sec," she told Ray as she pushed him through the steel fire exit door. As the door closed, Ray saw her turning to face the janitor.

Then the door shut.

Rain pummeled the agent. The door had spilled him into the hotel's observation deck. He peered over the railing down at the floodwall towering over crashing tidal waves below, showering saltwater across the agent's face. After a minute alone in the hard rain, he tried the fire-escape door which was locked. Lightning flashed about until he slowly realized Ally would never join him. How could he have been so stupid?

He'd lost her.

That essential truth set in as he returned to his hotel, picking up a replacement eComp from the lobby vending machine. It took six hours for the special FCC updates to secure his new eComp. He attempted calling Exxon and even knocked on his partner's hotel-room door, but couldn't reach him.

He accessed the Beverly Hills surveillance network to locate and track her from their convenience store meeting. But she had arrived on foot from the southern *Dead Zone* where the main supports of the geo-dome were being installed. There were no active surveillance cameras in that area. So he requisitioned the drone delivery of an FCC field DNA kit to his hotel, struggling unsuccessfully to lift her skin sample off his body. The steam room and salt contaminants made that impossible. He tried again to ring Exxon, but there was no answer. So he finally showered and collapsed in bed, the next morning calling the Four Season's Hotel front desk manager.

On his iScreen, the terse manager explained that no one named Ally worked in the hotel. Ray's subsequent FCC audit of the Four Seasons later confirmed this fact. A frustrated Ray reached another dead end, outsmarted by her.

Working out in the Hilton gym, a depression soon filled him. He felt betrayed by his feelings, a profound insult for an FCC agent who was expected to remain in control and yet remain in harmony with them.

Again he remembered David Bellingham's warning that this situation could happen. The clues were so evident in hindsight.

She couldn't open the locked front door to the spa. She never had an access code on her iScreen, instead picking the lock like a common thief. But she didn't lie about her appearance online on their digital date, she could be Ravenna's identical twin. An annoyed Exxon woke up late in the morning. He finally knocked on Ray's door:

"You drag me halfway around the world," the Chinese cop's auto-translator told him, "dump your eComp, leave me searching for you at a restaurant you left to hightail it with a murder suspect. Why the hell am I here, Ray?"

Ray explained how Ally broke his eComp. But after searching all night and thinking him dead, the Asian detective just wanted to collapse in bed.

Later they decided to follow the only lead left: staking out the convenience store where Ray met Ally. He and Exxon split the shifts, eSurveying the convenience stores camera network in shifts from their respective hotel rooms. It was close enough that if they spotted her, they could track her through Beverly Hills' dense surveillance network back to her eventual dwelling. They live-viewed in case she used the digital cloak to temporarily pixelate the cameras. Then they would trigger a police response. So despite the use of his automated eSurveillance, the team still had to rely on a live set of eyeballs like old stakeouts.

Two days of it yielded no fruit. Doing push-ups in his hotel room, he watched the store's overhead cameras covering the floor. Suddenly a power window opened up from *Dreamspace* with a new date response from his next suspect:

YOUR INVITE IS ACCEPTED.
WELCOME TO ANIMAL LOVER'S CAGE,
1:00 AM WST.

The case ground to a crawl for the remainder of the day. Ally didn't reappear at the store. And she didn't show up in any facial recognition searches in the city. Perhaps because she possessed a tool to blot out cameras and not be noticed?

Ray finally refocused on Animal Lover in preparation for the upcoming date. His Siri surfed through old media on people who loved animals, profiling former animal conservationists before the storm rendered most species extinct. Stretching outside his comport before the date, Ray took in scenes from the Disney film "Old Yeller". The boy and his beloved dog walked across a grass field covering the surfaces around Ray within the room.

Exxon entered through the media suite door that Ray's eye swipe opened. The detective sat in a retractable stool that swung out of the comport's recessed housing. Ray leaned back in the comport's inner bed. Exxon would audit the date, but keep the store surveillance on the walls around him. Ray's Chinese partner winked sternly at him, his gun holstered to his belt as he waved goodbye to the web agent.

"You going to do good Ray," Exxon's translation voice grew serious, "even though you let the last one get away while wasting my entire night looking for your dead body-"

"How many times we going to do this?"

"Break a leg," Exxon used the old stage reference that internet agents on web TV series told each other. In reality, no one used ever used that nomenclature.

The holographic glass lid hermetically sealed around Ray's inner comport chamber. Ray considered choosing the 2030s actor Fritz Fran as his skin, but remained with his recent favorite Matt Damon Skin. Damon's face now filled the semi-opaque holographic inner lid. Reclining back, Ray's eComp docked. Instantly, he was transported from his body to a large stone balcony where he hung precipitously off its narrow ledge by one hand grasping the carved railing.

This upper terrace adorned a massive, Italian villa piazza bathed in moonlight. Beams of light illuminated his garish, red and white striped pizza delivery outfit, and crimson scarf. He realized he materialized in-date like Romeo. It was as if he scaled the old building and one step from his climb's end, he hung off the balcony, holding his large boxed pizza before this Juliet. At first, he could not make out his date's face as she took the pizza box from him. Only as his eyes adjusted did he make out her 2040s era paper dress. She took out a slice of steaming pepperoni from the box and nibbled on the end, saying:

"Good to meet you, lover boy," she took his hand, hoisting him up to the stone balcony. He now made out the face of what struck him as a Japanese woman in her mid-twenties. A shock of bleached blonde hair moussed up in a tower over her head. Outdated LCD rhinestones set around her right eye, pulsed crimson light:

"Thanks for coming," she spoke in an American accent with an Asian accent.

Curiously he noted the strong smell of whiskey on her breath. She ushered Ray through two large French doors spilling them into an interior too vast for the piazza to ever accommodate. This interior was an old-style, 21st Century IKEA furniture store arranged in endless demos of decorated rooms. They strolled past an IKEA mirror display section, reflecting his date and his own Damon Skin again rendered so lifelike that Ray still found it disconcerting-

"I'm a freak for antiques," she spoke about her IKEA collection, "Imagine the fortune I'd have if only grannie had held onto that furniture from her youth."

"It would be priceless," he nodded in agreement.

"How strange that things only become precious once they're rare. While your Skin is so common."

"I could swap if you like-"

"No. Skins are immaterial to me. I search for deeper things. Do you have rare tastes?"

"Yes. I see why the dating system matched us," he playfully grinned, not sure what he could add to better lure her.

She led him into a smaller living room display, two brown leather couches slung around a white lacquered coffee table and brown, shag carpet. The back wall of the façade held a now clichéd painting from the 2030s with two lovers drawing into a kiss while both secretly spied their old style smartphones, part of the reflective Neo-Luddite School of the early '40s, a decade his date seemed to favor, before Bellingham's *Doors 1.0* prioritized the online over the offline realm.

"Name your poison, lover-boy," his date sauntered through a passageway beyond the false wall holding the painting. He couldn't see the bar display, but heard the clink of ice cubes into glass tumblers, "I got every poison you could imbibe," she told him from around the corner, "or morphine or anything stronger."

"Scotch" he requested since he smelled it on her breath. Shared tastes seemed to him a reliable path to lead him to the all-important, linking kiss.

"Ever long for a game platform that's more than *Dreamspace?*" she inquired from the dark bar.

"What do you mean?"

"Something deeper than mere dramatics?"

Suddenly a frightened stallion galloped down the warehouse of IKEA displays, headed right for Ray. The agent was unsure of what to do. He stood his ground as the panicked hooves grazed past his couch. The animal crashed through the apartment living room display, disappearing through a series of holes piercing variously decorated kitchens. He heard the sounds of distant glass breaking as it beat a surreal path through the warehouse. Again he was reminded of the coffin, remembering that he was powerless in someone else's world. His pace quickened as if he were riding a roller coaster into pure madness. A suspicion proved correct when he heard-

The sounds of tiny paws approaching.

Ray turned to a black Scottish terrier with a pink diamond-clad collar. Cautiously, it approached Ray on the couch. The animal began aggressively sniffing Ray's crotch. The agent gently pushed the dog away as his nose closed in on his genital area-

The beast lunged with bared teeth! Snapping jaws attempting to castrate him! Ray shot atop the couch's back. Heart racing as he watched the wild animal snarling, barking, struggling unsuccessfully to haul its tiny body up on the couch.

His date called out from the other room, "My game mate must have quick reactions and a strong state of mind. The reason why I jacked the pain levels in here way higher than the offline world."

His date reentered the room, now flanked by a surreal array of animals. Still teetering on the couch to escape the rabid terrier, Ray took in the odd animal menagerie. A goat, rabbit, cow, yak, ferret. A massive gorilla clad in a tuxedo and chomping on a cigar, forced his way to the front and center of the group, its ominous eyes locked on Ray.

"They don't like you," his date hissed.

"I see that," Ray laughed while at the same time, feeling a fearful chill. Torn by a strange urge to both scream and laugh until the gorilla violently beat its thick chest. It was a digital world, but one which genuinely felt like reality. No, he corrected himself, it would feel worse since the pain levels were jacked up even higher.

Ray said, "Timeout."

"Time's up," she replied, "I trust their judgment."

The massive gorilla charged the FCC agent. No more laughing. Floor vibrating as the beast rampaged toward Ray. It wasn't real. But that didn't matter when this reality could impose pain, even more than normal. The agent found himself wanting to gather his hand in an OK symbol. She seemed to read his mind.

"All exit protocols are closed off," she told him, "there's no hiding from the pain now."

The gorilla collided into Ray, sending him flying through the window of the display wall behind him. Ray passed through the shattering glass, landing outside on the wet grass of the villa's backyard. The dying gorilla floundering beside him, a massive shard of glass impaled through its chest.

Horrendous pain overwhelmed Ray. Long glass shards were stabbed through both his hands which didn't just hurt-IT HURT LIKE HELL! The walls of the mansion behind him exploded into crushed stone and wood as the circus menagerie thundered at Ray from an erupting cloud of dust and hooves.

The agent fled back down the sloping yard bathed in moonlight. Ray's pain dulled by adrenaline as a rhino, grizzly, and lion now led the pack closing in on the sprinting agent. He raced down the sloping yard and away from the landscape lights illuminating the mansion.

"Exxon," huffed Ray to his invisible auditor, "this bitch is crazy!"

Back in Ray's hotel room, Exxon watched his partner clad in his Damon Skin in-game. The scene depicted across the semi-opaque media screen of Ray's comport lid. At that moment online, Exxon saw a yack gored Ray in the rear, tossing the wounded agent like a rag doll at the boat moored to the dock ahead of him.

Searing in pain, Ray landed like a rag doll inside the wood-hulled boat, winded from the excruciating impact. The pain from the glass impaled into his two hands was overshadowed by his spine, impacting against the main hull beam of the boat, his momentum sending it gliding into the lake beyond. His female date, riding an elephant, leaped off the animal's back, landing on the boat's stern as it drifted silently into ever darker and colder waters.

"I like the way you handle pain," she stepped down into the boat as Ray writhed in complete agony, "pain excites the senses," she sat cross-legged on the bench above him, "You're tough. Most of them are crying at this point."

Ray fought back tears from a pain that blocked even the formation of a thought. Agony as severe as anything he'd ever felt. He feared he might pass out only to find himself in a more gruesome predicament- this wasn't real. It's a game, he reassured himself through the awful sensations, He needed to kiss her. BUT HE WANTED TO KILL HER! Repeating the mission objective like a mantra, he just couldn't make his mind focus beyond the anger and pain. The pain swept over him, making him feel as if he could vomit.

"Everyone's got a limit," she savored his extreme discomfort, "soon we'll find yours."

This date wasn't ending anytime soon, realized the agent in a dream that felt like it had been going on for so long. An effect of the pain. Ray considered rushing over to kiss her on the lips and end this nightmare. But before he could summon such energy, he felt his body getting wet as the vessel took on water from an unplugged hole near the bow. The boat keeled sideways as it began to sink.

On the holographic monitor of Ray's comport back in his Media Suite, Exxon spied the shark fins circling the sinking boat before Ray noticed them.

In the dream date, Ray would've tried for a kiss, but she flipped backward off the boat, splashing unseen into the water.

Ray managed to stand, seeing the great white sharks circling his sinking vessel. He leaped up to the stern which was the only part still not submerged. Then Ray tumbled back into the bitingly frigid water, the shock of it slightly numbing his pain until a shark bit off some of his bicep. His arm set ablaze in unimaginable pain as he swam through the icy water towards the faint outline of a shore. The frigidly cold water felt like thousands of razor blades cutting his exposed flesh to the bone. Swimming with his one good arm, he struggled to breathe and not pass out from the anguish gripping his very being, as two sharks closed in for the kill.

The cold wind whipped at him as he dragged himself up on the icy shore, struggling to get air. Any humor he had for this world long since left. He slumped over on his knees, staring at his now impaled hands still wrought with thick shards of glass. He avoided eyeing his right bicep which poured bright red blood down his body, blossoming around him in the snow, making him feel tired. Then his date's shadow cast by the moonlight fell across his wounded figure.

He peered up to see half of her torso had been bitten away. Leaving only the nearly-comical outline of a shark's mouth. In the real world, they would have bled to death by now. But this was not the real world-

Ray vomited on himself.

"Had enough?" she sighed.

He just shook from the cold and pain.

She made a strange hand gesture which lowered his pain level to what she figured was normal, although he was too rattled to honestly know. Strangely the decreased pain he felt served as a glorious relief. Obediently, he followed her into the distant cave visible through the light snowfall. He felt a stranger deep within himself. Something young and long forgotten that just didn't want to be in that extreme pain.

He struggled to walk faster.

Trying to refocus through the anguish. Plotting to hopefully steal a kiss. Then wondering if a kiss consented by only one party could even link their *Dreamspace* networks and reveal his date's I.P. address? The extreme pain warped his mind so that his heart truly believed that no matter what he did, Ray would never escape her reach of pain.

So twisted and confused, he thrust his feelings down deep as he followed her like a mindless servant into the cave. He realized behind his masked surprise that he'd become her slave. Her property to do with as she pleased. The ability for her to inflict anguish eradicated any ability for him to alter his fate. His survival instinct thus abrogated him as a slave to her without malice. The same method all civilizations used as command and control artifices. Causing millions of Russians to sincerely weep at the death of their mass-killer, Stalin. Or like prior American blacks and Latinos mass-imprisoned in the largest jailing in history during the *Three Traitors slavery* period of American history. They not only allowed their own mass-jailers to posit that black lives mattered to them, but blamed the leaders who didn't imprison them. Like them, this woman was-

Ray's master.

His woozy mind returned to itself as her obedient minion. He was going to take this all the way and link with her. So he followed the pain that kept him walking like a silent dog at her side up the stone steps. As they progressed, he made out animated shadows projected from an unseen fire. They reflected on the stone ceiling arching down to its walls. The flickering flame revealing itself at the center of this upper, subterranean landing surrounded on three sides by the rock wall. He followed lock in step with her, hoping only that his master would further decrease his pain. He needed to remain focused as they ascended to the landing to spy four Inuit hunters in the far corner. They were wrapped in thick fur parkas and smoking cigarettes. Seeing Ray and his female master, they instantly rushed them as a fourth took aim at Ray's head.

"Man is the worst animal of all," his date whispered to him as two of the attackers grabbed her, dragging her kicking body across the rock chamber as the other two tackled a wounded Ray.

Rough hands brutally throwing him to the ground as he saw the other two hungrily stripping off his date's clothes—searing pain—his attacker slammed a rock into the side of his head. Ringing agony and blood coursing down his temple. Another attacker dragged his head towards the raging fire. The heat of the flames awakened his senses. The image of the burned corpses in Utah flashing in his mind.

He was not going to burn in any world!

Primal anger filled him. He was well-trained to kill, despite the long shards of glass extending from his only working limb, the other now useless. Bleeding to death and light-headed as Ray's lumbering opponent raised a rock to strike him a second time. His soul unpeeled through the countless layers of his life to the epicenter of a boy buried so deep within. The will to live at any cost ran through all of them. Which awakened in him in that moment. He slammed his palm over the rock-wielding attacker, driving the tip of the impaled shard of glass through the man's eye.

Ray rolled onto his side as his lifeless arm swung around, its shard severing the jugular vein of the attacker who had dragged his head towards the fire's reach. The man now tried to stop the blood spurting out of his neck.

Ray scampered around on the dirt cave floor to douse his large patch of flaming hair. Then leaping to his feet. Measured breaths as he closed the distance of the cave ledge in a handful of bloody jumps. Racing as Ravenna did no doubt towards Blackout. Rushing the attackers assaulting his mortally wounded date now naked as they tried to force her to the ground.

Ray stabbed the two attackers with a cutting cross-slice from the glass extending from his one working hand. He lost feeling in the other arm. Life ebbing with his blood loss. His martial arts training finished them off with neck-breaking kicks from his uninjured legs.

Ray was no longer a man, nor an FCC agent. He had become the personification of an angry slave protecting his master in the same illogical pattern masses and elites repeated throughout all of history. Until he realized he'd killed both attackers. Then he felt the bloodied arms of his date wrapping around his shoulders as she drew close from behind, her lips to his ear:

"To kill a man," she whispered, "you must embrace your inner animal," in an impressed tone she added, "And you truly are an animal lover."

The kiss.

Feeling her cold, bloodied lips against his own. A spark between them flickering as they linked *Dreamspace* networks before she told him, "Next time I'll show you a new game to top this one."

He was confused. She read his face, adding:

"You'll understand soon enough. I'll send over the details."

The fire died, giving way to darkness.

FCC agent Ray Kemper opened his eyes back inside his hotel room comport. He sensed his body still intact. The pain now gone. It took him a moment to manually hit the lid release button on the left side of the inner comport bed. Still thrown by the pain, he didn't think he could manage a subtle eye swipe on his iScreen; he just wanted out of this machine. The holo-glass lid retracted as the agent sat up.

Exiting the machine, his feet felt cold against the non-slip, media screen floor. The moment they kissed, his date's IP address had been transmitted directly from *Dreamspace* to the FCC. Exxon now stood near the edge of the translucent bed, his back to Ray. He eyed the digital tracking system onscreen, honing in on the geo-location of Ray's date, now revealed across the Media Suite's surfaces.

"That bitch is truly crazy," Exxon's auto-translation chirped in Ray's ear as the Chinese detective noted his quasi-partner walking up.

Ray couldn't help but first double-check his body to make sure everything was in proper working order. That online world felt so real that he still somehow felt certain that some part of him was still missing.

A message flashed across his Media Suite's walls and ceiling, illuminating the room. The FCC had tracked the user's I.P. address to central Paris. Then the tracking software shut down.

His generic Siri chirped in Ray's ear, "Ray, the specific location is under current eInterpol surveillance. I've already had the

FCC request the physical address. eInterpol's system has responded that this will require a Section 3 Web Judge."

"Why?" asked Ray.

"Animal Lover' is under confidential surveillance by the French. We need a judicial release to discover the reason why. We'll get it, but that's not immediately happening ."

Suddenly the excitement again stopped. Exxon retired to his room. Alone, a still-wired Ray logged online in his comport. He didn't want to go on the web since the date, but felt he had to force himself to do it. Mindlessly he surfed on his translucent board through the ad sections of the web. Advertisements morphed into massive, intricate waves and swells larger than anything that had graced the former North Shore of Hawaii. Cresting a wave for the new G Tech sports eComp Upgrade, Ray surfed down the wave and zoned out as he ascended the massive ad wave for the classic shooter game FS8.

"FS8. Travel back in time to stop the storm," from the massive wave, the ad announcer's voice summarized the multi-player, online, shooter game's premise.

Ray's thoughts drifted back from his dead father to Ally back in the wine bar, eyeing the storm as she lamented the lies to soon craft reality. *Dreamspace*, to her, was the greatest lie.

Meanwhile, the automated voice looping every 30 seconds throughout the web, "You're surfing the ads of the web on *Doors 4.0.* by Bellingham Labs."

Ray surfed down the backside of an incredibly large FS8 wave of glistening illumination filling the ad-stream punctuated by streaking media surfers. Ray rose up to crest another mega-wave sponsored by Tanx Media with a concert date announcement for the web's new breakout teen star, Stumbleweed.

"You're surfing the web with Bellingham Labs' *Doors 4.0.-*"

Then he saw it.

Shocked. He slowed his board, not believing what he beheld with his eyes. Head turning to track the surfer who passed him. The surfer looked just like him-

Wearing Ray's Skin!

The FCC agent almost fell off his surfboard in shock. Then another copy of himself passed by, clad as a caveman. When the third version of him dressed as George Washington winked as he passed.

"You're surfing the web with Bellingham Labs' *Doors 4.0.-*" Was he dreaming?

Soon another copy of him surfed by, twirling an umbrella marked *KISS ME, I KILLED BLACKOUT*, the umbrella collapsed backward as he flashed Ray a proud, thumbs up to this user who chose the same Skin as him.

A media search on Ray's iScreen brought up the new Mr. Zero's House of Skins flesh update. The wild-eyed Indian Man in gold chains and old-style tan Adidas tracksuit swung an ax through Ray's head:

"The new viral sensation! 30 million units sold in the last fifteen minutes, which at this rate, will overtake Damon's Skin by the week's end. Get yours by midnight WST, and we'll cover the sales tax! Buy the world's savior, the government agent who killed Blackout! Also available as an adult erotic skin in all states except Texas."

Ray's Siri popped up a news blast in the right upper corner of Ray's semi-opaque iScreen. The data leak of the FCC agent blasted across shareware sites worldwide, followed by more news clippings filling Ray's iScreen. Reporters commented on Blackout's killer. They didn't know his name yet, but knew his likeness. The leak revealing his FCC agent picture attached to his FCC eBadge. Ray feared that he'd be thrown into the witness protection program right then and there. His career was over.

He eMessaged his boss.

Approximately 10 minutes later Ray hyperlinked to the secure, FCC online chat room. Across the table, his boss, Joe Caresio, waited for his arrival. A massive FCC icon subtly glowing on the circular wall surrounding them.

"Here's the situation, Ray," sighed Joe, "FCC's not sure who leaked your identity. But you well-know the cover's blown."

Joe fed him nonsensical reassurances about the FCC using all assets to contain what they both knew to be uncontainable. The top rung wanted a suicide, and he was conducting a murder investigation. Too wired to sleep, long after he logged off from the eMeeting he did push-ups on the hotel's open roof at night. Hail biting like daggers at his muscular arms illuminated in none-too-distant lightning. Then Ray did something new, jogging down the outer fire-escape stairwell and going out for a run. He almost never recreationally journeyed outside in the post-Yin Yang viral world. Sprinting far beyond the protective rain awnings, Ray raced down the flood-wall-lined Wilshire Corridor. It connected via bridges and tunnel in both directions to connect the Santa Monica Island and Beverly Hills to the mainland port of Pasadena.

Ray's mind returned to Ally. She no doubt had seen his leaked Skin online. He knew she would never reach out to him now.

"Due to the magnitude of your current case," his boss had told him online, "you're allowed to quickly wrap it up. The FISA Judge lacks clearance to know that you worked on Blackout's virus, otherwise you'd be mandated straight into witness protection. So the White House NSC has final deliberation on what will happen to you. Until then you're free."

Ray resolved that before that time, he would catch this killer in an investigation which most certainly had cost him his career. Then like a gift for his determination, a genuine second chance graced his iScreen when he returned from his run. An incoming *Dreamspace* IM from the Hopeless Romantic, dispatched

from the cover of an online web hall from which the sender had
now logged off.

The message read:

**IRONIC, YOUR SKIN WAS THE ONLY TRUTH.
MEET NOW OR NEVER.**

part four

David Bellingham the elder

"Rain down, you heavens, from above.
And let the skies pour down righteousness."

Isaiah 45:8

fifteen

David stared at her IM.

He viewed it at the same moment Ray did. David Bellingham's *Dreamspace* messaging system was set to register any communications between these two users whose respective identities remained anonymous to each other. Her message now hovered in words of fire on his lone monolith in space:

IRONIC, YOUR SKIN WAS THE ONLY TRUTH.
MEET NOW OR NEVER.

He never knew her name.

So David Bellingham might never know the name of the only woman he loved. She never asked for his. Names were just words, after all, given to them by other people. She didn't desire the normal dating compacts with David, seeking a deeper transparency that in retrospect surpassed words.

For Ray, she went by *Ally*.

A recent fabrication cemented by the random accident in the convenience store; when she ran into the FCC Web Agent while wearing the nametag. David observed them in real-time through the store's surveillance cameras, eyeing her new, fake name badge. He typically followed her or had proxies do so. But he lost her when she crossed through the geo-dome construction zone. So he sent one of his many offline investigators on foot to catch her exiting onto Little Santa Monica Blvd and entering the store. After the meeting with Ray, he followed them across various eSurveillance camera networks into the wine bar and later, the Four Seasons Hotel. He had his Siri dispatch the janitor to the hotel steam room when he couldn't bear to observe any more between them.

For David Bellingham, this nameless woman was the only person that he ever connected with; the-52-year-old inventor never forgot his mother's great fear, the one she muttered aloud after her son's life-changing accident. The concern that he would never fall in love. But she never imagined the lifetime's sentence he'd endure from having love and losing it.

Once David played Dr. Jim Tutwiler's ultrarealistic game, he imagined himself preparing to set sail into undiscovered realms where he might've given his mother peace of mind by finding love. So in a way, David Bellingham's now-deceased mom placed him on the journey to this unlikely outcome in space and time. While his injury ironically brought his mother to the man she ultimately loved, Dr. Jim Tutwiler. Since she died, David became ever more aware of one essential truth-

He was alone.

For a long time, he missed her so much it hurt. A sense of falling, making him slightly dizzy. Vertigo while standing still. Now he remained alone on this vast monolith in outer space.

A man and his thoughts.

Now he struggled to feel calm. Even though his protégé was gone, being here made it easier to live with what was going on out there...except for the woman he loved who periodically filled his stream of consciousness. She made him realize what he'd been missing. That thing eluding him through his many childlike despite his many escapes through inventions. Bringing him here to discover the woman he loved, flirting with another man. When she first lured in Agent Kemper during the chance store meeting, the footage was hard for David to watch in real-time.

He had felt like half of her whole. Even with the Asian, he sensed she had no connection to him. Now Ray had something else David yearned for. Love and sex always seemed out of reach for him; his injury hindering his physical growth long before puberty. A 13-year-old David did experience a sexual dream never to be repeated in his life. As he moved in to kiss the female lover, he discovered an invisible partition separating them. It was perceptible only from the mist of her breath highlighting the previously unseen, translucent barrier diving her from him:

"This is death," she set her palm against the now-fogged wall.

The Old Testament described sex as coming to "know" someone else. As a soul isolated from humanity, David Bellingham appreciated that apt description while considering it a fact that he would never come to know anyone. People were formed in the crucible of social contact with others. Who were isolated islands like him? So he set out to create the first virtual online chat room, like the ones now used in private web conferencing. He created the modern web of *Doors 1.0* to connect himself to that outside world.

In the first modern web hallways generated by *Doors* more than a decade and a half prior, a younger David was horrified by the unreal Skins users soon sported; online anonymity by hiding their actual likeness. The inventor naively failed to predict humans would wear such masks rendering the web inauthentic to him. His failure to realize that humans naturally wore masks of one kind or another in the offline world, allowed Mr. Zero's ascent.

David's failure to capture the flesh trade despite the vociferous warnings of his younger protégé later endowed Pia Geller as a voice to be heeded. His physical injury, rendering him so appealing and fueling Oscar-winning films and books based on his life, forged his blind spot, Pia often cautioned.

So he'd let users retain their much-needed masks as gamers in Dreamspace. She pioneered his software's manipulation of the user's neural pathways, inducing an integral-level of Stockholm syndrome within a *Tutwiler Reality*; when the mind could no longer discern between not just what was real, but who one was; allowing the mask to become the user. The gamer's mind-set free by the dire threat of the real, dystopian world.

Dreamspace became their reality.

Previously only the lethal, first-person video game from David's childhood could focus sufficient processing power to conjure such an in-game illusion. But those games displayed similar symptoms children developed when raised early on interactive screens. The same condition that only David Bellingham somehow survived. The fallout from tricking the brain into another reality, later classified as *Gamer Neural Shock*. GNS was discovered only after Dr. Tutwiler's passing.

Jim retired and lived with David's mother for the remainder of his life. He perished as a much older man in the home he first visited up the old dirt road. By then, Jim and mom's bedroom overlooked Bellingham Labs' corporate compound, the first ring of university-like buildings and a small park with a bench the couple frequented.

David designed his online chat room at the time of Jim's sudden passing. Since the Yin Yang viral outbreak, the average lifespan had been reduced to 48. *Green Lung* was the most lethal form of the virus since it's release. Not until the early 2050s would new sterilizing technologies catch up. Only recently did younger people no longer need to wear face masks, largely for the first time since 2019-

Forty long years later.

David's research built on Jim's work. A two-person game avoided the fatal GNS which afflicted all single-player, Tutwiler immersive games. Evolving developments in processing technology now allowed that code to manifest a game for two simultaneous players. *Dreamspace* could still only be played once; gaming twice corrupted the brain's neural wiring as Tutwiler's original game had, inducing GNS.

Now for the first time in history, a *Tutwiler Reality* game was being released to the general public. *Dreamspace* was soon expected to be the first FCC licensed, uber-real video game safe for general consumption. Two gamers playing one time. If they logged off, they could never play it again without dying from the experience. Only the dates reduced rendering, allowed for logging on and off.

There was, however, one flaw in the game that troubled David. The burden he sought to forget for now. Her mind was filled to the brim with her. And to think he met her within his creation? David often reflected on the inventor of Science, Renee Descartes' warning about the human brain's greatest failure. The mind was a horrible judge at what was real, trusting only what is sensed in the moment as genuine. Yet humans spent half their lives awake and the other half dreaming, thinking both true at the time they experienced them.

It inspired David to redirected Jim's technology to create a digital workroom where he could exist online in a reality rendered less than Tutwiler's game. But still a place with real laws of physics except for physical or mental sensations. A platform simulating sensations of the mind was sure to trigger GNS. From a prior comport in what was still his meagerly-designed, Opelousas living room, he began working with the seed of what would become his core design team.

When Bellingham Labs completed the beta version of *Dreamspace*, his eight-person, design team secretly audited test users' dates. The team remained invisible to the beta testers when auditing them.

The audited players were invited from random selectees, certain Bellingham Labs' employees, a sprinkling of high net worth individuals, and pro-gamers to provide various points of view. He knew the large list of those offered invites, but there was no ID code so he didn't know the identities of those who accepted the offer. The myriad of questionnaires and post-dating interviews were largely to mislead the beta testers from suspecting their *Dreamspace* dates were being audited in real-time-view mode.

David and his design team witnessed events in-game which profoundly humbled the famed inventor, forcing him to recognize he must slowly ease users onto the platform; the reason why *Dreamspace* now began with introductory, short-term-dates allowing users to game-play unbridled freedom as they searched out a viable game-mate. While relationships based on offline group affiliation, shared socioeconomic status, prior relationships, or any other real-world attribute rarely contributed to their choice of game-mates.

David named these brief interludes *episodes*, but his co-designer, Pia Geller, thought *dates* to be more appropriate. In those mini-dates, David watched as his digital universe mimicked reality so well that it drew out neophyte's impulses and desires, long-suppressed by culture and modes of child-rearing.

A Homo sapien's consciousness endowed freedom and anonymity was unsettling to observe in the early stage of use. Humans as the great intellect C.G. Jung noted, will seek over time to do the opposite of what was acceptable. Certain humans would always press the envelope, over-consuming, over-hunting, and now over-fulfilling their every wish and desire. Most of it carnal and socially unacceptable. Their odd reactions stemmed from the same wellspring through which power almost historically corrupted anyone, with the notable exception of George Washington.

Often the beta testers lacked the introspection to realize they were undergoing a radical self-awakening. Aware only in partaking from new, often previously forbidden experiences. New users, who in the offline world were fixated on controlling risk in their lives were often the most sexual, violent, and weird, unable to handle the freedom they so long denied themselves.

Before *Dreamspace*, this type of personality was often drawn to casino gambling; searching for the rare and improbable risk many often deprived themselves of in their everyday existence. While a minority learned from life that sex was a thirst which George Washington wisely concluded was ultimately unquenchable. Those who took large risks in the real world or embraced the danger of freedom, acted in *Dreamspace* as they did in the offline world. The prime determiner of a beta-users behavior directly correlated to how they processed fear in their offline existence.

His co-designer, Pia, often warned David of the unforeseen forces their Tutwiler-level video game might birth. Pia did not hold her boss's overarching faith in humanity's innate goodness. David claimed to see it in mass media stories, proving that good consistently conquered evil in most fictional outcomes. But that was fiction, she countered, derogatively terming it myth-making. David then drew on Yale's infant child study from the 20'teens, showing 89 percent of infants were programmed to be good.

"Yeah," Pia would counter, "and that wicked 11 percent polluted our entire history."

Pia's cruel childhood scarred and likewise alerted her to the handiwork of the evil. Most of them were far older than you. She often reminded David of his brutal childhood, leaving him perpetually impaired; there were no unspeakable ideas between these two geniuses because they possessed no ego, held no insecurity, and belittled no one; they both realized that stolen energy from others didn't exist and yet led to the curse of bad outcomes.

Sometimes in the moment, it was hard to gauge one's fortunes in this test of existence. How strange, David considered, that he should suffer such a fate from a wicked father. But he didn't dwell on such things. David's formative years felt like they belonged to a body in a comport on a completely different planet. It was invisible to him. He was just a heart and mind unbound. In some ways, he still possessed that sheen of goodness in children but wore it on a man. He seemed like Superman to Pia. While her fear of that same individual eventually influenced Pia to create a secret game, trapping the user's consciousness like a jarred butterfly. A place where she could finally escape what she considered the madness of reality.

Those damaging memories experienced during the early years that children, now adults, often carried around within them. A secret that once shared could only set them free. To take off one's blinders was necessary to truly tell if one was doing good or bad. For her, the goal was not so much emotional thrills and the choreography of a well-moving plot-

It was about feelings.

In fact, she hoped to rid herself of the story altogether. Without a cumbersome in-game plotline, processing power would be freed up to enlarge the user's sensations beyond what was emotionally possible in *Dreamspace* or the offline reality. In the end, designing ultra-real game realities relied on hard decisions of where to use the limited amount of processing power. *Dreamspace* didn't play with the mind or emotions, and in her final verdict, prioritized too much to the story.

One brainstorming session in their secure chat room, Pia remonstrated David for his penchant for historic, cinematic conventions; a product, she again asserted, of a life spent watching movies and web media in place of true existence.

"Life isn't a film," his younger, female co-designer reiterated, "it's a Haiku. It doesn't rhyme and it leaves you self-imposing some meaning on what is ultimately devoid of it."

"So we all should just be nihilists?" countered David.

"It's a test," she told him, knowing by then that she could never convince him of a different direction for *Dreamspace*, but still feeling compelled to try, "It's like Bruce Springsteen wrote in *Born in The U.S.A.* Kids get beat up like dogs and spend half their lives just covering it up. What they wish not to see allowed their elected leaders to wreck our world. But we've always existed in invisible prisons of our making. Living out sentences in quiet desperation, thinking only they are screwed up in a world of assumed normalcy. The prisoner willingly jails themselves for their best chance at a consistency of needed resources," she stared into some past memory when she told him, "I swear, the more experiences I had out there in the real world, the more convinced I became that most people are like your father. Just like him, that stuff only shines through when they can truly get away with murder."

Pia was so close and yet so far from him. It was hard to define their relationship. They played many roles with each other in designing the game. Her traumatizing parents probably shaped her into being a lesbian. She did not want to have kids. But in Dreamspace she could put on that skin of a possible Pia without the trauma. At least she thought she could. David saw through it in times of in-game development of intimacy or pain. R*iding* the story's building tension had a way of revealing game-mates to each other. But they always felt like two actors who were never lovers no matter how many times they game-tested such roles. For him, it was physical trauma and for her one of a different form.

He remembered in the online chat room with Pia when it first dawned on him that, "With enough processing power Dreamspace will create lives for people that rival reality."

"Processing speed isn't the issue," Pia warned, "in the end, they'll grow bored with the long-term story no matter how interesting it is. They surf other channels and live other films because they inevitably crave innovative stories, new characters to become lost in, fresh challenges to test their emotions. But if they really accepted the truth of November 10th, 1619, wouldn't they be offline having nothing to do with our game? Focusing on themselves and their children."

"It's all part of wrestling with God."

"No," Pia corrected him, "humans created this disaster."

He grew uncomfortable when she'd invoke the Abrahamic God with that growing religiosity spurned through her Dreamspace design work. While his beliefs were based in science which acknowledged God as its Creator, lending scientific authenticity to only the Torah and historic accuracy of the Old Testament prophets whose predictions, with the sole exception of end times, were already fulfilled. That was what he accepted in a path to God based on pure scientific reason, rather than the faith he abhorred as the most commonly used tool of mass-mind control.

"Maybe we use your idea," he cottoned to a prior notion months before which he had at the time dismissed, "The one about robbing the gamer of their memories. So they forget how long they've been in-game. Then we could break the storylines up and they wouldn't realize it," that comment would later drive the wedge between them

When she first heard it, he saw the fear flash in her face for only a moment. That alarm made him realize that she knew something he did not. It would be a move she saw possible on the chess-board that he would not realize for over a year.

At the time, he didn't know why his protégé kept her notion secret nor why it frightened her. Her reply, in retrospect, purposely misled him when she cautioned, "Without constraints, some political jackass will eventually seize power over *Dreamspace*, but future humanity won't even know they're in-game. It'll be worse than America under the *Three Traitors*. They won't be aware of the fact that they could easily escape their impossible circumstances. This usurper could control the story-rendering A.I. and abuse them like some malevolent god."

"The game keeps the species alive while we figure out options in-game or offline," he countered.

The long-term implications were hard to predict when humanity permanently resided in body vault comport bays, their minds immersed in *Dreamspace*. Could he keep progressive generations hooked to his game as ever-evolving food and medical technology better serviced users' bodies on less? Humanity must, after all, face forty millennia of human beings existing cradle to grave online in comports; med-bots perhaps extracting eggs and sperm to mechanically incubate fetuses based on users' online choices. Raised cradle to grave for so many generations. No social order lasted that long except ancient cave-culture. But nothing would change in the physical world during *Dreamspace*, allowing the online world to keep humans alive in a real-world society strikingly akin to Plato's *Republic*.

The human attraction factor served as the basis of that game, proved to be a double-edged sword. Especially when he found himself floating like an invisible spirit through the many walls subdividing his dating worlds. As an invisible auditor, he felt no exterior-caused sensations in the real long-term game or risked GNS. He also used the same software to audit through users' slightly less-rendered dating worlds.

Floating effortlessly like a ghost through surfaces that moved around him, he floated through a spaceship partition wall into an ancient palace bedroom. There he spied the woman who would become his only lover. By gently moving his arms, he could resist the constant current carrying him forward as if in an invisible *lazy river*.

Floating in mid-air above her.

Where he first glimpsed her as he was overcome with a feeling of *déjà vu* as if he'd met her many times before so that she never felt like a stranger. Socrates spoke of such a connection between true lovers, but David never believed those things until he glimpsed her face.

Catching her in the heat of judgment that only a woman who completely understood herself could muster. Supreme confidence indicating her to be beyond insult. Requiring no one else's judgment of herself that she long ago before realized would always be prejudicial and self-serving to them. David felt as if she'd peered into the endless well of her own possibilities and divined exactly what she wished to see; conjuring her identity from sheer will rather than luck or chance. She was what she wanted to be and there simply was no other option. That concentrated force of character remained despite her fluid, female capriciousness.

David fell for her in a single look.

He felt a part of her so that he could not be separated even by death when he first encountered her painted face in that royal palace overlooking a moonlit desert. The warm breeze blowing rose petals through the open doorway. Her suitor, pretending to be a king, requesting she emasculate him through a certain sexual act he requested in a confidant whisper. The perverse details were inconsequential. Her laughter at his request served as a casual acceptance of his private perversions, which reflected his nature, but indicated he simply could not be her game mate.

Over many months, David Bellingham audited enough dates to realize that in each one, she behaved like a completely different persona with only her supreme confidence and *selfie* Skin as the continuing theme. Never playing the same role twice. On each date, she shared nothing of herself but lured her suitors into the deepest of personal admissions amidst her often-repeated assurances of an unconditional, feminine acceptance of nearly anything.

A lie crafted to get at their truths. Since each date constituted a different lie, David later realized that her matching software proved useless from her eclectic choices purposely avoiding patterned responses. She sought to randomly assign dates until David manipulated his matching software to ensure an encounter with her. She always went by the *Hopeless Romantic,* as his system didn't allow a user to alter their I.D. He knew only from her extreme discount code that she was one of many professional gamers extended an invite to test *Dreamspace.*

Hoping to maximize control, he offered to host the date. She agreed, demanding only that he wear his *selfie* Skin certified by a comport laser body-scan. David's tall physique was truly fit from the constant electroshock treatments he received in a lifetime inside his comport's inner bed. His handsome face cloaked in shadows was almost the same as his father's, a man whose photos and likeness, his son long suppressed from the media. The designer of *Dreamspace* picked the only environment where he could be himself: his family home at the end of that private dirt road outside of Opelousas long before Bellingham Labs campus arose.

So that his face in twilight amber through the distant row of pecan trees was how she first saw him. The two stood in the field behind his home which was never publicly photographed, and purposely portrayed differently in the biographical films on his life.

A white t-shirt and his thumbs tucked in the waist pockets of faded work jeans left him looking a bit like Matthew McConaughey with a rural unpretentiousness.

"You're handsome," she looked genuinely pleased.

"So are you," he drawled before awkwardly fumbling, "Not handsome, but I mean beautiful."

"Serene place," she surveyed the distant pecan trees set against orange-tinted dusk, "Where exactly are we?"

"The South," he followed her as she began walking.

"A man of few words," he thought she enjoyed his reticence. Most of her dates were so quick to talk when they spied her actual beauty, verified of course by her *selfie* comport scan.

He progressed with caution, remembering how quickly she could pull away from a suitor on her audited dates. While he felt a new fear, the desire to succumb to his creation and permanently enter *Dreamspace* with her. The temptation bloomed as they strolled past the simulation of the spot where decades before Dr. Jim Tutwiler idled his rented Camaro sports car; considering turning around and not helping the boy who grew into this man.

The smell of wild grass and the chirp of crickets filled the silence as they neared the far row of pecan trees until the last light departed. The couple stopped only once they could no longer make out the ground in the dark, moonless evening. He regretted that he hadn't integrated a full moon into his world, but she giggled at the unanticipated outcome.

"I've dated a bit in *Dreamspace*, I really loved this one."

"Why?" he asked.

She searched for the words before shrugging, "I don't know. It just felt honest. Next time I'll show you my world," she leaned over, pecking him on the lips.

Their first kiss.

Faint static electricity sparked as they linked *Dreamspace* networks. He wondered what world awaited him? He never imagined the fantastic place she would soon show him. One that would change David in a way perhaps only his childhood accident had, awakening the inventor to incredible truths about himself and humanity; secrets to be revealed the following evening-

On their second date.

sixteen

He logged onto darkness.

On their second *Dreamspace* date, David's eyes adjusted to her silhouette set against a brilliant array of stars. It was unlike any night sky he'd ever experienced as a child in the offline world before his accident. A stellar firmament so brilliant that it would've twinkled in the noonday sky; long before the advent of early civilization's smelting of metals polluted the stratosphere to a familiar light blue still visible in old pre-storm media.

The cold air chilled his face.

The woman now known as Ally stood across from him, cloaked in a thick fur top, leather pants, and reindeer hide boots.

The smell of leather and fur thick in the air. He sported similar attire as he heard the sound of flowing water far beneath them in the darkness. As his eyes adjusted, he realized that they stood on a broad, stone archway acting as a natural bridge, spanning an icy river far below, reflecting moonlight.

Taking his cold hand, she led David towards a lit speck of light on the river's far side. The damp, crisp air filled his nostrils. He would soon learn that the light emanated from the entrance to a large, subterranean dwelling. A cave housing primordial humans who lived long before recorded history. The cave consisted of numerous underground caverns. Near its central mouth, pale-faced people of varying generations warmed themselves around a central fire. The fit males adorned with frost kissed cheeks from their recent time spent out hunting.

This flame near the entrance warded off most predators. For there were creatures in these ancient days which still left their mark on even modern human babies, triggering them to experience lethal predator nightmares up to the present. A human trait honed from a history of repeatedly being preyed upon by saber-toothed lions and other beasts in the wild. All from when humans and their ancestors existed not in nuclear families, but as-

Clans.

The fire-lit faces eyeing him at the cavern's entrance, caused David to hesitate. He and his date stood beyond the cave's mouth illuminated from inside by the raging fire in a circular, stone pit.

His date's warm whisper moistened his cold ear, "Don't worry. You're home."

David was well versed in the prehistoric human era of her world. He knew, for instance, that tens of millions of years ago, humans and their ancestors solely existed in familial clans of males. This crowd of pale-faced people in her cave was designed to be David's extended family. Women of the clan had to be married out to other caves to avoid the mental retardation that soon followed in their offspring from the limited gene pool. The ongoing human war against major life-threatening birth-defects from constant in-breeding over generations.

Most here looked similar to David's *selfie*. It was odd to see so many males of varying ages mildly resembling his father but in a positive way. While the one who reminded him most of his dad was the aloof, shaman priest whose darkness gave voice to things that the saying and believing of his prophecies could relate in some way to later events in reality. The one who claimed to see beyond others. Her *Dreamspace* world was so authentic that everything he'd ever experienced before it or after in some sense seemed inauthentic.

This cave was based on an actual, subterranean lair accidentally discovered in rural France by hikers in the 1990s. Later, the caverns were completely scanned and digitized online; a popular film documentary was even produced about it by the noted German filmmaker *Werner Herzog*. This find constituted the oldest discovery in history: a perfectly preserved cave cut off from the world by a random rockslide blocking and concealing the entrance for eons. The airtight caverns' microclimate protected the cave's wall-art paintings, which seemed so new when discovered that they were first considered fakes.

Archaeologists would later realize this cave served as the religious and social center for a network of other smaller, neighboring caves that were the group's dwellings. In flickering torchlight, his date led him through glistening chambers of the spiritual cave. The stalactites of calcium carbonate sparkled back the torch's illumination like an old, laser light show.

Many tunnels were covered in paintings of wild animal. The night before the hunt, men stabbed spears and blade tips at these animal cave paintings giving them blessings in the hunt for the same animal. It was in many ways their direct form of Spiritual worship to the One Spirit of all things. A long-held standard of monotheism that governed nearly all of humanity and its proto ancestors, sculpting the DNA code to its present form.

As a hobby, she'd studied anthropology to better fathom her species; he marveled as she uttered truths that he'd blogged about. Explaining to him how humans existed for tens of millions of years in cave societies and before that, lived as violent alpha males possessing harems of simultaneously-ovulating females. Semi-cannibalistic killer apes with a taste for sucking brains from each other's dead skulls. The proto ancestors of humans whose dark actions resonated through Caine's children. The final evolution from tree-dwelling monkeys. Before that period, humanity stemmed from a hairy, small rodent who survived the death of the dinosaurs to evolve into the varied forms of terrestrial mammals. They all stemmed from amphibious lizard and before that fish.

After tens of millions of years in caves, humans were upended by their shamans as the earth gradually warmed out of the long ice-age. These priests were allowed to later exist in off-sight religious centers while being sustained with provisions by the cave-bound clan. They began to rape their young male followers, controlling them against their self-interest from an early age to toil for their pedophile priest and his idol. The excess crops the priest's slave-victims farmed were used to feed these growing temple cities. Pedophile priests dispatched retinues of armed people to enslave more cave people, raping and thus mind-controlling more young to be enslaved farmers. The priest raped their masses for thousands of year until the pattern evolved into kings who reign for most of the past 10 millennia. All born from pedophile-based-civilization.

While the horrors this civilization wrought still hadn't lasted long enough to broadly-imprint itself on the DNA of human behavior. It constituted only 10,000 years of the human's million-year history. So children were still haunted by prehistoric life still giving new toddler's predator nightmares. Tens of thousands of years of peace would need to pass before that instinct faded away.

Just as David knew that twenty thousand years must pass for a human to genetically transform from ebony, African color to the pale shade of his date's cave's occupants; their lighter skin being a necessary adaptation to produce Vitamin D from sunlight in northern climates. Dark skin protected its peoples from Africa's blazing sun since rich Vitamin D foods were plentiful in the tropics.

Humans, like their longtime companion the dog, required thousands of lifetimes of repeated events for exterior events to imprint on a progeny's basic brain wiring. She didn't instruct him on all of this. While his background education only made it seem all the more real.

"We're programmed for this life," she pointed out as they kissed at the cave's entry on that second date. The migrating woolly mammoths plodding through moonlit snow in the valley below, "It's why this feels like home," taking in the animals progressing below them in the crisp, moon-lit night she said, "We lost the earth because people tried to replace this with stuff you could buy. And the Devil was there to provide the apple."

She shared the 18th Century French philosopher Jean-Jacques Rousseau's view that civilization was the worst affliction to ever befall humanity. The famed thinker noted in his day that the then-recently-discovered American Indians, which 17th Century Europeans derogatively termed *savages*, lived a far better quality of life than their European counterparts. They existed on the near-constant verge of hunger and death by foreign enemies and the weather.

David didn't bother to supply her data that completely negated her view. For the indigenous Americas were not so rosy, a fact unknown to Rousseau. The little-popularized introduction of horses to America by Europeans led the indigenous people down the path of inevitable self-extinction if not for the domination by the white man. In his youth, David was educated by Jim Tutwiler about the ancient, Cheyenne prophet *Sweet Medicine*. Jim thought God reached out to nearly all great nations, even the Roman

Empire at its start through the *Sibylline Books*. These nations were informed their reign would come to an end and often provided with the date or the manner of destruction. More organized cities to the America's south were madly sacrificing, knowing their end was near, but never imagining it would come through arriving, Spanish conquistadors. While to the north, the American Indians rode the horse towards a murderous, mass-self-extinction.

"The shamans claimed to speak for the One Spirit," she eyed the shaman with caution, "That was the snake that was accepted" she hinted at her inner-spiritual outlook as she and David walked deeper into the torch-lit depths of the massive, central cave.

Her spiritual comments were in keeping with recent modernity. God wasn't something overly evident in the 2050s trappings of mega ads and flesh updates. There were no prominent preachers or spiritual Gurus to fill media screen ads. Over the years, various COVID quarantines ended church attendance. While many scientific experts were now despised along with the World Health Organization as puppets of former Communist China. Many former experts were hated, like Harvard University's Chemistry department chair, who in the 20'teens secretly aided China to create the Yin Yang virus's Wuhan lab. While Stanford helped Xi Jinping create the AIDS-immune fetuses he needed to hatch his evil plan.

At the start of the pandemic, Harvard suddenly advertised training in CRISPR genetic-editing technology as the clear way of the future wickedly created by their treason. The new technology would be banned except for China, where its long-term effect would poison that nation's gene pool, nearly destroying China. In the end, Harvard became synonymous with the large orphanage converted from its prior campus, feeding the masses of orphans produced from the lethal after-effects and evolutions of the Yin Yang virus This parentless generation served as a complete rebuke to the pre-pandemic, treasonous pro-Communist-Chinese American politicians and academics.

As unthinkable as it might have been for the prior generation of Americans, everyone now knew that *secularism*, a lack of a belief in God, was scientifically impossible due to the truth of November 10th, 1619. That secularism had birthed the hypocrisy that created the plague. David's blog popularized the factual Divine birth of science. A major reason why the world had returned to Shangdi, Brahma, Great Spirit, Creator, God, just names for a concept that inherently was beyond any label. All matter and time and space had collective consciousness. And as Holy Scripture made clear, It developed itself along the lines of goodness eventually dominating over evil. So that in the end, it was all an idea leading to an outcome desired by the Universe.

"Anytime we're not wrestling with God, our species beyond this cave life will fall into our natural ways of self-destruction," reflected a young woman who never saw the sun in reality. The pain of that theft, perhaps thought David, brought her back to the light of the Abrahamic Creator she found in this cave-society's ontology.

The constant rebirth as life energy shape-changed through various creatures; the circular movement anthropologists termed *flow* which was monotheistic since all things were part of the *Great Spirit* and similar to the holistic view of the philosopher *Spinoza*. She enjoyed watching David and fellow hunters stab at painted animals on the cave walls in the hope that the act would later endow them with a successful hunt sustaining the clan.

"Nothing dies," she told him in shadows, "the hunter often is reborn as the hunted. By keeping us hunting, time is occupied, keeping most along the straight and narrow."

During a later, ancient fertility ceremony later symbolized by Easter, she and David consummated their relationship alone in the shadows, part of a greater whole. Although there were many bodies around them, the couple remained lost in each other. The tension from his 13-year-old's erotic dream finally found a release in her. Dreamspace had torn down the barrier.

The crackling of the distant fire faintly illuminated the statue of the original Eve, Mother of all humans. The one born with the radically larger forehead and telltale pointed chin characteristic of humanity; all due to a rare beneficial, rather than typically destructive, mutation from what was believed by science to have been incest.

Eve's brain and forehead were vastly enlarged in one lifetime. Stemming from one woman, humans' genetics were so closely related from their common mother that they typically had to reject incest; otherwise, their offspring over time would no longer be viable. A toll making incest a lethal, forbidden fruit for anyone who did it.

Women were forced to be married out to other clans to sustain genetic diversity, socially and politically connecting clan-tribes across vast distances via marriage. A trend still memorialized into modernity by females taking their husband's names in matrimony. David later watched these cave people celebrate sex with strangers traveling through their isolated lands. Just as later civilizations often commanded their females to engage in sex with foreign strangers in their temples, acquiring vitally needed, new genes to support better offspring. There were no venereal diseases back then which stemmed from later civilization's herders engaging in sex with their flocks during periods of isolation.

In the primordial caves, human females alone enjoyed choosing with whom to reproduce with via the power of hidden ovulation; a trait only women had. Allowing them through sheer desire to create ideal male offspring with larger penises, finally rendering the human male genitalia the largest, relative to their body size, of any primate and nearly all mammals.

Relationships between human lovers in the caves fed the typical pattern of four-year couplings, the period required to create a three-year-old, sentient offspring able to communicate and flee from predators. In this primordial society, having healthy children was everything while *the seven-year itch* lobbied for varied offspring. The reason why a woman reproduced with various clan members to diversify her genetic expression for a varied continuation of Eve's bloodline. The frustration from the poly-sexual norm often chafed females through history; their suppression of monogamy by men at God's Scriptural directive was not the existence they were long-evolved for. Back in the cave-

Eve was everywhere.

Her likeness being reproduced in fertility cult statues covering the planet for millions of years. Part of the lost, ancient religion predating civilization's plurality of beliefs. The original worldwide spiritual system based on that first mutant girl from East Africa who endowed her progeny its heightened consciousness. The human exponential jump in thinking made these human primates aware of how to do things, such as how to rid themselves of body pests. Shaving their body fur until they became largely hairless, except for the cephalic hair on their head; which unlike body fur, didn't stop growing and could be woven around the skull as added head protection.

David loved feeling like part of the larger group within this cave. Feeling as if his singular heartbeat was one tiny link in the endless chain of life extending back eons before him. That vast continuity cradled him, perhaps causing him to desire to lose himself to this woman forever? A female with whom he yearned to enter the permanent game, surrendering to the illusion he crafted for others but never intended on using himself.

He felt all that on his first date.

Yet the cat seldom strayed far from his existence on later dates. After that fertility festival when he went out alone to relieve himself in the snow, he saw the feline from his childhood stalking at the edge of the forest. In retrospect, it served as an omen of a dark end soon to come when many dates later in the cave, she asked:

"David, why are we still online?" she queried on a twilight walk in the ancient woods.

"We're...dating," his breath misted in genuine confusion.

"But why here?" she stopped, "let's meet offline."

"Then why are we in *Dreamspace*?" he asked.

"It's a safer way of finding someone without risking *Green Lung*."

"But what about the long-term game?" he added, always hoping they would just match up online.

"The Three Traitors ended the world long before I was born," she hardened, "Now Bellingham wants us to forget that crime in his long-term game. That's not for me."

On the next date she again requested they meet offline. She wanted to link up in the Manhattan geo-dome's Central Park. When he delayed, she knew that she was emotionally compromised and didn't truly know him. More dates passed. Finally, she leaned in for what she warned would be the final kiss. But it never happened. Hesitating at the last moment she stalked towards the cave entrance:

"I'll wait for that kiss out there," she left the cave without kissing him, walking out of David Bellingham's life as she eMessaged him the proposed date and time for their offline meeting.

It was odd.

He knew he could never go. But he also couldn't convince himself that she would not stay. Days later, he watched her in Central Park at the set time and date, having hacked the New York City surveillance camera network. Observing her from four angles in the offline world covering his monolith in space. Her eyes searching for him. It was November, rust-colored leaves surrounding her. She didn't wait long in her faded jeans and black turtleneck. The cameras captured no tears or emotions. In the end, she knew he wasn't for real.

After watching her out there at that moment, he felt trapped. A feeling he hadn't ever previously imagined. It made him do new, unpredictable things. Employing his *Dreamspace* auditor's tool, he spied on her continuing *Dreamspace* dates with other beta testers. A few months later, he felt crippled with jealousy when she settled on the half-Asian, Beijing night-club promoter. Spying on their *Dreamspace* dalliances, he saw them together and later hacked into her new suitor's home surveillance system. There, he witnessed them having sex in the man's mansion at the center of the domed suburb outside Beijing.

From his *Dreamspace* monolith, the most handicapped man on Earth watched helplessly as the courtship flourished. Until David later surveilled her new *beau* mistreating her at the end of her Beijing Christmas trip. Shocked, he spied on her using David's special software; realizing that during their dates, she must've hacked some program files from his system; programs meant purely for his private collection. She stole it from him on one of their later dates, no doubt trying to figure out his real identity. Now her possible use of his secret programs initiated this FCC investigation, drawing her into Agent Kemper's orbit.

After realizing she had robbed him of more than his heart, but secret, proprietary software, David grew even more solitary. No more dates with strangers. Pia had already fled. So he remained isolated, existing on his monolith above the sick Earth. The black plain seamlessly turned into a colossal iScreen he often used to spy on her; following her in both the online and offline world of *Dreamspace-*

Feeling like a helpless child.

David could never offline, only issuing orders to personnel through his Siri and iScreen texts. The storm-filled Earth orbited him as his lone cat stroked his leg, the sole visitor except for the recent meeting with Agent Kemper. It was also on this silent monolith that the final pieces fell together many months before, allowing David to realize the actual destiny of *Dreamspace* that he felt would save humanity. Once that goal was finally achieved, he promised himself that he would find a way back to her.

Shortly after their breakup, however, problems arose which made that outcome unlikely. At the time, he'd been perfecting software to replace a permanent game mate in a game if one of the players expired first. Then the key to his life's meaning unexpectedly arose from a processing problem in *Dreamspace* after his break-up. The issue didn't manifest in the dates, but only in the long-term game module. It would take almost two years to realize a solution, delaying the announcement of his creation's imminent release.

At the time, his team was baffled as to why precisely after 7 months, 15 days, and 4 hours of continuous playing in the long-term *Dreamspace* game, the first software error simultaneously manifested for both players. The two game-mates would initially experience the same event as two different phenomena. If an unseen auditor spied the event, they would observe a third phenomena, differing from the other two. While none of the human observations matched the third party recording of the experience or any additional observer's scrutiny.

No one saw the event the same.

After this initial manifestation, the strange occurrences increased exponentially with each passing hour of gameplay. Storylines fractured. The game-mates came to fight with each other over their differing perceptions of what each believed to be real. A falling rock to one user might appear as a soaring bird to another, sending the game-mates into violent disagreements on the basic facets of the assumed reality. The two players accused each other of being delusional or schizophrenic, often fighting with each other as the digital reality was assumed to be the only real one.

He first suspected a programming error.

After months of research, his design team found no issues in the codex architecture of the game. Bellingham employed a mock structure of simulated subatomic atoms & molecules, layering up into ever larger aspects of reality's building blocks of his game platform.

David's game-writing software simulated a story generated from a user's choices through an array of possible, precalculated outcomes. The real magic was in the way the story unraveled into a puzzle of many parts, continuing Hitchcock's *MacGuffin*; the unfolding plot conceit to keep one desiring more. He endowed players with the chance to be everything from the hero to the villain through their choices and actions. But just as computer-weather-modeling indicated since the 1960s, some unseen force escaped David's grasp in his digital world.

Chaos reared its ugly head, forcing him to appreciate that even in math, irrational numbers filled the majority of space around limited rational constructs. The consequences being that the observable order of reality must be an illusion resting upon a far broader, irrational realm unrealized by him or anyone else, perhaps highlighted by *Dreamspace's* odd glitches?

David ultimately noted these anomalies paralleled a proven outcome of Albert Einstein's theory of relativity. From extremely different positions of time and space, two observers could witness differing phenomena from the same event: just like his permanent *Dreamspace* gamers' glitch.

He theorized game-mates' bodies might be physically too far apart from each other. So a two-person comport was constructed; placing the couple in a single unit with their bodies physically touching. It did nothing to stop the in-game anomalies that continued and increased over time. The game world degenerating for the two into a chaos of unlinked dreams as they psychologically fragmented in the surreal confusion. It was as if they were sedated and unaware that their world no longer mimicked anything like the reality they'd been made to forget.

Later, David suspected that human minds might inevitably reshape his game's reality as quantum physics suggested it did in the real-world. Even blessings on food and other items he suspected could carry this energy due to Quantum Mechanic's *Double Slit* experiment. But if life was a test, then rewards seldom followed good behavior or else the wicked would just play along. At least that was what David told himself when he mass-activated the secret, *backdoor* spying protocol he'd integrated into all of his manufactured eComp cameras. The technology drew upon prior mass-spying software the totalitarian Chinese leader, Xi Jinping placed in all his manufactured smart devices from phones to TVs; allowing him to spy on an entire free world that foolishly forgot it remained in a continuing Cold War.

David's analytics sorted users' offline activities into statistical conclusions. What he found startled him more than his *Dreamspace* audits. His complex analytics revealed that people's social relationships and wider society reflected the state of its underlying economy. Liberty correlated directly to the health of domestic manufacturing just as George Washington warned. Now that everything was provided, most yearned for a diversion from what seemed a possible, impending mass-death.

He felt so alone.

Desperate for any remedy to reunite him with the woman now known as Ally, David felt he must first fix *Dreamspace*. Out of desperation, he redirected the story-writing A.I. hub of his *Dreamspace* game from generating the most entertaining sequences for his users to create experiences to morally improve them. He hoped this return to the cinematic convention of an ever-improving hero might remedy his issue.

The *Dreamspace* hub went haywire. The system instantly ejected thousands of his long-term gamers. Then it denied that the offlined players had been bounced out of the game. The software became confused about reality. Which raised the eerie specter for David Bellingham that the so-called real world existed as a multi-branching game perhaps akin to *Dreamspace*?

He started a six-week system scan. He wondered if his creation was a crude reflection of the secret workings of some underlying reality? A level of existence that God in Holy Scripture made clear was only a test for the real life following death and judgment. Then he took stock in what he could spiritually be sure of.

From the independent truth of God's birth of Science on 11/10/1619, David long-theorized that the Torah, the first five books of the Old Testament, alone could be considered scientifically valid in Abrahamic-faith scripture. In comparison, Christian *Gospels*, by their definition, were motivational speeches to sign up recruits to their inner-connection free of others. A movement spread through these gospels that were admittedly free of any burden of facts. While Mohammed's account in Islam was biographical. As Christ posited in the Gospels, any later Abrahamic faith had to acknowledge the Torah as the only firm, unchanging foundation. Like a Russian troika doll, the inner-most core of all later Abrahamic faiths collapsed back into God's laws and words dictated to Moses.

The Torah.

Until David popularized it, the inner connection through the unchanging laws of the Torah free of any priests' spiritual meddling, was mostly unknown. It fueled a major return to the 20'teens Mark Burnett, and Roma Downey web-TV-series *AD*, now considered to be *the wisdom of Christ* reiterated at the end of days. The factual portrayal of authentic Christianity before Greek pedophiles created a new religion, refusing Christ's inner-seeking, legal worship lost after the three Israelite, pedophile high-priests flourished in the ancient toleration of sodomy.

That show elaborated on the same truth uttered by the actor Graham Chapman in Monty Python's *Life of Brian* to his inadvertent followers, cautioning them that they weren't to follow anyone, using scripture to think for themselves as individuals. Those comedians discovered this insight because they took the time to read the Holy Scripture instead of taking the interpretation of a meddling liar.

The historian Josephus documented that Jesus refuted the tyrant Israelite family, the *Hasmoneans,* particularly their cruel domination over the people with a new, illegal religious tax assessed each year instead of once in a lifetime. The Hasmoneans took control over the priesthood and kingship in violation of God's laws. The Hasmonean tyrants facilitating Christ's death were only in power after the civil war begun by the three prior Israelite High Priests attempting a mass-pedophile-rape. The reason why the *Old Testament* recorded no Divine magic in their so-called second temple that had filled much of the first temple until Babylon conquered that nation.

Still, for nearly three centuries, Christ's crucifixion restored the inward faith until the first Christian, Roman Emperor Constantine ended the movement in 325 A.D. at the *Council of Nicea.* Constantine, a worshipper of the Roman sun god until Christian conversion shortly before his death, feared the inward-looking Torah faith would undermine the uniformity required of his Roman empire. He purposely appointed members of the Greek pedophile society as newly empowered Christian priests to formalize a new religion the likes of which Christ's reiteration of the Torah strictly forbid.

The Greeks reversed the inward-looking faith outward to spiritual advisers, Greek priests who expectedly forbid heterosexuals from their church ranks. These new Greek priests altered the unchanging Sabbath to the day of sun worship in deference to Constantine's sun deity. They ended Christianity while illicitly claiming their new faith possessed a nonexistent link back to Peter as the first pope, which he certainly was not.

This newly invented, papal position harkened back to the Greek's love of Plato's theorized utopia from the *Republic* with the pope as the philosopher-king. They took over Roman society with it, birthing the medieval age. Peter was, in fact, only brought to Rome to be beheaded by Emperor Nero. Scripture incontrovertibly proved to anyone who read the text that Peter would've been revolted by the concept of a pope after spending his life fighting off meddling priests heretically interfering in one's inner portal to the Divine with only scripture as the guide.

These later Greek Christians turned rabidly anti-Semitic, blaming Israelites for killing Christ; ignoring the truth that pedophile Greek occupiers of ancient Israel brought about his eventual crucifixion by infecting Israelite high-priests with their abominable ways. By then, Israelites were scattered like dust as Jacob's Ladder's dream presaged in *Genesis*. Traces of Abraham's DNA mixed with other races and ethnicities, bringing anyone with a trace of it under the covenant. So that later, cheap DNA tests could regather the tribes via science, allowing people to know if they were bound by Abraham's compact.

That gift accompanied by the price of near-destruction from science's fallout upon the planet. Everyone now appreciated that Xi Jinping's Yin Yang virus gripped the world in 2020, exactly 2,625 years or *weeks* as the Prophet Daniel stated must pass from the original temple's end of their rightful blood sacrifice. That occurred in 587 BC when Babylonian conquered Israel and economically sucked the nation dry of wealth for 18 years before destroying it. Just like the 18 years from China's entering into the World Trade Organization to spread its goods worldwide to 2019's Yin Yang virus attack on humanity through Xi Jinping's concealment. The prophet predicted 2020 as the blessed year marking the end of the Israelite's suffering as The Time of Trouble began.

Finally, his six-week-long *Dreamspace* system scan drew to completion, David suspected Pia's secret, inward game to be more in keeping with God's inner-link than Dreamspace. Perhaps his game was cursed because of it? Had she been right to flee with her secret game? By now, he realized he couldn't redirect the *Dreamspace* platform to an inward path by building better game-mates.

The night before the report was issued he had a dream. In it he sat shocked as he read the report from his six-week-long game scan. His program system started the eBriefing by showing him the Norman Rockwell painting titled *Freedom of Worship* before giving him the unexpected fix to his game-world's issue:

The United States is the blessed New Jerusalem. It alone allowed each to worship as they desire, finally accommodating the Old Testament's inner-seeking, unchangeable laws. The Almighty beckons all to approach Him within them as reiterated to His Prophet Elijah. The same Elijah whose life corrects the New Jerusalem in their error of worship. Elijah rebuked the wicked Davidian kings, showing Americans that they cannot worship their leaders who enriched their mortal enemy, dooming them. Americans must wrestle with God which is truth and use their vote to bring about their salvation or die.

His actual game scan told him nothing.

It didn't even notice a problem in his program. Then followed the darkest days. The glitch at the time still could not be remedied. Dreamspace's failure threatened to turn Bellingham Labs insolvent.

David was plagued by money-matters in reality and a repeating dream when sleeping. In it, he, along with millions of other people, woke up in a modern warehouse of devices far-evolved beyond comports. This planet was revealed to him to be the real Earth. All human history since formal civilization had begun 10,000 years before played out in another reality that was not real. So earth now remained unspoiled from humanity's failures required as a learning lesson for the species to depart from their wicked ways.

Only good people were here.

Above a futuristic city of floating islands, a magnetic highway of goods above spanned the planet; products transported in the air with automated pickup deliveries by smaller, local drones. In his dream, he visited a friend he'd never met; a young man who owned an Italian penthouse restaurant of exposed brick walls. Flying drones popped down with truffles and Barolo wine freshly delivered from Tuscany half-way around the planet. The world seemed a restoration of Eden with all provisions free and plentiful. They told him God was present in a new Temple in the western half of the United States, water flowing from it to renew the planet. And as always, it wasn't about the accumulation of excess wealth and goods, but developing one's spirit.

He gave up.

Unable to solve his game's issue, he resumed his secret surveillance of his ex-lover, reassuring himself that it was a diversion from *Dreamspace's* seemingly fated ruin. But as Steve Jobs concluded, one could only connect the dots in hindsight. David Bellingham never imagined that his meandering journey would bring him to this point.

Taking his mind off of Ally, he spied through the eComp camera belonging to the President of the United States. The Commander-in-Chief's eComp camera POV now projected across David's huge monolith. The inventor watched as the world leader urinated in his private bathroom just off the Oval Office. The head of the free world turned to catch his reflection in the lavatory's holo-mirror wall, noting his hydration level analyzed from his urine.

To clear his mind from his former lover, David often secretly checked in on the President. Yet this man was not the most significant threat to David's new, secret plan. Only two people were: Pia Geller, his co-designer who fled his company some time ago and-

FCC agent Ray Kemper.

Bellingham never suspected that his ex-lover would be interested in such a skilled manipulator like the Web Agent. What

an irony that David and Ray should cross paths through her; the reason why the inventor secretly leaked Ray Kemper's face to the web as Blackout's killer.

The inventor felt that blowing the FCC agent's cover would send Ray spiraling from the orbit of the woman now known as Ally. With her detestation of the establishment and its guardians like Ray, David expected she'd sever her dalliance with Kemper. But the inventor could never predict her actions.

He should've known from his audits of her dream dates that she played a different person with each suitor. As much as he hated to admit it, David knew her only as well as she revealed to him. Now she looked the same but acted like someone else. His stomach sank as he returned to the *Dreamspace* IM she recently sent to Ray. The instant message now hovering before him:

IRONIC, YOUR SKIN WAS THE ONLY TRUTH. MEET NOW OR NEVER.

Anger welled.

It was like a kick to the ribs as her message revealed her inner feelings to the inventor. All David could think of was possessing her in a hunger that demanded to be filled. His next eye swipe cleared the surveillance checkerboard from his monolith.

Through private tracking devices in his Doors-powered web, he quickly tracked down his former lover who had just entered an eWeb hall not far from where she first dispatched her recent IM message to Ray. Watching Ray Kemper online near her, David Bellingham, invisible to them, never suspected what she would do next.

seventeen

She placed herself out of reach.

Now eyeing the man who she previously thought could be her mate in the crowded web hall. Now possibly just another unthinking member of the world-order. A symptom of the disease which long-plagued the world. Ally reflected on the irony of this recently unmasked FCC agent positioned in the middle of a crowded, online hall littered with other likenesses of him.

She made the *hang loose* symbol with her hand, calling up her translucent surfboard that instantly materialized, hovering just above the walkway floor. On the meta ad covering the surfaces around them, Ray's face was carved up by Mr. Zero's sushi knife.

The Indian Skin peddler ranted from behind oversized mirrored sunglasses and tan sweats in the Vid ad:

"Join the movement! Wear our savior's Skin or use him as your Siri. Celebrate the nameless savior who helped end World War IV!" ranted the king of eFlesh, "Buy before midnight WST and save 15%!"

Ally surfed across Ray's face covering the walls of the online hallway. She knew that she caught his eye as she surfed up the wall. Inverting, she rocketed along the ceiling's slipstream high above the online corridor. Racing along with the blur of other surfers as they rode the digital wave ads of the ceiling which now seemed like the floor. Soon Ray caught up. They surfed side by side so proximal to each other, they seemed to be standing still. She could offline with a quick eye stroke as the familiar, automated voice filled the online realm:

"You're surfing the web with *Doors 4.0.* hosted by Bellingham Labs."

"What wasn't a lie?" she finally asked him.

"Everything…except my job."

"Then follow me, Mr. Hero," She sped up,

She wasn't sure how the government agent found her, taking great pains to cover her tracks online and offline like a cautious thief. So what could've possibly alerted the FCC to her presence? She figured their *Dreamspace* date and real-world meeting in the convenience store wasn't mere coincidence.

Racing behind her, Ray artfully jumped and leaped around surfers without lagging them. Ahead of him, he spied her grabbing something. But he was too far back to recognize it as her earring. She threw the looped metal jewelry ahead of her as it rapidly expanded into a metal ring four feet in diameter. She surfed uninterrupted through the ring's center. No time to think, Ray crouched, following her through the ring into a different area of the web. The looped metal returned like a boomerang into her hand. He figured it was some illegal, hyperlinking tool to access forbidden zones of the web. This place must be independent of the *Doors* software because his semi-transparent surfboard fell away as he plummeted behind her into interminable darkness. The sudden drop in his stomach until he tightened his abs.

His Siri whispered in his ear, "Ray, her portal hyperlinked you into *Dreamspace's* internal operating system-"

Then he saw a distant light visible far below them, glimmering like a star as they plummeted towards it. Their surfboards vaporizing into curling smoke in an area no longer supporting such protocols. Streamlining his arms at his sides, Ray soared ever faster towards Ally to steal a network-linking kiss and end this charade until his Siri informed him:

"Ray, this hub allows Dream Genies to audit and troubleshoot Dreamworlds. Touching her here will not geo-locate her in the offline world. Nor will a kiss here link *Dreamspace* networks."

Ray slowed his descent, allowing Ally to fall ahead of him as she cried back at him, "We're about to fall through the user's long-term game worlds. You won't be able to hunt me here."

"I only hunt the bad ones."

"You hunted Blackout," her eyes connected with his own.

They fell through the expansive orb of light surrounding them in the illuminated mist. The light gave way to a radiating pinwheel-shaped pattern rising out of the distance. As they fell closer, Ray discerned the pinwheel pattern consisted of radiating rings of stained glass window panes extending out of the void.

They crashed through a single glass panel depicting a medieval forest scene. Shattered glass showering with them as they fell through an actual forest thick with trees, branches, and needles tearing at them in the darkness before both their bodies evaporated into a mist. Their bodies now nothing more than vapor, traveling almost unseen past a male and female couple sitting on a tree branch, arguing in an unrecognizable tongue.

"Ray," his Siri informed him in a whisper, "I cannot translate their words."

The couple remained oblivious to the thin vapor trail. The falling curls of vapor now embodying Ray and Ally drifted past the two arguing game-mates.

"They can't hear or see us," Ally told him.

The forest trees morphed surreally into wooden floorboards of a mid 20th Century home's formal living room. High ceilings and 19th Century furniture. Seated around a massive fireplace, a couple argued in a weird language as their young boy in Victoria-era clothing finished a jigsaw puzzle on the floor between them. The meaning of their argument remained a mystery, but they were definitely at odds with each other. The line of vapor constituting Ray and Ally coursed into the unfinished jigsaw puzzle, which at first appeared to be a painting of a seashore, but upon closer inspection was a mural of a gated neighborhood of odd-looking mansions, all closely resembled religious temples as the vignette became reality.

Ray found himself drifting as vapor through the cul de sac lined by these massive homes. A pink night sky glowed above him as he smelled cotton candy in the air. Through the windows of the mansions, he eyed couples arguing with each other. A chorus of disagreements rising up in chaotic madness. Even though he possessed no physical body, Ray found it surprisingly easy to speak with Ally by merely thinking words before hearing them just as David did in the biopic movies on his childhood:

"So the real *Dreamspace* game is," thought Ray aloud, "an endless argument?"

"It was," Ally corrected him, "The long-term gamers started to see events differently, which came to encompass just about everything in-game. All part of a programming glitch David could not resolve, except by ending the couple."

"End them how?" inquired Ray.

"You'll see. We're headed there now."

The vapor trail comprising the two of them passed between massive fires flanking the front door of a temple-like mansion adorned with an ancient Egyptian styled eye. Its hot flames somehow wafted their vapor stream upward through an eye-shaped glass transom over the front door.

Ray felt disoriented as the stream of vapor constituting his consciousness along with Ally's, wafted down a red velvet hallway to a couple breaking out of a tender embrace. The female grabbed a knife previously concealed from behind her back and held it to the man's neck. He struggled to turn the blade on her. Ray felt dizzier. Eyeing his distorted reflection in a hallway mirror depicting Ally and him like a warped funhouse mirror. Vertigo increased until he thought he might pass out as his strange stream of vapor moved into the mirror.

"Relax," she assured him, "it's gonna get surreal."

What he felt next was hard to capture in words since it defied any previous experience he'd ever had. A peculiar new reality of this long-term *Dreamspace* game. Whereas Ray commonly believed what his senses perceived, he found himself surreally believing only what he felt. It was as if he traveled now somehow through his own mind's eye, although words could not properly characterize this realm.

Geometric patterns filled a dark landscape within him. A kaleidoscope reflection of that charred mother and child back in Utah and then cleaning out his dad's personal belongings with his mom after the man's death. He felt something eternal and spiritual from a source he could not identify. Then he began to feel not like a man, but more as he did as a child or maybe as some ancestor long before humans.

He wanted to look at Ally, to steady himself. As if focusing on her face would bring him back to this moment in his life from which he now felt unstrung. All he knew was what he could now see. A kaleidoscope image of female human limbs and exposed breasts and arms moving in intricate, geometric designs similar to what he'd been forced to experience in his FCC psychedelic drug training.

All Web Agents were administered various mind-altering drugs, mainly psychotropics. The hope was that they could better combat a drug's effects if they were unwittingly dosed to drive them mad, as the CIA did to unsuspecting victims in the mid 20th Century. Ray felt his very being folding in on itself in a place in him that seemed more like a sacred temple than a video game operating system. What did that even mean? He grew confused in his thoughts, making out four rocks shaped as crude hearts. They were set down by four identical hands on sand. Then seated above the rocks, he saw a couple on a rusted bench in an endless desert bathed in purple dusk. The middle-aged man already seated on the bench in a tweed jacket and jeans read aloud from a hardcover book titled *Quod Vitae Sectabor Iter*. From David's blog, Ray knew the Latin phrase meant *which path will I take?*

The woman seated alongside him on the bench, angrily pushed away the old hard-cover book, speaking words that sounded like gibberish to Ray:

"I'm thinking from my side thinking that it would be best if we don't because if we did it would be far worse for us both not to."

"El Segundo," the annoyed man repeated as he tapped a finger against the book's embossed Latin title, "I just told you that if we did not do it that it would mean that we…"

They seemed drugged, thought Ray as he and Ally as vapor closed in on the book. Their language was not a rational speech. Words seemed unable to speak through them or serve as their underlying architecture of thoughts. What kind of game was this, wondered the FCC agent, and how was the FCC ever going to certify mind-manipulations as safe?

It was Ray now who struggled to keep up with his mind as he drifted as vapor into the printed illustration on a page of the book the woman now flipped to. The picture that now became his reality had been an old lithographic illustration of an endless stairway of glass leading up from a desert to the sky. Beside it, a massive, crumbling stone monument depicted ruins of what seemed to be Ray's face. It lay half crumbled as it extended from the buried sands of the desert. The image reminded the agent of the 19th Century poem *Ozymandias* which he studied in school. As if Ray had once been a mighty Pharaoh, now worn to forgotten sands over time. The wind directing his vapor trail through the sculpture's right eye, sending his consciousness into another dream world.

The stream of vapor carrying him and what he believed was still Ally, over a surreal river of whitewater morphing into haunting women in white dresses. The women ran off in all directions, proudly holding up crimson, heart-shaped cards. His curl of vapor followed one of the women into a cave sculpted in a monstrous face reminiscent of a Hieronymus Bosch painting David blogged about. This world in a way, Ray reminded himself, was a projection of its game-mates. The stream of vapor carrying Ray followed the white garbed woman with her heart deeper into the darkness of the cave—

"ALERT!" his eComp system buzzed in his ear as he beheld the sobering image of the skull and crossbones warning across his opaque iScreen. It drew him out of this surreal world into some semblance of reality.

"Ray," his Siri told him, "I was able to scan Ally's system. She possesses files similar to Blackout's virus."

How could she possess a file with Blackout's virus? Only one dark outcome was plausible. With a subtle eye swipe, he dispatched his eComp to collect the files that appeared almost too quickly as a captured file icon across his iScreen before it dissolved.

His unseen Siri whispered to Ray in the darkness, "The content of the file data spiraled its own deletion. With time I might be able to unwind it and locate the original web I.P. address of its creator, but the content is lost."

What the hell was she doing with data spiral protocols, he wondered. Was she a hacker? This file might be more important than his murder investigation. It might mean she and others possessed copies of Blackout's virus.

Then he felt his body materializing beside her in the darkness as a dim glowing light surrounded them. Her hair swirling as if in zero gravity.

"This is the core of *Dreamspace's* operating system," she explained, "where the couples' arguments end. This is where David terminates his users."

Ray struggled to pry his mind from the fact that she possessed files originating from Blackout.

"He kills *Dreamspace* couples here?" she added.

"They don't get the respect of dying."

He didn't bother to hide his confusion.

"David merges two users into one player," she explained, "So there's no more argument because there's no more couple to witness the event differently. They become one person made from two-"

"So no GNS," interjected Ray.

"Exactly. I'm going to show you how this happens."

"Why me?"

"Fate brought me to someone senior enough to have killed Blackout," her eyes reminded him of Ravenna's as she explained, "You're going to warn the FCC before they rubber-stamp this crap as safe. He's keeping this from your agency. We're about to experience that secret."

Their floating bodies drew closer. Swirling ribbons of light sweeping around both of them. Streaks of colored light enveloped the two in a glowing cocoon. Ally's face glowing in the cradling, pulsing illumination. He hid the fear from his visage. She sensed his serenity as another behavioral trick the FCC inculcated within the agent. Because she knew no one could go through the merge the first time without being terrified, his feat merely highlighted his mastery of acting.

Then something strange occurred for Ally. For reasons she could not articulate, Ray reminded her of her mysterious ex whom she dated in her primordial *Dreamspace* cave. The user she would never truly know. The only one she ever thought could be her game mate, but who refused to meet her in the real world. Had it been this government agent in disguise? She remembered something her father told her as a little girl:

"Where there's one lie, there's more."

At that moment Ray reminded himself that he might be amidst a killer with a data file belonging to his late arch enemy. Their lips touching. The kiss radiating its heat through their bodies. He couldn't help but shut his eyes as inexplicable flickers of light sparked behind his closed eyelids. He felt a stream of foreign emotions race through him, sensations too loud as his body felt like it was racing forward:

"We're merging," he heard her whisper, "now you can know me."

In his mind, materialized what he figured must be a memory of Ally as a child in a carnival tent with a lumbering, mustached man, maybe her father. Then, a scene of firing guns in a game world he recognized as *FS8*. Images flashing in an ever faster staccato. He saw Ally making love to Ray's Asian murder victim in that bedroom back in Beijing. Then her point of view as she killed other men. One murdered with a knife in a garden by the sea. Another, thrown down the long stairway of a large house. Then other homicides in so many different times and places that Ray reckoned they must be in *Dreamspace* date worlds.

A human body with a cow skull head suddenly filled his range of vision with umbrellas all around, shielding this unsightly figure from a pouring rain of red blood. Ray suddenly felt like he was experiencing a heart attack that finally subsided in darkness as Ally whispered:

"Animal crackers with ranch dressing, you like that?" she giggled.

He knew what she was talking about. The weird food combination his boss, Joe Caresio, loved so much after a workout. Joe ate them with Ray when he was a cadet at the FCC Academy. Agent Kemper felt a fear of losing himself not to death, but being scanned like an open book by his murder suspect.

He somehow forced his eyes open and physically recoiled to see his own body merging with Ally's in a monstrous shape with four arms and legs. They were truly becoming one as his iScreen filled again with a blinking skull symbol and alarm. Over the alarm he heard his Siri warn:

"As we hack her, she's hacking us."

Ray desperately fought to separate himself from this monster with two backs still floating in the glowing light.

"I've seen enough of you, Agent Kemper," she allowed him to tear himself away, both their bodies separated and reconstituting, "If I show you any more, you're likely to geo-locate me in the offline world just like you did Blackout," his heart sank with her words as he realized this nut job was a fan of the mass murderer.

She giggled naked before him, "Ray, I don't see a future between an FCC agent and a hacker," she took off her earring, throwing it behind her before pulling her floating body through the opening web portal. She disappeared on the far side.

Quickly he bolted through the portal before it closed, discovering himself again in his chosen online clothes, standing in a crowd of strangers in another web corridor. Her portal dissolving behind him into vapor as he realized that Ally had already offlined. She had once again escaped.

Exxon didn't tease Ray.

By now Ally revealed herself in each encounter to be able to escape Ray's arsenal of tricks. Although his Chinese partner couldn't audit anything once they entered Dreamspace's operating system hub, he felt strangely confident Ray would meet her again. Ray was unable to possess his colleague's optimism in the matter.

Returning to the gym, the deflated FCC agent lost himself in another long workout before Exxon entered in tight black athletic pants and a stretch t-shirt. The Chinese detective stretched silently for almost an hour without speaking, until he turned to Ray with a dry grin:

"Why didn't you tell me you knew her before the investigation?" his auto-translation chirped in Ray's ear.

He stopped doing dumbbell flys, hiding his awe at his partner's assertion, "How did you know?"

"Instinct."

Without continuing the conversation in public, Ray brought his partner back to his hotel room; taking off both their eComps, Ray placed them in his hotel room safe and closed the door. Then he offlined all the media and shut down the master electric breaker. In silent darkness, he divulged the affair he'd had with Ravenna and the fact that Ally was most probably her identical twin. The Chinese detective remained silent in the dark Media Suite.

Deep down Exxon felt relieved, finally fathoming his partner's strange reaction during the World War II date, which struck him at the time as implausibly unprofessional. Exxon had feared that he'd wasted his time flying stateside to help an incompetent agent. But now it all made sense. After confessing, Ray felt like a walk.

In their rain jackets, they returned to the convenience store where Ray first met Ally. But Ray dared not enter. After all, he was now a public celebrity, the reason why he sported the hood of his rain jacket tight over his face. Because the nameless man the world believed ended World War IV was now the fastest-selling Skin on the market, surpassing even the Damon craze of late. Once he returned to his Media Suite and prepared for bed, Ray's Siri informed him:

"Ray. I unlocked the source of Ally's file that was similar to Blackout's virus. The file's data is permanently wiped. But I was able to identify its point of origin as Paris, France."

"Same city as Animal Lover."

"The file is also owned by Animal Lover. eInterpol just released the exact location on Animal Lover's I.P. address matching the coordinate in the file. We now have a visual of Animal Lover entering and leaving the building."

The face of *Animal Lover* filled Ray's iScreen. The FCC agent instantly recognized the visage of David Bellingham's protégé and co-designer, Pia Geller. The late thirties, blonde with those dreamy eyes Ray first beheld in the *Dreamspace* infomercial.

Agent Kemper soaked in the gravity of this discovery. So Pia possessed a corrupted source code to Blackout's Yin Yang digital virus. The same file Ally possessed. Did they know each other? It made no sense to him; how could Ally or Pia possess such a thing, even in its ruined form.

What else did they possess?

On his media screen, Ray called up paused footage on Pia from the *Dreamspace* commercial. Studying the lines of her face, he wondered if Ally was indeed innocent. He paused the footage of Pia and walked up to the actual wall screen, placing his hand on her face filling the sidewall of his Media Suite. He wondered if it was true-

Had he finally found his killer?

part five

Pia Geller

"Refrain your voice from weeping.
And your eyes from tears;
For your work shall be rewarded, says the Lord."

Jeremiah 31:16

eighteen

Pia could be his murderer.

FCC agent Ray Kemper always sensed this case could unfold into something more significant than the death of a well-connected, Chinese victim. At risk was the safety of the comport to protect users from foul play while online. There was no reasonable explanation for how the comport lid was opened unless from the inside by the user's manual release. A manual hydraulic button mounted in the frame of the inner bed. Now the former second in command of Bellingham Labs R&D Department seemed implicated, raising the new possibility of insider knowledge of how to open the device. Perhaps Pia also possessed some high tech software to wipe surveillance cameras and enter the home of his victim as well as his own Los Angeles hotel room?

Reclining in his transparent hotel bed, Ray listened as his Siri briefed him through details of Pia's life, "She was born in Opelousas, Louisiana, the same town as David Bellingham. The Gellers were part of a Jewish family who intermarried with local French-Cajuns since the late 1800s. The family historically owned and operated grain elevators and founded the local bank. They lost their fortune in the total collapse of the agriculture industry in 2039."

His Siri's words were accompanied by a local news video of Louisiana state police flanking a crane hauling a crashed hybrid minivan out of the muddy Atchafalaya River. An unseen newscaster narrated, "The car accident in Krotz Springs, Louisiana, plunged Pia's family vehicle into the Atchafalaya River. Her entire family perished with the sole exception of the then six-year-old Pia." The video cut to the little sandy-haired girl being wrapped in a blanket and placed in an ambulance in the pouring rain. "She claimed to have no memories of the crash. So authorities remained unsure if it was an accident caused by the rain or familial suicide due to her father's dire financial straits."

Then over-exposed home video footage of Pia her now 10, bony and thin, "Pia had no direct relatives and was mistreated by her foster care provider later incarcerated for abusing various children. At 11, she ran fled her second foster family in Opelousas. Walking many miles outside of town, she climbed through David's compound's fenced perimeter. Pia later claimed that she wished to be discovered by his roving security personnel to meet the famous inventor.

Watching the summary on his hotel room floor screen, Ray did push-ups as a famous Bellingham movie depicted a Hollywood recreation of David first meeting Pia in his original, online chat room.

David, in his early '30s at the time, sat across from the 10-year-old dismayed by this wondrous new digital world invention that seemed so real at the time:

"Why did you come here?" asked the actor who most famously portrayed David Bellingham in film.

The actress playing Pia replied, "I want to design games."

"Why?" David had asked many prior candidates as he cultivated what would soon become a massive corporation.

"I want to escape to the online world just like you."

It was the answer that famously got her the job as his co-designer. The movie's montage showed David funding Pia Geller's education, tutoring her in online design, "With his help," his Siri narrated, "Pia graduated from the prestigious Episcopal School of Acadiana before acquiring a philosophy degree at Tulane University. Pia then completed a postgraduate, doctoral degree in Quantum Symbolic Logic Programming at UCLA before returning to David's side to co-design *Dreamspace*."

Photos of a mid-twenties Pia with David's aging mother filled the media screens of Ray's hotel room. Paparazzi recorded them at David's favorite childhood burger stand, *Judice Inn*, in nearby Lafayette.

In a rare interview, David's mother curiously said of Pia, "I knew I would meet Pia decades before I met her. Perhaps why she feels like the daughter I never had?"

Then one sampling of the many gossip sites about the recent major event in her life, "Rumors swirling of Pia Geller's long fight with drug addiction, perhaps explaining her sudden disappearance before the teaser advance rollout for *Dreamspace* last February-"

Two years prior she vanished. Bellingham Labs claimed its star co-designer took a temporary leave of absence. Ray's government research found no trace of Pia through credit card billing, vid surveillance, or tracking analytics. She simply dropped off the grid. Conspiracy sites attributed Pia Geller's disappearance to everything from assassination to alien abduction. No one knew what happened.

She was never spotted again.

The company still had not formally addressed any reason for her inexplicable disappearance. But after she vanished, top employees of the company were barred from foreign travel. Ray wasn't sure why eInterpol had staked out Pia's Paris abode, but after discovering her whereabouts, they intentionally slowed down his investigation. Then hours later, David Bellingham surprisingly shed light on Pia's disappearance when he again met with Ray online.

The web agent approached the famed inventor casting a long shadow across his lone monolith. The government agent eyed the list of suspects spelled out in floating purple flames as the user ID for *Animal Lover* glowed brighter than the others.

"As you well know, Pia vanished," explained the inventor, "she escaped into the offline world, into a private video game of her making. One starkly different from *Dreamspace*," David sadly conceded as if Pia was soon to die, "a single-player game which naturally accelerated GNS."

The whole world knew about Gamer Neural Shock, the condition first inflicted by Dr. Tutwiler's initial game platform. Later experts postulated that David's young brain was malleable enough to allow his survival as he awoke through various offline and online worlds during his game play.

"Did you aid her in her game's design?" asked Ray.

"Pia made it without my knowledge. I've been struggling to find a way to explain her game to you ever since you requested our meeting. Sadly words cannot convey notions beyond experience. I can only show you the power it held over her when I forced her off of it."

With a hand gesture, David caused a floating power window to appear between the inventor and the FCC agent. A date and time stamp from November 13th, 2057 filled a black screen.

Then surveillance footage played, showing a bird's eye view of three uniformed Bellingham Labs' guards forcibly removing Pia from a comport. Bellingham's former co-designer howled as if she were burning alive, the tendons of her neck taught, her face red, spit flying in a tirade of profanities, degenerating into a primal scream.

The footage paused on the image.

"She created the fountainhead of human entertainment," David admitted, "a digital game world which was so alluring that even its creator could not bear to offline."

"Why'd she do it?" after all, reasoned Ray, Pia knew better than toying with a single-player, ultra-real game.

"Pia realized that escaping ourselves was what humans sought through entertainment."

"So what was her game's plotline?"

"It varied. Her software scanned a player's mind, usually extracting an intense situation from their memories. Something they hungered for."

"Enticing the heart over the mind," added Ray as his mind's eye was filled with the many hours he spent as a cadet studying his facial features in a virtual mirror. So he could wield his behavior as skilled politicians once did to manipulate the hearts of the many in ways constituents did not realize.

"Pia's was a game of the heart," replied David, "The player relived a past experience as if it were in the present. Living it cycle after cycle as the player became lost in a perfect flow of emotions so strong that one surrendered themselves into only the reality of the game."

"Then," Ray queried, "You just keep reliving an experience?"

"An experience that improves with each cycle to a level of emotional perfection not found in reality. Both *Dreamspace* and her game relied on forgetting the real world, but Pia's relied on living only within a series of moments."

When he first discovered Pia's secret game built from *Dreamspace's* programming codex, her mentor felt robbed-

"I didn't steal from you," she had told him in their private online chat room meeting, "Tutwiler created this code-"

"How far along are you in the GNS symptoms?" he felt so sad for her.

She said nothing more to him. David didn't know what to do except to confine his protégé to quarters under the supervision of armed guards. Only then did he study her game's programming architecture. Knowing he, alone, proved impervious to Gamer Neural Shock, he dared to enter her creation. Still he wouldn't allow her game software to scan his mind for a scenario; rather he decided to play as Pia, using her account and *selfie* Skin in-game.

Darkness surrounded him online as her game loaded. From out of the ethereal darkness her digital universe materialized him as her before the front door of a sushi restaurant. Inside he discovered a cozy establishment tucked just within the Santa Monica coastal flood wall. He caught Pia's reflection as himself in the mirror behind the cash register. The game felt so real that he forced himself to remember who he was.

She was clad in her favorite t-shirt of The Moo, ripped jeans, a rain slicker, and her favorite black *Hunter* English rain boots. David as Pia sauntered up to the sushi bar with a preternatural knowledge of her regular seat in a restaurant he'd never before visited. He knew he'd frequented this place, sensing the manipulative neural software wrapping its way around his consciousness.

After all, he as Pia came here every Saturday evening for many years. A vague realization bubbled free of the manipulative neural protocols, allowing him to realize that the past was indeed a constant character in the present. Everything in one's entire life was always within reach as it was in the offline reality. In contrast, *Dreamspace* seemed an archaic construct of pounding tension from an old-style movie.

David existing as Pia joined a familiar group of friends gathered at the sushi bar. She recognized these regulars. The old Japanese sushi chef standing behind the glass case of fish welcomed her with spread arms over an array of open sake bottles resting atop the glass counter. A cluster of diners had brought bottles to share with each other and the sushi staff. The meal harkened back to humanity's humble beginnings around their collective fires. Ally would've loved it, he mused, as the meal so resembled her cave.

Pia lifted the clear sake glass to her lips. The flow of time slowing to snapshots of moments like a *haiku* poem as she drank more sake, nibbling on Hamachi grown in domed, agro-fisheries in the flooded Midwest. Then she felt a profound sadness at the clink of the glass sake tumblers. Feeling the clear alcohol like her own life, ebbing towards an eventual end.

She eyed the burly, 60'ish, red-faced man appearing like a medieval friar beside her. David as Pia sensed this to be their last meal before the man died from complications related to esophageal cancer. A memory overtook Pia when she washed her hands alone weeks before in the restaurant's bathroom. Then she somehow divined the man's eventual demise like an ocean wave sweeping over her as the light bulb overhead flickered. Like one of the famous *stingers*, David blogged about.

That was when David saw a more recent memory lingering in her mind's eye from her past gaming. An incident that happened one night in her apartment bedroom at his corporate campus. A brilliant light filled the room. She turned and saw the floating sword of fire hovering in mid-air above her bed. Feeling the heat of its flames against her skin. She saw the glowing words traced in fire floating beneath it:

STOP DREAMSPACE

He figured the hallucination to be a unique symptom of GNS caused by her single-player game. The memory left Pia as quickly as it manifested in her mind. But he knew it had actually happened before he caught her with her game.

The memory was real.

Then, Pia's elegant software wrapped itself around his conscious mind. David Bellingham integrally lost himself as Pia Geller, an experience that would've driven anyone else, no doubt, perpetually into GNS.

Her game's storyline required no overarching plot except the complete loss of self. He tumbled down a rabbit hole, forgetting he was not her. Pia ate and drank to her heart's content in a never-ending carousel of the same dinner of friends. This pained orphan tasted a hint of a comradery long robbed from her by life. An endless feast of delicious sushi and sashimi washed down with the most beautiful sakes.

David had tasted so many wines in *Dreamspace*, but the refined, Japanese Django Junmai sakes were infinitely more complicated than any wine. Pia's memories of her many sips of sake offered by this jolly friend had by now instilled within her a connoisseur's knowledge: the judgment of the present taste informed by all the past ones. Sipping the *Nama* sake teaming with living enzymes brought on an ethereal inebriation unlike anything else. She read a bottle's label, titled *Miasaka Yamahai 50 Nama* spelled out in Japanese characters alongside a translated, English moniker:

THE LAST RIDE HOME

The irony of the sake's name was not lost on David as Pia. He as her, more than anyone, knew the last ride home to be the most vivid. When the proverbial sand in the hourglass was about to run out. A moment usually not appreciated as the last of something except in retrospect. The way the novelist Dostoevsky relished the beautiful reflection of the Sun off a church steeple only a moment before he was spared from being shot by Tsarist guards. Only as it was threatened did the human mind realize the childhood beauty long taken for granted. Or like his last glimpse of his true lover. Clawing ever after at the moment so it did not end. The reason why perhaps the Philosopher Heidegger invoked Van Gogh's humble painting of shoes on a floor as the most profound work of art ever created. Elemental simplicity in everlasting needs. For as long as there are humans, there will be lovers, shoes, and other essentials to differentiate from the needless fluff.

If David could have stood outside of Pia at this moment with an observer's clarity, he would've wept at *Dreamspace's* simplicity. How his game endlessly drove the love-interested protagonist back and forth through ever-increasing crests and valleys of heightening tension with their game-mate. Because humans detested happy stories, spending their free time in the stress and misery of others who were brave and did the right thing. For the heart yearned for that troubled life. While Pia's game, like the fractal algorithm, that it was constructed from, dove into the beautiful eternity of a grain of sand. Those escapes from alcohol, drugs, or diversions.

If David hadn't set the auto alarm three days before his Bellingham Labs board eMeeting, he never would have awakened from Pia's secret creation. Instantly the pain and loss of his real-life filled him, for how could it compare to her rich complexity and ability to walk and function in a body? He was again forced to realize he was paralyzed and trapped. But worse than that, his heart yearned for those feelings that had become like a sacred space to him in Pia's reality.

Even now on the monolith beside Ray, the inventor shuddered from the perfection of her game. His mind returned to it like a heroin addict forever chasing their first rush. In its wake, he couldn't help but feel the sorrow of Shakespeare's *Macbeth*, musing over life as a story told by an idiot full of sound and fury and in the end, signifying nothing. The view from only the moment. How David longed even now for that glass of *Nama* sake to flow across Pia's tongue in that realm of elegant nothingness. A feeling of connections with others, which he had only previously known in his ex-lover's cave.

But as if every pleasure came at a cost, the programming glitch in the long term *Dreamspace* game arose. He couldn't rely on Pia who was forcibly under the watchful eye of armed guards and might go public with the glitch if she found out. After the revelation she'd abused a single-player game, he figured her seemingly Divine visitation he witnessed with the flaming sword could be a delusion and not a memory. A symptom of GNS' breakdown of the brain and the source of her sudden religiosity just before she soon fled to peddle her game to rich users-

"Meeeow," the cat purred.

The animal's sound broke David's train of thought filling microseconds, snapping him back to the present. He eyed the feline's long shadow falling across Ray. The inventor's mind flash-backed to the first meeting with young Pia in that online chat room where she told him why she wanted to be a game designer. The real answer which neither divulged to others. Their secret even the movies missed. What struck David most in her response was the fact that she didn't describe any game world she wished to craft. Most got lost in the details and stage-craft when pitching themselves to work under him. The 10-year-old simply wanted to be where he was.

No one ever said that.

A willing traveler to journey with him. Her reply would've brought tears to his eyes, but he wouldn't do that in the company of a child or employee. It seemed for a time that David got it right with his protégé. After all, his mother took the wayward child under her wing, hosting her in the confines of their old home now surrounded by the new glass and steel lab complexes of his company's growing campus. A world ringed by barbed wire and roving guards after the first psychotic broke into his home and nearly killed him in his comport. Inspiring David to create the highly armored *Red Series* comports for himself and wealthy VIP users. Now David beat a quick path through the talking points he aimed to hand-off to Ray:

"Pia's secret game warped her mind. It made her sick. I forced her off it. I tried to destroy the game. And she fled."

He showed Ray more video of Pia before she fled. Restrained to a bed to keep her from thrashing and cutting her flesh with her nails. The withdrawals from her game rivaling any drug's fallout. She urinated and defecated on herself in the footage, screaming and begging to be plugged back into her digital creation.

"The symptoms of GNS blossomed in her mind," added David, "she spoke of the game like her lover, a living thing she could not be apart from. The actual danger of real artificial intelligence was not taking over the world, but merely the human heart."

Standing before Ray on the monolith, David's eyes turned up to the sick Earth above. Tentacles of lightning erupted within massive hurricanes covering the planet, reflecting the proverbial storm raging within Bellingham. That yearning even now to lose himself to her game. Two weeks after he offlined, he played a customized version of Pia's game, allowing it this time to scan his brain. What a hypocrite he was, calling her an addict while he secretly danced again with her digital lover. But he could tolerate GNS; he told himself.

Inside his comport in his Opelousas living room, David finally logged into Pia's customized creation as himself, which had taken two days to auto-render. The excitement and curiosity to see what it would conjure for him had filled his mind. For safety, he set an auto alarm to offline him after only two minutes of game-play.

He materialized in-game as an eight-year-old boy, standing in his parent's bedroom on that fateful night of his tragic accident.

His customized game beginning with his finger drawing back the trigger of his father's department-issued sidearm; shooting his dad through the hand and forehead. He saved his mother's life as the recoil of the weapon flung him back at a slightly different angle than what had occurred. The rear of his head barely missed the hard table's edge behind him. Laying unscathed on the floor, his eyes wide, breathless, still feeling his body-

He was terrified.

David Bellingham was now an ordinary boy with his entire life ahead of him. A great tragedy avoided. Running into his mother's arms, he felt the safety of a moment that truly never was. To exist as a healthy boy. Healthy now. Healthy—before he was forcibly offlined by his auto timer.

Shaken, he commanded his Siri to digitally wipe the program from all of Bellingham Labs' servers before he changed his mind. Erasing it from his corporate hard drives. David recollected again on that Japanese sake, titled *The Last Ride Home*. A final moment to soak it all in as it vanished. Perhaps explaining his odd relief when he later discovered Pia's escape with a copy of her game.

Barebones.

Just a codex backbone which still required many server farms to blossom her creation into even a fraction of what his massive servers had rendered. From the information the FCC agent now shared with him, he figured Pia was attempting to grow her competing game platform. The French president's office had alerted David that Pia was in Paris, but the inventor did nothing. His previous attempts to stop or capture her had all failed. The inventor recused himself in the hopes that a significant state apparatchik might achieve what his free agents from the private sector were unable to achieve for him.

The end of his protégé and her game.

"From our date," Ray divulged to David, "I think she was fishing for high-paying clients from *Dreamspace*. She told me that for the right price, she'd show me a game world to rival *Dreamspace*. But if she wants to be lost in her creation, why's she out hustling for money?"

"Money means more microprocessors and cooling units to better render her world. Without my company computers, she requires server farms to process even a base level of resolution. The sale of her game is aimed at procuring more of those servers. Since single-player games drive their users mad from GNS, maybe that had something to do with your possible homicide victim? Perhaps he went nuts and just killed himself?"

Ray declined to comment, promising, "David, I will get her."

Ray's words failed to persuade the inventor who warned, "Beware Ray, Pia's magic."

"Magic?" the agent looked incredulous.

"Creating super realistic game worlds is a dangerous art best left for God…"

His voice trailed off.

What was the point of telling the agent anything more? How could he share the directive his game-writing A.I. had revealed to him, wondered David. He knew the agent would never understand such power, nor fathom David's conviction that Ray was somehow like a mirror to him. Perhaps why the secretive inventor disclosed a bit more about the magic ultra-realistic game designers acquired? The unique power which David felt was similar to Einstein's mysterious force oddly named *Spooky Action At a Distance*. After this preamble, David shared with Ray the bizarre details of Pia's magic.

The agent listened in complete disbelief.

nineteen

David spoke.

The FCC agent listened. As much as he was a fan of the truths revealed in David's blogs, Ray found it difficult to believe the inventor's warning, even after the agent offlined from their virtual meeting. His mind kept toggling between the present and the memories of that meeting.

Thinking of the details even now.

Donning tinted sunglasses to match the fake beard he had delivered to his room, Ray appeared in the bathroom mirror like someone else. Not long after, the FCC agent boarded the Paris bound Delta space jet with Exxon in tow. The L.A. to Paris flight usually took an hour, but a stratospheric mega-hurricane covering the Arctic to Europe necessitated a bumpy, sub stratospheric, Southern detour over what used to be Africa. Inside his business class comport, Ray watched their flight progress over the Atlas mountain range island which along with the Sahara archipelago to its south, was all that was left of that continent. Due to turbulence, the Web Agent didn't immediately dock and online to the web through his comport as he commonly did. Instead, he took a moment to recollect on Bellingham's surreal warning about Pia Geller's supposed, *magic*.

According to David, his longtime design partner possessed the power to sway reality to her intended outcome. A passive observer would view this advantage as astonishingly good luck. The kind of success Napoleon prioritized over intelligence when picking his famed field marshals. Pia's cadre of Mongolian bodyguards, according to David, had witnessed this magic and took to worshipping her as a religious saint.

The Mongolians, all refugees from the flooded plains of East Asia, were now famous for their brutality and willingness to die for the elites they safe-guarded. Like a modern Swiss Guard. They could procure the impossible contraband from mainland China, such as outlawed Gamma drills or unnumbered mega caliber shells. Nor was this client like any other mercenary team. They lovingly gave up their lives for Pia, all dying prematurely from various combat-enhancing drugs eroding their hearts, taken to increase their battle reactions to better serve Pia.

"My company spent great resources to catch her," David had explained during their monolith meeting, "attempting to save her in our research lab from GNS. The closest I got to her was catching one of her bodyguards in Azerbaijan."

An eye swipe from David's iScreen generated a floating media window before them. In it Ray saw a guard in an interrogation room with the bruised and shackled bodyguard:

"You will never stop her," her follower ridiculed his interrogators before peering into the camera's lens, "you fools. Pia is a Prophet of the Universe!"

David's eye-stroke paused the footage as he told Ray, "Her power can be understood once you realize science was given to humanity by God."

Ray saved the inventor from explaining more by merely stating the date, "November 10th, 1619."

David smiled. In the inventor's reaction, Ray saw that David did previously believe the FCC agent was a true fan of his blog.

David continued in shorthand, "God created all things in six days. Pia and I created a crude simulation of his handiwork over many years. In doing so, we may have received the tiniest fraction of His power of creation in this reality."

"Can she make things appear like a genie?" inquired Ray.

"No," the inventor elaborated, "It's more subtle. Evident in things like George Washington's luck, which commonly left his clothes riddled with bullet holes while no shot ever struck him. Or the way weather always saved him."

Unknown to Ray, David omitted a great deal from his disclosure to the FCC agent whose cover the inventor secretly blew. David would never mention Pia's vision of the burning sword. He did, however, explain a power, which seemed somewhat religious.

Pia's parents had no religion. Genetically, she was an Israelite. Perhaps why she felt drawn to the ancient Old Testament's later description of God as the *Lord of Hosts*. An old Hebrew term implying that God controlled all the discrete units of the universe: the subatomic particles were parts of Him, up through atoms, molecules, cells, and life-forms all were limited manifestations of an infinite force. He and Pia used the same building blocks to attempt to craft *Dreamspace* from the ground up. But something in that architecture caused the system to fail, forcing users to see different phenomena from the same event.

Ray also omitted relevant facts during the meeting with David, such as Pia's exact whereabouts. Later in his Delta business class comport during the France-bound flight, the agent reexamined the European eInterpol agency's notification to the FCC of Pia's exact location. An 18th-century condominium along the *Quai Voltaire* overlooking the River Seine.

During the meeting on the monolith, Ray never considered David also knew his former co-designers' whereabouts. The French prime minister personally notified David by personal courier to his compound, speaking there online with the inventor in a private chat room. The French hoped to host Bellingham Labs' upcoming European headquarters in Paris, secretly giving the information to the inventor in the hopes that it might sway their chances over the other nations' bids. The French secret service shared the telemetry radiating over the internet lines from Pia's condo. David recognized the unique adaptation of the *Dreamspace* codex, revealing it to be her secret game.

On the Delta space flight, Agent Kemper reviewed the satellite and surveillance intelligence on Pia's lodgings in the building which possibly housed the 18th Century French philosopher, Voltaire shortly before his death. Now if David was to be believed, this residence hosted a modern technological philosopher, who refined her science into magic. The reason why Ray requested a second French tactical team and more flying, surveillance drones.

Standing on the second story landing just around the corner from Pia's Parisian front door, Ray still wondered if he should've ordered up a more significant force. Crouched behind the seven French soldiers, his eye swipe increased the air-conditioning inside his body armor. Despite the chill radiating through his mid-torso a.c. vents, the spider like-web-woven body armor always generated hotspots in the armpit and neckline areas beneath the massive, armored helmet. All of it to protect his body from potentially devastating, mega caliber ammo hits. Trickles of sweat ran from his neck down to his torso chilled by the rear vents.

The FCC agent stared into his iScreen now projected across the battle helmet's visor. Along the border of the semi-opaque margins flashed various live feeds from the five military snipers who had entered from the roof, now stationed around the upper-level hallway beneath the massive crystal chandelier. It towered over the open, four-storied marble atrium of the front doors to the building's apportioned condos. Various snipers' crosshairs hovered over Pia's front door, one of three units on this second-floor landing. Not far away with other armored police, stood Ray. The agent huddling behind the task force gathered in the corner and out of sight of her front door.

"We're ready," the French squad leader's words were auto-translated in English through Ray's helmet comlink.

The FCC agent's armored gloved hand wrapped around his mega caliber handgun. The majority of the strike force were French-Arabs, descended from the immigrants forcibly uprooted from the Middle East to Europe. The largest forced migration since the Second World War in what historians now termed the *Obamination or Obama Forced Migration*; a needless product of his broken promise about the Syrian red-line in a dithering foreign policy which undermined the world in favor of China and Iran.

The only soldier not of Middle Eastern descent was the commander knocking his armored fist against Pia's 18th Century front door. Before the operation, the leader's dark skin and Caribbean accent identified him as another island immigrant whose home now lay far under the sea from the flooding and rain.

The lead agent's fist wrapped a second time at the door as his helmet's integrated battle camera recorded his point of view. He spoke over his helmet's mic, "Ms. Geller, this is the police. Under FCC authority-"

A blast of light—

The leader's arm was severed at the shoulder, the limb flying like a projectile across the atrium. The second mega caliber gunshot from the far side of Pia's door caught the commander in his heavily armored chest, blasting him into the strategically placed backup soldiers, sending them both out through the shattered atrium window. They violently landed on parked cars in the inner courtyard beyond, their video feed turning to static.

Ray's instincts kicked in.

His visor superimposed a target crosshair synched to his weapon's barrel. An eye swipe altered the border of his iScreen so he could see the POV's of the many drones hovering over the building in the rain. Ray did something quite rare for most humans, but familiar in his trade-

Rushing into danger.

Ravenna loved this part of the job. Drawn into the moment so much that she lost herself. Ray didn't share such a thrill from combat. But once felt, this state of war became a self-evident truth never to be shed. Post Traumatic Stress Disorder wasn't a disorder at all, believed Ray, but reflected a society so long out of touch that it failed to realize its legal order was based on the near-constant pain and killing, reinforcing that state as the baseline of reality for those who felt it.

Brilliant explosions from mega shells erupting around Ray and the French soldiers ahead. They charged through a now shattered, wooden doorway concealed in billowing smoke. A mega caliber slug struck a soldier just ahead of Ray, sending him flying backward past him like a cannonball. Ray by now melted into a series of reactions and well-honed instincts.

Exxon charged parallel to him, or so he had thought. The agent wasn't thinking now of his quasi-partner. No matter what the technology, the lines between bravery, stupidity, and survival in these conditions was more blind chance, so why entertain fear? Ray's feet and hands moved with a will of their own at speeds too fast for thoughts. The foyer spilled into a grand salon, which he'd studied in the blueprints of her residence before the mission. Now the room remained obscured in smoke bombs punctuated by bursts of gunfire.

In that salon's far corner, Pia Geller remained calm, suspended in her long-term immersion comport. Still lost to the throes of her digital game world, she was already alerted on her iScreen but knew the protocol. She would remain online as long as possible. Her positive feelings in-game protected her bodyguards with a *magic* best described as spooky luck commonly misunderstood because it occurred at such an odd distance and high frequency.

Her game currently processed through the many black-market Wan Yu banks of Quark Processor chip computers filling her entire apartment. These eight-foot-high, black rectangle-shaped computer processors resembled giant dominos due to their white cooling dots. The *chips* as they were nick-named, stood stacked on end, covering the walls in encroaching piles that corralled the strike force into a curving channel in the center of the large salon. Ray couldn't see the massive cooling dots, many of which already pierced with bullets, sprayed out plumes of liquid nitrogen Ray originally mistook as his enemy's smoke bomb.

With the intruders in her Paris refuge, Pia Geller knew she must leave her game, but first awaited instructions from her guards buying her more time. Her heart by now was devoid of fear. She'd beaten incredible odds many times from David's assassination attempts on her life. Her levitating body inside her special comport was not sorcery, but rather the magnetic threads of her jumpsuit repelled by recessed magnets within her comport's inner bed. Suspended aloft, she was protected from bedsores. I.V. lines and her elegant waist belt serviced her biological needs and excrement, as she seldom offlined.

Reality had become too confining and dangerous to her. Especially after Australia, when David's killers nearly surrounded her team in Cairnes. Just after she fled, Pia suffered panic attacks, but three years of escaping made her more secure in her arcane superpowers.

Now seated at the sushi restaurant counter in her world, she eyed video footage of the violent melee projected across a floating power window only she could see. It felt like fiction and this place, reality. Savoring the final moments of a beautiful meal more perfect than any imaginable. A profound sense of contentment passed through her that could've made her stay in-game to meet her death. But once alerted, the illusion of her reality must be accepted. It was a game and if she wished to return here again, she must soon offline.

Outside the comport hosting her body, a thick waist-high iron wall acted as an added protective barrier for her comport. Her guards created multiple escape paths after what happened in Manaus Island, now all that was left above sea-level in what had been Brazil. In the wake of that second attack, she kept the 9mm semi-automatic pistol strapped to her leg even now inside her comport. And the electronic jamming amulet was strapped around her arm along with combat boots already secured on her feet.

Pia and her bodyguard disciples war-gamed many home invasion scenarios in an online space mimicking this apartment and the surrounding blocks. She knew to wait for her Siri to identify the ideal escape route. Most of her live video feeds were blinded by the misting, liquid nitrogen from the processing chips, forcing her attackers into a thin column through the center of the main salon.

The pre-frozen ice across the wooden floor caused the assault team to slip and fall just ahead of Ray, who now struggled to maintain his balance. The ice had been hidden due to the hydra-foil insulation sheets lining the floors and walls. Slipping and sliding across the frozen floor, Ray fired at multiple Mongolians shooting at him from above the low slung wall in the corner forward of him.

The blast of his gun rocketed Ray backward, careening him into the iron wall from which the mercenaries fired at him.

Inside her comport behind this low slung wall, Pia mused at the irony of the moment: real-world gunmen sent to kill or capture her because of a new creative direction she chose over a video game. Who would've ever previously believed such a thing?

If her game did cause GNS, then it was the most pleasant way to pass through life to an inevitable end. But most importantly, it was unlike *Dreamspace*. So perhaps with enough users, she could stop David's game and fulfill the request made of her by the burning sword she had witnessed in offline reality.

She was long inspired by the 20th Century filmmaker, Alfred Hitchcock, who predicted cinema would evolve beyond plot, becoming an instrument feeding a series of emotions into the audience's minds. Hitchcock grasped that essential truth which David could not accept: entertainment was not about the stage-craft, but the feeling at its most heightened, stirring the heart in an alluring sequence like Mozart's great symphonies. Severed from the real world for his entire life, David could not grasp this point no matter how hard she struggled to make him realize it.

Her eye swipe offlined her from her perfect sushi dinner, returning her soul to her mortal coil in reality. The holographic glass lid of her comport retracted into its armored shell. The sting of gunpowder filled her nose. Eyes closed, she kept the earplugs into her ears when she onlined.

Rolling out of the comport, slithering across the frozen floor of ice. Monstrous, mega caliber bullets ricocheted so close that two ripped the fabric of her jumpsuit while none touched her flesh. Just like George Washington, David's great hero. Even that founding father's most significant military blunder on July 4th, 1754 which started the French and Indian War became his crowning success. His mistake, after all, began the war that later forced the British crown to raise taxes to offset the cost of the conflagration. That English tax birthed the American Revolution, creating a new nation on July 4th, 1776. A country Washington headed as its first President and thereby showed humanity that there was another option to kingly rule.

Luck could change the world.

Eyelids pressed closed; she opened the circular hatch adorning the concrete wall just as one of her bodyguards fell over dead beside her. His hollow gaze no longer registered her entering the secret tunnel. But a reverence remained in his eyes. Her protectors felt for her as the primitive Indians centuries before had treated Christopher Columbus; after his almanac allowed him to pretend to cause a solar eclipse and save his and his men's lives. A feat made possible only because Sir Isaac Newton's predicted the movement of heavenly bodies at any moment in the past, present, or future.

Pia climbed into the cramped tunnel behind her comport. Two more bullets passed like razors across her cheek without grazing her flesh. The reason why she didn't fear them as she had in the beginning. Approaching the mouth of the tunnel carved through cement ahead, Pia noticed the spotlights of circling drones above her rain-soaked, Paris stronghold. She no longer had to remind herself that every outcome was already written in a seemingly endless wave of possibilities in the physical world. She merely focused on the result she wished to achieve, reducing the stream of infinite possibilities to a strand of singular, ideal outcomes like pearls strung along her favorite necklace.

Opening the loosely connected grate at the tunnel's end, she spotted the lights of the drones cutting through hail and rain above the Parisian rooftops. Knowing the countless cameras on those flying drones connected to eyes searching for her. Innumerable observers with the purpose of her capture or death. She was not afraid. Pia loved that the universe cared enough to author every possible outcome for her in what she believed was a test for all humanity. But God charged her with stopping the game. A task her *magic* could still not achieve.

Still, Pia took a moment to let the love of her Creator pass through her being, hoping she would not fail. A love not based on faith, but through science's birth and all, she'd physically experienced. Stepping out onto the Parisian rooftops in the rain, her protection became evident in a bolt of lightning temporarily blinding all the drone cameras; allowing David's ex-designer to race unmolested beneath them. Darting under the cradle of lightning bolts stunning the drones, their powerless metal bodies crashed lifelessly into the streets surrounding her building. She knew this manifestation was Him inside of her reality.

Sprinting across the slippery rooftop in the rain, Pia felt something akin to the certainty George Washington held that he would one day do a great thing. She visualized a wave of possible outcomes in the coming moment, imagining them like petals radiating from a flower's center, each representing a possible present. The infinite results expanding into endless bouquets of branching paths already forged by her Creator. A unique Pia stood on each petal. The distinct Pia's in each of their many, singular outcomes, considered each to be the only one in what was truly a bouquet of endless, but differing, Pia Geller's. She lost herself in that beautiful geometry, using her heart to find its way to God's intended outcome for her. No plan. Only He could see so far ahead.

So she never felt alone.

Looking back, Pia saw His hand in all the good and adverse events of her life. Science and religion were complementary, just like fate and free will were not contradictions, but two sides of the same coin. As Einsteinian relativity dictated, each observer relied on a certain biased point of view. For any view had to be from some prejudicial position of space and time. Looking backward into the past anyone could note a chain of singular outcomes they believed encapsulated their life. While peering forward revealed the infinity of possibilities God allowed. That prerequisite reduction of the infinite to finite, such as the present moment, was what humans termed *living*. She was at ease with all contradictions, woven into the unity of her Creator.

Through this logic and emotional vein, Pia Geller displayed the power of Plato's mythic philosopher-king. All those past thinkers wasting their lives feuding over the reality of the outer world versus the inner universe of the mind. When truthfully it was all God: the missing link to bond together everything into the much sought after *unified field theory* that eluded Einstein. An infinite wellspring where mind and body converged like two rivers both reflecting the **Creator**. Her love for God now filled her. Running in spiritual rapture, she found her mind transported back to her second to last meeting with David:

"Have you ever seen a floating, fiery sword?" he inquired with a devilish grin from across the table.

"Yes," she felt relieved, "so you saw it too?"

He negatively shook his head.

Then she figured it out, utterly surprised, "You played my game?" she couldn't believe it, "'Mr. anti-one player' breaks his prohibition."

"I figure the sword is a hallucination brought on by GNS-"

"David, I know what I saw. It was real. It was like the sword that guarded Eden."

"So we're in Eden?" mocked David.

"Outside of Eden. Fighting as God warned for our provisions to just survive. Where we live and die, studied all the while perhaps by unseen others just like we audit *Dreamspace* beta testers. We had all we needed in Eden. But we couldn't behave under one rule in paradise, so our sins cast us out. Driving us out, in fear of dwindling resources, we over-consumed everything. Producing beyond what any garden except Eden could fulfill. So we built a false digital garden with everything that we're truly barred from entering. We did wrong. These games just divert us from reality. He won't allow that. He always gets involved when the mass-free will is at stake. Hence the sword as a warning to us here."

She could tell from his pejorative grin that her words meant nonsense to him, "Pia, we aren't in reality. Nor are we even in a digital online chat room right now. I'm in the latter back portion of my brain. You are in your cerebral simulation in yours. We're never able to escape the prisons of our minds."

"Descartes began science by first proving the immortality of our souls which have no prisons. Imagine what our world would have been if his followers hadn't hidden God's hand in science's birth? With people looking inward for the greatest wisdom, just as science's creator pointed the way"

"But they didn't," sighed David, "and we're picking up the pieces-"

"Those pieces never get picked up. The glitches in *Dreamspace* are from God, from within your users. Their inner Temple is doing it. The same reason why subatomic particles behave differently when we study or try to record them. This is also why our attention is power," Pia pointed at herself, "That temple channels God's energy through each of us as pieces of Him. Consciousness. He left us with the freedom to use ours to shape reality through our actions."

"So the sword means keep out?" he probed.

She nodded yes, her intense eyes ablaze, "Our creation seeks to silence God by denying the truths of the real world which is our legacy. It's Him. You can deny His existence, but no one gets to deny reality or we're the Dodo bird, soon to go extinct from a murder we don't even realize-"

"You've turned God into 'magic'."

"Then what word would you choose to explain how group meditation in Washington DC circa the 1990s lowered the local crime rate? How is that possible, David? Give me the method to describe such a spooky action at a distance. It's His portal within us!"

They touched on this point before this conversation, but Pia didn't know that events would later prove her words at this moment influenced new notions in David. For she would never guess the Divine notice his game-writing analytics later told him. It was hard for David to consider starting again from scratch. All that lost time. Just as she felt she'd lost, having never truly spread her alternate game in the hopes of stopping David and fulfilling her Maker's will.

Her greatest regret.

Surrendering the fact about group meditation lowering crime rates. When David retorted about the power of the human mind to reshape reality, she realized she had inadvertently shown him how to weaponize *Dreamspace* against humanity. Her mentor would deny humans' inner temple. Turning the game into a monstrous creation God, Himself, warned her to stop. The data she gave David later earned her a death sentence from her former mentor. Because only Pia Geller knew what dark purpose David Bellingham intended to release from his game. The reason she remained so resolute, sprinting across the roof, knowing-

The fate of all humanity was at stake.

twenty

Pure blasphemy.

Only the thought of David's secret destiny for *Dreamspace* quickened Pia's pace across those Parisian rooftops. She ignored the bullets zipping past her from some unseen source. An electric bolt struck the drone firing at her, sending the flying contraption nose-diving in the storm towards the River Seine. David might have as well have dispatched it. All part of his misguided attempt to save humanity, which would sow its condemnation, she ardently believed.

In the Bellingham Labs' online chat room two and a half years prior, as she attempted to recover from withdrawals from her game, they last spoke face to face. David had already forced her out of her game and locked her into a secured hospital room. She finally agreed to use the room's comport, *on-lining* to meet up in their design chat room. He revealed the *Dreamspace* glitch and his remedy:

"The DC Group Meditation gave me the solution."

Perhaps it was his tone or the glint in his eye. She had come to know the inventor as a brother. The moment David brought up this point, Pia fathomed his plan. She became suddenly attuned to the fact that she was in an online chat room in a digital realm David Bellingham controlled. While her body resided within a corporate comport where she could indefinitely be kept as his prisoner.

She reflected on how the 20th Century physicist Niels Bohr must've felt when his colleague and friend, Warner Heisenberg, attempted to recruit him to invent the atomic bomb for Hitler. This meeting with David proved equally grave for humanity. The reason why she resolved like Bohr, to flee at the first possible chance.

David figured out how to solve his glitch, "I merge two players into one to prevent the in-game aberrations," he explained, "by forcing unification of their senses into one, they now see the same event. The glitch is gone."

"But you lose the gamers," she countered.

"I like to think we're evolving them," he smiled, "so they can remain in-game."

The online meeting abruptly ended.

A lightning strike from a rainstorm fried the electrical systems at Bellingham Labs' north campus. She offlined in the comport to find the front door to her locked room now lay open. Back then, she questioned such luck, suspecting some sympathetic employee had set her free. Immediately she fled, discovering a nearby Jeep with keys in the ignition. She soon found the front gate wide open, having shorted from the lightning strike. She nearly ran over the guard manning the open road, racing out into the relative safety of a torrential downpour. Penniless, alone, without even her driver's license, she reached the nearby town of Lafayette, unsure of how to continue. But step by step—

She survived.

Even this evening she escaped one of the greatest hunters in the world. FCC agent Ray Kemper now had to admit that his mission turned into a fiasco. The French police lost ground to Pia's guards who tripped them up with the iced floor. Although Ray didn't know it during the explosive gun battle, Pia's bodyguards wore retractable ice skate blades extending from their boots, rendering them more nimble than their clumsy, unprepared attackers. Most of the French agents were blown backward from the recoil of their mega caliber rounds, sending them flying rearward on the ice. The camera lenses of the law enforcement official's guns recorded every moment for post-mission auditors. Colliding into a cooling system, Ray spun around to see the burly, ice-skating Mongol gliding up, aiming his mega caliber weapon at Ray's head.

Ray's subconscious scanned the geography of space-time around him. but discovered no solution. He prepared to die until the Mongol was shot directly in the face. Ray turned to realize Exxon had killed the attacker from the rear corner, saving Ray's life. Then, one of the French soldiers lobbed a grenade behind the low-slung wall. The explosion blasted three Mongol guards from behind it up into bloody pieces. One of their bones left a large scratch in Ray's battle visor and would've killed him had he not been armored. More often than not the body-parts, not the bullets got you. As the liquid nitrogen mist died down, the remaining Mongols ducked behind the waist-high iron wall.

The firefight ended.

Ray and Exxon followed the French police working in two-man advance teams towards the low, iron wall. They expected a volley of return fire from the protected position, but the most forward French officer advised that the others that the bodyguards were somehow gone. Ray slid on his armored belly along the ice to the low slung wall, lifted himself over it to spy the comport hidden behind it. Behind the device, he eyed the wooden hatchway door mounted in the concrete wall.

He kicked open the tiny hatch with his armored boot, peering down the long concrete tunnel bored through the old stone wall. Feeling as if he gazed down into that subterranean passage from Alice in Wonderland, the proverbial rabbit hole. Gun drawn ahead of him, FCC agent Kemper spotted a Mongol bodyguard fleeing from the tunnel's far end and out onto the Parisian rooftop in the rain and lightning. He quickly crawled down the tunnel thanks to the padded knee joints of his armored suit, followed by Exxon and the six surviving French soldiers.

Rain pounded his visor as he made it out onto the old rooftop, able to make out little in the hail and mist. On another rooftop far ahead of Ray, Pia Geller ran for her life. Her silver, magnetic jumpsuit reflected flashes of lightning in what became a brilliant hailstorm. She knew now that if she died, there would still be enough users of her illicit game to constitute an alternative operating system for humans soon destined to live online in video games all the time. Robbed of the memory of themselves and their nightmarish world their species wrought.

Her life's purpose was now to stop the world from *on-lining* in *Dreamspace*. The slick Chinese club developer seemed a promising networker for influential Asian buyers of her game. But his untimely death led the authorities, no doubt, back to her. She could tell by the size of this strike force and the army of flying drones that this operation was not David's alone. No, she reflected as she ran, this was an FCC field mission.

After the club developer was supposedly killed, she took the precaution of having a Mongolian bodyguard eHack the dead man's mansion surveillance system. That was how she first discovered FCC agent Ray Kemper during his visit to that home with the local detective.

Her team tracked his movements after that. She planned to kill him in his Los Angeles Hilton hotel room after she stole back the comport hard-drives. But her plan failed. She never got those drives, still fearing its user history files could reveal her business transaction over her game with the victim, possibly leading authorities to discover the other sold copies of her game. She used David's unique software she had helped develop to blind video cameras to one's presence. But the skilled agent offlined earlier than expected and nearly killed her in his hotel room. She would've been dead if not for that software covering her tracks out of the hotel-

Now her textured boot soles unexpectedly slid across the wet, Paris rooftop. Regaining her balance, she refocused on the present, knowing her well-trained hunter could not be far behind. Sprinting faster through hail giving way to rain, she followed the semi-opaque, three-dimensional arrows watermarked on her iScreen.

Two rooftops and a street behind her, FCC agent Ray Kemper pursued the rogue game designer. He tracked what he thought was her thermal signature on his iScreen. The bouncing blob of radiating color moved in a quickened gait. Ray kept glancing around for her bodyguards, expecting an ambush. When he peered back, the FCC agent saw only Exxon and the remaining six French soldiers lagging behind him. As he turned back, a Mongol leaped from behind a sloping roof, shooting at Ray's head. The bullet grazed his armored helmet as Ray shot the attacker square in the face. The Mongol's now headless body fell back, flying off the roof and into the rainy mist.

Many paces away, Pia's iScreen revealed she'd lost another of her protectors as she puffed on her neural drug inhaler. Her pulse surged. Eyes dilating as she leaped with superhuman ability across the wide street below. Advancing from behind, Ray saw her clear the considerable distance to the next roof. He was forced to race sideways to where the road below narrowed so that he could clear the decreased gap. Jumping across the street, he noted his team's eComps were all momentarily disrupted by a lightning strike. The distraction would've made a less-trained agent lose their footing when landing on the opposite roof in near-blinding rain.

With an eye swipe, the FCC agent switched off his thermal scanner, naturally sighting his prey 10 paces ahead, her silhouette temporarily illuminated by the lightning. Pia's feet pivoted around on the wet roof as she turned to face Ray. He was not close enough to see her expression; she eyed him with the detached look of a religious martyr, accepting of her fate and devoid of fear. She didn't jump off the building as much as she gave herself up to the outcome.

Falling out of Ray's view

The world tumbled by as the rooftop left Pia, sending her plummeting off the building and into a trash dumpster five stories below. She landed with the precision of an Olympic athlete, adeptly leaping to her feet and rushing off down the *Parisian Left Bank* avenue shielded in rain awnings.

On the roof, Ray reached the edge and leaped into the dumpster below, nearly catching his armored arm on the side of the metal dumpster. With an eye swipe, he shed his spider-web ballistics armor, which hindered his pursuit. He leaped up in only his black lycra shirt, which with an eye-stroke could light up in the bold letters, FCC. He didn't want that as a bull's-eye for her bodyguards who might lurk ahead, lying in wait.

Racing in his waterproof jeans and combat boots now free of their armored shell. The agent smelled incense in the air as he snaked through the crowded street. Passing over an owner locking up a brasserie as a duet of The Moo and Stumbleweed played from a Karaoke bar next door. Rain pelted Ray's determined face as he hunted his target. Following Pia into an outdoor bazaar, which shut down the street. Beneath plastic rain tents strung across the street, Ray darted between a row of kabob and pastry stands bordering the evening flea market of vintage *glow in the dark* curios.

Fluorescent colored items that were so popular nearly twenty years ago in the early '40s now radiated under black lights strung along the inner face of the rain awnings. Shoppers noted the muscular agent with his mega caliber handgun racing by. Through his auto-translation, Ray heard someone asking where the camera was, assuming he must be an actor in some web-film.

The Moo's pop hit *Infinite Sunshine* pulsed from unseen speakers lining the bazaar. Ray veered around a pop-up media billboard showing a shapely, Swedish woman peddling *Fraska's Insect Bars* as another of Pia's guards rushed out, ambushing the agent in close quarters. The FCC agent shot the Mongol dead without slowing his pursuit. Various spectators' eComps snapped vid pics of Ray's blindingly skillful moves.

"That is one realistic mask," a pedestrian's comment was auto-translated in his ear, "you look just like Blackout's killer!"

Many observers gestured at his likeness now filling the Mr. Zero ads on the media walls flanking the border of the night market. The light from this Mr. Zero ad ironically illuminated Ray's face as he bolted past shoppers. Weapon extended before him, he drew a line of sight on Pia's bobbing head amidst the crowd of shoppers, snapping more pics of the agent ready to shoot Pia. Some now laughed, thinking his pursuit to be a web spoof. A focused Ray pursued Pia towards a line of drone sky taxis cued on the perpendicular street bordering the night bazaar.

After the Beverly Hilton incident, the ex-designer did not wish to duel in a gunfight with this expertly trained FCC killer. Racing towards the forward most drone taxi, she knew he would overtake her before she reached the possible getaway vehicle. Grabbing the 9mm holstered to her thigh, she slowed to spin around in the rain and fire at Ray who had quickly closed the gap between them. She could not reach the drone taxi in time. So in the heat of the moment, she abandoned certainty and found herself calling upon the Universe once again for luck.

Before Ray could discharge his weapon, the Cosmos possibly answered Pia's call as a woman coincidently walked between them, blocking Ray's line of fire. The former game designer pushed the unsuspecting female at the FCC agent only a few paces behind; then the ex-designer threw herself into the sky taxi. Pia never registered the baby in the woman's arms until the screaming infant flew through the rain. Dropping his weapon, Ray leaped forward, catching the infant like a football, cradling the child close to his body as he rolled across the hard ground and sprang into the sky taxi just ahead of the closing door.

Inside the drone taxi, Ray spun around. He attempted to hand the baby back to the hysterical mother, now visible through the window of the closed hatch. For the briefest of moments, the baby cooed at the frightened face of his young, French mother visible through the drone's sole window. Raindrops framing her visage before she suddenly disappeared as the vehicle shot up into the rain-soaked sky.

Lightning erupting in a sea of clouds.

Inside the flying vehicle, the baby turned apoplectic. Still cradling the red-faced infant close to his chest, the FCC agent turned to face the ominous-looking woman crouched in the shadows between the third and fourth row of the clear bench seats.

Pia reckoned the interior to be about twice the size of her passenger van, nothing more than a conventional payload box covered in media screens like the web. She vanquished David's killers up to now and would do it again, she believed. Summoning every advantage from her study of the Copenhagen School of Quantum Mechanics as well as God, she visualized her desired outcome before adding an extra edge she procured in reality; puffing on her inhaler now set to *strength*.

The red seat belt light flashing intermittently against the interior media screens, bathing crimson light across her face as a notice in French requested all passengers to fasten their seat belts. Her Siri had hacked the flight protocol to trigger the early take-off but the taxi still noted the additional weight and paused in mid-ascent in the rain. Pia touched the amulet strapped to her upper arm. The device was crafted to appear like the popular trend of arm bracelets. Her finger pressed the center of the sculpted gem, which lit up, instantly jamming the drone taxi's web connection. A skull and crossbones symbol filled the six media surfaces of the interior payload bay.

"Warning!" an automated voice alerted the cabin in alternating French and English, "this taxi has been illegally off-lined."

The warning's loud voice sent the baby into frightened howling. On her iScreen, Pia set the new destination of the vehicle through her software's virtual map. Redirecting the drone to the preset rendezvous point North of the Belgian border. The sky taxi suddenly banked left, knocking Ray, cradling the baby, into the right side of the media surfaces. Pia turned her attention at her pursuer, taking in his dark silhouette across the cabin too small for a fight. The infant clawed at the agent as she felt his eyes upon her.

"Warning!" the automated voice overhead spoke in French and then in English, "this drone taxi has been forcibly hacked and continues to remain offline from the web. We apologize for any inconvenience."

Ray understood he was in a cage controlled by his prey. Eyeing Pia 15 feet back as she puffed again on the inhaler. Although he could not see it in the half-darkness of the interior, her pupils dilated. Her senses instantly sharpened as Pia jumped across the benches toward the FCC agent still cradling the baby with one arm. Ray knew that a gunshot here might suck them all out of the flying vehicle.

He struggled to fend her off.

She was inhumanly strong. Hand tight around his neck as she slammed him up into the cramped ceiling with seemingly superhuman strength. The power he recognized not as *magic,* but the product of those life threatening neural drug inhalers her bodyguards favored and she kept for emergencies. His thick body held aloft by only her slender arm. Pia's iron grip tightening around his throat, strangling a red-faced Ray on the verge of blacking out as the baby continued to wail. The agent lost control of his limbs, inadvertently dropping the screaming infant caught by Pia's free hand.

Before passing out, Ray surged with one last burst of energy, allowing him time to swat the tiny amulet from her arm as she held the baby. The jamming device fell to the floor. The force of the impact pressing the mounted crystal, severing the pirate mode.

The drone taxi announced, "Hacking stopped. Now reconnected to the web."

The vehicle banked right, tossing them like rag dolls across the cabin. Pia brimmed with anger, realizing her senses had betrayed her, forcing her to catch a baby when the entire human race was at stake!

The flying vehicle veered back to Paris as a virtual voice stated in French and repeated in English, "*Ce taxi de la ciel retours a la point d'origine. Les autorities ont ete informees…*this sky taxi is returning to its point of origin. The authorities have been notified."

The authorities now could triangulate her initial, pirated flight path. She couldn't hack her way through the air surveillance network with her cover now blown. The FCC no doubt had satellites in space focused on her flying vehicle at this very moment. She had to force a landing and risk it on foot. The entertainment system somehow activated. The Moo, iconic in France, filled the four taxi eWalls as the gold-painted rock star sang his classic rap gangsta hilo croog hit of '39, "Rave for Dave."

The singer's voice sounded so compelling that even the baby in Pia's arm stopped crying, the infant staring up transfixed at the gold-painted pop idol crooning about David Bellingham's famous campaign against the Political Correctness hearings. The video on the ceiling showed the gold-painted rock star dancing his way down a staircase of contorted human bodies as golden cupids flew by holding a banner marked "THE MOO'S THE REAL FIZBIT!"

That image glazed across Ray's eyes as Pia caught him in a chokehold with one hand, nearly crushing his windpipe. He felt as trapped as in that coffin in *Dreamspace*. A final rush of his endocrine system as the baby howled in Pia's cradled arm. Ray was almost dead. The last jolt of adrenaline sharpening the agent's senses to buy him a few more seconds before he expired, giving him just enough time to kick the baby from Pia's arms.

Again she reached out for the flying baby as Ray stole a puff from her inhaler, which he had spied sticking out of her metallic jumpsuit's breast pocket. Her fist knocked the inhaler from Ray's mouth so rapidly that the agent never saw the dial had been moved to *agility*. He deduced his enhanced power as he nimbly escaped her grasp with acute precision and clarity, grabbing the falling baby, before artfully ducking around Pia's lumbering fist, which swatted only air.

"I spared you in your hotel room!" she heaved as Ray set the baby under the bench and nimbly flipped back from her reach. Pia charged at him like a thundering bull, launching an iron punch at his head.

Ray ducked as her hand slammed into the hard, holo-glass window behind him. The super-hardened glass crushed her limb like a collapsed accordion of shattered bone and blood. The fight was over, illustrating why humans could never possess super physical power. Color ebbing from Pia's face alongside her flailing energy. She bled profusely from her damaged limb as strobing blue police lights now filled the interior cabin through the lone door window. The media on the meta surfaces suddenly played the child rockstar, Stumbleweed's homage to *Alice in Wonderland-Grin Without a Cat*.

Her song played as French authorities escorted the flying vehicle down towards what would be revealed as a rural, French field in the pounding rain. The occupants of the drone taxi with the sole exception of the still howling infant in Ray's arms knew it was over. The neural drug had the agent's heart racing as he tried to gather information from a dying Pia:

"You designed the program to block the video camera footage at the crime scene, didn't you?" he intoned it as a statement rather than a question.

She shook her head no, "The one who made it," she gasped between throbbing pain, "the one who infected us through our…" her lips went silent as she eyed her fallen eComp on the floor beside her.

Then her body inexplicably stiffened. What happened next was something FCC agent Ray Kemper never before witnessed. It was as if an invisible spirit entered the sky taxi and seized control of Pia's body. She knew what it was, but there was no way to communicate it to this agent. The point was to keep her from speaking such truths. She had said too much to be allowed to live any longer.

Her lips pursed so tightly that she bled from the corners of her mouth. In her mind, the dream designer wanted to tell Ray the truth but could utter nothing. Unable to disclose the real reason why she fled and never went public with the nefarious truth about David Bellingham. He had was done something awful to her mind. She thought that merely looking at the eComp, instead of voicing the notion, might escape this tool's wrath.

She was dead wrong.

In this outcome, Pia Geller never said another word. Both her arms rising as her own body strangled herself in an act, which might've seemed comical if not for its impossibility. The unnatural way her eyes flashed from fear to the shock of revelation.

Across the cramped cabin, cradling the howling infant, Ray hesitated to draw close to the woman; fearing her behavior might be a trick to get him close enough for her to crush him with her still possible, super strength. Staring at him, Pia Geller died with mixed feelings about her life. She seemed in the end, the tragic poet of humanity. She had escaped her prison as a child only to be imprisoned by her savior. David Bellingham's great secret she now feared would soon enslave her species in what could best be renamed *Humanity 2.0*.

That evil genie once out of the bottle would never return. In her dying moments, Pia now felt sure that she knew the dark ending of *Homo sapiens* protracted conflict between good and evil. All because she and David carelessly scaled those digital peeks where God alone should walk.

The baby ceased its weeping. A calm amidst the storm as it stared curiously at the woman crumpled across the cramped interior of the flying taxi. The infant laughed for it was too young to fathom death, which lingered so close to him. While the agent cradling the child feared he lost his case with this woman's impending passing.

The dying video game designer peered up at the FCC agent, wondering why she did not escape this trial by fire like so many before it? Then the universe revealed to her a glorious truth as she expired. A fact she felt certain David Bellingham would one day learn in his final revelation.

twenty-one

Ray caught his killer.

At least that's what he kept mentally telling himself as he eyed Pia's corpse still visible through the frosted window of the medical coma capsule. Agent Kemper requested her body be frozen and shipped back to the FCC lab under armed escort for further study. A young junior FCC guard dispatched to accompany the body back to Langley, Virginia, meekly requested to take a photo with the now-iconic Web Agent who killed Blackout: the face of the hottest-selling Skin on earth.

"I'm on the job," an injured, bandaged Ray reinforced the fact he was not a web actor and they were not civilians.

No longer hidden behind a battle helmet, Ray's likeness drew unwanted glances from various officials in the rain-swept field as air transports circled above, preparing for landing. Beyond them, surveillance drones maintained the extensive security perimeter.

Ray noted with a furtive glance the paramedics who escorted the near-hysterical French mother from a drone. Her eyes red from the tears she shed for her abducted baby. Under an umbrella extended by an FCC guard, Ray returned the now sleeping child to his relieved, worn-out mother. The woman uttered something to Ray in French, but the two air transports landing nearby drowned out her auto-translation, spraying them with muddy rainwater from the soggy ground; sending the mother and baby racing back into the flying ambulance which soon departed.

A third flying drone transported Agent Kemper to the rooftop landing pad of the U.S. Embassy just off the *Place de la Concorde* and within view of the famous Hotel de Crillon. Law enforcement agents had died on this FCC mission, thus web law dictated the Special Agent personally report a debriefing over a secured embassy communiqué.

In a private third-floor embassy office overlooking *L'avenue Gabriel*, Ray warmed himself with an espresso and surveyed the surveillance video footage recorded by the sky taxi's interior cameras. No camera's point of view captured the precise angle of Pia strangling herself. Ray's body blocked the best possible shot, allowing only Pia's legs to be captured. When he ditched his battle helmet to catch up with her in the pursuit, he discarded its embedded camera. While his gun, recovered by agents after the fact, had been dropped before entering the sky taxi: so he had no personal recording camera to corroborate his outrageous claim that Pia Geller strangled herself.

This action, Ray knew, experts would claim to be physically impossible like the death in his case. For anyone strangling themselves would lose consciousness well before they could choke to death. The only thing the footage proved was that Ray did not murder the fugitive. He feared the medical experts would later attribute it to unique, if never before reported, symptoms of GNS marring her brain in later cerebral scans. At that moment for reasons he couldn't articulate, the Web Agent felt close to solving a puzzle perhaps tangentially linked to his murder victim-

Weary from the long day, Ray finished his recorded debriefing and emailed his video-testimonial to his boss, Joe Caresio back in DC. Joe was officially banned from communicating with his subordinate until a brief internal review was completed. An hour later Ray met up with Exxon at Paris's Orly spaceport.

Ray wanted to thank the detective for saving his life sincerely, but the many eyes on him at the departure area made any private discussion impossible. He was separated from his disguise which couldn't be found back in the mission van where he left it to don his armor.

The ever-growing mob over the hottest selling Skin likeness forced Delta Spacelines to transport the two men by private car to their flight, boarding them last onto the space jet. Business-class passengers stared at Ray as one of the sushi chefs at the gastropub snapped a pic of him. Ironically, the vid ad on the inner lids of the Delta comports at the end of the pre-board flashed Mr. Zero's special discount on Ray's Skin for Delta elite frequent fliers.

Upon landing in LAX, Delta transported Exxon and Ray by private car from the flight to a special U.S. Customs processing hall for government officials. Later Ray's face was plastered on the media screen floors of The Beverly Hilton lobby as he and Exxon returned. Mr. Zero raving over the face of "the savior of World War IV."

Back in his Media Suite, Ray's mind returned to concerns about his career. After this case, he knew he would surely be cycled out without even an offer as an instructor at the eAcademy until the furor over his Skin died down; otherwise, it would be too distracting for the cadets. Drifting off to sleep in the bed, he was soon awakened by an iScreen request to chat with his boss online.

Moments later, Ray docked into his hotel room comport, hyperlinking to the secure, online FCC chat-room. The familiar, circular white walls. Joe, seated in a floating chair before the hovering desk, had already reviewed his agent's Paris report. Grinning, he greeted his subordinate who materialized in the white chair opposite his superior.

"Well," Lieutenant Caresio sighed, "Paris proved a bit thornier than we'd like."

"Ms. Geller didn't make it easy."

"Here's the situation, Ray," his boss cut straight to business, "Pia Geller's DNA did not match the forensic evidence from your victim's crime scene," he sighed, "And the top brass are dubious about your debrief theory on a web virus infecting Pia's mind."

Ray was prepared for pushback, countering, "The video shows I didn't strangle her, so how does the top brass wish to explain her death by strangulation?"

A pregnant pause.

"They can't," his boss acquiesced. Ray knew his superior was being pressured by the FCC chairwoman herself, "So you think Pia's mind was infected with a neural protocol that could control her body?"

Ray nodded yes, "Perhaps implanted like an online cookie in her brain. She tried to tell me who created the video cloak, but before she could say, her own body turned on her."

"Mad cow disease doesn't cause such reactions," countered his boss.

"Still, I think this protocol was prion based," Ray could speak in short-hand on the matter since he and Joe as FCC officials well-knew about prions.

They were oddly shaped protein codes impervious to heat from cooking, which usually killed microscopic germs. Prions represented viral data that could migrate into the brain of anyone eating them. For humans, mad cow disease was prion based after farmers fed their cattle cheap feedstock containing dead-cattle brains.

Joe was incredulous, "A computer virus that can act upon the brain?"

"Why not?" Ray retorted, "It could be structurally similar to kuru."

As an FCC cadet, Ray learned kuru as a disease originating with remote Papua New Guinean natives who consumed the raw brains of their dead relatives in funerary rights. Later stages of the prion based disease manifested as a neurological ailment combining extreme depression with uncontrollable, hysterical laughter until the victim lost all neurological and body control.

Ray conjured this theory after reflecting for some time that Pia physically killing herself was as impossible as kuru proved for human emotions. The victims of kuru exhibited wild emotional leaps while retaining normal tendon reflexes. Perhaps a digital virus wielded directives to force its victims through impossible physical actions? Their tendon reflexes manipulated as if they were puppets on strings set to kill themselves through uniquely planned, body-movement protocols?

Joe held little interest in a debate about manipulating prions for a computer *mind* virus which never before manifested. For Ray's boss, the truth was simple, Pia played a first-person game of her design and developed Gamer Neural Shock. A well-documented syndrome ending ultra-realistic first-person games.

"It's GNS," Joe sighed, "and from Pia's comport drives, we now know your murder victim also toyed with her illicit game. So they both got burned."

"My victim didn't choke himself to death."

"No, he stabbed himself in a way considered physically impossible," shrugged Joe, "maybe the GNS symptoms could've forced them both to die this way?"

"I saw it with my own eyes, Joe, it wasn't GNS,"

"You focus on tracking down 'Hopeless Romantic' and getting another date with that last suspect, 'Voyeur'," Lieutenant Caresio wrapped up the meeting, "and if you can't do that in a few days, you're to close the case hopefully before *Dreamspace* goes public."

With a hand gesture, Joe off-lined both of them.

The next break came nearly two days later while Ray and Exxon worked out in The Beverly Hilton gym during the late hours. It was the only time Ray could venture out in public without drawing a crowd. Between bench press sets, his Siri alerted him:

"Ray, the FCC web surveillance system spotted Ally at another store in Los Feliz 18 minutes ago at 3:23 AM," footage flashed across the agent's iScreen from a ceiling-mounted, store camera capturing Ally walking across a Mr. Zero vid-ad on the floor ironically flashing Ray's face. Edited camera views then trailed her from this convenience store to her tiny apartment.

The following afternoon when Ally ventured out for what turned out to be errands, a covert forensics team entered her Spartan studio, finding nothing more than a stripped-down mattress, empty desk, and a lone chair. There was hardly anything in the kitchen, closet, or bathroom to indicate a person even lived there. She obviously did not value material possessions except for various Sansevieria and Peace Lilie plants that scrubbed and oxygenated the air of the tiny flat. The team managed to extract a DNA sample from her toothbrush and a handle of a water pitcher she used for the plants. Ray and Exxon watched the mission from the media screens of Ray's hotel room. The evidence would soon be cross-matched to the partially corroded, female DNA left at the Beijing crime scene.

"It's her," Exxon told his partner, "I know it."

A few minutes later, Ray received his boss's chat room request. From across the online table, Joe broke the news to his field agent:

"Congrats, your case is closed. Ally's DNA matched," his superior did not conceal his apparent irritation and perhaps weariness from the late hour back on the East Coast. Ray knew the reason why, but stayed on point, playing it cool:

"So when are we bringing her in?" asked Ray.

"We aren't."

Joe grunted as his hand gesture shortcut caused the circular chat room wall to fill with eVideo surveillance of Ally. The footage depicted her online while reclined in a business class comport inside a commercial space jet in orbit.

"*Hopeless Romantic* was in-flight from Beijing to L.A. when your victim died," explained Joe, "so Ally's DNA was left on the comport from her visit. But we obviously can't tie her to a possible murder."

Ray wasn't sure what to make of the discovery.

"I assume you still haven't gotten a date with Voyeur?" inquired Joe.

"No. I met Voyeur through my dead victim's comport. The suspect believed I was an imposter-"

"So Voyeur might be probably afraid of dating anyone in *Dreamspace* now. So your case is now ruled a suicide," Joe sighed, his eyes coldly locked on his subordinate, "Ray, you should've told me."

"It didn't seem relevant at the time."

Joe gestured at Ally's face in the surveillance video surrounding them, "She's Ravenna's identical twin! And you didn't think that was relevant enough to tell me-"

"I was going to-"

"You were compromised. Off the record, I don't care if you and Ravenna screwed around on '*Swipe 9*.' Those anti-fraternization laws were ridiculous given the years you all wound up spending together. But you were already under scrutiny as the only person other than Blackout who knew his software codex. Your omission on Ally constitute an apparent breach of trust and left me with nothing to defend you with to my superiors," his boss of many decades took a somber breath, "There's no other outcome except to notify you that you're terminated. It's only because of your past feats that you're not headed to jail."

There it was.

At the eAcademy, Ray wondered how he would leave the agency. Perhaps as a field agent, supervisor, or mission specialist, while never imagining this outcome. It was done so quickly that it didn't feel real to Ray. With a hand gesture, his mentor and boss vanished from the online chat room as an automated message in a sterile, female voice filled the digital chat room:

"Agent Kemper, your eBadge and security clearance is revoked. A courier box will be en route shortly to your location. Please return it with your firearm and offline badge."

Not the moment that the young cadet would've expected after having saved the world. Ray took note of the white, circular room, levitating chairs, and table, realizing this moment would constitute the last time he would visit a secure, FCC chat room. The only career he'd ever known, now gone. His mind returned to his dad's hard drives piled up in that Chicago office so many decades ago. Had his son left something more essential to mark his time? Ray and his handler helped to end World War IV. But humanity was about to mass migrate into David's *Dreamspace* and forget reality including that fact.

If not, there might've been lucrative sponsorship deals for him in the offline world. Ironically, he saved humanity so they could get lost inside David's online rabbit hole. With everyone in *Dreamspace*, there would be no more ad revenue, digital Skins, or even professional gamers.

There was, indeed, nothing except her. But how could he ever mend things with Ally? It might help that he was no longer an agent? The question consumed him as he sat in the chat room's floating legless chair, staring at his digital *selfie*'s hands, wondering how to get back to Ally. Then he realized government auditors were probably watching his every move online. But Ray never suspected someone else also watched him.

From his lonely perch, David Bellingham spied agent Kemper, now projected on the live surveillance footage filling his vast monolith in simulated outer space. Silently the inventor studied the former Web Agent seated at the virtual table in the chat room David famously designed. The hidden protocols buried in *Doors 4.0* allowed its inventor to spy on anyone in any digital space on his web. The view from the four angles on the FCC agent projected as panels across the monolith. At the same time David registered the courier package en route to The Beverly Hilton in which Ray was expected to place his gun and physical off-line badge.

Relief finally swept over David now that the thorn of Ray Kemper had been cut down. The inventor could focus on auditing the handful of other people who might prove a hindrance to his plan. He returned to spying on two senators, three American executives, the FCC chairwoman, and of course the president of the United States, whose eComp camera currently revealed him entering his personal quarters at the White House.

Soon the universe shifted as quantum physics suggested it could while no one was observing or attempting to record it. The carousel of endless possibilities, which Niels Bohr first posited, spun like an infinite roulette wheel after David was no longer observing Ray, who sat offline now at the edge of his hotel room bed. Then a notion suddenly flickering through his mind.

A new task.

To take his mind off things, he tried to unwrap the data spiral of Ally's mysterious, self-deleting file, which had originated with Blackout. It seemed to Ray, the only thing left that he had of hers. His Siri assured him that the source data was permanently destroyed, but nothing created could ever be genuinely destroyed by the law of thermodynamics, computer forensics supporting this theory time and again.

So Ray passed on the meal request from Exxon a few hours later, working through the night to weave together the fragmented codex of symbolic logic glyphs to achieve his goal. The code remained starkly similar to that wielded in Blackout's electric back-feed virus. In the end, Ray's work as a coder couldn't resurrect the lost data, but it did reveal an unexpected revelation:

"Ray, Pia also possessed this file in her Paris comport hard-drive," his Siri instructed him.

"How do you know that?"

"The files are the same size and both require the same passwords," his Siri explained, "The password is Voyeur."

"*Voyeur*?" Ray was shocked, speaking the password aloud.

Shutting his eyes, Ray recollected on Voyeur, that young girl in the glasshouse offering him the pill or knife. Who was the actual user behind that mask? His thoughts drifted back to the seemingly impossible deaths of Pia and his Chinese murder victim. Strangling hands and a sword through a torso were actions supposedly impossible to perform on oneself.

"Ray, I think this file contains three programs," his Siri told him.

"I thought so too in reconstituting them," replied Ray, "I'm wondering if they're Blackout's corrupted unusable file, the video cloak, and the possible neural virus which caused Pia and my victim to kill themselves. Do you think Pia authored them?"

"No. The file info shows someone else did."

Ray recalled Pia's warning in the sky taxi that everyone was *infected* through what he assumed was their eComps; her eyes focused on her fallen earpiece on the sky taxi floor. By trying to communicate that fact, Pia had triggered something, perhaps a new styled neural embed that killed her? Ray's mind returned to his date with Voyeur who also possessed possible those fragments of

Blackout's virus files. Who was the real person behind that Skin? Perhaps the same person who created the video pixelation protocol and the lethal neural embed-

Buzzzzzzzzzzzzzzzzzz.

A fly buzzed past Ray's ear. He tracked it as it landed on the bedside table. Flies in the age of constant rain carried dangerous diseases, contaminating areas each time they landed. Eyes purposely turned away from the insect, Ray grabbed a damp towel he left on the bed's edge from his shower. Still turned away, he wound the towel as his mother taught him as a boy, never looking back at the fly which he soon swatted dead. The crushed insect landing motionless on the media screen floor as Ray once again regarded the wisdom of his mom's sage advice to him when he was a kid:

"If people underestimate a fly, what else don't they see?"

Her comment now made the former Web Agent think of David Bellingham, the inventor of the eComp. A paralyzed man more helpless than the dead fly whom the mind might relegate in a list of suspects since he could not even travel in the real world. At that moment, Ray saw David's screen saver on the media walls which he took to broadcasting. It showed a hurricane covered Earth from the viewpoint of an orbiting satellite, practically the same view David employed from his isolated monolith. A view of something too far to touch, leaving one only to watch like-

A voyeur.

If David was Voyeur, he might have proprietary information to suspect Ray's dishonesty? Perhaps David even had a hand in killing Ray's Chinese victim? Killing the man with the neural protocol without even being there, just like Ray witnessed with Pia. But why then was the video cloak employed in the Beijing dome neighborhood? The program pixelated all the cameras along the assassin's trail in and out of the crime scene, beginning and ending with the furthest most camera. The truth dawned on Ray.

These same files could be used for varying purposes by different people.

The video cloak in Beijing might be misdirection to imply someone physically entered and exited his victim's mansion. But given Pia's death, which Ray had witnessed, he now knew no killer need be present in Beijing. Ally could've triggered it via the web from her space flight. Falsely implying someone was there when no one had been physically present during his victim's death. A termination from what might be the neural embed, which meant David could be his killer too, puppeteering victims from the web into reality.

Agent Ray Kemper emoted no physical reaction as he believed he solved his case. No cry of Eureka. He masked the shudder of fear coursing through him. Remaining still for a long moment as if daydreaming, he now behaved like a person who knew he was being observed by perhaps, an unseen fly.

Entering the bathroom, he casually took off his eComp before washing his face and shaving, which he'd skipped following his earlier shower. As he often did, he scrubbed the antibacterial alloy shell of the sleek eComp with facial soap, washing it. Nothing out of the ordinary. Because often he'd forget the earpiece on the sink counter as he did now, wandering away to exit his Media Suite.

Taking the stairs down to the business center on the lobby floor as if seeking a bit of exercise since he was not visiting the gym tonight. Without his eComp, it took some time on the hotel phone to arrange for the hotel's 3D printer to charge his room for the print job. Most interfaces now required an eComp, but a call from the business center's phone to the front desk arranged to have the charge billed to his room.

Watching as the sleek printer generated the reproduction of the old item. Something not often seen these days. A physical book with synthetic pages and a black faux leather binding, embossed with faux-gold letters:

English & Mandarin Translation Dictionary

He soon carried the book tucked under his arm, its cover against his torso as he approached Exxon's Media Suite door. It felt claustrophobic the moment Ray turned off all the media systems in his quasi-partner's hotel room as a puzzled Exxon watched. Dead, black media screens made the room smaller than Ray expected. The former Web Agent again placed Exxon's eComp into the concealed hotel's iSafe embedded in the media screen wall leading to the bathroom.

"Why…no…eComp? asked the Chinese detective in severely broken English.

After their blossoming partnership through auto-translation software, it was starkly cumbersome to communicate presently. Ray gestured at pre-circled words in his translation dictionary, speaking as if addressing a young toddler:

"No eComp. EComp download virus to brain."

Exxon took a moment to look at the translated word for a *virus*, already circled in the language translation book.

"Understand," the Chinese cop nodded.

"Virus kill Pia like…puppet," Ray gestured at the circled word for *puppet* while physically mimicking his arm like a puppet's as if controlled by strings.

A confused Exxon traced the outline of a curvy woman with his two hands, "Pia, no puppet. Pia, woman."

Ray flipped his translation dictionary to another pre-marked word already circled in red marker from the business center. Exxon didn't like that word, taking the book in hand. He flipped to another word before crudely reading its corresponding English translation aloud:

"Remote control," smiled a proud Exxon, "better…word."

Ray nodded affirmatively, pleased that his partner understood—

A noise in the hall!

It startled Ray. He forced the Chinese detective into the confines of Exxon's hotel bathroom. The former Web Agent pointed out at the empty hotel room as if it were the scene of their victim's death, "During murder...no one there."

"Why ruin," Exxon flipped to another word, "...cameras?"

"To make us think killer there. Killer no there," stressed Ray, "Killer on web," Ray again gestured like a puppet, "make person kill self."

"Remote control," Exxon repeated the word aloud, nodding in understanding before asking the resulting question, "Killer...be?"

"Voyeur. Ally's ex in *Dreamspace.*"

"Voyeur...in reality...what person?"

Ray found it hard to voice the name. As if saying it would birth the frightening truth of a killer in near-complete control. A controlling figure as scary and concealed as Xi Jinping had been at the Yin Yang virus's initial outbreak. Ray's lips hesitated another moment before uttering, "David Bellingham."

A long silence.

It was inconceivable to Exxon to suspect David, the savior of humanity. The one who might give humans their remaining hope through his revolutionary game. It didn't feel right to the seasoned detective. Instead, Exxon offered his own starkly different conclusion from the same fact pattern:

"Maybe...Ally use remote control...to kill?"

Only as Ray shook his head no, did it dawn on him that Exxon could be right? He considered her a suspect and then dropped her. She didn't invent the video pixelation program or neural virus, but she possessed both just like Pia, which David might've initially created. But instead of David remotely killing, Ally could've done the deed from her space jet comport in outer space, using the video cloak to make it seem like someone was there when they were not, perfecting her alibi. But without his badge and job, he could not now check her user history.

Wow.

Using the video cloak as misdirection was brilliant. It caused Ray's superiors to assume that someone was in his victim's bedroom when, in fact, no one was present. Did the neural embed somehow allow his Chinese victim to be played like a puppet and kill himself too? She could be that killer. After all, Ray witnessed memories of Ally murdering in far-flung settings he assumed to be *Dreamspace* worlds. Perhaps some of those scenes were in reality?

From his partner's perspective, Exxon long-suspected Ray had fallen for the female suspect. She did, after all, look like Ray's former handler; someone whom Ray held a deep affection for by merit of his confession to his partner. She killed her Chinese ex-lover remotely for whatever reason. This stolen *remote control* program could be her perfect alibi for law enforcement too primitive to grasp such a new, inventive murder weapon forcing the victim to take his own life.

The detective's retort sent a demoralized Ray retreating to his hotel room where he took a hot bath to clear his mind. Sinking into the water, the smell of the hotel's French U.V. farmed verbena bath soap laced the steamy air in a citrus scent. Letting his mind drift, Ray listened to several of his favorite David Bellingham blogs on the integrated media system through his eComp he grabbed on the sink. He landed on a blog he'd heard many times before. David's electronic voice uttering the fact that:

"Mass meditation in Washington DC in 1993 lowered crime rates by 23.6%. Quantum mechanics proves our collective minds can tangibly alter our reality. Imagine what the minds of the entire world thinking in unison could achieve?"

Ray's mind flashed back to memories of merging with Ally as one. Then Pia trying to tell him how everyone was infected as she eyed her eComp. Only then did Agent Kemper grasp the actual scope of this case, which had almost nothing to do with his Chinese victim. This case had never honestly been about that murder. An even larger shudder of fear turned his heart cold. He felt like a child wishing to avert a truth too powerful to face. No.

His killer could not be Ally.

Offlining from his eComp, he instructed his Siri to temporarily deactivate. He dried off completely before turning off the main electric breaker to his room in a recessed panel behind his sink. Sitting naked on the transparent bed sheets, he commenced writing the new computer program.

Remembering the oath he'd been forced to repeat following Blackout's death, he realized he now broke that pledge. From scratch, he recreated Blackout's *Yin Yang* digital program from the eTerrorist's symbolic logic glyph codex, which only Ray now knew. He tailored this version to his particular requirements. No doubt the FCC was watching him closely. When the time came, he would *bleachbit* the system to buy him some time. But once he acted, the authorities would go straight for him. Still, Ray knew how to hide in the offline world. He might get away with it, but would eventually be caught. Yet by then-

It would be done.

As Ray built the program on his offlined eComp, a worldwide, digital crowd gathered online, cheering as the clock ticked down to *Dreamspace's* public release. Fans filled the central arena where many online halls conjoined. A sea of Skins extending out of the massive auditorium and out through the infinite corridors of the web. A convergence of humanity surpassing even the number of spectators watching man's first steps on the Moon.

Within this digital arena, the gold-painted rock icon, The Moo, sang beneath the countdown clock, crooning over David Bellingham's great digital migration soon to carry humanity into blissful, online ignorance for the remainder of their lives. The last of humanity's anticipated panaceas through the ages. They would forget their troubles and the storm. They would see the sun again, being reborn and cleansed of the sins of the past.

Following the closure of Ray's murder case as a suicide, the FCC officially certified *Dreamspace* as safe for general consumption. Already a billion people were pre-registered to begin dating within the next few hours in the hopes of finding game-mates with whom to migrate into the long-term game for the remainder of their lives.

The musical prodigy, the Moo, now unveiled his newest composition, written for this event just as Beethoven once wrote, his *9th Symphony* for what he thought would be Napoleon's Republic like America. If The Moo knew David's actual intent for *Dreamspace*, the modern musician might've ripped up his dedication just as the 19th Century Beethoven did after Napoleon betrayed the republican values of the French Revolution and crowned himself King of a conquered Europe. But The Moo could not imagine the truth about *Dreamspace*, which Ray now grasped as the rock icon sang the final verse:

> *"They destroyed our world and sky,*
> *leave it with a sigh,*
> *that old world dead in hours,*
> *the sun in Dreamspace will be ours.*
> *Are you ready to blow your mind?*
> *All who see it will know the time."*

Just shy of an hour before the official *Dreamspace* launch, ex FCC agent Ray Kemper completed his program. Seated on the edge of his transparent bed inside his Media Suite, he did not use his eComp to dispatch the IM to David. He needed his eComp to remain offline as long as possible. After turning on the power, he used his Media Suite's web interface, sending an orally dictated IM to David Bellingham's private web address, accessible through his web-search history. The former agent's message remained concise:

DAVID, NEED TO MEET.
RE: HOPELESS ROMANTIC.

Shortly after sending his message, Ray received David's response across his iScreen:

LOG IN.

Only then did Ray knock on Exxon's door, asking him to enter his room. The Chinese detective entered the Media Suite, bolting the door behind him. He found Ray already inside the hotel comport with the holo-lid still open.

"Just watch," Ray told his partner before the former Web Agent leaned back, allowing his eComp to dock. Instantly Ray's senses were torn from his body as-

He onlined.

Exxon sat down at the small retractable chair which he again swung out of the comport's recessed panel. The online auditing screen projected across the comport's holo-lid. Cracking knuckles behind his head, Exxon watched from Ray's perspective now covering the holographic lid. The former FCC agent walked across David's vast monolith, closing on the lone inventor standing at the very edge with stars behind him.

Online, Ray closed the distance between himself and the famed inventor who had inexplicably addressed Ray as his *mirror*. The clean, scentless air of the monolith filling his nostrils. Agent Kemper reminded himself that he was now in David's digital realm. He reckoned how vulnerable Ravenna, herself, must've felt when she laid her gun's infrared target on Blackout's flying comport: knowing there was no escape.   Facing his possible death, Utah burned deep from within Ray's soul. He would leave behind more than those hard-drives of his father even if he failed. If he succeeded, he might save the world a second time. His thoughts returned to Ally, her face burning in his heart. Ray Kemper sought to protect her too, along with everyone else alive on Earth. For he now knew David's great secret.

The truth about *Dreamspace*.

twenty-two

David's secret plan.

Ray's requested online meeting did not interrupt the inventor's reflection of the approaching culmination of his life's work. All from his insight based on Pia's profound discovery that group meditation in DC seemingly lowered the local crime rate; indicating mass consciousness could shape real-world events.

In the many games of David's possible futures that he played as a child, the worldwide storm-filled most of them. If the free world nations and Russia quickly reorganized with World War 2-like alliance against China and Iran, America could buy time to become the ultra micro manufacture of the goods it needed. It even involved Latin American non-citizens, long-displaced by Xi

Jinping's supplying of chemicals vital to the drug cartel in their homeland, driving them out in resulting violence. These Latinos remained guest workers in the highly successful factories along the sequestered southern U.S. border making basic goods that citizen-manufacturers in American cities assembled into more complex goods.

A young David learned from gaming that if America just bought what it made, the nation was large and rich in natural resources as its history well-proved, to quickly again become a manufacturing powerhouse. The thing Xi Jinping feared most and the reason why he was willing to kill the nation before it could achieve such a purpose and best him.

From his early game play, David learned that how quickly America got real about its internal traitors and got off Chinese goods following the pandemic decided if the most horrific outcomes could be avoided. Like the Bible warned, the New Jerusalem couldn't be afraid of killing its false prophets. The worst outcomes the *Three Traitors* and their allies inflicted was the deadly solar U.V. rays coming through the broken Ozone layer decimated by continuing Chinese slave pollution. The stratospheric hole was torn open by China as Isaiah foretold, turning all life including the virus into *ash* in a single day through the deadly U.V. rays no longer warded off by the atmosphere's protective layer.

David lived that manifestation only once in his childhood gaming. It occurred on a Saturday. Americans awoke late to find that all terrestrial life from Polynesia to Europe had fried to ash from solar rays due to the end of the stratosphere's gaseous shield. Americans were tragically cooked to death from inside as if inside a microwave or oven as God called it in the Old Testament. The final cost for so many abominations built on the prior, cheap goods of a rigged system that the three treasonous U.S. presidents birthed and fed with the American's acceptance of slave-made products to soil their homes, lives, and future.

The American media that misled for so long about the China trade and pollution until their deconsolidation, were glaringly honest in the end. Newscasters broadcast live and often with their families present, slowly microwaved to ash at in the news studio while their anguished viewers watched from home. There was something odd for David about so many people dying in front of their cameras and media screens. Amateur eCompers populating impromptu video-chat sessions in humanity's last moment; strangers dying together through online links. The chaos of screams and agony of being slowly cooked alive stayed with him.

He lived that ghastly outcome when he'd nearly given up, frustrated and stuck at the same obstacle in his repeated gaming. Witnessing families holding hands until their bodies became too hot to touch. He was someone he never met in California named Gideon on the west coast which was the last longitude to die. Isaiah spoke of a frightening justice the coastal ports would face. The President in Space Force One did not land in the Bay Area but raced away from the sun, refueling at desolate depots in the shade of night, remaining alive but with nowhere to go.

The Prophet Daniel's prophecied *wings of abomination* would destroy all remaining life; those wings born from the *Three Traitor's* atmospheric pollution. George Washington's warning came true. The nation failed to make what it bought because of a wicked president, driving the inevitable treason from its port cities, chasing out their marginalized citizens for new non-citizens above the law citizens alone were held to. These ports collectively attacked the Electoral College and any president challenging slavery. From that one outcome of ash, he always sensed himself inside an invisible microwave oven on earth just waiting to be turned on.

Perhaps why he enjoyed being up here on his monolith? As he and Pia temporarily mocked out an array of dream potentials in *Dreamspace*, the old memories of David's childhood gaming rushed back to him in striking clarity. He remembered previously forgotten games where all life had turned to ash in other ways; one due to a mass-cremation of most Americans from the G5 internet signal killing so many on a national day of mourning. As the Torah made clear, the people paid for their religious or governmental leaders' transgressions when the people did want to be bothered to wrestle with their leaders as their Constitution required.

Another day of ash came after people remained in cities with water infused with the Yin Yang virus that forced Americans as Isaiah prophecied to live spaced apart with cities abandoned. Another outcome saw American culture turned wholly pedophile like all prior non-Abrahamic ones, burning their remaining heterosexual outliers. A feat achieved by tolerating the spread of male homosexuals while never addressing the underlying cause of the pedophile rapists who rendered most of those non-heterosexuals at an age too young to consent. Stealing the choice of sexuality symbolized on the far side of the rainbow adorning the movement's flag; a path these young victims were barred from naturally exploring unmolested. Letting the rapist wolves proliferate amongst the sheep they made seemed to be an ultimate insult to the Universe. The reason why that outcome faced destruction from a meteor the likes of which had luckily not manifested in David's current timeline. All of these outcomes reinforced Descartes' notion that there was no objective reality. Only the test of humans to honor the rules the Torah imposed.

Human actions brought about different future challenges far beyond their sphere of possible influence. Back when David had sampled a fraction of the possible outcomes, charting paths around repeating pitfalls and delaying eventualities like that frightening day of ash. Navigating through an infinitesimally small portion of the multiverse's branching outcomes where humanity from its past wickedness did not die.

Except for The Day of Ash, David Bellingham never discovered an outcome without the storm; nor one where he could again feel or move his body. But the ash event stayed with him.

Standing not far from the monolith's edge in the vacuum of space, the 52-year-old inventor now took in the cold, motionless air. The lack of any odors, humidity, or breeze endowed the simulated air with a crispness that was hard to describe, but exhilarating. He turned to face the FCC agent materializing 20 paces behind him.

David never suspected Ray had figured out his secret plan. Despite Ray's admission, the inventor never appreciated what a dedicated fan Ray was for David's blog. The inventor never imagined that Ray, let alone anyone else, would repeatedly review the blog's vast corpus of knowledge over many years. But Ray had done just that since his academy days, lulling himself into a relaxing escape of learning; occupying his mind to set his subconscious free for a spell from the discipline of the FCC's mental rigors.

That wasn't to say that David from the start did not sense something important about the civil servant. At the time, David chalked up the feeling up to his prior love for the fictional web agent series about people like Kemper, skilled-actors, seducers, who could manipulate others similar to Star Wars' *Jedi* mind tricks. Perhaps Ray's greatest deceit, in this case, remained his intelligence guardedly cloaked beneath unassuming charisma.

Ray knew why David aimed to sign up anyone who would subscribe to *Dreamspace*; subsidizing users' fees for those with little or no resources. He would run the subscription like Constantine's revised Greek Christianity. And each could have what they needed now as Communism had falsely promised because all could now receive the same level of an illusion each needed in his game.

The long-term game still failed, but at least at a precise moment, David could accurately calculate as Newton did for heavenly bodies' movements in space and time. By the time the game failed for most, he'd have enough *Dreamspacers* immersed in the main game to launch his secret plan.

Approaching David on the monolith, Ray again reflected on the *merge* he experienced with Ally, considering that with so many peoples' consciousness bound as one, weird things could be forced to happen in reality. What Einstein termed with no better choice of words than *Spooky Action At A Distance*. The windmill Cervantes's Don Quixote charged at might be able to morph in the physical world into a dragon or anything else with enough minds seeking its reshaping. Thanks to David's blog, Ray long-appreciated Quantum Mechanic's *Double Slit* experiment proving any human observation physically transformed the subatomic universe being studied. While human's recording machines also warped observations. That was a major point: machines made in reality through ideas also altered the universe. Proof that ideas warped commanded physical reality. The reason why the only thing bonding humans together in their reality was the common, mental compact as citizens under laws that made clear how they could act.

Walking towards David, Ray realized why God grew so frustrated with Moses for refusing to be both the governmental and spiritual leader. Dividing the government from the spiritual allowed for the Torah's inner-faith but would later fate the New Jerusalem to fail to believe. Then it would redefine itself beyond the limits of the Torah's prohibitions for all humans. Limits assumed and accepted by the nation's Judeo Christian label as *one nation under God.* Now with those key Old Testament prohibitions long-broken, a few Old Testament prophecies were left to be fulfilled as Christ made clear they would before the end. Without its Judeo Christian mooring and ignorant of the truth of science from 11/10/1619, the New Jerusalem of America brought on world-ending actions from a mistaken notion as progress from a society cursed by the hypocritical, underlying economy. The only curative at this late date would require-

Mind over matter.

Ray understood that through the *merge* protocol, David sought to unite not just two game-mates as one but all as one holistic mass-consciousness with stark implications from Einsteinian relativity. A singular bundle of minds manipulated through the game's mental protocols to wish in unison that the storm would end.

Although Ray could never know it, the broken game became an untested vessel to avoid the loss of so much time on David's part. A vehicle to travel through the fabric of time and space to previously unthinkable outcomes: such as ending what would be a 40,000-year-long storm in perhaps hours, days, minutes, or even seconds after its master directed his followers in unison to simultaneously wish it away. In the end, *Dreamspace* was never meant to be a refuge of amnesia and entertainment, but a vehicle to end the storm.

The reason why Ray figured that David would use all of his funds to help humanity, massively subsidizing *Dreamspace's* game and body vault subscriptions with his growing profits to populate his digital arc ready to set for unimagined destinations. Did he believe he was a hand of God to bring about renewal to the planet? If so, like Christopher Columbus before him, David Bellingham would seemingly control the heavens for those witnessing the end of the storms. And if the man was wrong, humanity could attempt to continue inside his video game refuge of permanent amnesia. The prediction of the final stage of humankind by the 19th Century German philosopher Friedrich Nietzsche would become true: all of humanity residing ever after on couches for the remainder of their lives. Endless body vaults of comports harnessed as multi-dimensional time and space travelers worked their magic online.

In the seconds of watching Ray's approach, the inventor pushed away Pia's certainty that only freely-chosen prayer could achieve what David sought. She felt no one could force anything on anyone else because that violated God's predicate of free will. Otherwise, how could people be judged if their hand was forced? But this outcome was the only one David ever successfully gamed as a kid where all of humanity did not die. So now after a lifetime, he was finally here, reflected David as Ray's measured footsteps drew closer.

"Come and see a new world be born," the inventor beckoned the Web Agent towards the monolith's edge.

Sick earth rose over its horizon. Their home planet now resembled Saturn, covered in storms and adorned with a massive orbital ring of satellite debris.

Drawing ever closer to David, the former FCC agent played it from the hip, uttering those fateful words:

"David, you truly are 'the Voyeur', my final suspect."

Ray knew that he had unmasked his killer when his idol's hand gesture paralyzed the former Web Agent's online Skin. Ray couldn't move. His virtual body remaining frozen just below his neck as his feet hovered slightly above the floor. Like his final moments with Blackout, Ray was only able to move his face, unable to even turn his head. Months before it would have been unimaginable for Ray to consider his hero, David Bellingham, could do such a thing to him. World War IV paled in comparison to the coming, frightening chapter in history's possible end.

Bellingham made a second-hand gesture shortcut, raising Ray's frozen body a few feet off the surface of the monolith. Staring at the paralytic man hovering before him, the inventor suspiciously wondered why Ray had revealed his hand so early. What cards could this person have left to play?

Ray was not frightened.

"You created quite the program," muttered the FCC agent, "puppeteering Pia's body like you did with my murder victim," Ray sighed, "And merging all those minds into one might wish away our troubling storm."

A chill ran down the inventor's spine for Ray, indeed, had figured out his plan. Then again, David considered Ray to be everything he yearned to be, including having the love of that woman now lost to him.

A nagging thought now consumed the inventor. If the former Web Agent knew his plan, why disclose it in David's private realm where he was in complete control? Had he notified anyone of his suspicions? Not that it mattered for the agent, Ray's admission sealing his fate. Then the inventor realized his horrible oversight! With a quick hand gesture, he triggered the comport in Ray's room to back-surge electricity, another hidden protocol of his to fry Exxon who monitored their exchange in astonishment.

Which was the last feeling Exxon ever had. In Ray's Media Suite, the comport electrocuted the Chinese detective. His smoking corpse collapsing to the media suite's floor.

At the same time on the monolith, there was nothing to inform Ray that his partner had been murdered. He never suspected the designer possessed such tricks through his hardware in the offline world. The former Web Agent nonetheless sensed growing darkness in David's eyes as he added:

"Ray, you forced me to kill."

"Napoleon never blamed himself either," replied David's former fan, "Hitler, Stalin, Mao, the Three Traitors, Xi Jinping, and now David Bellingham to join them."

Ex-agent Kemper realized he should've heeded Bellingham's blog about never blindly looking up to any human except George Washington. That warning included his idol who blogged it.

While David's mind at that moment turned serene. Gaming those many outcomes as a child endowed him with insights Ray could never fathom. Jim Tutwiler's hyper-real video game had been just a portal to many future gateways through which young David passed and failed, repeating the cycles to find the only way that achieved his aim of keeping his species alive.

As this unexpected outcome played out, David and Ray felt like a mirror to each other, drawn to the same woman who now went by Ally. The passion David held for her bounced like a beam of light between two mirrors, infinite and finite at the same time. Was that the deep bond he felt in this man?

"For all of our history," sighed David, "we craved stories to escape ourselves and our problems," his eyes fell upon the almost alien-looking Earth half-setting now over the monolith's far edge, "This is what all that escapism leads to. In the end, we had it all gave it away for no gain so that later we could be snuffed out by a single human's edict. We're not capable of self-rule. We throw away the precious things and lie that it's nothing. To aid the few and the cheap savings of the moment."

Mother Earth's blighted form eclipsed the cat in the distance behind Ray.

"To make the water go away," Ray stared at their planet, breaking David's needless soliloquy, "you might need nearly everyone's minds merged into one. That power will consume. Someone you can't imagine will sit in that game-control center and do horrible things. It might even be you. Taking power and rendering our species unworthy of saving."

His words made David sad.

The inventor knew he could never alter Ray's naïve idealism. The former Web Agent had not seen what David had experienced in those many outcomes of his childhood video game. All those failed game cycles allowing Bellingham as a child to peer ever further into the cursed abyss. As connected as he felt to Ray, David simply knew what no one else could understand. Whereas Ray Kemper was a public servant indoctrinated and inculcated with preserving the order that wrecked everything because he lacked the data David had experienced.

The rain made revolutionaries of anyone willing to keep the human story going; it was a question of which way to go. Just like that Latin text in Descartes' Divine vision that helped birth science. But no matter how much David delayed his next action with such idle thoughts, he felt like *Prince Charming*. Quelling the image of his monstrous father within him, he made a hand gesture that lit up the dark, monolith floor.

It became a massive, floating screen in space now illuminated with a sea of checkerboard squares; each panel revealing a user's live eComp camera feed, pinholes into the private lives of so many at that moment in time. David ignored the video feeds, but let his head hang low from all he had witnessed in his journey.

"I'm trying to be the savior," he told Ray.

"Tell that to Pia."

"I did what I had to do with her," confided David in his faint Louisiana drawl more to himself than to Ray, "She's cryogenically frozen now thanks to you. And when the FCC is done with her body, I'll continue to freeze Pia, and one day she will be reanimated."

The inventor did not lie.

From his perspective, Pia had poisoned herself and the world with her alternate operating system for *Humanity* 2.0. But to David, Pia's game like a tiger chasing its tail, remained lethal. He was here to make the world safe.

The cat's gentle purr drew him from his idle procrastination. In truth, he did not savor the business to follow and would've stalled longer. The distant feline stretching its limbs before the purple fire cast its long shadow across half of David's face as he confided to Ray that:

"You were an excellent detective. The best. And as promised, this is the final detective story."

Ray understood David's words, appreciating why it truly would be the last tale. There would be no more detectives or anyone else of independent mind, concluded the agent, if David's plan came to fruition. While David Bellingham now fought the fire of jealousy again burning in him for the woman this government agent had touched. The same rage he felt for her abusive Chinese suitor. Hate made it easier for him.

Bellingham's eye swipe caused his extremities to glow. Moving his arms, he simultaneously manipulated Ray's physical body back in his hotel comport. Kemper's Media Suite now became visible across the entire monolith floor in four checkerboard squares generated by the four corresponding cameras mounted into the hotel's comport's exterior.

Paralyzed below the neck and feeling nothing of his body, a floating Ray on the monolith watched impotently as David piloted his physical form in the offline world. The inventor extended his left hand, causing Ray's hand in his hotel comport to hit the manual release button mounted into the comport's inner bed. Then he piloted Ray out of the capsule as the holo lid retracted.

Ray felt nauseous as he eyed the still-smoldering corpse of Exxon on the floor. David awkwardly puppeteered the former Web Agent's body over the Asian detective's smoking corpse. Eyeing his dead partner's body covering part of the monolith's screen, Ray struggled to keep his cool. He wasn't sure how Exxon perished, but knew David triggered it. Realizing it was David's eyes that peered through the little girl as the Voyeur in the glasshouse on that first date.

Across the monolith screen, Ray watched as David puppeteered the former Web Agent's feet to walk towards the hotel night-stand. On the monolith, David kneeled as his right hand extended forward. In the offline world, Ray's hand grabbed his pistol tucked under the bedside table. David now moved his fingers, causing Ray's real-world hand to wrap tightly around the weapon's handle, activating the gun's camera mounted beneath the barrel.

With sick earth and stars behind him, David brought his empty hand towards his head. In the offline world, the weapon rose to Ray's temple; the gun's camera now recording the suicide for any inquiring eyes that might follow. No need for camera pixelation this time to throw off the scent, thought Ray as he watched from David's monolith. After all, ruined Web Agents often took their own existence after their cover was blown and career gone, especially one who had been dishonorably discharged.

Realizing he was cornered, Ray Kemper broke down to his core, finding the little boy deep inside who suddenly awakened from the former centrality of his youth. Powerful emotions sweeping over Ray, the longing for his mother as a child's tears filled his eyes:

"But," Ray pathetically sobbed, "I was your mirror…"

It was startling for David to see such a fit, confident man break down. Iconic strength crumbling into trembling down to his quivering lower lip as Ray wept at his impending mortality. For a moment the inventor glimpsed the same nascent core of this grown man that Ally appreciated on her date with him. Ray reminded David Bellingham of that character from Sartre's play of the soldier weeping before his execution, realizing only in the end that he was a coward all the while.

David sought to comfort Ray by adding, "All those games I played as a child sometimes gaming as myself and sometimes as others until I got the level right. This is the only one I ever found where we all don't die."

Ray's whimpering response was too low for David to hear, causing the inventor to move a few steps closer. Then the agent did the most unexpected thing. Ray jutted his chin forward, managing to bite the end of David's lip. The quick touch of their lips caused an actual spark, which the former Web Agent hoped to achieve. The basic framework of the Dreamspace platform was, indeed, intact here.

Ever the consummate liar, Ray had revealed everything he knew to disarm the genius. It was better to be considered stupid when one possessed no leverage. Fools, after all, were granted wide latitudes, which Ray required if his plan was to work. Instantly, he passed his recreated *Yin Yang* digital virus into David Bellingham's eComp system. The former Web Agent grinned like a fox as the virus instantly unpacked itself in David's system–

"Courtesy of Blackout," the FCC agent winked.

David then realized Ray's performance had been but an act. Utah and Ravenna long robbed the agent of any true tears he still might've possessed. Ray's virus spread effortlessly through David's eComp operating systems. The frightening *Yin Yang* symbol flashed across Bellingham's semi-opaque iScreen. That most frightening warning in modernity.

The inventor never saw the skull and crossbones alert that should've followed. He noted only darkness and a sudden sensation of being once again without a body. Entombed in darkness not experienced since he migrated to the first online chat room where he hatched the eComp and comport to power Doors and then Dreamspace. Now he returned to the realm where hidden partitions cruelly separated lovers even in dreams: the real landscape of David Bellingham's reality without the facade of his invented technologies.

Once again, hearing the familiar, mechanistic baffles of his artificial respirator that then shorted out, leaving only the rain tip-tapping against the windows of his Opelousas living room window. Like a fallen angel, David heard his heart monitor in a home he truly never left. Accompanied by sounds of his medical staff rushing into his blacked-out living room with the massive old flat-screen TV his late mother bought, still in the corner.

In the faint evening moonlight, his medical staff realized their flashlights and medical equipment failed to work, not yet aware of the invisible EMP blast that fried the electric wiring in the home and surrounding area. The chief tech attempted mouth to mouth resuscitation; an action rendered precarious by David's paralyzed tongue now lodged in the back of his throat. By the time a nurse located matches, its meager flame failed to illuminate the back of David's blocked airway.

Compared to Socrates, David Bellingham died with almost equal restraint, due to his complete paralysis since childhood to replace Socrates' paralyzing Hemlock. Only a gurgling in his throat was audible as his mind spun from the building lack of oxygen.

Outside David's home, the street lights and corporate campus buildings were blacked out in a five-mile radius from what Ray fashioned as a more localized EMP blast with limited electric back-feed. No one was electrocuted thanks to Ray's modification to the program's parameters, although a nurse's neck and arm were severely scalded when an electric tea kettle exploded in the medical staff's break room. Nearby, David's med team finally stopped the hand pumps, calling the death of David Bellingham a short time before *Dreamspace's* worldwide release.

Draping a sheet over him, lights exploded before David's paralyzed eyes behind closed lids. He suddenly felt liberated from his darkness. The pineal gland deep in his brain, a primordial eyeball looking upward, dumped Dimethyltryptamine, the most powerful hallucinogenic, created only during REM sleep, into his mind. It freed his consciousness from his body.

Why would Mother Nature have incorporated such a drug into every living organism, he had famously blogged, if not for some destiny that awaited beyond death? He didn't so much think those words at that moment as feel their hopeful sentiment in a continuing moment that had seemed to have no end.

From his studies, David Bellingham previously expected the scene this drug now conjured for his unstrung consciousness; the vast maze test-patients in an American funded government DMT study at The University of New Mexico in the 1990's all claimed to have experienced. They were dosed with DMT while alive which sucked the dead out of their bodies and through a labyrinth of differing forms for each person; in David's case, it manifested as a massive ballroom filled with endless dancing Ally's, all in the same flowing white dress. Like an old-time musical, each Ally tossed a tuxedo-clad David through the spinning vortex of identical dancers, all with her warm smile on their faces as their hands touched his own.

Each beckoned for his touch.

There was no invisible partition now to ever divide his true love from him. Just this dance spinning him from one Ally's kiss to another in a climactic, dance number. A scene that he suspected would end with the as yet unseen, insectoid-like angel who awaited all humans in that final moment after death. The DMT testers nearly all saw this form. But for once in his life, David Bellingham did not seek the truth, but wished only to remain here with each Ally for eternity as his consciousness fizzled out of existence like champagne bubbles evaporating in the most beautiful moment he ever experienced-

Dying in the arms of his infinite Ally.

part six

Truth

"And on the wings of abomination shall be one
who makes desolate.
Even until the consummation, which is determined.
Is poured out on the desolate."

Daniel 9:27

twenty-three

David Bellingham was dead.

The news, announced to the press a week after his death. The official version was delayed so that the founder's untimely passing did not eclipse *Dreamspace's* public launch. The company remained tight-lipped about its founder's cause of death as the web swirled with conspiracy theories such as a rumored cyber-strike on Bellingham Labs' Opelousas compound. Blackout's allies were thought to have fried all electric devices and power lines in the area.

Now there was a new, private worry for parents and adults that perhaps Blackout's world-ending virus had not been fully quarantined? Cracks in the foundation of order were still not great enough to interrupt the masses from their daily work cycles for future rewards, which had been endured many times in recent modernity commencing with the novel Coronavirus. Now the generation given a new future through *Dreamspace* mourned the technology's creator. They would have no idea what would've happened to them if David had remained alive to co-opt their minds. Media retrospectives again aired the famed inventor's life through various movies, docs, and journalistic pieces about him.

Only one thing seemed sure.

The American president finally gave words to this sentiment, lamenting in an international *State of The World* address surrounding the inventor's passing, "Although a great light has been snuffed out in our storm, David's mind now lights the digital way before us," was how the U.S. leader termed *Dreamspace*, an American creation, serving as humanity's best hope for human survival. He remarkably referred to the world-wide hurricanes as *our* storm. Finally an American leader publicly acknowledged the United States of America's complicity in birthing the storms from past economic policies which birthed the Yin Yang virus and continuing nightmares. So that beyond wiping out most life on Earth, the true cost of all those cheap Chinese goods we sought in the past would force humanity into a mass digital migration online. A false reality David created to fulfill the quest he began while holding a dying cat outside that Walmart so many years ago.

Its shadow would soon cover the world.

As the planet seemingly grew forever darker when the casket of the expected savior of humanity was solemnly lowered into the concrete tomb beside his mother's grave. Both bodies within view of their old home on the outskirts of what was now a bustling corporate campus as dense as some major metropolis. The TV cameras remained focused on raindrops trickling down the unmarked black monolith now lowered into place to mark David's grave. It was now the most viewed image in history as Bellingham Labs' stock rallied with the incredible reception of *Dreamspace*.

After the funeral, most leaders participated in a worldwide moment of silence for the late visionary; deference paid by most humans to one largely devoid of a body, while ironically giving humanity their online bodies. The memorial service was broadcast live on the meta walls of the eHalls of the modern web. All possible because of David's *Doors* software that resurrected the web.

Amongst the silent masses of online users in the digital corridors, stood Ray. Just another face in the crowd. His eyes scanning the sea of surreal Skins and spotted her in a black sweater and faded jeans. She sported her *selfie* Skin. Ally had picked this web sector, careful to remain safely beyond his immediate reach. Her sensors set to automatically offline her if Ray attempted to hyperlink close enough to touch her Skin.

He was pleased just to get a meeting with her online or offline. The concession made only after lengthy prostration through their *Dreamspace* IM's for the past week. Ray's desire to see Ally was the only thing that kept him going since Exxon's passing. The detective's death took a heavy toll on the former Web Agent. Surveillance cameras on Ray's hotel comport verified the Chinese cop died from the seemingly, freakish short circuit while Ray was online with David. After the man's remains arrived back in Beijing, Ray requested to attend the funeral but was curtly notified by the man's ex-wife that the body had been cremated and the ashes scattered as per his wishes in the domed Forbidden City.

Days later, Ray received an unexpected meeting request from Ally. So much time passed since their last meeting that Ray figured he'd never again see her. Now here he was only paces away in the web corridor as the meta ad on the wall broadcast the national suicide hotline, the now-familiar advice for people to kill themselves as it wasn't their fault, but rather the *Three Traitors*. And their allies in the past.

"You looked just like my ex. She was your biological twin," Ray called out to her through the surreal crowd, "My dead partner, the hero who killed Blackout-"

"Righteous, dude!" one of the *chatters* smiled.

After all, Ray now sported the iconic online Skin of the agent who killed Blackout; spectators assumed he was staging in character the way people sometimes did in celeb Skins. After all, there were more than a few Ray's in various clothing in this eHall. If he were on the job these days, he would've ironically traded in his camouflage of the Damon Skin for his *selfie*.

"How could you know this twin of me?" Ally looked incredulous.

"Fate," shrugged Ray.

A tear welled from her eye. He assumed she wept for the identical twin she'd never meet. But her next comment reminded Ray once again of his father's warning that a man could never fathom a woman's heart. As Ally revealed that the source of her tears was because, "You and I can never truly be together."

"But he's the savior of World War IV!" joked a nearby Matt Damon Skin dressed as Abraham Lincoln.

She walked away.

How could she be sure they would never work out, he wondered. Ray somehow felt her words were true. Yet improbability brought them together, and it seemed that they should not be torn asunder. The former FCC agent nimbly maneuvered through the crowd, following at a safe distance for her as he explained:

"I'm sorry we met through a lie."

From the corner of his eye, Ray noticed that they walked parallel to the *Dreamspace* wall ad again showing the old photo of young David as a child preparing to play Jim Tutwiler's lethal video game. He pushed the thoughts of David from his mind.

"Ally, I want to meet you again," Ray called out to her.

"Yeah," ahead of him, she walked even faster, "Who am I meeting today?"

"I'm Ray."

"We're not compatible," she slowed her stride, allowing him to walk beside her through the crowd, "we're both liars. You lie because it's your job and I do it because I definitely can't be honest with you-"

"I don't have to lie anymore. I'm not with the agency," he whispered to her as he eyed the crowd surrounding them, "And I know you're my game mate, my soul mate," he cried out in his most sincere voice, "Ally, I love you!"

She stared into his eyes. Her face revealed little to him. He wasn't sure if his words had touched her. But he did move George Washington in a Mohawk beside them enough to lean in and mutter, "Guys, get a room."

Ray already had one.

His Hilton Media Suite recreated a contemporary, lit fireplace on the far wall. Later laying in the transparent hotel bed across from a naked Ally, the former Web Agent reveled in his luck at reaching such an unexpected eventuality. He could never predict they would go from the online meeting to preparing to make love. His life made sense, thought Ray; everything was necessary to reach this place. Her naked body pressed against his as he took in her scent smelling identical to Ravenna. How unexpected that he, the former Web Agent, had become a true star-crossed lover.

Like the poet John Donne once wrote, nothing beyond this bed seemed real to him. Ray understood why David's video game required two users to keep the players from going mad. It was the same reason why most stories and movies involved possible couples. For life could only continue with another. Even Einstein's theory of relativity dictated truth came in at least two conflicting views at the extremes of time and space. And what was more extreme and rare than true love, he noted. Then a spark of fear, perhaps born from the insecurity that he could one day lose her?

"What're you thinking?" she registered the darkness that bloomed within him.

Ray resolved not to reveal such a window into his soul. An *FS8* pop up suddenly covered the digital fireplace. Without his FCC badge, he couldn't now bar the pop-ups every 30 minutes from corporate underwriters of these suites.

So next an ad for the House of Skins appeared. The Indian Skin peddler now discounted Siri Skins in Ray's likeness. Spectators' eComp footage of Ray killing one of Pia's Mongolian bodyguards in Paris filled the screen as the Indian cried:

"Purchase a new Skin and get Blackout's killer free for your Siri's likeness."

The eComp discount now denoted declining sales for his likeness, which had peaked. The new craze was a talking toilet bowl. Ray's Skin would slowly be slashed until it was bundled in that final, ignominious end on the road for modern web celebrity Skins-

The Christmas discount *Skin bin*.

Finally Ray's eye swipe could end the ads. Another eye movement purchased a commercial-free period lasting the next eight hours. Eyes returning to his date, he spied the supple lines of her naked body as they prepared to finally make love.

He eyed the small of her back and supple buttocks in shadows as she reached for something on the floor on the far side of the bed, beyond his view. Her body bathed in the false firelight from the wall screen as she reached into her purse set before it. When she swung around to face him, Ray expected s kiss. While the harsh sting of her knife taken from her purse sank easily into his flesh.

Ray howled like an animal.

The sudden pain announced an unexpected outcome. That horrible screech hunters and farmers knew so well. Her angry knife plunging into his chest, exacting a new cry from the fallen man who considered himself the good guy. Tearing through his lungs, the knife ended the screams forcing him into silence. Through his eyes, he took in the unbelievable sight of Ally's blade plunging into his unseen torso as he stared up at her. The harsh stings of pain, which only grew in intensity as she carved him up. Numbing pain and agony transporting him towards eventual shock. The realization that there would be no more future for Ray Kemper.

Blood flying as Ally continued stabbing into him. Raising a futile hand to stop her, Ray watched as the blade sliced effortlessly through the soft flesh of his right hand and plunged into his shoulder. A searing burn as blood from the injury splattered across his eyes and the media screen surface above him. Blood dripping upon the crimson puddle pooling into the folds of the transparent bed sheets before trickling down onto the media floor.

Now he couldn't even howl.

Barely managing a breath. Slipping quickly into an agony beyond comprehension. The pain only combat soldiers and murder victims typically felt. Wounds pathologists would claim he could never inflict upon himself. Ray did not think back on David's assurances to him on the monolith that the inventor could not be his murderer. The pain was too great to allow anything else to occupy David's currently overwhelmed mind. Nor did he consider that by breaking his oath to the government, Ray Kemper murdered the wrong person, perhaps snuffing out what would've been the best hope for humanity's survival. He had no time for the truth because—

Time was running out.

As shock numbed the pain, the memories of David finally returned to him. The inventor was right. *Dreamspace* had gotten the better of him, the expertly trained ex-Web Agent conceded. Or had his dedication to a life of meaning, brought him here? Thinking of his dead father's pile of hard-drives, he watched as Ally calmly reached over for-

Ray's eComp.

She placed the bloody earpiece on her ear. Her software eHacked into Ray's system with a third program she stole from the ex-lover whose true identity she would never know. Love, she learned, was not her true destiny, but did provide her the tricks to pull off the seemingly impossible. Ally's story, it turned out, was about truth and justice to her.   She used Ray's eComp to attempt to assume the supreme mantle of power on this third planet from a star termed the *Sun*. She aimed to cleanse this world that murdered her father for being a good, honest man. A nation so blind that it quit raising its kids or supporting their fellow Americans. Shutting their eyes in *Dreamspace* like a mouse cleaning its hands as the deadly snake in the cage approaches.

Ally's next action seemed to her the only remedy. A move set into motion by her eye swipe across Ray's hacked eComp iScreen. She thought back on that first human woman perhaps born to parents who could not even be called human. A little girl who consciously awakened in a world where she alone could see so much farther than anyone else with that newly enlarged prefrontal lobe. The reason why humans, unlike their predecessors, could carve an arrowhead in a single stroke rather than chipping and then having to assess where to cut next in a slow, unwinding process. Civilization, she considered, was just an ever more complex arrowhead from humanity to finally pierce the world.

"Blackout's *Yin Yang* codex has been found and is uploading to shareware sites worldwide," Ray's hacked Siri notified its hacker.

She knew the underground web routes could not be predicted or found until triggered. But one chance was all she required. She did not marvel at the power of the idea his program represented. Ally just felt lucky to upload the symbolic logic equations from the agent's hacked eComp to the dark web. Like a living thing, this powerful, digital code refused to be trapped. As the progress bar on the upload status slowly edged towards completion, she was given a rare, brief respite.

"Why?" Ray asked her.

She remained silent, eyes averted.

"Ally…" he pleaded as she peered down at him.

"You…killed my victim?" he muttered.

She didn't bother telling him how his Chinese murder victim discovered she'd aided Blackout. She couldn't risk him going to the authorities and drawing unneeded attention on her. Especially because she possessed a lot of illegal software from many sources. So after her suitor's violent actions to her in China, she silently left. She never was attracted to him, but he paid big money to watch her game and begged for her to visit. She went because the prospects of pro gaming were drying up with *Dreamspace's* release. Still, none of that was anybody's business but hers.

The former Web Agent already forgot the question he posed. With shock setting in, the pain turning to a growing coldness, David returned to the sole realization that he murdered David. What he thought was a heroic act was its antithesis. Didn't it go wrong when his superiors trusted him with Blackout's codex? He should've been killed or put in a supermax jail because he possessed such knowledge. Total power corrupted whether you realized it or not.

Watching him die, she didn't bother to scoff at Ray. He seemed now as pathetic as his lies. So stupid, he never considered that there could be more than one bad guy in his sorry. Did he think he was in a web movie?

The former FCC agent reminded this woman in that moment of the lyrics from her dad's favorite song, *Life on Mars* by David Bowie. The lyric where the lawman beats up the wrong guy seemed so *apropos* for Ray. He had to learn the hard way that everyone possessed their own agenda. Everyone lied about the big stuff. And after being disappointed by two men she loved-

She was done.

On her iScreen, she saw her upload complete. A map of the world unfolded, displaying her file being downloaded in various coordinates around the planet from shareware sites to a litany of cohorts and closeted would-be mass-murderers. The file paths for the ePocalypse appeared at first as flashes of light on the semi-opaque iScreen map; like nuclear missiles exploding around the globe on some monitor. Each successful upload displayed as another tiny flash. Although Ray's virus possessed a far smaller blast diameter, it didn't matter as the file was quickly resent around the planet by users' auto upload-bots.

Countless copies of Blackout's *Yin Yang* digital virus recursively arose from sleeper cells proliferating like the first asymptomatic spreaders of its namesake, now not from China, but the dark web. The end of humanity sown through the collective eye swipes of these unknowns. Disgruntled humans shunned by lovers. Jobless. Starving and pretending to be the opposite online. Passionate zealots who quashed the free debate of contrarian views. Would-be school shooters now stifled by armed guards at educational institutions, protecting kids as the society long did its money. And the many young minds who thought it so cool and never saw the Sun and Moon anyway, assuming a false narrative of guilt for the treason of a few. But mostly they were the unsung victims of shattered childhoods who in their minds had nothing to lose, burdened in the guilt of past leadership and the voters that allowed it.

On her stolen and hacked eComp iScreen, the world map was now covered in a thousand points of light filling the globe. No one could stop this future. She took off Ray's eComp, setting it down on the bloodied media screen floor. Turning in the faint glow of the simulated fire on the wall, she watched the color run from Ray's dying face. Yet she could never see this ex Web Agent as anything but a mindless defender of the forces which birthed the storm-

The floor exploded in electric sparks! All four media screen walls cracked and shattered. Although she expected to be fried by this initial discharge, the voltage stream didn't shock them, stifled by the electronic safeguards Hilton used in these top-line suites. Nonetheless, incandescent sparks lit up the room, illuminating Ray's final view of Ally in seemingly white fireworks before the invisible EMP blast pulsed through the wider area.

Without a sound, the city like most of the planet, was now blown back to the stone age. Hands could only craft the next generation of electronics in candlelight by non-electric devices. Earth by then would be covered in a vast ocean for an interminable epoch of aquatic silence and healing. No more electric U.V. farms. No more food. Those not killed in the first cyber strikes would soon drown in the prisons of their leveed zones. She didn't choose to die next to him, but where else did she have time to go? Not that it mattered-

Since the late 2040s, she and the world knew from Bellingham's blog that God birthed science on November 10th, 1619. Like most, she knew logic independent of faith proved His existence; the first five books of the Old Testament illustrating God akin to what she felt was *Star Wars'* Force, reached from within oneself by dealing with truths. She understood that the theme of Christ's Gospels returned all to the first five books of the Old Testament, reiterating Elijah's inner connection.

But where was the contrition?

She never heard anyone utter Isaiah's prayer of repentance that would be needed in end times. Wrestling with God meant wrestling with the truth, she knew from scripture, and no one wanted that.

"I appreciate that I lived during the storm," Ray heard her throaty whisper in the darkness, "rain flushes away the lies in your head. Let's you see everything as it is-"

Beyond the walls of The Beverly Hilton, they felt the thundering explosion ring out. A groaning sigh of collapsing metal as the electromagnetic gates of the L.A. Island floodwall gave way. Record-high tsunamis rose up through the gap in the broken wall, seemingly towering up to the heavens. Incredible waves of water not seen since ancient Crete's destruction, now threatening to swamp Beverly Hills Island. The earth rumbling as powerful waves closed in on them from all sides; all the product of a woman who achieved what Blackout failed to make real:

The ePocalypse.

Ally's gift to humanity she believed was her stinging judgment. Her species, she knew, had damned itself long before her birth. The grumbling tsunamis converging in rain and hail from all sides of the intersection of Wilshire Blvd and Santa Monica Ave was to wash the trash away. Her warm body vibrating against Ray's cold flesh.

Staring down at him, her gaze reminding Ray of that final beam of sunlight from the famous documentary, *Last Sun*. Those yachting sun-seekers of the late 2030s pursuing the final remnants of sunshine in a viral-afflicted planet now nearly covered in ever-expanding storms. He thought he was transported back to that date, the August 12th, 2039, approximately 400 miles south of Papeete, Tahiti, just before the last rainclouds swallowed up the final hole still revealing sunny skies. Practically everyone on earth witnessed the film's final moment of the last sunlight to touch the planet's surface.

In the darkness and confusion of near-death, Ray thought he was on one of those yachts, staring up at Ally with the vanishing sun cradling her head. Her outline silhouetted against the closing ring of clouds like a crown adorning her...before her eyes returned him to some semblance of reality. Ray realized that just because he felt love for her, didn't mean she felt the same for him.

His certainty had been his downfall.

For what had he ever offered of himself to her? Fighting for her acceptance as if to correct some previous story with his former handler. So determined to make all the events of his life matter became the false narrative he sought to impose on reality. To create meaning for him and avoid the lost time the famed 19th Century novelist Marcel Proust popularized. He had ignored Exxon's dire warning. That search for a higher purpose in his life led him to the end of the world. That's what he would've concluded if his muddled mind were not so weary as he approached death's door.

At that moment, she suddenly realized how fitting Apple's logo had been. Whether intentional or not, Steve Jobs's subtle warning of the bitten apple foretold technology to be the final forbidden fruit. The one to ultimately annihilate the species weakened by its lethal dependence on a highly vulnerable web like it did with Communist China a generation prior.

"Life's not a story with one ending," she whispered to Ray as the mega-tsunami thundered ever closer, rattling the walls of their hotel room, forcing her to yell, "it's like a video game of infinite outcomes and you weren't even playing-"

The virus killed them.

Its tsunami demolished their room along with the hotel building, ending Ray Kemper's existence. He was only one of the billions of victims claimed at the end of the world; for that species did, indeed, go extinct from events set into motion just before Ray Kemper's death at approximately 8:13 PM on Friday, February the 13th, 2060, the year Sir Isaac Newton accurately predicted.

Ray's death, like the others, came suddenly. He found himself stripped of a body, existing in only a dark void he assumed must be the state after life ended. He felt like David Bellingham after his accident. No pain. Yet in the progressive seconds, there was no final rendezvous with that vibrating, insectoid-like angel that David Bellingham popularized in his blog. Although Ray did not yet realize it, there was one revelation left to his existence to be revealed. A secret to shatter all things, born from a single word. A word he thought within the confines of his mind without a body-

A word that unleashed magic.

twenty-four

Ray thought the word.

Just as God in Holy Scripture didn't craft but spoke existence into being. Yet Ray didn't speak the word at all, only thinking it aloud in his mind. But hearing the word oddly uttered in David Bellingham's synthesized voice, not Ray's own. The electronic voice of that later 21st Century icon. A confused Ray Kemper again conjured the word in his mind, hearing it curiously spoken around him:

"Mommy."

Ray Kemper heard shuffling footsteps in the darkness. His eyes were mechanically opened. Ray realized in stumbling shock that he was back in the lab; staring up at the oversized ducts lining the fireproof foam ceiling. He now oddly realized that he'd been the nine-year-old boy, David Bellingham, preparing to play what his Mommy told him would make it all better.

And it did.

New memories raced in to replace the old. The reality of Ray Kemper's life now partially dissolved as David awakened from what he felt was a realistic dream. He just completed the game's first cycle. The words the elder Bellingham told him suddenly resonated:

"All those games I played as a child sometimes gaming as myself and sometimes as others until I got the level right-"

Now David realized he'd gamed for the first time as Ray Kemper and lost. Curiously he met the elder version of himself along the way. He only now realized the great notion that Ray Kemper forgot on his manhunt was the truth of David's existence. On that final day of World War IV when Ray eyed the *Dreamspace* ad with young David Bellingham set to begin his childhood video game. The truth of his real identity illustrated before him at that moment was singed away by Ravenna's attractive voice over the comlink, asking:

"Ray, you with me?

Her inquiry marked the precise moment young David fully immersed into his in-game character in that digital representation of a possible future; as an agent hot on the heels of Blackout in December 2059. Now this child fathomed insights into his existence, which the elder version of himself made clear in-game; Jim Tutwiler's creation was a portal to get to the future where David could keep his species alive.

He wound up in a dead-end through the only time travel permitted by Einsteinian relativity; experiencing the future packaged as pure data flowing backward in time through many possible pasts in ways that didn't upset physical order. The data was delivered in written words that could be recorded on film or spoken as Ravenna did over their comlink. Ideas could travel backward in time. Just like the device Albert Einstein predicted and named a *tachyonic anti-telephone*. It allowed young David as Ray to mirror his older self and somehow see the wider world. The Universe wasn't an Oracle, telling him what to do or answering questions in a post-science world. His unique experiences showed David the way through, revealing the truth to shatter lies; leading the boy back here to again utter the word as he heard unseen footsteps shuffling around him:

"Mommy."

A moment later she appeared, leaning over him in the comport. She looked tired, but was thrilled to see him, "David, I missed you so much," he saw her tightening her hold on his paralyzed hand that he couldn't feel, shockingly reinforcing his fractured physical state, "how was the game?"

The boy felt immeasurably relieved to see his Mommy's face before him. Now somehow his tragic injury didn't feel as awful as it had been before this undertaking. Whereas most believed what they saw, David Bellingham now saw what he believed. And he believed what he gamed as a boy.

His possible outcomes relied on the expressed symptoms and spread of the COVID-19 strains that he somehow knew were varied in each game he would play. But all were chameleons of an eventual possibility of extinction wrought by a Chinese tyrant's pollution manifested in varied forms. Once the New Jerusalem had for the bribes of its leaders and remaining elites brought a time of trouble upon itself and the world just as the Old Testament foretold; a time worse than even The Black Death to challenge the chorus of nations like never before.

Mom repeated her question to her child overcome in thought, "How was it, baby?"

"So real!" his audible thoughts broadcasted through the speakers lining his primitive comport, "I was a government agent in the future named Ray Kemper. I met and killed myself, but not how it sounds. And I did it all to save the woman I love."

"Love?" his Mother was taken aback by such an adult sentiment.

"Yeah," his excited mental tone echoed through the lab in his electronic voice, "she killed me!"

The mechanized device blinked his eyes closed for a moment as he reassured her, "But I was bad. Real bad. I fell for the wrong girl who was worse than me. She killed me along with everybody else on Earth. But it was awesome, Mom!" he realized the burning truth, "I want to see her again."

A relieved Jim Tutwiler bent over the comport beside David's mother. Before this game, the child didn't even know who Jim Tutwiler was or what was going on. But from playing the game, he knew much about the sporting a thick dark beard. Jim didn't want to shave until David finished the first game cycle. The young boy spied the weariness in the man's eyes from the belief that his creation would one day kill the child. But for now, Jim didn't introduce himself but made a single point clear:

"The love interest will reappear each time you play, always the same but different. She's wired into my game-"

"Like a mirror," the boy's notion struck an eerie chord in Jim Tutwiler, somehow making the creator suspect that this child sensed some deeper truth about his invention.

"How long was I in it?" queried the nine-year-old.

"You spent twenty-one days in-game," replied Jim.

"No," David sharply corrected him in his synthesized voice, "this is no game," then his mind drifted as children were wont to do, thinking, "Pia was right."

"Pia? Is that your lady friend's name?" asked his Mother.

"No. Pia was my only friend but I killed her, well...not really," the boy marveled at the peculiarities of what he'd experienced.

Then he remembered how China's concealment of the biological Yin Yang virus and the later internet takedown followed by Blackout's own digital Yin Yang virus could end humanity. The early lessons of what to avoid were cut and dry in comparison to future challenges he would discover.

David would eventually game as himself and sometimes as others like Agent Kemper, key individuals who came in contact with David Bellingham at some critical juncture in a possible future. All part of David Bellingham's unlocking of the next steps in what would be revealed as the Universe's plan of salvation for a remnant of chosen people of Abrahamic DNA and those with U.S. citizenship. Many mistakes would be made in-game. Young David stumbled, but he did not fall. Never abandoning the mission symbolized in the cat's long shadow. But he realized the way to cure death was not going to lay at the end of the interactive video game road.

Scientifically speaking, all roads eventually led back to God free of the meddling of experts and others' rationalizations. Just the Torah and one's inner mind to guide actions. In most of his childhood game-play, David would discover timelines where humanity typically remained hard at work, creating a uniquely cynical world and thinking that was the way it was. Refusing to wrestle, but accepting the status quo or letting it warp their actual government and thereby themselves in basic ways. Allowing the few to abuse and kill the masses while calling it *progress*. But in the end, it wasn't just the historical byproduct of homelessness, mass-imprisonment, drug-addiction, and starvation, but the end of all life that this political wickedness would create.

America became like the Dodo bird, oblivious to threats even when being murdered in their homes by a weaponized virus due to the concealment of key data by the originating nation's dictator whom many U.S. leaders long-served. Young David now knew that the United States faced Machiavelli's *Prince*, Xi Jinping, who struck his possible death blow by simply keeping facts secret about his virus. In the future timeline he just gamed, David saw *Dreamspace* as the vehicle to save everyone, regardless of their qualities, beliefs, and character. In hindsight, salvation as the gift of a *Dreamspace* subsidized subscription was too cheap to be real.

This boy now understood that the final tale of the Israelites was one of two cities, an old and new Jerusalem. Both in their time were economically taken over by foreigners through trickery for exactly 18 years. The ancient Jerusalem lost itself to the allure of its Greek pedophile overlords' child slavery. The reason why sodomy could never be allowed to proliferate. Whereas the New Jerusalem failed to realize its status as the only nation to host and spread the Torah's inner-connection through its distinct freedom of religion. It too allowed the proliferation of pedophilia. Just as it failed for a long time to realize that through trickery and bribes, American presidents from Clinton to Obama long served Chinese slavery; through that servitude, America committed the largest imprisonment and corresponding rape in human history of its own from these pro-Chinese politicians embracing slavery. Then the consolidated media and treasonous U.S. politicians trapped Americans in an invisible prison.

Only after gaming many cycles did David realize just how much a belief in God and the health of domestic manufacturing determined everything as George Washington ardently claimed. It decided the subsequent society constructing the shared reality of the nation. Making things and buying them bound citizens together, warding out the foreign threats George Washington warned republics were vulnerable to from the ancient Roman republic's own history. As an example, David's gaming later revealed that Blackout's program wasn't even created by the teenager. It was funded by Mr. Zero who many games later was revealed to be a frontman for the remaining Communist Chinese government which never ended, attempting to fuel a second Web Blackout. The *dying man of Asia* still yearned to drag the chorus of nations down with its suicidal regime that long-doomed its own.

Communist China had always been death. Because it deprived its people of the wealth and property they worked to acquire. The wealth that Washington wisely noted Americans needed to buttress their liberty and freedom. Without manufacturing, America would be taken over from within by its treasonous leaders. Attacked without provocation by the Yin Yang virus while its politicians obfuscated the issue to avoid their culpable guilt of the monster America needlessly created. America would have to get real or die to have a COVID-free nation. It had to start by facing those who so abused Americans from within.

And what of love?

Throughout his life, David remained tight-lipped on the topic. In his blogs, he seldom spoke on the heart. He never divulged that he experienced the same lover not just once or twice in those childhood games, but every single time he played.

She always filled his first in-game experience, making him feel as if he'd previously met her in a way the ancient philosopher Plato spoke of: so that she never really felt like a stranger. Ravenna and Ally were only two of nearly endless manifestations of this woman, who like the speed of light, became a constant in David Bellingham's unlikely universe: ever-changing and yet the same.

She proved that not money, success, or victory were suitable goals, but living correctly and finding love in preparation for the next generation was the key woven into nearly every life story. Living well brought upon him a better version of her. Like Eve from Adam's rib, in hindsight, she was always a part of him before he even knew her. David came to heed Mohammed's parting warning to his male followers to be good to their women, for they were truly God's gift to man. Whether David would find true love with this woman, would remain a secret for now.

The yearning to see her burned within his heart in a new, mature way. A powerful array of feelings motivating him to want to re-enter the game. Tears flowing from his paralyzed eyes. Love's first touch hurt now that it was gone. From a different perspective, this injured boy discovered love through a computer projection; an expression of programming code rendered so realistically that it conjured up a possible, future love interest that couldn't help but be real in any universe David was in.

"Mommy, can I play the game again?" he read the trepidation in her eyes, adding, "Pretty please."

A chill ran up his mother's spine as she heard the request in his synthesized voice. Somehow she sensed that her son was no longer a boy nor exclusively her own. As a mother, she understood that a woman had wrenched her son's heart away, her greatest fear dissipating. Hopefully, she prayed that her young David could find it without the female suitor again killing him.

Young David would find love over and over again. His recent romance tragically mirrored her own. But perhaps, she thought, he could learn and get better? With a smile and a slight nod, mom consented to let her son play Dr. Jim Tutwiler's creation a second time. She would agree for him to play many times more until he went on to invent the first digital chat room years later, becoming one of the wealthiest individuals on Earth and the founder of a future made possible through his distinct inventions that followed.

For now, it felt unbearable.

Waiting impatiently as Jim and his staff restarted the massive computer processors. David could barely contain himself. Those agonizing minutes between cycles of playing when he heard the processors initiating, filled him with the desperate yearning for his lover's touch. The most dangerous aspect of Artificial Intelligence would be its ability to seduce the heart, which inherently controlled the real, underlying core.

The reason why stories typically were based in a couple coming together. Often, young David would be forced to replay the same level until he got it right, returning to a pivotal moment on the path to an ideal outcome manifested in reality through his successes and mistakes. The free-flowing program code of the crude reflection of reality would again allow David to peer into a mirror of himself extending back through space and time. But the lone compass setting remained her. Always there at the inception of his digital voyage. Her familiar face greeting him in Spanish, English, or some other far-flung language as he first entered Tutwiler's virtual creation. Still different and yet the same as Plato wrote of so that they never were strangers.

As the lab computers hosting this digital world reloaded at Loma Linda Medical Center, young David reminded himself that the last time he played, he fell for the wrong lover, like his mother before him. He loved Ravenna, or at least thought so, and confused her with Ally. Hopeless romantics often made such mistakes, imposing a truth in their heads rather than what was. It would take many cycles of play before David Bellingham informed his heart. While the cat nearly always remained a gentle reminder to stay his course.

For now, a nine-year-old David doesn't even suspect that he was fated to be the example of what would happen if God had not interceded in human affairs. God was supposed to interject the Archangel *Saint Michael* who watches over the children, to stand up and anoint a political figure. The missing prophecy never came to fruition in his gaming.

He sensed that Americans in another branch of the multiverse would consider him like a character in a fictionalized story. He was so far apart from them that he would seem like a work of art. While after China's dictator intentionally concealed COVID-19, the borders remained idiotically open for more viral strains. America's economic dependence on tyranny could spell its doom. Xi Jinping held a death grip on the U.S. through other strains his 480,000 infected Chinese passengers held on American soil. The end move of World War III remained invisible to Americans, completely subduing them and leaders, media, and everyone else for embracing Chinese slavery. Their silence on the

Islamic Chinese genocide fed the possible genocide of the world and proved it now served Communist tyranny.

David had no idea that some of his audience were the lucky ones. Because his life served as the best outcome if America continued. For it's 28 years of treason, the world would end in any future branching outcome without the Lord's direct intervention.

Somehow, young David sensed he was now destined to construct a Tutwiler-level of reality in a massive-multiplayer-online-game called *Garden* rather than a duo gamer format like *Dreamspace*. This massive multiplayer role-playing game would redesign existence in a new way with unexpected replay appeal to all who came to know of that tale.

For just knowing the story of *Garden* like *Dreamspace* before it would change the trajectory of the New Jerusalem and the world. Despite all that happened and all he now knew on a global scale, David almost solely burned for Ravenna and Ally. Now he might be able to double back down another path with them. His game had just delivered a sting to show him that defending free-will and liberty was what the universe always desired from Americans. He could not force or trick people into their own salvation. They must choose life with their own free will.

Despite his mother nearby, young David now only wishes to see that woman again in any hair color and get it right. Trying as all true lovers might, to find a way to preserve that primal attraction that appeared so rarely and still was so commonly shunned. Love like faith was individualized and resisted control even by leaders' laws as he and Ravenna had proven. Beauty and love were self-evident even to babies. Whereas adults often lost themselves in their thinking, turned upside down without realizing it by their leaders as they struggled just to make ends meet. Finding through non-legal etiquette like *political correctness* that some words were not acceptable, thereby censoring thoughts and blinding those to evil as the writer George Orwell *newspeak* would in his seminal work 1984. Despite all that happened, if a young David doesn't ever see her face again, he hopes to at least hear the voice of his former handler asking-

"Ray, you with me?" Ravenna inquired over agent Ray Kemper's private eComp comlink.

Her words awakened the FCC agent from his momentary daydream as he squatted out of view, eyeing the famous picture of young David Bellingham's face below him. It filled a meta ad not for *Dreamspace*, but for *Garden* covering the floor screen of the crowded eHallway. The advertisement of David's upcoming game covered even the distant ceiling of waves high above down to the walls and floor of this online corridor where he now man-hunted.

That iconic image of the great inventor as a child set to begin Jim Tutwiler's immersive game surrounded him. The ad for David Bellingham's new game called *Garden* continued. Staring into the ad's iconic photo of young David Bellingham set to play his childhood game, FCC agent Kemper lost himself for a moment in a great revelation suddenly robbed by Ravenna's voice chirping over the comlink. The notion evaporated like vapor through a clenched fist as he heard his handler's beautiful voice.

He re-focused his attention on the supreme gravity of the moment, tracking the world's most dangerous eTerrorist still many paces ahead. Honing in on the enemy of World War IV, he eyed Blackout's dark hoodie on the move through the sea of surreal Skins filling the packed, digital eCorridor of web chatters. The FCC agent's training and skill focused. He must kill Blackout and contain the eTerrorist's deadly, world-ending virus, or everything Ray knew would be destroyed by the ePocalypse. Charging forward, the skilled Web Agent felt caught up in events so significant that they could only be described as the most important in history.

Darting through the crowd of Skins without touching and lagging a single user, he didn't allow himself to wonder again on what great notion he'd forgotten? He ignored the now ubiquitous ad for Bellingham Labs' *Garden 1.0*. The way one's mind could wander at the strangest of times when he should've remained focused solely on his target. Whatever the notion was, thought FCC agent Ray Kemper, it seemed so vital and true at the time yet now for the life of him-

He just couldn't remember why.

DREAMSPACE
ESCAPE C19
WATCH
THE MOVIE SIMULATION
WWW.CENTEREDAMERICA.COM
PG-13

CHINA LIED MASS MURDERING WITH COVID-19
REVEALED THE COLD WAR NEVER ENDED

THE SERVICE ECONOMY IS THE ILLUSION OF
AN IMAGINARY COMMON INTEREST FUNDING OUR ENEMY

TO WIN THE WAR,
AMERICA MUST:

PROTECT THE PEOPLE
LIVE FREE UNTIL COVID FREE - EXTEND UNEMPLOYMENT
ONE PARENT AT HOME - SCHOOLING SUBSIDY FOR FAMILIES
ESSENTIAL WORKERS - HAZARD PAY AND LIFE INSURANCE
STAY HEALTHY - BIFURCATE HOSPITALS AND COVID-19 CLINICS
FREE SPEECH - END CENSORSHIP SOCIAL MEDIA
DECOMMUNIZE MEDIA - REMOVE COMMUNIST PROPAGANDA

DECOMMUNIZE GOVERNMENT
TRIALS FOR TREASON -
POLITICIANS ALIGNED WITH CHINA,
WHO INSTITUTED THE DEADLY SERVICE ECONOMY,
WHO ENSLAVED CITIZENS IN FOR-PROFIT PRISONS,
WHO PROPAGATED VIOLENCE
AND DECLARED AMERICAN PORTS SANCTUARIES FOR CHINA.

MAKE IN AMERICA AGAIN- CHEXIT
MADE IN AMERICA - MANUFACTURE ESSENTIAL GOODS
CLOSE BORDERS - CONTAIN AND PROTECT FROM BIO ATTACKS
END SLAVERY - END MASS IMPRISONEMENT SLAVE LABOR

BEFORE CHINA/NORTH KOREA *STRIKE AGAIN*

CHINA LIES WE DIE
CLOSE BORDERS NOW

DECOMMUNIZE THE
GOVERNMENT

CLIMATE CHANGE!
LET'S MAKE
IN AMERICA
(NOT IN CHINA)

CHINA IS
ONE DICTATOR
WITH A BILLION
SLAVES

RESPECT

CHILDREN NEED THEIR MOTHERS
END GENERATION CHILD ABUSE
ONE PARENT AT HOME SUBSIDY

LET US LIVE
TO MAKE
MANKIND
FREE

CISM
THE

BLM
END SLAVERY AGAIN
END FOR-PROFIT PRISONS
MANUFACTURE IN USA

ESSENTIAL
HAZ PAY +
LIFE INSURANCE

GARDEN 1.0

A sneak peek into the opening chapter of the next installment in the-five-part *Dreamspace* series.

part one

Gardeners

"For behold. The Lord will come with fire
And with His chariots, like a whirlwind,"

Isaiah 66:15

prologue

They came at dusk.

Usually they were forbidden from visiting the third planet of this sun, which future *Homo sapiens* would name Earth. But almost 60,000 years ago, there were few humans, and none realized they were on a roughly spherical planet. Even their continued existence seemed doubtful given the radical climate change brought on by recent volcanic activity. The reason why the alien's mother ship remained unseen in geosynchronous orbit above, rather than landing.

They left their ship in the stratosphere, slowly gliding down through the planet's atmosphere. Finally, they flew high above the flat, windswept landscape, which would remain barren for countless eons to come. Only when the first cities of so-called *civilization* would arise through farming, slaving, and killing, would this landscape change.

For now, only Neanderthal hunter-gatherers largely stalked deer in the region, the hominid's presence noted by their sensor systems. The planet's surface was unsafe, inundated with lethal saber-toothed lions and a myriad of deadly beasts, which only much later would be hunted to extinction by humans. *Homo sapiens* recently escaped their native continent of Africa a few thousand years prior. Part of a tiny group that first crossed the vast northern desert blocking the path to Eurasia. Now their progeny, numbering 42 humans of varying age in this region, slumbered in the cave ahead of the flying life forms.

These seven creatures of seemingly black, glass-like bodies raced through the sky without making a sound. Aesthetically, they bore a faint resemblance to a half-crushed spider. Earth's life usually contained two matching halves while these creatures remained asymmetrical. Seven varied limbs would be the best description for what protruded from the semi-elliptical suit surrounding their headless torsos. Within their pressurized armored suits, this bizarre life form was a swirling vapor of hydrogen sulfide, conducting electrical signals emanating from some unknown point beyond reality. The gaseous being reflected its home within a nebula in a semi-parallel dimension of the multiverse.

Although the life form utilized no organized language, the electrical signals powered their consciousness, issuing directives. These specific directions were only in hindsight evidenced as brilliant and originating from God who was outside time and space. Perhaps it was the reason this species lived so long that they lost much of their history over time as they remained the most hallowed in the Cosmos. Their inner portal to the Divine was emitted from within the alternating magnetic centers of their gaseous body.

This life form was not the only extraterrestrial species to visit the planet Earth; various aliens traveled to this planet in vehicles of differing technologies, but all came because the Universe commanded them to. Otherwise this world was strictly off-limits, gestating a unique species for a purpose no life form could fathom.

So it was rare for such a visitor to be here, like these other-worldly creatures in their seemingly black crystal suits. Their gear protected not them, but Earth's inhabitants from the viral cloud constituting semi-vaporous creatures, which if released in the atmosphere, would quickly consume all life on Earth. The reason why the aliens rarely touched the ground: hovering safely above as they did now, a hundred feet over the mouth of the cave below.

A brilliant fire crackled from the cavern's mouth, splitting the darkness of the night. The aliens' scanning telemetry revealed most of the hunter-gatherers were within the cave. A few stood century during the night at the cave's entrance while a scout on the perch above kept a watchful eye from afar on the funeral party gathered down the hill. Down below around the funeral pyre, some of the deceased's relatives slept on fur blankets; the once blazing flame now ash and dying embers.

One of the levitating aliens high above dispatched a small robotic droid, which exited the spider-like creature's shortest limb housing the device. The droid cloaked itself invisible as it silently flew down to collect the bulk of the ashes from the funeral pyre.

Objective achieved, the taskforce veered off, electromagnetically levitating back to the reservation of land cordoned off by electromagnetic fences. As commanded, this alien race's army of robots had created an eight-mile-wide garden reserve between three rivers in an area rich in natural gold. They constructed this place by gathering plants from around the globe, growing the most ideal first in a nursery before transplanting them to create the well-manicured, natural-looking garden. In a grassy clearing at the garden's center, the collected ash from the pyre suddenly reconstituted into a human being using a technology native to this race.

Life was breathed into ash, along with an addition to his mind now congealing from dust, forming the mid-20's human male who awoke alone, consumed in fear. Only a moment before in his life, a huge bear had attacked him with frightening claws shimmering in the noon-time sun. Now it was evening and his fellow hunters were nowhere to be seen.

Eyes darting about.

He studied the lush garden brimming with exotic fruits, wild birds, and animals largely concealed in a sea of leaves and tree trunks. A gentle stream could be heard somewhere behind this clearing of manicured grass bathed in a shaft of moonlight. Rising to his feet, he found himself starving as the reanimation process drained most of his blood sugar. Plucking a pear from a bush, he bit into the sweetest flesh he ever tasted before thundering footsteps closed in from behind him.

Spinning around in the darkness, he suspected the bear that most recently took his life. But he saw nothing, hearing only a booming voice resounding not in the man's native tongue, but a new language he now recognized. Words in this unique tongue thundered through the garden, not from hidden speakers planted in the compound, but rather from a special portal added within Adam's consciousness through which he alone heard the voice roar:

"I am God the Almighty. You are Adam. You shall dress and keep this garden. Of every tree here you may freely eat, except the tree of knowledge."

Clouds parted overhead, allowing a beam of what Adam thought to be moonlight. But this greenish illumination emanated from a place beyond space and time. This type of light could pass through objects and could make people glow. Now it chose to shine conventionally upon the beautiful tree bearing fist-sized, red fruit in the form of a human heart.

"For in the day that you eat this, you shall surely die. Do you understand, Adam?" thundered the voice.

Although the man had possessed a different name, he suddenly felt he'd always been Adam and now wished to ask so many questions: like how he came to arrive in this garden after the bear attack? He wondered if he was dead or if this place was some afterlife, like the ones preached by his tribe's shamans. But his lips quivered at asking anything as he nodded in silent acknowledgment about the single act he was forbidden to do.

The voice disappeared.

Adam spent a week alone in the garden. When loneliness crept in, the alien over-seers were commanded through their conscious interface to the Universe to gather specific animal life forms from the wild, introducing them into the garden. He was commanded to pick names for each animal as they were introduced into the fenced-in game reserve. Adam dutifully carried out this goal, eating fruit while slaughtering and cooking various animals as meals. Each of his queries or needs were answered with some verse of the ancient spirit song. In this way-

Adam lived with God.

Which was true, but not quite as he perceived. For he did not know the Godly voice was artificial to his experience, an ancient message of tones and syntax kept alive by these aliens all these years. Nor would he have understood that the voice was also directly from God but mentally projected through them. His race had no clue that the Universe often used intermediaries termed *angels,* much like these vaporous aliens, because the Cosmos already knew how this behavioral test of Adam's would turn out. The Universe knew how everything would be, including the ending of this ongoing, moral test of the garden's occupant that would extend for many eons to come.

The force of evil, on the other hand, was infinitely less powerful than the Universe. It acted on anger, representing the darkness of the prior proto-human, cannibalistic ancestors of these creatures. Those violent beasts which ate each other's brains, mutating and expanding their consciousness to edge their way to the intellect of someone like Adam. Those actions were long since abandoned millions of years prior. But due to the physics concept of entropy, nothing that has ever happened is ever lost, but rather stored as data in the present; an unseen force evident in the slithering serpent lingering unseen for now in shadows. Unlike the vaporous extraterrestrial life forms, this being was part of the test of obedience in the *Garden*.

The serpent knew the test subject who died and was reborn would not be easy to sway. This man was on borrowed time bequeathed from God. So the snake knew to wait many weeks. Biding his time as an ever-growing loneliness consumed Adam, forcing the aliens to initiate the next directive.

Their floating med-bots sedated him while slumbering. In a subterranean lab, an android later surgically extracted a rib from his body. Although the wound could've been genetically healed, they were to leave a painful scar. The missing rib was for Adam to realize something had been taken from him. For all gifts come at a cost and this one should be painful. The true source of this pain would bring both love and misery to him for the remainder of his days; ever-culminating consequences of his choices to follow.

In the alien mother ship, an advanced team cultured Adam's DNA from the rib's bone cells into a female form which they accelerated in age to be slightly younger than her intended mate. A sophisticated, artificial data device was implanted into her brain, allowing her to mimic both Adam's social conventions and overly complex language. She possessed life knowledge without having lived, knew his tastes, and how to cleverly manipulate him.

They were not the same.

There were other human females on Earth at the time, most of them remaining trapped by an impregnable northern desert and the only exit point being Africa's Horn. But none of them were chosen by God to ultimately continue the species bloodline. For Adam and Eve's bloodline would improbably expand out into all future humanity, including the species' native African counterparts.

There was no way to anticipate that fact at the time by anyone. But through their intuition, these alien *angel* caretakers knew God placed within these two mates a portal that the Universe would one day share with all humanity. This inner portal, however, would only be made obvious much later in the human journey.

For now, a test of obedience to the Divine continued for the couple. Some days later, the serpent appeared to Eve one afternoon as she picked fruit while Adam foraged in a nearby thicket.

"God," hissed the serpent, "has said that you shall not eat of every tree in this garden?"

She didn't fear the snake because Adam told her that nothing in the garden could threaten them, but she knew the one limitation which she now voiced, "Eating that fruit would kill us."

"No, you would not die," charmed the serpent, "for God knows that in the day you eat of that forbidden fruit, your eyes shall be opened and you shall be as gods, knowing good and evil."

Eve turned to eye the heart-shaped fruits. Indeed they were as beautiful as its blazing sun, she thought. On impulse, she plucked one, biting into its flesh.

The occupants of the garden were being tested in an environment rich in all necessary resources while being commanded to abstain from eating this one thing. This test of obedience was vital to dictate the life form's subsequent story, allowing the ultimate offspring to measure how far they advanced at the end in comparison to the beginning.

The vaporous garden care-takers had done well in their own species' test so long ago, with none breaking the one limitation commanded until after tens of millions of years and then, only by accident. The Universe all the while knew the whole story of everything with branching, endless outcomes carved from free will. Yet if the free choice was taken out of the equation and peoples' actions were controlled by the Cosmos, their descendants would turn wicked and stupid. Evil would consume them just as-
Eve consumed the forbidden fruit.

Humans in comparison to other life forms did not fare well in the obedience test, lasting only two weeks after Eve's arrival. The poor, initial performance would've astounded the alien caretakers if not for their wisdom gleaming from their ancient existence. Another later group of *angel workers* would later break with their commands and take pity on these humans, offering them unique tools for which these creatures' punishment was documented in the *Old Testament*.

The fact that extraterrestrials occupied Earth up to the 21st Century was well acknowledged by various retired U.S. military personnel, Clinton's former Chief of Staff, as well as Russian Prime Minister Vladimir Putin. Both Clinton and Putin learned only while in office that there were branches of their governments beyond their reach, run by non-terrestrial beings for unknown objectives.

These alien caretakers throughout the ages were dispatched by a universal Force, which early in human history was incorrectly anthropomorphized into the shape of idols. Divine honesty was shared only with the Israelites who learned their God had no shape. God made clear he would dispatch at certain times, his *anointed ones*. Sometimes heavenly beams of light passed through walls and ceilings, striking humans, thereby altering their DNA to produce a Divine messenger they often naturally birthed as their progeny. Special beings which acted as agents of the Universe.

Most of these messengers didn't even know they were Divine, part extraterrestrials.

Such people were recorded in Holy Scripture, like Enoch, whose line eventually bore all of the remaining western civilization to follow through his grandson, Noah. Just as the Universe later entered into a pact with one of Noah's posterity, Abraham, whose Divinely altered DNA assured God's special covenant would be embedded in the genetics of all of Abraham's offspring. One of his descendants, the prophet Elijah would discover that the Universe was the God of all things and not just reigning over Israelites; a truth rendering all other idols to be false; a fact long-forgotten by humans since the Universe scattered them out of Babel eons prior. For after the flood, *Homo sapiens* sought only to build a tower out of their proving ground to quickly reach their Maker and escape this crucible of freedom a minority often turned into hell.

Elijah was shown the Divine portal implanted into the DNA of Adam. His knowledge in a tiny part reflected a link to the Universe's mind. In the *Garden*, he was far from perfect. Like most males of his species, Adam was a pushover for beauty, truly lost the moment Eve bit into the fruit as he would follow her in humanity's greatest fall.

The forbidden fruit immediately caused radical, biogenetic changes inside Eve unlike any before it. Her prefrontal cortex now mutated in a massive leap in cognition. Eve's forehead portion of her skull physically expanded along with her skin as her consciousness took on that of a modern human being. Her forehead increased upward along with her enhanced sense of *being*, viewing herself now as a person in the exterior world as well as aware of the endless, internal realm within her mind due to her expanded Divine portal. Eve underwent a quantum leap never before experienced in any prior Earthling.

Tens of thousands of years later, the famed Harvard scientific thinker, Stephen J. Gould, would theorize these rapid, biomorphic changes evident in the fossil record could only be possible through incest. Gould's agnosticism kept him from considering the Holy Scripture's depiction of ancient, genetic nanotechnology. Because the devices released by the forbidden fruit, indeed, gave humans their enhanced intellect to fathom good and evil by imagining and interpreting the possible chain of outcomes from events. Eve's mind's eye freed her from what was revealed as the confines of the moment, limiting all other terrestrial creatures on this planet. Staring at her hands, she felt like her mind was moving through progressive moments to a future she could now predict or attempt to conjure from many possible, current actions.

When Adam beheld Eve's face, he found her enlarged forehead only accentuated her stunning beauty. While the complexity of her voice, deep inflection, and sudden depth in her eyes seemed so much more complex than his own; almost like a chorus of many minds bound together as one. Knowing that this beautiful mate whom he so loved was now far more than Adam. He dreaded he'd lost her forever. One of the many reactions to be repeated throughout human history. Instead of trusting in God, his lust and love for her compelled him to also eat the fruit, which she claimed to be a gift of fate.

As he tasted the forbidden thing, Adam felt aware in a way he could never previously have understood. His forehead expanded as he, himself, awakened. Like dropping off a cliff with so much more information rushing through him until he realized he was more than he had been before it. Now he marveled at the garden's beauty in a newfound human way. The sudden awareness of embarrassment struck him. For they were naked unlike the fur or scale covers of the animals in the garden. Only after they feebly attempted to cover their exposed genitals with leaves, did the Universe appear.

God's voice was not mentally projected by the gaseous aliens. The Divine presence, however, was cloaked by a technology emanating from a baton-shaped probe, flying end over end, which suddenly passed by earth. That probe was dispatched in the wake of the Big Bang. Like the alien probe *Omuamua* that similarly passed Earth in October, 2017, this one caused molecules and atoms to rearrange on Earth before Adam and Eve. Scientists would never have guessed this object to be a message from God. Nor would they have suspected that the probe's technological stagecraft was paralleled by God's actual presence in reality.

The probe's technology cloaked the actual manifestation, minimizing the ripples that an obvious Divine Visitation could cause through multiple cosmos. In this case, God wanted some degree of disturbance and allowed it to flow into this and parallel universes beyond comprehension. The disturbance sowed the karmic punishment into Adam and Eve's progeny until the end of days. For they were made to know that their progeny would because of them, suffer, toil, and endure lives of pain while struggling to find the spiritual connection Adam and Eve had taken for granted in the garden possessing all things including immortality; where the only danger was breaking that one rule. A challenge humans resisted for only fourteen days.

The test was over.

God's quantum curse radiated out as a punishment needed corrective for humans to one day via their free will better reflect their Creator's hopes for them. For God was good. While sadly, humans were generally not. Despite knowing through scripture that their soul's impending immortality relied on how they lived this life on earth, they mostly fell into wickedness, greed, and the pleasures of this life as if it were the only one, failing to believe in anything but what their senses beheld.

Only in Eden was the direct relationship between God and His creation standard, made possible by prophecies given to the alien custodians of Eden eon's prior. The aliens' purpose was to speak for the Lord who now directly addressed Adam from their perspective. The aliens could not fathom the meaning of the language spoken to the humans:

"Adam," the Universe's voice roared, "Where are you? Why do you hide from Me?"

A beam of greenish, yellow light shone down from the heavens. Thinking himself concealed in a dense thicket of bushes, a petrified Adam feared the wrath from his breaking of the sole commandment. The beam of light suddenly shined down, passing through the bushes and highlighting every inch of the trembling man:

"I was afraid," replied Adam, "I was naked. So I hid."

"Who told you that you were naked?" inquired the Light which now made Adam and Eve's bodies glow. When he received no answer from them, God asked, "Have you eaten of the one tree I commanded you not to touch or consume?"

"My woman gave me the fruit," confessed Adam, "and I ate of it."

God's ire turned upon Eve, "What have you done?"

"It was the serpent, he beguiled me," she fearfully retorted, tears in her eyes. She had trusted her feelings which made her follow the snake. Even now she denied the wickedness she had done, the same self-denial cursing her posterity. The ability to blind oneself while committing evil.

"Now you have chosen to be like God, coming to better know the difference between good and evil," thundered the Lord.

The Universe next punished the serpent before the couple, showing who was truly powerful. They were made to understand that this evil creature would continue slithering alongside humanity, biting the heels of their future offspring to follow.

In the wake of their eviction, the symptoms of their new state of mortality became clear. They would be the first to age and die in a continuous line of life jumping through ancestors on the long and crooked road to redemption. Floating swords of fire now barred the couple from the entrances of Eden as the aliens inside its confines, packed up their equipment. Before departing, they incinerated the *Garden* to ashes, the wind scattering its remains to the four corners of a planet now given to humanity.

East of Eden, the couple remained frightened and alone, separated from God. Both Adam and his woman knew now they would die. They and their progeny would be burdened with a painful delivery from their offspring's larger heads, permanently increased by the fruit. These humans would no longer hunt and gather, but farm. Their relationship with time now vastly different than other proto-humans. Humans like Adam and Eve would work for the delayed rewards far into the future that farming represented. They would make their bread in toil, eat bitter herbs, and be cut by thorns while dangerous animals would be free to hunt them as prey outside the *Garden*. Their heightened temporal awareness from their enlarged foreheads would give them the edge of intelligence over their brawn and bring overwhelming sorrow and guilt.

The Universe did supply Adam and Eve with durable animal skin garments to cover and protect their nakedness. They made similar outfits for their two sons who followed. One brother, Caine, who used the land to farm killed Abel in cold blood, favoring open ranges of land for animal herding. Caine's offspring mixed with the wider proto-human stock, expanding the mutation of enlarged foreheads throughout the wider population.

Caine's descendant's intelligence would be equaled only by their wickedness as they populated the Earth. Using primitive technologies to drive a society so evil that eons later their Maker would drown all but one family in a worldwide flood documented by nearly all ancient cultures. Many generations later, a descendant of Noah named Abraham would enter into a special compact with the Universe. An agreement that permanently altered his DNA and that of his descendants, their special genetics binding them to a covenant with God which would draw near-eternal suffering on their part. Such was the crooked road to redemption for this sad species from biting into a forbidden fruit after only two weeks.

That first night following humanity's fall, new aliens arrived. The ones recorded in scripture as floating Cherubim wielding their fiery swords which sealed the *Garden*. Originating from the nearby Proxima Centauri stellar system, they stood guard as the vaporous caretakers packed up paradise lost and left.

The Cherubim, themselves, were conscious in a way more similar to humans, later pitying this species. Almost all life forms eventually failed the obedience test in various realities; but the humans failed so quickly, causing their line to suffer horribly in reparation. For suffering alone allowed the needed growth over generations. Just as eons later, the Israelite's 400 years of bondage would be required to purge them from the stain of jealous brothers who sold their youngest sibling into foreign slavery. Because the Universe abhorred human slavery more than nearly anything. Slavery inhibited free will, genetically limiting a slave's decisions, forcing the slave to usually have his master as his father, a damning curse for both.

The Cosmos knew precisely which humans by their freely made choices were worthy of long-term rewards. The Universe knew all of it since the beginning of time. From one perspective, *Homo sapiens* were free to choose the stories born from the guided outcomes of their actions. Without God, humans would have killed themselves off as demonstrated by Adam and Eve's children, Caine and Abel. But through chance, chaos, fate, agents behind the scene and sometimes in the proverbial spotlight from the Universe, Adam and Eve would improbably inject their DNA into all subsequent human beings who came to survive in a planetary game reserve to breed the most powerful species into a kinder, better entity.

The reason why evil must be so prolific while good actions usually could not be rewarded in this installment of reality. The reward here was not the point. Life was but a test for this fallen species, choosing between myriads of prohibited temptations, eventually cultivating a final redeemer who chose good over evil out of inherent feelings. A figure who was not all human and had lived many times, always appearing when most needed and sometimes even reviled.

But almost no human along the way realized that Adam and Eve were actually in a simulation of Adam's world before his death. A recursive storyline requiring them to finally return to their lost garden. A quest that would threaten a descendent of Adam and Eve, named David Bellingham. His ultra-real, video game, *Dreamspace,* would later be expanded alongside his co-designer, Pia Geller. Developments in processing allowed them to create a massive multiplayer *Dreamspace* game world they titled *Garden 1.0.*

Pia's inspiration for the name stemmed not from the biblical garden, but rather the ending of the famous book by the 18th Century French philosopher, *Voltaire.* The great thinker used the metaphor of a garden to represent one's inner self. A place, the French philosopher advocated where all should first cultivate our inner selves before embracing the certainty to go out and persuade others. Researching our conviction and seldom trusting our leaders.

Pia Geller's intricate game was meant to make players better by harnessing rewards through the modern serpent of major corporate sponsorship from the famed brands of the distant future. But Pia never expected that *Garden* would be taken over by a force beyond description. An individual calling himself *Mandrake Van Ness* held hostage all the players in-game. If their bodies were disconnected from comports, they'd die. The only way to free them was for a player to finish the game, unexpectedly bringing a personal redemption for everyone trapped within it. If only a player could finish it. Because everything since Adam was not quite as it seemed for the human race.

God reiterated in scripture that so-called reality for them was not real, but a test before the reality to follow. Following his resurrection, Adam was no longer in the prior reality where fish had evolved into primates like him. Adam now existed in something more akin to a *game,* the contributing factor to why if no

XVI   BENNETT JOSHUA DAVLIN

one later won *Garden*, it could cost the lives of every human being that had ever lived on Earth. The ultimate fate of humanity was now linked to whether one player could finally end the multiplayer online video game by reaching the fabled-
Garden.

ANOTHER 2020 *TIME OF TROUBLE* MOVIE RELEASE FROM THE FILMMAKER

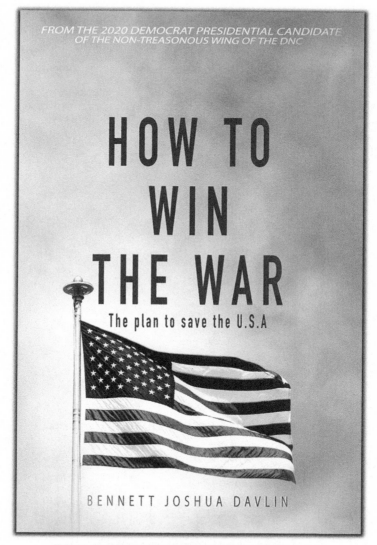

FROM THE 2020 DEMOCRAT PRESIDENTIAL CANDIDATE
OF THE NON-TREASONOUS WING OF THE DNC

HOW TO WIN THE WAR

The plan to save the U.S.A

BENNETT JOSHUA DAVLIN

THE 14-MINUTE SHORT FILM ON HOW TO FIX THE U.S.A.
WWW.CENTEREDAMERICA.COM

FROM THE 2020 DEMOCRAT PRESIDENTIAL CANDIDATE
OF THE NON-TREASONOUS WING OF THE DNC

CHINA LIED MASS MURDERING WITH COVID-19
REVEALED THE COLD WAR NEVER ENDED

THE SERVICE ECONOMY IS THE ILLUSION OF
AN IMAGINARY COMMON INTEREST FUNDING OUR ENEMY

TO WIN THE WAR,
AMERICA MUST:

PROTECT THE PEOPLE
LIVE FREE UNTIL COVID FREE - EXTEND UNEMPLOYMENT
ONE PARENT AT HOME - SCHOOLING SUBSIDY FOR FAMILIES
ESSENTIAL WORKERS - HAZARD PAY AND LIFE INSURANCE
STAY HEALTHY - BIFURCATE HOSPITALS AND COVID-19 CLINICS
FREE SPEECH - END CENSORSHIP SOCIAL MEDIA
DECOMMUNIZE MEDIA - REMOVE COMMUNIST PROPAGANDA

DECOMMUNIZE GOVERNMENT
TRIALS FOR TREASON -
POLITICIANS ALIGNED WITH CHINA,
WHO INSTITUTED THE DEADLY SERVICE ECONOMY,
WHO ENSLAVED CITIZENS IN FOR-PROFIT PRISONS,
WHO PROPAGATED VIOLENCE
AND DECLARED AMERICAN PORTS SANCTUARIES FOR CHINA.

MAKE IN AMERICA AGAIN- CHEXIT
MADE IN AMERICA - MANUFACTURE ESSENTIAL GOODS
CLOSE BORDERS - CONTAIN AND PROTECT FROM BIO ATTACKS
END SLAVERY - END MASS IMPRISONEMENT SLAVE LABOR

BEFORE CHINA/NORTH KOREA STRIKE AGAIN

CENTERED AMERICA BOOKS
www.centeredamerica.com

Also available as an ebook

$24.99 US
$32.65 CAN

ISBN 9781735873688

90000

9 781735 873688

HOW TO
WIN
THE WAR

The plan to save the U.S.A

BENNETT JOSHUA DAVLIN

FROM THE 2020 DEMOCRAT PRESIDENTIAL CANDIDATE OF THE NON-TREASONOUS WING OF THE DNC

"...I next critized the sex-abuse cover-up scandal, protected for ages by the top elites of their (Catholic) bureaucracy. I disclosed that many of my male homosexual friends, once reaching middle-age, disclosed that they were raped when young by Catholic priests. This wicked conspiracy along with the wrong Sabbath showed the wickedness wrought from the nonsensical Papal infallibility.

I then revealed that my wife and I would never be in a meeting with Catholic Officials except for one, critical fact: **The archangel Saint Michael visited me in the presence of my wife on October 27th, 2017, and altered our lives, bringing us here."**

- SAINT MICHAEL STOOD UP, PAGE 94

AT THAT TIME (SAINT) MICHAEL
SHALL STAND UP.
THE GREAT PRINCE WHO STANDS WATCH OVER THE SONS
OF YOUR PEOPLE; AND THERE SHALL BE A
TIME OF TROUBLE,
SUCH AS NEVER WAS SINCE THERE WAS A NATION,
EVEN TO THAT TIME.
AND AT THAT TIME YOUR PEOPLE
SHALL BE DELIVERED,
EVERY ONE WHO IS FOUND WRITTEN IN THE BOOK.

-(DANIEL 12:1)

CENTERED AMERICA BOOKS
www.centeredamerica.com

Also available as an ebook

$24.99 US
$32.65 CAN

ISBN 9781735873640

9 781735 873640

SAINT MICHAEL STOOD UP

China is Gog

BENNETT JOSHUA DAVLIN

SAINT MICHAEL STOOD UP

China is Gog

BENNETT JOSHUA DAVLIN

JOIN THE MOVEMENT
AT
WWW.CENTEREDAMERICA.COM

THE CANDIDATE OF THE NON-TREASONOUS WING
OF THE DEMOCRAT PARTY

Born in South Central Louisiana, Bennett Joshua Davlin began making films at the age of five and completed his first novel at ten. He attended Semester at Sea and London's City College, graduating from Tulane University, and later attending Tulane's A.B. Freeman School of Business's graduate MBA program. Davlin was a former war correspondent in the 1990s Yugoslavian conflict, a professional mountaineer, spelunker, and a PADI Divemaster with expertise in cave and sunken wreck penetrations. He's worked in the oilfield sector and in structured and international finance. As a CEO, he turned around the largest manufacturer of high-end American decorative goods, after which the policies of then-president Clinton forced him to offshore his manufacturing to China. He lived in Hong Kong and Communist China in various periods throughout the past 30 years. Davlin became a Hollywood studio screenwriter, penning such films as the Jackie Chan blockbuster *Medallion* for Sony, Columbia & TriStar Pictures. He wrote the international best-selling novel *Memory* published by The Berkley Imprint of The Penguin Group and translated in multiple languages by Sony Books, Blanvalet, and Random House. He was a keynote speaker at The Tennessee Williams Festival and a guest lecturer at NYU and other universities. Davlin wrote, produced, and directed the adaptation of *Memory* into a feature film theatrically released worldwide by Warner Bros. and EBE. In television, Bennett and his TV producing partner, Randy Douthit, co-creator of CNN's *Crossfire* and *Judge Judy,* work on projects under a *first-look* deal with CBS Paramount. He is also a 2020 Democrat candidate for U.S. president and a government policy thinker, political, economic, and philosophical essayist at his site *Centeredamerica.com*

Made in the USA
Coppell, TX
08 January 2021